THE
WOMAN
ON THE
LEDGE

THE WOMAN ON THE LEDGE

RUTH MANCINI

CENTURY

1 3 5 7 9 10 8 6 4 2

Century
20 Vauxhall Bridge Road
London SW1V 2SA

Century is part of the Penguin Random House group of companies
whose addresses can be found at global.penguinrandomhouse.com.

Penguin
Random House
UK

First published by Century in 2024

www.penguin.co.uk

A CIP catalogue record for this book is available from the British Library.

ISBN: 9781529909807 (hardback)
ISBN: 9781529909814 (trade paperback)

Typeset in 11.75/16.63 pt Times New Roman by Jouve (UK), Milton Keynes
Printed and bound in Great Britain by Clays Ltd, Elcograf S.p.A.

The authorised representative in the EEA is Penguin Random House Ireland,
Morrison Chambers, 32 Nassau Street, Dublin D02 YH68

www.greenpenguin.co.uk

For my mum, with love always

Prologue

Monday, 19 December

I wake with a start, my heart racing. There's a second or two of confusion as the morning light creeps through the slats in my blind. Then I hear it. Banging. Male voices, shouting.

'Open up. Police!'

For a second or two I am so heavy with sleep and fear that I can't move a muscle. My stomach tugs and my mind whirls. They've come for me. They've finally come for me. Then it starts up again, the banging. It's loud. They're at the front door, I realise with alarm. Someone's buzzed them in through the communal door. They can't have rung my buzzer; I'd have heard it. In a flat this small, it sounds as though they're already in my front room.

George, my cat, springs off the bed and darts underneath the wicker chair. I push my covers back quickly. 'Coming!' I shout, but my voice comes out high-pitched and thin. I hope they can hear me; I don't want them to start breaking down the door. I reach for my jeans and pull them on as quickly as I can, then grab a clean T-shirt from a pile of laundry that's sitting on top of the chair. I grapple with my nightdress, yanking it off, and

1

pull the T-shirt over my head, catching my arm painfully on the bedroom door handle as I run down the hall.

'I'm coming!' I call again, gripping my sore arm. I reach up and grab the key from the ledge above the front door. My fingers are trembling as I slide back the security chain. 'Just a second,' I plead. 'I just need to unlock it.' I turn the key and push up the latch.

They swarm in. Huge men in uniform and stab vests in my tiny hallway. Two, then three, then four of them; they push their way in, invade my space, as if I'm the dangerous criminal they think I am.

A female cop is here now, thank God.

'Tate Kinsella?'

'Yes.'

She takes my forearm and lifts my hand, snaps a handcuff over my wrist. 'Tate Kinsella, I'm arresting you on suspicion of murder,' she says, and then rattles off quickly, off pat, 'You do not have to say anything but it may harm your defence if you do not mention when questioned something you later rely on in court. Anything you do say may be given in evidence. Got that?'

I nod.

They search my living room and bedroom then, while I stand in the kitchen with the female cop, the handcuffs clamped heavy and tight round my wrists. I run my tongue over my teeth and glance around the kitchen, my mind spinning with all the things I need to think of, but being shackled so close to a complete stranger, I can't get my thoughts straight. The roof of my mouth is bone dry.

'Can I get a drink of water?' I ask, nodding towards the sink. The counter next to it is piled up with plates and dirty dishes. Last night's empty wine glasses: two of them. Smears of ketchup and grains of egg fried rice on the worktop. Wine and a takeaway: the kind of meal you eat when you've got something to celebrate. The cop's eyes follow mine. I wonder if she's already profiling me.

'Not now. Later,' she says.

'My cat,' I say. 'I need to make arrangements.'

'What arrangements?'

'My neighbour. Please . . . I need to call her. My phone . . . it's by the bed.'

'We'll sort that out for you.'

'She lives two floors up. She has a key. I just need to ask her to feed the cat.'

'Like I said, we'll sort that out.'

Another ten minutes and I'm escorted out of the flats. My heart hammers in my chest at the sight of the blue and fluorescent yellow chequered police vehicle, parked incongruously next to my little Corsa on the narrow street outside. It's mid-December and the air is fresh and cold, but the police have taken my coat and all my jumpers. I shiver in my thin T-shirt as the back door is opened for me and I'm pushed down into the rear of the car.

We travel the short journey to the police station in silence, the female cop driving and her male colleague next to her, me in the back, just the occasional staccato crackle of the police radio and the male officer's low-toned response floating around on the periphery of my thoughts. We pass the Middle Eastern restaurants and shops of the Edgware Road, the bookies and the

3

cash converters, Upper Berkeley Street, Portman Square. It all looks the same, but not the same. I walk these streets most days, but everything looks new, like it does when you come back home after a holiday. Will I ever come back again? My heart thumps against my chest. It's just a palpitation. It's nothing, I tell myself. I'm bound to be anxious, but now – more than ever – I need to stay calm.

One thing I'm glad of is that I won't be going back to that office, ever again. My stomach wrenches at the thought of it. Peering over the edge of the roof terrace. Seeing her, her broken body on the pavement looking like nothing more than a pile of clothes. A person-shaped pile of clothes. Her shoe in the road. Her handbag hanging, caught on the spike of a railing. I replay it over and over in my head; the indescribable pain she must have felt as she hit the ground. And then I'm crying again. Every time I see her broken body, I feel winded, as if I can't breathe, as if I am the one who has fallen twenty-five floors from a London roof terrace to my death on the pavement below.

We pull into a gated entrance at the back of the police station and the car stops. I'm taken through a yard full of police vehicles and into an empty room with concrete walls and black plastic crash mats spread across the floor. I'm told that this is a holding cell and that we have to wait because we're in a queue to get into custody. After a few moments, the officers speak through the intercom and we're buzzed in.

I'm now in a stark foyer with a single high desk. I sit on a bench, flanked by the two officers. The female officer takes off my handcuffs, finds a small box of tissues and puts them on the bench next to me.

'I'll get you some water,' she offers.

'Thanks.' I rub my sore wrists, take a tissue out of the box and wipe my streaming nose and eyes. The female officer disappears and leaves me with the male one. He's young, clean-shaven, fair-haired, pimply. He looks a lot like my nephew, Josh, which comforts me a little as we sit there on the bench, side by side.

The female officer returns with a plastic cup and hands it to me. I take a gulp. It's ice-cold, but welcome. I swallow down the rest.

'You want some more?'

'No. It's OK, thanks.'

We wait a few moments longer and then the sergeant behind the desk waves us forward. He asks me a series of questions about my state of mind, which I tell him is fine, although obviously it's been better. He reads me my rights, which I tell him I understand. He offers me a lawyer; I accept. He tells me that he'll get me the duty solicitor. I'm then given a blanket and shown into a cell. They take my shoes and my clothes and give me a sweat top and joggers to wear. The door slams shut and I lie down on the bed and close my eyes. I won't sleep – I don't need to sleep – but I don't want to look at the metal toilet in the corner, which has no seat or lid. I don't want to look at anything. Even with my eyes closed, everything is so alien – the clothes I'm wearing, the coarseness of the blanket against my fingertips, the slamming of cell doors, the jangling of keys.

I draw my knees up to my chest. I have so much to think about, so much that I need to go over. There's so much I need to say to my lawyer when he or she gets here, but my hands and feet are cold and my mind is numb. The blanket isn't warming me but I don't know if I will be allowed a second one and I don't want to draw attention to myself by asking. No matter how much I try to focus on my breathing – in for four, hold for five, out for six or seven – I just can't get it all straight in my head.

When the lawyer arrives, they come for me again. There's a tap on the tiny window in the door and this time the jangling of keys is for me. I'm handcuffed once more, but only briefly; they take the cuffs off as I'm shown into a small room, where the lawyer is waiting. It's a woman – in her late thirties, I'd say, a similar age to me. She has wavy fair hair pulled back into an untidy knot and she's wearing a fleece top, jeans and trainers. She's not what I expected; I thought they all wore suits. But I'm wearing a blanket, paper shoes and somebody else's tracksuit, and so her casual appearance immediately puts me at ease.

'Hello, Tate. Sit down. I'm Sarah,' she says. 'I'm your lawyer. Is that OK?'

I slide onto the bench opposite her. 'Sure,' I agree.

'You have a choice,' she smiles. Her eyes are kind. 'If you decide you don't think I'm the right lawyer for you, you can ask for someone else. And everything you tell me is completely confidential. I have to tell you that. I'm not allowed to step outside this room and tell anyone what you've told me.'

I nod.

'Except,' she continues, 'what we both agree that I can say on your behalf to the police or in court or to my colleagues, if I need to.'

'OK.'

She moves a finger across the trackpad on her laptop. 'Your

name's Tate Kinsella, is that right? And your date of birth is the eighth of June 1984?'

'Yes.'

'Good. OK.' She sits back and looks at me earnestly, her forehead creasing. 'So, Tate, do you know why you're here?'

'Yes.'

'You're accused of the murder of—'

'I know,' I say quickly. 'I know what I'm here for.'

'And how do you feel about that?' she asks. 'Are you doing OK?'

I look back at her, surprised. It's strange how everyone's asking how *I* am when they think I killed someone. I suppose I'd expected a little more hate.

'I'm OK,' I say. 'A bit shaken. But I knew. I just knew they were going to arrest me for this.'

'Yes.' Sarah moves her finger across the trackpad and narrows her eyes as she peers down at her laptop. 'You made a statement. You told the police and you told witnesses at the scene that you'd been with the deceased inside the building – that you were there with her before she died. You told them that it was all your fault.' She looks up at me, questioningly.

'I didn't mean it.' I shake my head. 'I was confused. I thought . . .'

Her eyes move back to the page. 'And then you retracted that. You said that you didn't even know she was in the building.'

I lower my head into my hands. 'I didn't.'

'But you were there.'

'Yes, I was there,' I agree. 'In the building. At the same

7

time. But I wasn't *with* her. I didn't do anything wrong. I told the police that. But they didn't believe me.'

'No,' she agrees.

'Look, I can't explain any of this. I don't know how – or why – it happened. Well, I have a theory, but it's kind of . . . crazy. It's . . . it's pretty much off the wall, in fact.'

She looks me hard in the eye. 'Tate, I have to warn you . . . If you had any involvement in this, you need to say nothing. You need to stay silent. Do you understand?'

'No. I need to tell them!' I protest. 'I'm innocent. I didn't do this. I need to tell them my side of things.'

'You already told them your side of things.'

'But they didn't believe me! They arrested me.'

'Exactly,' she says. 'So, telling them your side of things doesn't necessarily mean they're going to let you go. It doesn't work like that. And as you've already discovered, it can end up tying you in knots.'

'But I'm innocent!'

'Then tell *me* about it,' she says. 'And let me advise you. That's what I'm here for.'

I pull the blanket closely around my shoulders, although I'm warming up nicely now. I can feel my feet. I can think again.

She moves her laptop towards her and waits for me, her eyes lowered, her shoulders poised.

I sigh. 'I don't know where to start,' I tell her.

'Start from the beginning,' she says.

PART ONE

PART ONE

1

Friday, 9 December

I weaved my way through the crowded room towards the glass door that led out on to the terrace. Spirits were high and the Christmas karaoke was in full swing. My line manager, Dan, and his PA, Hayley, had just done a not too shoddy Elton John and Kiki Dee. Now, our CEO, Jerry Seager, was up, singing Elvis. Emboldened by a captive audience and a quantity of vodka, he'd pulled open his shirt buttons and was gyrating his hips in an enthusiastic parody of the King.

The bar was on the top floor of a twenty-five-storey office block in the heart of the City of London. As I reached the door, I spotted several people from my department congregating in the smoking area outside. I stopped short. I'd had my fill of idle office chit-chat. In truth, there was no one at the bank that I connected with other than Dan – and Hayley, perhaps. I had no interest in the associates' cars or their skiing holidays or who was in line for the biggest bonus, and they definitely had no interest in me and my senescent acting career.

I crept past them round the corner and climbed the narrow fire escape to the upper level of the roof terrace. The cold air was sobering, as was the view. When I got to the top, I could see the white lights of Tower Bridge twinkling in the distance, the river beyond snaking its way eastwards towards the docks. Behind me, across the water to my right, the Shard rose out of the night, its lower levels shrouded in darkness, its tip contrastingly bright. I lit a cigarette and breathed in deeply for a moment, enjoying the view and the solitude. When I'd finished, I stepped forward, moving a little nearer to the wall of the terrace, curious to see how close I could get, what the view was like down to the street below. I've never been good with heights and I felt my knees weaken, but something perverse inside me was drawing me closer to the edge. It was as if I was daring my own brain to stop me from jumping. Someone once told me that this is the true meaning of vertigo.

I reached the railing that bordered the building. I gripped it tight and peered over, and there it was – that long, sheer drop. I felt my stomach somersault as I looked down for a moment or two. And then, to my right, out of the corner of my eye, I saw her. A woman with dark, wavy hair. She'd climbed up one of the angled skylights and over the railing, and was sitting on the other side, on the ledge of the wall, her legs dangling in mid-air.

I hesitated. 'Hey,' I called out to her. 'I really don't think you should be sitting up there.'

She didn't answer. I moved closer.

'Seriously.' I spoke quickly, feeling giddy. 'It's not safe. You're going to fall.'

She turned her head and looked at me. 'Can you just . . . leave me, please?'

I hesitated. 'I don't think I should.'

'I just want to . . . I just need a minute.'

'And then you'll come down?'

She hesitated, turned her back to me, then shook her head.

I felt myself shiver. 'If you're thinking about jumping . . . please, please don't.'

She didn't answer.

'Come on,' I said, gently. 'Things can't be that bad.'

Her voice wobbled and cracked slightly as she said, 'Oh yeah? You wanna bet?' She picked up a bottle of wine that was on the wall next to her, tipped back her head and took a long slug.

'Do you want to talk about it?' I persisted.

'There's nothing to say,' she answered. 'I've fucked up everything. I've really, *royally* fucked up.'

'How have you fucked up?'

Her shoulders shook and she started to cry.

I said quickly, 'Look. My life's a complete car wreck. I should be the one jumping.'

She didn't answer.

'Seriously,' I said. 'I'm a thirty-eight-year-old out-of-work-actress-slash-office-temp-slash-dogsbody. I live on my own with a cat.'

She looked round. 'You're an actress?'

'Yeah,' I said, relieved. I'd got her attention. 'Well . . . I'm trying to be.'

'What have you been in?'

'Nothing you'd have heard of,' I admitted.

'Have you been on the telly?'

'One advert. Years ago.'

'Which one?'

13

'Carpet Palace? I was the woman on the flying carpet. The one that flew through the window and landed in that couple's living room?'

She looked at me blankly.

'Yeah. Anyway. I haven't had any decent work in years. I'm twenty-one grand in debt. I'm not qualified to do anything except act. Actually, that's not true. I have OCR Level Two typing, but my speed sucks and I have RSI. So I do a lot of photocopying, and scanning, and shredding. Which' – I knew I was prattling – 'will be really useful if I ever get a part as an insanely bored office temp. But in the meantime, it's totally, insanely fucking boring. And guess what? My brothers and sisters are all married with kids and they're all multimillionaires.'

'Seriously?'

'Seriously.' I nodded. 'Every one of them. They all have the big house, the nice car, the designer clothes, the expensive holidays.' I paused. 'They're living the dream. And then there's me.'

The woman stretched out her arm and offered me the wine bottle. I stepped forward, reached up and took it from her.

'Are they really all millionaires?' she asked.

'They really are.' I wiped the rim of the bottle with my sleeve and took a slug of wine. 'I'm not kidding. One of my sisters owns a chain of hotels. And my oldest brother floated his company on the stock market before the crash and pocketed fifty million. He went from being rich to super rich overnight.'

'If they're so rich, why don't they help you pay off your debts?'

'They all ganged up and came to an agreement that they wouldn't do that. They think I need to get my shit together, learn to help myself.'

She nodded slowly. 'Nice.'

My phone bleeped. I pulled it out of my pocket and looked at the screen.

'Boyfriend?' she asked.

I shook my head. 'It's just Amazon. Delivery tomorrow.'

'What have you ordered?'

'Shoes,' I said.

She nodded again and started crying.

'It's a bit late, to be honest,' I said. 'I wanted them for the party.'

She cried harder.

'Hey.' I moved closer.

'At least you have a boyfriend,' she sobbed. 'At least you have a fucking boyfriend.'

'What?' I frowned. 'What makes you think I have a boyfriend?'

She hesitated. 'That message you just got.'

'From Amazon.'

'Oh. Yeah. OK.'

How drunk *was* she?

'So, *do* you have a boyfriend?'

She was looking hard at me, waiting for my answer. She was wobbling on the wall. Panic spread through me. I wanted to say no, but I didn't want to lie either. What if Dan came up here looking for me?

'Sort of,' I admitted.

She sniffed. 'What does that mean?'

'There's someone,' I confessed. 'But he's not really my boyfriend.'

'How is he not really your boyfriend?'

I hesitated. 'He's married.'

She looked at me, unblinking.

'See what I mean?' I said. 'Car wreck.'

She thought about this for a minute while the wind lifted the corner of her coat and smacked it against her thigh. She pushed it down. 'Do you love him?'

'Yes.'

'Does he love you?'

'I don't know. Maybe.'

'So, there's hope,' she slurred. 'You have hope.'

'He's married,' I reminded her. 'He has a daughter who he adores. He's never going to leave his wife.'

'How do you know?'

'I googled it.'

She smiled, suddenly, through her tears. 'You googled it?'

'Oh, you know. I googled how many times men leave their wives and it's only, like, five per cent or something.'

Her grin widened.

'What?' I asked, smiling back.

She shrugged. 'I don't know. Sorry. That just sounded funny.'

'It's what you do when you're desperate.'

'Tell me about it,' she said.

I watched her in silence for a moment. She didn't move, but I felt we'd made progress. I didn't want to blow it by saying the wrong thing.

Eventually, she sniffed and wiped her eyes. She asked, 'Can I have one of your cigarettes?'

I quickly pulled the packet from my bag and held it out to her.

She reached for it, her fingers not quite touching it. 'I can't quite . . . Can you move closer?'

'Come down,' I begged her. 'Please. Where do you live? Maybe we can share a cab home, or . . . or we could go and find a bar or something. We can talk some more.'

She considered this for a moment in silence and then, to my surprise, she turned, gripped the railing and levered herself up onto her knees on the wall. She ducked down through the railing and slid down the skylight. I quickly moved next to her, positioning myself between her and the wall.

I tapped out a cigarette. I passed it to her, flicked my lighter and lit it for her and then held out the wine bottle. She took it, breathed out a plume of smoke, took a slug of wine.

'What's your name?' she asked me.

'Tate.'

She frowned. 'Come again?'

'Tate. T-a-t-e.'

'Unusual.'

'Yeah. I think my parents were hoping it would make me interesting. We're all monosyllabic. There's Fern, Heath, Blair, Skye. And me. What about you?'

'Helen.'

'Oooh. Get you. You have syllables.'

She pressed her lips together and sucked in her cheeks. 'My surname's "Back".'

I looked at her, straight-faced. Hell and back. I didn't dare laugh. She was still too close to the edge of the building. She could yet change her mind, clamber back up the skylight and throw herself off.

'Just kidding. It's Jones.' She grinned and let out another plume of smoke.

I smiled back at her, relieved.

'So, tell me about this married man,' she said.

I hesitated. 'Who do you work for?'

'What?'

'Do you work for CPF?'

'Who?'

'The French bank I work for. We're on levels twelve to nineteen. It's our party that's going on in the bar tonight.'

She shook her head. 'No.'

'So, which floor are you on?'

She took a puff of her cigarette. 'The tenth.'

'Tenth?' I scratched my head. 'Is that Cowan McCauley?'

'I'm just a temp,' she said. 'I don't really know anyone.'

I tapped a cigarette out of the pack and lit it. 'Me too. It sucks, doesn't it? No one really bothers getting to know you. It's like you're invisible.'

'So why are you here?'

I shrugged. 'Office Christmas party. You have to make the effort, don't you?'

She crushed her cigarette butt with her shoe. 'I dunno. I don't see why, if you're only temping.'

'It's long-term,' I told her. 'I've been here four months already.' I paused, then said, 'OK. Truth is, the guy I'm seeing.' I flip my head towards the building. 'He's inside. I work with him. He's my boss.'

She pressed her lips together, shook her head knowingly.

'Yep,' I said wryly. 'So that's why I'm here. Only . . . it's pointless really. He never talks to me when we're at work. In fact, he makes a point of avoiding me. So, you're right. I don't really know why I came.'

She passed me the bottle. I took a slug and passed it back again. 'What about you?' I asked her. 'Why are *you* here?'

'I came to throw myself off the roof, remember?'

'Shit. Sorry,' I said. 'But you're not going to any more?'

She looked wistfully away towards the tip of the Shard. 'You kind of put me off.'

I gently touched her arm. 'Come on. Let's call a cab. Things may look different in the morning.'

'I doubt it.'

'Well, if they don't, you can call me. OK?'

'Seriously?'

'Yeah. Seriously. Give me your phone.'

She pulled her phone out of her pocket and handed it to me. I tapped in my number and pressed send. My phone bleeped and I handed hers back to her.

She looked at me quizzically. 'Why do you care?'

I said, 'Because, whatever you think you've done – or not done – you seem like a nice person.' I added, with a smile, 'And anyway . . . us office temps have to stick together, don't we?'

She thought about this for a moment, then shuffled forwards. She lowered herself off the skylight and jumped down onto the roof next to me.

2

Monday, 19 December

My lawyer, Sarah, stops typing. 'So, she worked on the tenth floor?'

'No.' I shake my head. 'She lied. She didn't really work there.'

'She didn't work at . . .' Sarah swipes the trackpad and scrolls up. 'Cowan McCauley? Or she didn't work on the tenth floor?'

'She didn't work in the building.'

'Oh. I see.' Her eyes flicker up to meet mine. 'So . . . why did she lie?'

'She shouldn't have been there. She blagged her way in.'

'And why did she do that?'

I look her in the eye. 'She wanted to kill herself. That's what she said.'

'There are other ways to kill yourself.'

I nod. 'But she knew the building. She was confident she could find a way in. And 225 Eastcheap is high enough to . . .' I pause and close my eyes for a moment before opening them again. 'It's a hundred metres high. Three hundred feet. That's just about optimal, apparently. It's pretty much the perfect height if you want a guarantee that you won't survive the fall, but you also don't want too much time to think about it on the way down.'

Sarah frowns. 'She told you all this?'

I look down at the table. 'Yeah. It should have been an alarm bell. All of it. Her instability. Her lies. But I felt sorry for her. And I liked her. She had a bit of life about her.' I look up. 'I know that sounds like a weird thing to say in the circumstances, but she didn't seem crazy. She just seemed like someone normal who'd got maudlin and drunk too much. There was nothing . . . unhinged about her. I guess I wasn't completely convinced that she was serious about jumping.'

'Well, I can see why you'd draw that conclusion. You managed to talk her down.'

'Yeah,' I snort. 'And look where it got me.'

'So, if she didn't work there . . . how did she get in?'

'She said the guy on the door remembered her face. That she'd worked in the building a couple of months previously. It was the evening. There was a party. She somehow convinced him that she was someone's plus one and he let her in. You can't get into the bar or onto any of the floors without a pass, so I guess he saw no harm. They had more security upstairs on the door of the bar. And beyond that, there wasn't really anywhere else she could go.'

'Except . . . the roof terrace?'

'Yes. You can access it directly from the twenty-fifth floor, without having to go through the bar. There are no security cameras on the roof either, of course.'

'And she'd know that?'

'I guess she made it her business to find out.'

Sarah glances across at the sheet of paper that's on the table beside her laptop. 'So, 225 Eastcheap is a high-rise building with twenty-five floors. Can you tell me a bit more?'

'Like what?'

'Describe it to me.'

'OK. Well . . . there are lots of different companies there. It has a gym in the basement and a bar at the top. I think some of the floors even have sleep pods. No one really works late or at weekends at the bank,' I explain. 'But some of the US law firms in the building work into the night.'

'What about security?' she asks, still typing this up.

'There's a security office with cameras on the ground floor to the left as you go in. And then there's a desk next to the lower-level turnstile where the security guys also sit. During the week, in the daytime, you usually have to flash your pass at them as you go through the turnstile. And then you can go up or down, but you need your pass again to get into the corridors on the different floors.'

'It still seems as though this woman went to a lot of trouble,' she says, lifting her eyes from the screen of her laptop.

I nod. 'I know. I agree.'

She looks into my eyes searchingly. 'Go on. You managed to talk her down from the roof. What happened next?'

'I called a cab, we went down the stairs – all twenty-five flights because she said she had a phobia about lifts. And then we went home. We dropped her off first – she was on my way. Or so she said.'

22

'What do you mean?'

'She said she lived in Kenrick Place, just off Baker Street. I'm in Paddington, so it made sense to share a cab and split the fare. So, the cab stopped in Kenrick Place. She got out. We said goodbye. She said she was OK. She seemed OK. I told her again to call if she needed to talk.'

'And did she?'

'Yes, she did. The very next day.'

3

Saturday, 10 December

The following morning – the morning after the party – I'd woken early, but I dozed a little and didn't get out of bed until noon. I made tea and toast, then spent the afternoon lounging on the sofa, eating crisps and watching an old Hitchcock thriller. I'd exchanged messages with Dan, I tell Sarah, which had left me feeling alternately thrilled and dejected. He was on his way over. We'd spend the evening together. I'd go out for groceries. I'd cook. Don't go to any trouble, he'd said. Things were a little tricky at the moment with Emily, his daughter. He probably wouldn't be able to stay too long. A takeout, then, and a nice bottle of wine.

It was settled. I'd have a bath and wash the dishes, hoover the flat and empty the bins. Then, another message. Something's come up, he'd said. He couldn't come over after all. I messaged him back, worried. What had happened? It's nothing, he'd said. Nothing to worry about. But Maddy, his wife, had to go into the City to meet someone. It was important. He now needed to stay at home. He had to look after Emily.

I knew all about Emily. She was fifteen, and old enough to be left home alone for a few hours. But she was going through a rebellious phase, running with the wrong crowd, smoking and drinking and God knows what else. These kids she was hanging out with were a bad influence. One evening, she'd managed to sneak out without her parents knowing and hadn't come home until dawn. Dan and Maddy had been beside themselves with worry. Dan needed to keep an eye on her. If he went out for the evening, then so would she and she was meant to be grounded. Any chance she could get and she'd be off.

We ended the call. I swallowed a couple of headache pills, lay back on the sofa and dozed lightly for a while. When I woke again, I felt listless and low. I should do something for the weekend, arrange something, but I'd left it too late. All of my friends would have plans. They didn't know about Dan – I was too ashamed to tell them; they wouldn't approve – but even so, I didn't want any of them to think they were my last-minute option. So, when my phone rang and I saw that it was Helen, I was quite glad of the diversion.

'Hello, Tate,' she said, speaking rapidly, her voice unsteady. 'I'm really sorry about this, but I need to get to the point. I've lost an earring. I've looked everywhere, but I can't find it. It must have fallen out last night.'

'Oh no,' I said. 'Were they expensive?'

'They're diamonds!' she exclaimed, almost accusingly. 'They're precious. Unique. And irreplaceable. They were the last thing my gran gave me before she died. They're . . .' She paused, then I heard a sob. 'They're all I have left of her. I have to find it. I have to get it back!'

'Do you want me to call the cab company?' I asked. 'See if that driver last night can take a look in the back of his cab—'

'No.' She cut me off sharply. 'I've done that already, but it's no good. They say it's not there.'

'OK. Well . . . God, I'm sorry,' I told her. 'I don't know what else to suggest.'

'The office. Eastcheap. We need to go back to the building and check. Now. Will you come with me?'

I thought about this for a moment. It was Saturday evening. That was quite a big ask. I wanted to say, 'Can't it wait until Monday?' but I was guessing it couldn't, or she wouldn't have suggested it. I supposed the sooner Helen retraced her steps the more chance she had of finding the earring. But why did she need me?

'Erm. Well, I suppose I could,' I began. 'But—'

'Would you?' she interrupted gratefully. 'And can you bring your security pass? I can't find mine. I think I must have dropped that too. I'm not going to be able to get in otherwise.'

I hesitated. The rules at CPF were strict. Although it was a bank, there was no money on the premises, but even so, I wasn't meant to swipe anyone else in. I'd only just met Helen. I barely knew her. I didn't really feel comfortable about this.

But, on the other hand, she sounded desperate and I didn't feel comfortable with that either. I'd said she could call on me, hadn't I? And besides, there should be someone from security behind the desk. If they hadn't found her pass and they didn't like the idea of her going into the building, she could just wait for me in the lobby while I went up and looked for the earring on my own.

'OK,' I agreed finally. After all, it wasn't as if I had any-thing better to do. 'My car's outside. I can pick you up on the way if you like?'

'Don't worry. I'm in a cab already. I'm round the corner from you. I'll be there in . . . like, five minutes?'

'You're . . . on the way to my place?'

'Yes. That OK?'

'How do you . . . how do you know where I live?'

A pause. 'Park East. Sussex Gardens? That right?'

'Yes. That's right.'

'You told me last night – don't you remember?'

'No,' I confessed. 'But . . . OK. See you in a minute, then.'

I dressed hurriedly in jeans and a thick sweater, opened a tin of Sheba for George and grabbed my work security pass. When I got down to the entrance, a cab was idling outside and Helen was leaning out of the back window, smiling and waving. She seemed much calmer. 'Forget the car, we'll take the cab there,' she smiled. 'If we find that earring, I'm going to be buying you a very large drink.'

I got into the back of the taxi next to her. She gave the driver the office address.

'Did you call security?' I asked her as we headed through Mayfair on our way to the City.

She looked worried. 'No. Why?'

I shrugged. 'You're meant to give them a heads-up so that they know who to expect in the building. You know, so they can put the main lights on and stuff. At six p.m. on a Saturday, I don't know who in security is going to be there.'

'Well, that's OK. You have your pass, don't you? We can

get in. We won't be long. And the lights are motion-sensored, aren't they? We'll be able to see.'

'Sure, but . . . I still think we should call security.' I reached for my phone.

She hesitated, then said, 'Please don't call them.'

I frowned. 'Why not?'

'Well, it will just be easier, won't it? It will save me getting the third degree.'

'They might have your pass, though. Someone might have handed it in,' I pointed out. 'And they might have handed in your earring too. Don't you at least want to ask?'

Helen turned and gazed out of the window in silence for a moment, then turned back to me and said, 'Look, Tate, I . . . I don't want you to call security. I don't have a pass. The thing is . . . I don't actually work there any more.'

'What? What do you mean?'

She sighed and looked down into her lap. 'OK. So, you know I told you how I fucked everything up? That was one of the things I fucked up. I lost my job.'

'So you don't work there?'

'No. I used to. I used to work for Cowan McCauley on the tenth floor, like I said. But then I got fired.'

'When?'

'A couple of months ago.'

'Oh. God. Right. I see.' I glanced across at her. She turned her head and looked out of the window. I followed her gaze. We'd reached Victoria Embankment and I could see Waterloo Bridge up ahead. We were probably only another fifteen minutes away from the office. I wanted to know why she'd been fired, but at the same time I didn't want to drag up the past and upset her.

'So . . . what were you doing there, then? Last night?'

Helen dipped her chin and made an 'Are you really asking me that?' face.

'You went there just to . . . just to . . .' I began.

'Kill myself. Yes.'

'But that's . . .'

'Insane? I know.'

I hesitated, taking this in. 'But how did you get past security then?'

'I knew the guy on the door. He always . . . well, he liked me,' she admitted. 'We always flirted a little. You know? I told him I was there for the CPF party. Gave him the name of one of the secretaries, said I was meeting her in the bar. He radioed up to one of the guys on the door upstairs and—'

I looked up sharply. 'Hang on a minute. Which secretary?'

'Hayley Allbright. You know her?'

My heart leaped. 'She's . . . she's my boss's PA.'

'Ah yes. Dan . . . the man.' She smiled and raised her eyebrows knowingly.

I stared back at her in dismay. Oh my God. What the hell was I thinking, talking to a complete stranger about me and Dan?

'I didn't think you knew anyone from CPF?' I cleared my throat. 'I asked you and you said . . . well, you didn't seem to know who . . . Never mind,' I said. 'So, is she a friend of yours?'

'Who?'

29

'Hayley.'

'Oh. No.' She looked at me sheepishly. 'I just said that to get in.'

'But you know her?' I persisted.

'Well, yeah.'

'How? How do you know her?'

Helen turned to face me and then her eyes widened. 'Oh, God. You're worried. You think I'm going to . . .' I felt her hand on my arm. 'Tate, I met her in the bar a couple of months ago, that's all. It was shortly before I got the sack. We just got chatting and I told her things weren't going too well at Cowan McCauley. She said there were openings at CPF and that I should call if I wanted her to put a word in for me. She gave me her number. And that was that.'

'And did you?' I persisted.

'Did I what?'

'Call her.'

'No. I didn't call her.'

'Why not?'

She frowned and moved her hand away from my arm. 'Because I didn't. I didn't want another job. Not at that particular time. Things were really bad for me.' Her eyes misted up.

'Right. It's OK,' I said quickly. 'You don't have to tell me.'

'And *you* don't have to worry,' she said, her eyes wet but shining. 'I'm not going to tell anyone what you told me last night.'

My stomach jolted a little. What did I tell her? I cast my mind back to the previous evening. Oh Christ! It was all coming back to me now. There was a second conversation about Dan. Now I remembered. I'd talked about him. A lot.

She reached out to me again and took hold of my hand, gripping it tight. 'I meant what I said, Tate. Honestly.'

I looked back at her apprehensively. 'What *did* you say, exactly?'

'That your secret's safe with me. One hundred per cent.'

I shifted in my seat. We were both a little the worse for wear on the ride home last night, I knew that, but – until now – I'd thought she was in a far worse state than me. And yet, it seemed, she remembered more of the conversation than I did. And now that she'd brought it up, what she was saying was ringing an uncomfortable bell.

'So, who else do you know at CPF?' I asked, my heart racing a little.

'No one,' she reassured me. 'I told you. I didn't go for the party. That was just an excuse to get in.'

'But . . . what if someone had recognised you?'

'Who? It was a CPF party.'

'What about Hayley?'

She shrugged. 'Like I said, I barely know her. I'd have just made some excuse.'

I stared at her in silence for a moment.

'I'm on your side, Tate,' she insisted. 'I'm not going to tell anyone. Really. And I'm not going to try and top myself again either, if that's what you're wondering.'

I took a breath. 'Honestly?'

'Honestly. I just want to find my earring. Last night was . . . then. And this is now.' She turned to face me. 'I wanted to be with my gran,' she explained, softly. 'She was my rock. I missed her so much. I just wanted to . . . I thought it was what

I wanted. But you really helped me, Tate. I realised after talking with you that . . .'

'That there's always someone whose life is more fucked up than yours?'

Her mouth curved into a smile. 'Something like that,' she said.

4

When we pulled up outside 225 Eastcheap, Helen followed me out of the cab and through the revolving glass door into the lobby. There was in fact no one from security at the desk and, for a brief moment, I hesitated while Helen watched me expectantly, her eyes on mine. I then pushed aside my reservations and swiped us both through the turnstile and into the inner quadrant.

I paused outside the lift, but Helen shook her head and said, 'We came down the stairs, remember?'

We walked on along the corridor, past the glass-walled courtyard and through the double doors to the foot of the stairwell. Helen stopped as the lights blinked on and glanced up at the cavernous ceiling above us. 'I feel bad,' she said. 'Making you walk up all these stairs. Why don't you go back and get the lift up to the twenty-fifth floor? You can check the roof terrace for me and then make your way down the stairs, while I start here and work my way up. We can meet halfway, or wherever. It'll save time, won't it? And it'll save my legs – and yours.'

I hesitated, feeling uneasy again. I was responsible for her being in the building, so I really ought to stay with her. But, on the other hand, what she'd suggested made a lot of sense. She just wanted to find her earring, and we'd do that quicker if we split the search into two. There was virtually nowhere she could go without a pass, after all. And – the thought that was hovering at the back of my mind – there was no way she could get to the roof terrace before I did, not if I was taking the lift and she had to walk up twenty-five flights of stairs.

'OK,' I agreed. 'Why don't we say I'll meet you in the stair-well on the fifteenth . . . or somewhere around there? Or you can just stop on the stairs when you get tired and wait for me to come down to you.'

She nodded. 'Sounds like a plan.'

'Don't go into any of the corridors, will you?' I asked her. 'I'm sure this goes without saying, but if the cleaners or any-one else come along and open the door for you, you mustn't go in.'

'Of course not,' Helen reassured me. 'Why would I? I didn't go onto any of the floors yesterday. If I see the cleaners, I'll ask them if they've found anything. But otherwise, I'll leave you to speak to them on Monday. That sound OK?'

'Sure. I'll definitely ask around on Monday. Just don't do anything or go anywhere that will get me into trouble, will you?' I pleaded.

'I promise,' she smiled, nodding her head again vigorously. 'I'll be right here.'

She gave me a description of the missing earring, glanced around the floor intently and then headed off up the stairs, scanning each step as she went. I walked back through the doors to the inner quadrant and pressed the button for the lift. It arrived within a minute and took me straight up to the twenty-fifth floor. I passed the entrance to the bar, peeping in through the glass. It was locked, empty. I then remembered that Helen had said she'd gone the other way round the quadrant to avoid the door staff at the bar, so I turned and retraced my steps. I carried on to the emergency exit and the inner fire escape that took me up onto the roof, scanning the ground as I went.

Up on the roof, it was cold and dark, with just a single motion-sensor emergency light casting a weak white spotlight onto the immediate vicinity. Across to my right, I could see the tip of the Shard all lit up, a beacon in the night sky, but the vast majority of the roof was in darkness. I pulled my phone out of my pocket, switched on the torch and retraced the approximate steps that Helen and I had taken the previous night. I flashed the beam over the skylight and onto the wall, then down over the ground where our feet had been. I spotted the empty wine bottle, which was still on the concrete beside the skylight, along with our cigarette butts, so it didn't look as though anyone had been up here to clean. But it was hard to see much, and it was also a little frightening. I could see the edge of the building, but it was too close for comfort in the half-light from my phone. I resolved to tell Helen that I'd do a further search on Monday, maybe get security up here, get them to take a proper look.

I headed back down into the building, flashing my torch around into the corners of the stairwell that housed the main fire escape, then walked back along the corridor, past the bar this time and then past the lift. I turned the corner and went through the door to the main staircase. I leaned over the banister and peered down into the stairwell to listen for Helen, but I couldn't hear any sound. I guessed that she must still be much further down.

The emergency lights on the stairs were better than the one on the roof terrace, but I scanned the concrete steps with my torch anyway, shining the beam back and forth and into the corners as I went. When I got to the fifteenth floor, I peered down again and called out Helen's name. My voice echoed down the stairwell, but I got no answer. I leaned on the banister and waited silently for a moment and then continued down to the fourteenth, thirteenth and then the twelfth, where I leaned over the banister again.

'Helen!' I called. 'Are you there?'

There was no answer. I walked over to the door to the corridor and peered through. I wondered if the cleaners were on one of these floors and whether she'd seen them through the window and – for whatever reason – had gone somewhere else to look for the earring instead. I pulled out my phone and found Helen's number and pressed the call button. It went to voicemail. I started to feel uneasy again. Where was she?

She must have gone back down the stairs, I concluded. There was no other way. My heart sank as I contemplated the possibility that she'd been followed in and questioned by security. Or . . . maybe she'd found the earring. Yes! Maybe she'd found it straight away and was waiting for me on the ground floor.

My spirits lifted a little. I hurried on down, not bothering to look for the earring any more. When I got to the ground floor, I called Helen's name one last time, then opened the door that led into the quadrant. I walked over to the turnstile and peered across to the seating area of the lobby. There was no one there, nor was there anyone sitting at the security desk. I looked across to the office, trying to catch sight of any movement inside, but the door was closed. Maybe she was in there, being questioned by security? Maybe she'd been frogmarched out of the building? Oh God. I could just imagine Dan's solemn face, his forehead etched with disappointment as he told me that I'd really fucked things up for him. Maybe he'd even say he had no option but to let me go.

I glanced around the quadrant towards the high glass window that bordered the small, impeccably manicured courtyard to my left. I walked over to the door and pushed the security bar, then my eyes moved across to the lift. All of a sudden, it hit me. What if it was just bullshit about her having a phobia? What if the missing earring was all a ruse? What if she'd simply waited for me to check the roof terrace and come out to the top of the stairwell – and then, when she'd heard me call down, she'd come back out here and taken the lift straight up to the roof?

Anxiety clawed at my gut. I ran over to the lift and glanced up at the indicator above it. It was on the twenty-fifth floor, but that's where I'd left it, so that didn't mean anything, did it? I hammered on the button, and then hammered again and waited a moment. I put my ear to the door of the lift shaft and listened. I hammered and hammered at the button repeatedly while staring up at the indicator light, but it remained lit up on the twenty-fifth. I froze. What should I do? Should I alert security? But then what if Helen had just gone to the toilet or was waiting outside the building? And if the lift was stuck or – worse – had been switched off, what could security do anyway, except run up twenty-five flights of stairs with me?

I turned, looked back past the turnstile towards the entrance, through the glass that fronted the building, imagining a glimpse of Helen under the streetlight outside. Then I ran back through the door to the staircase and launched myself up and round, up and round, one hand on the rail, my handbag slipping off my shoulder and down my arm and flapping against my leg. Up, up, up I went. I counted the floors. Fourth, fifth, sixth. I glanced up through the stairwell. Seventh, eighth, ninth. By the twelfth I was completely out of breath. I paused momentarily and wiped my damp forehead with my sleeve, pulled my thick sweater off, and then carried on up. Finally, I reached the top and crashed, panting, through the double doors. I ran past the bar. The lift doors were open, but I didn't stop to find out why. I rushed through the fire-exit door and clattered up the escape and out onto the roof. 'Helen!' I called, my voice loud in the cold, still air. 'It's me. Tate. Are you here?'

There was no reply.

The security light blinked on as I ran forward and its beam caught a glimmer of something shiny on the concrete ahead of me. I pulled my phone out of my pocket and tapped the torch on, moving closer, pointing it down. It was glass. Broken glass, all over the ground. I hesitated, confused. Had it been there before? I couldn't remember. I shone the torch towards the wall, to the place I'd last seen the wine bottle. It was gone. My heart pounded. I waved the torch back and forth around the roof terrace in a wide, desperate arc. I could see what looked like the neck of the wine bottle lying on the ground near the skylight. I stepped unsteadily around it towards the edge of the building, grabbed the railing tight and looked over. An ice-cold chill ran through me.

There was something. It was dark, but down on the pavement, lit by a nearby streetlight, there was a pile of ... something. A small crowd had gathered and traffic had come to a halt in the middle of the road. People were calling out and someone was pacing up and down. Drivers were getting out of their cars. I felt my fingers slip and slide as I lost my grip on the railing. It was obvious. Whilst I wished with every fibre of my being that it wasn't true, that this wasn't happening, there was absolutely no doubt in my mind. Someone was lying broken on the pavement below.

5

Monday, 19 December

Sarah reaches into her bag and pulls out a pack of tissues. She pushes them across the table towards me, then waits while I lower my head and sob into my arms.

When I stop crying and look up at her again, she asks, 'Did you know then? That it was her?'

'No.' I pull a tissue out of the pack in front of me and unfold it. I'm shivering. I have to cross my arms and clutch my shoulders to keep them still. 'I tried to get to her, but there was already a crowd of people around her. The security guy from our building was outside and there were other security guards from other buildings telling people to get back. No one would let me near her. I tried to explain what had happened, but it came out all wrong. I blamed myself. I didn't know then what I know now.'

Sarah pulls her laptop towards her and swipes the trackpad, then presses her lips together while she squints at the screen in front of her for a moment or two.

'So . . . what are you saying, Tate?' She lifts her eyes to

meet mine. 'You think that Helen did this to frame you? To set you up?'

'Yes,' I agree. Then, watching her face, 'Maybe. I don't know.'

'But why?' Sarah asks. 'Why would she do that?'

'I honestly don't know. I have a theory, but you probably won't believe it.' I hesitate. 'I don't even know if I believe it myself.'

Sarah keeps her eyes fixed on mine, then she leans back in her chair and folds her arms. 'I'm going to be completely honest with you,' she says. 'What I'm struggling with here is why anyone would believe a story like that in the first place. The missing earring. The missing security pass. It seems so . . . so obviously contrived.'

'I know! I'm a bloody idiot!' I start to cry again.

'I'm not saying that, Tate. We all do foolish things and, of course, hindsight is a wonderful thing. I'm just trying to understand why you would put yourself in a position like that for a complete stranger?'

'Because I'm lonely!' I cry out. 'Because I live on my own with a cat! Because I have no one to talk to – or, at least, no one whose life is as messed up as mine.'

'OK. OK,' she murmurs.

'And she wasn't a *complete* stranger,' I argue. 'At least I didn't think so at the time. She used to work for Cowan Mc-Cauley and she knew Hayley. That's what she told me. She knew Hayley's name!'

'But she didn't work for Cowan McCauley, did she?'

I shake my head. 'I honestly don't know. Dan spoke to

someone at their HR department last week, but they said they couldn't release that information to him. Data protection, apparently.'

'We'd have to make a disclosure application,' Sarah agrees. 'And what about Hayley? What did she have to say?'

I wipe my eyes. 'She'd never heard of her. Dan spoke to her. She didn't remember meeting anyone called Helen from Cowan McCauley in the bar.'

Sarah nods slowly. I notice she's not typing up what I'm saying any more.

'She was a good liar,' I insist. 'I know it sounds obvious now, but she was really convincing about the earring. And she was really upset.' I hesitate. 'OK. I suppose . . . I suppose, deep down, if I'm honest with myself, I knew that something wasn't quite right. But by the time she admitted that she didn't actually work at Cowan McCauley any more, I was worrying more about Dan. You know, whether she would tell Hayley or someone else about us. And by the time we got to the office, I was feeling pretty snookered. I mean . . . if I didn't swipe her in and let her look for the earring, she might be angry with me and then what would she do? I guess I . . . I just wanted to keep her onside. That's all I could really think about.'

There's a knock at the door. A custody assistant enters. 'Sorry to interrupt,' she says. 'But the sarge says we need to take your client for documentation now.'

Sarah advises me to cooperate and so I stand up and follow the custody assistant out of the door. We go down a corridor, through the custody suite and into a brightly lit side room. The custody assistant takes me towards an infrared scanning machine where she takes each of my fingers and presses them down onto a scanning pad, rolling them from left to right to create a fingerprint impression on the computer screen. It's uncomfortable, but I follow the instructions, nodding and pressing as she does this for all of my fingers, thumbs, palms and the sides of my hands. I sit still for my photograph to be taken, then open my mouth wide while she swabs it. All the while, I'm conscious of Sarah, who is standing in the doorway, watching in silence, her presence simultaneously comforting and disconcerting. She's good, I can tell. She's in my corner. That's her job. She's looking out for me. But does she believe me? That's the question. If she doesn't believe me, then nobody will. The police won't. Why would they? I'm their prime suspect. I must be, or they wouldn't have arrested me. I'll be charged and sent to prison, without question. And then . . .

And then it starts up again. The same series of terrifying images, the same series of questions that have been playing on a loop since the police banged on my front door and arrested me. Can I do this? Can I really do this? Am I strong enough? Do I have what it takes to see it through?

When the custody assistant is finished with me, the female detective comes in and asks for the passcode to my phone. Sarah has already told me that I don't have to give it to them, but there can be consequences to refusing and they can break into it anyway. I give the passcode to the detective. In exchange, I'm given a plastic cup of weak tea and a hot microwave meal that's meant to be lasagne and am shown back into the consult-ation room. Sarah follows, sits back down and opens her laptop. I slide onto the bench opposite her.

43

'OK?' she asks.

'Yes.'

Sarah swipes the trackpad, clicks and peers at the screen in front of her. 'So, you were up on the roof terrace. You looked over the railing and you saw someone on the ground below.'

I nod.

Her keyboard clickety-clacks as she types. Her eyes flicker between me and the screen. 'And then?'

'And then I ran down.' I wipe my eyes. 'Or did I get the lift? I can't even remember. I was in such a state. I just remember that the security guy was outside. He wouldn't let me near her.' I shake my head, bewildered. 'And then the police arrived.'

6

Saturday, 10 December

Inside 225 Eastcheap, I pushed at the revolving door, but it wouldn't open. The security guy must have locked it. My heart was hammering in my chest and my knees were weak. I could see through the glass that a small crowd had gathered. It was the weekend and the streets weren't that busy, but the commotion had drawn what people there were out from the nearby shops and bars. I could hear a siren in the near distance, getting louder and louder. I tried again to get the door open, but it was stuck, so I ran back through the turnstile, along the corridor and back through the double doors to the stairs, then went down a level to the lower ground floor, where I remembered there was an exit at the back of the building, past the gym that led into the underground car park. I let myself out and hurried through the car park, then ran up the slope and out onto the street behind.

When I rounded the corner into Eastcheap, people were milling around on the pavement and on the road or standing talking in small groups, hands over their mouths, expressions of shock and disbelief on their faces. One or two people had their phones out and, to my disgust, were holding them up in the air. I crossed the road, then began to push my way through the group, but my path was blocked. There was more than one security guard present, including the one from our building. He put up his hands and said forcefully, 'Stop. You can't come through here.'

Another male voice called out to me, irritated, 'Step back, please. Move away.'

'You don't understand!' I shrieked. 'I was with her!'

The security guard took hold of my arm and steered me gently back the way I'd just come.

'I was in the building with her!' I swallowed a sob.

'You know her? The woman who fell?' a woman asked.

'Yes.' I turned to face her. 'I didn't realise . . . I didn't mean this to happen. Oh my God. This is all my fault.'

'You'll need to wait for the police,' said the security guard, looking me up and down. 'Wait here, please.'

I did as I was told. I waited. And then the police and ambulance were there. Bright lights, vehicles moving in and blocking the road. Uniforms everywhere. Paramedics swooping in with equipment. Police cordoning off the street and dispersing the crowd.

Then I noticed the security guard pointing to me.

A uniformed police officer appeared by my side. 'I understand you may know the victim?' he asked me.

'Yes,' I replied, breathlessly. 'I was there. I was with her. Before, I mean. Not when she . . . you know . . . when she jumped.'

'She jumped?'

I nodded. 'I think so.'

'I'd like to take a statement from you straight away,' the officer said. 'Is that all right with you?'

'Yes. Of course.'

I walked with him to a police car. He opened the passenger door for me and indicated for me to get inside. I lowered myself into the seat and waited while he talked to a colleague. I'd never sat in a police car before. I stared out into the darkness of the road in front of me, at the headlights of the emergency vehicles. It was dark and light at the same time, and I felt as though I was dreaming – or had got caught up in someone else's nightmare, more like.

The officer spoke to another officer, who turned and squinted at me through the windscreen. My officer then walked back to the car and got into the driver's seat next to me. His radio crackled. He lifted his hand, flicked a switch and it fell silent. In the gleam of the headlight, I could see someone in a paper suit bending over and something being put into a plastic bag. I realised that it was her shoe and I suddenly felt sick.

The officer took a notebook out of a pocket in his vest. 'So, can I start by taking your name?'

I turned to look at him. He was a thin man in his fifties with glasses and grey hair. 'I'm sorry,' I said, putting my hand over my mouth, 'but I need to . . .' I quickly opened the car door, hung my head out and threw up onto the road outside.

'It's the shock,' he said, when I sat back up again. 'It's a natural reaction. I'll get the paramedics to check you over, though.'

'It's OK. I'm OK.' I fished in my pocket for a tissue and wiped my mouth.

'Do you need some water?' he asked.

'It's all right. I'm OK,' I repeated, and took a few deep breaths. 'My name's Tate Kinsella,' I said finally. 'T-a-t-e. Kinsella.'

He wrote this down. 'Occupation?'

'I work there.' I pointed to the building. 'I'm an office worker. I work for a French bank on the fourteenth floor.'

'It's Saturday. You were working today?'

'No. But I went into the office.' I added, 'I went with her.'

We both looked ahead through the windscreen to where the paramedics were kneeling, surrounded by police.

'Is she dead?' I blurted out.

The officer hesitated, then said, 'I'm sorry. Yes.'

I stifled a sob. 'Was it quick?' I asked him. 'Would she have been conscious when she hit the ground?'

'I'm sorry,' he said. 'I can't answer that.' He waited for a moment, then asked gently, 'Can you tell me what happened?'

I swallowed hard and nodded. 'We went into the building together, but I lost her inside. She was . . . depressed. I knew she wanted to jump. I tried to stop her, the night before. I *did* stop her. And then she wanted to come back and I should have known, but I didn't realise . . .' I caught my breath. 'It's all my fault,' I said. 'For letting her into the building. We used my pass. She didn't have one. She doesn't work there any more and I shouldn't have let her in.'

He wrote this down. 'So, what's her name?' he asked.

'Helen. Helen Jones.'

'What's your relationship with her?'

'I . . . I don't know her. Not really. I met her for the first time last night. There was a Christmas party. She was up on the roof terrace. She was obviously suicidal. She said her life was . . . fucked up. "I've fucked up everything," that's what she said. She'd lost her job at Cowan McCauley – they're on the tenth floor – and . . . I don't know what else. I just got talking to her and I stopped her from jumping and we got a cab home. I gave her my number, because I felt sorry for her. I wanted to make sure she was OK. And then she called me. Earlier this evening. She said she'd lost an earring – a valuable earring, a diamond, she said – and she wanted to go back and look for it. But she couldn't get back into the building because she didn't have a pass, so she asked me to come with her and swipe her in. But I lost her inside the building and then by the time I realised why she really wanted to get in . . . what she was *really* there for . . . it was too late. I ran up onto the roof terrace to try and stop her, but . . .' I sobbed. 'She'd already jumped. I was too late.'

'Do you have an address for her?'

'She lived in Kenrick Place. Baker Street. That's what she told me. We stopped there in the cab. It's a building just on the corner of . . .' I cast my mind back. 'I . . . I don't know the number, but . . . I think I could show you the building, on a map.'

'Did she live with anyone else?'

I shook my head. 'I don't know. I don't think so.'

He asked, 'Do you have any contact details for her next of kin?'

I shook my head again. 'No. Like I said, I barely knew her.

I think . . . I think she lived on her own. But I don't know any more than that.'

'And can you describe to me in a bit more detail what happened this evening.'

I told him, from the start. From the phone call about the earring to the cab journey to swiping Helen into the building and then leaving her at the foot of the stairs. Then not being able to find her. 'The whole thing must have been a ruse,' I said. 'The lost earring, her fear of lifts. But I believed her because . . . well, because she said she was OK. She said she was feeling OK now and I believed her because I thought, after all, if she'd really wanted to jump, she could have done it last night . . . couldn't she?'

My voice rose, forming a question, seeking reassurance, but the officer didn't answer. He wrote down what I was saying and then began to read it back. His radio crackled again and a voice said something in police jargon that I didn't understand. The officer folded up his notebook and tucked it back into his pocket. 'Can I ask you to wait here for a moment, please?' he said.

'Yes, of course.'

He got out of the car and walked over to talk to another officer. More police appeared and my officer put his hand on his hip and scratched his head, then turned to look through the windscreen at me. The other officers all followed his gaze. They talked some more and then, finally, my officer walked back towards the car.

'What's going on?' I asked as he slid into the seat next to me.

'We're still trying to establish the victim's identity,' he told me.

My heart thumped. 'You're not saying . . . You don't want me to identify her, do you? I'm not sure if I—'

'No,' he said quickly. 'It would need to be her next of kin.'

I turned to face him. 'But it's her. Helen? Right? I mean . . . she had a phone and a handbag and . . .'

'We have her handbag,' he said. 'We're just looking into that. But there are some identity documents in her possession which suggest that she's . . .'

'She's what?' I frowned, confused.

'There seems to be an anomaly here.'

'What kind of an anomaly?'

'Who else did you see in the building this evening?'

'No one. The building was empty.'

The officer licked his lips. 'I'd like you to come down to the station with me, if that's all right with you? We've still got some enquiries to make, but I'd like to take a further statement.'

'Am I under arrest?' I asked, my heart beating fast again.

'No. No, you're not under arrest. But you're a key witness and you've been very helpful. If it's all right with you, I'll take you to the station now?'

I sighed. 'Whatever I can do to help, I will. Of course I will.'

'Thank you.' He started the engine and reversed back into the road.

When we got to the police station, he parked at the front and we walked through the main entrance into a foyer. I was taken into a small room and offered a cup of tea. The officer disappeared and a friendly middle-aged woman in plain clothes came in and sat with me. She introduced herself as a victim support officer and told me that she was here to help me at this difficult time. She asked me about my friend, then said she could get support for me if I needed it. I was informed that my officer had gone to talk to his superior. After a bit, she went away to check what was happening, leaving me with a leaflet to read. When she returned she said that the case had been passed on to CID. We were just waiting on a change of shift, she said, for someone to be assigned the case.

Several hours passed. I drank more tea and was given repeated reassurances that it wouldn't be much longer. Eventually the door opened and a female detective entered. She took a seat opposite me and placed a notebook on the table in front of her. 'Hello, Tate,' she said. 'I'm DC Gallagher. Can I call you Tate?'

'Yes,' I agreed.

She hesitated, and then placed a pen on top of the notebook. 'Tate, we've been able to speak to the victim's husband.'

'She has a husband?' I asked, surprised.

'Yes. And fortunately, he's been able to come straight away.' She paused and watched my face. 'He's been able to identify the body.'

My heart beat faster. 'And was it Helen?'

She watched me warily. 'No,' she said, finally.

'What?' I said, sitting forwards. 'But it has to be. I mean, if it's not Helen – who is it?'

'Her name was Madeleine Blakely.'

I gazed at her. '*Maddy?*'

'I understand you knew her.'

'Yes,' I stuttered. 'I mean . . . I didn't *know* her. I've met her a few times, that's all. She's been into the office. I work for her husband, Dan.' I stop. 'It was *Maddy* who fell from the roof?'

She nodded.

'But . . . how?' I asked, bewildered. 'And what was she doing there?'

The detective continued to look at me, her expression sombre. 'We were hoping you might be able to help us with that.'

PART TWO

7

CITY OF LONDON POLICE

Pre-interview legal briefing

OFFICER(S) NAMES:

DC Karen Gallagher

DC Robyn Heaton

BRIEFING LOCATION:

Farringdon Police Station

TIME: 12:15 P.M.   **DATE:** Monday, 19 December 2022

LEGAL REPRESENTATIVE DETAILS: Sarah Kellerman

DETAINED PERSON(S) DETAILS:

Tate Elizabeth Ann Kinsella   **DOB:** 8.6.84

OFFENCE: Murder, contrary to Common Law

The CIRCUMSTANCES are:

At 19:25 on Saturday, 10 December, an ambulance was called
to Eastcheap, EC1, following reports that a woman had fallen

from the roof of a commercial office block. The woman was later identified as Madeleine Blakely. On first responder arrival she was in cardiac arrest. Life was pronounced extinct at 19:48.

It's believed that the deceased had gone to the building to meet a person known to her. She had in her possession her husband Daniel's employee security pass.

Preliminary results of the post-mortem reveal the cause of death to be the impact from the fall, which caused heart failure. They also reveal that the deceased had sustained a fresh injury to the left side of the cranium above the ear. The injury is believed to have been caused by a blow from a glass object, sustained prior to the fall from the rooftop. The weapon is believed to have been an empty wine bottle, fragments of which were found on the roof terrace and have been sent away for forensic analysis.

There are no CCTV cameras on the roof terrace. Enquiries relating to CCTV from the entrance, lift and corridors are ongoing. No CCTV footage will be shown in interview.

At the time of this incident your client worked in and had access to 225 Eastcheap. She told witnesses at the scene that she was with the victim before she fell. In a subsequent statement to police, she put herself on the roof terrace immediately after the victim had fallen. She later denied having been with the victim or having seen her at all that night.

We believe that your client has an unrequited romantic interest in the deceased's husband, Daniel Blakely, which has led to obsession. We have reason to believe that your client was the person that Madeleine Blakely had gone to meet that night. We wish to question your client about her involvement in the death of Madeleine Blakely.

Your client has no criminal convictions. We are not prepared to disclose anything further at this time.

8

Monday, 19 December

I stop reading and look up. '*Obsession?* It wasn't a bloody *obsession*! And it wasn't unrequited. We were in a relationship. We were . . .' I put my head in my hands. 'We were together, for God's sake!'

Sarah pulls the laptop back round to face her and waits in silence.

'I knew he'd do this,' I whisper.

'Who?'

'Dan.' I meet her gaze. 'I knew he'd deny our relationship if anyone confronted him with it. He was worried about his daughter, Emily. He didn't want her to find out about us.'

'Either way, this gives you a clear motive for murder,' Sarah says. 'And they now have your phone. So, what will they find?'

'Nothing.'

She frowns. 'No calls, no messages – nothing at all?'

'I deleted everything. Dan insisted.'

'The phone experts can sometimes retrieve deleted messages,' Sarah points out.

'They won't find anything.'

She raises an eyebrow. 'Are you sure about that?'

'Dan's the head of information systems at an international bank,' I explain. '*He's* an expert. He knows everything there is to know about tech security.'

'And what about his wife?'

'What do you mean?'

'Will the police find messages between you and Maddy?'

I shake my head. 'No. Of course not.'

'Do you have her number stored in your contacts?'

'Maddy's number? No! Why would I? Why are you even asking me this?'

'Because,' Sarah explains patiently, 'the police are going to ask you about your contact with her on the day she died. And because I need to know before we go into the interview room whether they might find anything to incriminate you.'

'Well, they won't, because they're looking for the wrong person. They need to find Helen, check *her* phone.'

'Helen,' Sarah repeats. 'OK. Let's talk about Helen. What happened to her that night?' she asks. 'Where did she go?'

'I don't know,' I concede. 'I was with the police for the rest of that evening. I tried calling her and the next morning I went to Kenrick Place, to the building the cab stopped at, and I asked around. No one knew her. I asked the police to find her.' I gesture towards the door. 'But it doesn't look as though they even tried. They haven't even mentioned her. But she's involved in this. I just know she is.'

Sarah observes me silently.

'Maybe they're not interested in the truth.'

'Maybe they're not interested because they have you at the crime scene. And because they have a motive for you – and they don't have a motive for anyone else.'

'OK.' I take a deep breath. 'I know it sounds strange, but I think Helen may have done this for me.'

'For *you*? You think Helen killed Maddy . . . *for you*?'

I lean forward. 'Because I helped her. To say thank you. In her own warped way . . . to ingratiate herself with me, somehow. To be my friend. Because she's crazy,' I add quickly. 'I think she could be really unstable. I think Helen called Maddy – pretending to be me – and arranged to meet her at the office. Told her to come up to the roof terrace and then . . . took her by surprise. I'm assuming she hit her with the bottle we left there the night before.'

'But . . . if Helen was *helping you* by killing Maddy, why would she then disappear and leave you in the frame?'

'I don't know,' I sigh. 'I haven't worked it all out yet. But what I *am* sure of is that I shouldn't have told Helen about me and Dan. She took an . . . *unusual* interest in my relationship with him. And she said some *really* weird things.'

Sarah frowns. 'What things?'

'OK,' I tell her. 'I missed something out – from the Friday night, the night of the party. After we left, we didn't go straight home. We went to a bar. We were driving through the West End and Helen asked the cab to stop. We were somewhere in Soho. She didn't want to go home; she wanted to talk, she said. I can't remember where the bar was. We went down some steps into a cellar. I remember her ordering a bottle of wine and then putting her hand over her glass every time I tried to top her up.

I must have drunk way more of it than she did; I barely remember getting home – but I do remember asking her what she'd done that was so bad that she'd want to kill herself. She didn't say much, just something about a relationship that had gone wrong and how it was all her fault. But there was something really sinister about the way she mentioned this relationship, as if she'd done something really terrible and had nothing left to lose. That's how it seemed. And after that, she just kept diverting the conversation back to me and my relationship with Dan, asking me questions about him. About us.'

'What questions?'

'I can't remember exactly, but she seemed intrigued – almost excited – by it. It was like . . . it was like I was talking her through the plot of a TV thriller rather than her realising what a mess I was in. But I talked about Dan because . . . well, because she was so interested, and because I needed someone to talk to. And because she wasn't judging me, like I knew my friends would. So I told her way more than I should have done.' I pause, then sigh. 'I told her how amazing it was when I was with Dan, but how hard it was when he left me and went back home to his wife. To Maddy. And Helen kept saying things like, "But you deserve to be happy too, Tate. She's got everything – she's got a great big house and money and a daughter and a successful career with one of the biggest publishing houses in the country."' I pause. '"She's got everything and you've got nothing." That's what she said.'

'She knew that about Maddy already?' Sarah asks me. 'About her family and her home? Where she worked?'

I rub my forehead. 'I don't know if I told her or . . . or if she knew that already. But I remember the conversation getting really weird. And I remember this clearly: at one point, she leaned forward and she said, really softly, "You and Dan could be together, you know. If you wanted it badly enough." And then she just sat there, smiling at me.'

I watch Sarah for her reaction. Her brow is furrowed. 'OK,' she says after a moment. 'And then what?'

'That's all I've got,' I admit. 'Look, I know it's not much to go on . . .'

'No,' she agrees.

'But Helen's DNA will be on that wine bottle.'

'As will yours,' she points out.

'But when they test it, they'll be able to identify her, right?'

'They'll find a mixed profile,' she tells me. 'Which may weaken the forensic evidence against *you*. But they won't test for her at random. They'd have to arrest her as a suspect and have a sample of her DNA to compare it with first. And at the moment, it doesn't seem as though they have any other evidence that would give them the grounds to do that. If they did, they'd be pursuing her and not you.'

'But that's crazy!' I cry out. 'She shouldn't even have been in the building. She was trespassing!'

'You let her in,' she says. 'So that's a moot point, actually.'

'I didn't let her go up onto the roof, though!'

'Can you be certain that she *did*?'

She waits for me.

'No,' I concede finally.

'So, it's possible, isn't it, that the police are not going after

Helen because the CCTV doesn't support what you told them? Because they have no proof that she was even there?'

'But she *was* there!'

'On the ground floor. That's where you left her.'

'Yes.'

'But you can't say for sure that she didn't just turn round and walk back out of the building again.'

I exhale, heavily.

'Thing is, Tate . . .' Sarah leans forward and speaks gently. 'You've put yourself on the roof at the relevant time. You gave the police an account that turned out not to be true, which caused them to think they were investigating a suicide when it was in fact a murder. The information you gave them would have affected how they dealt with their investigation in the crucial first few hours. In retrospect, it could well look as though you were deliberately misdirecting them. And then, "I didn't do it. Someone else was there with me and they ran away before the police arrived."' She winces. 'It's a bit of a cliché, if I'm honest.'

I look back at her in horror. 'Are you saying that they think I made Helen up?'

'It's possible,' she replies hesitantly.

'And you?' I demand. 'Do *you* think I'm lying?'

Her eyes flicker to meet mine and her face softens. 'I wasn't there, Tate. I have no way of knowing for sure what happened that night. And I'm not here to judge you. I'm here to protect you.' She leans forward again. 'But protecting you includes preventing you from putting forward an account which . . . which might not stand up to scrutiny. It's better to make no comment until you know for sure that this is the defence you want to run.'

I think for a moment. 'Someone put me in the frame,' I say finally. 'Someone told the police about me and Dan. And as far as I'm aware, the only person who knew about us was Helen. Dan wouldn't have mentioned me to the police unless they asked him about me outright. If they did, he'd have denied that anything had happened between us, to protect Emily, but he would never have deliberately pointed the finger at me.'

Sarah looks doubtful. 'He had to be pretty suspicious of you, though, didn't he? His wife is attacked and pushed from the roof and you just happen to be there at the same time.'

'No,' I protest. 'No. He asked me, and I told him about Helen. And then he said he'd help me find her. He *believed* me,' I add pointedly.

I watch her face. Her expression is neutral but I can tell what she's thinking. She thinks I'm deluded. Nonetheless, as I launch into my account of the telephone conversation I'd had with Dan, she calmly swipes the trackpad and begins to type.

9

'It took him three days to call me,' I say. 'I'd left messages, but he was grieving, obviously, and he had Emily to think of and I didn't want to be needy. I tried my hardest not to bother him, but I couldn't eat, I couldn't sleep. I felt so guilty.'

'Guilty?' Sarah eyes me cautiously.

'About us. About our affair. I thought that Maddy had found out about us,' I explain. 'I thought it was all our fault.'

'You thought it was suicide?'

'At that stage, yes. The police didn't tell me Maddy had been attacked. Dan and I met at work, and so I thought that she was maybe making some kind of statement to the two of us by killing herself at our workplace. I was thinking all sorts, to be honest, trying to get my head around it. But then Dan called me and he told me that she'd been hit with a bottle, that they'd found the broken bottleneck on the roof and that it had . . .' I stop, take a deep breath and squeeze my eyes shut for a moment. 'It had Maddy's blood on it,' I say finally, my voice breaking up. 'He said that they thought she had been knocked to the ground and then pushed over the edge.'

Sarah takes this in. 'So what else did he say?'

'He wanted to know what I was doing at the office that night. He was suspicious to begin with, but then I reminded him that he was supposed to come and see me that evening, that I was going to order a takeaway for us and he was going to pick up a bottle of wine – we'd had it all planned. He didn't come because Maddy had to go out to meet someone. It was *him* who cancelled on *me*, not the other way round.' I pause, then add, 'I don't want to tell the police any of this, though. There's no point. Dan will just deny it.'

'And you have no evidence that he'd arranged to come over to see you?'

I shake my head. 'Like I said, he insisted that I delete all our texts, our call history, everything. He told me how to prevent anyone from retrieving the messages by installing some software on my phone. He told me that it was over between us; he said that he had to think of Emily, that he couldn't risk her finding out about us, that it would destroy her. I was devastated, but what could I do? So, I agreed to delete everything. And then he said that I mustn't call him any more because he had a family liaison officer with him almost every hour of every day.'

'So, was that the end of the conversation?'

'No. I begged him not to abandon me. I told him that I was really scared the police were going to arrest me for Maddy's murder. I told him about Helen, about how I'd met her, about the missing earring. I admitted that I'd swiped her into the building and lost her inside.'

'And what did he say?'

'He was upset with me, obviously – especially when I told him that I'd let on to Helen about us, about me and him having an affair. But I was desperate and in the end I think he felt sorry for me. I asked him – I begged him – to help me look for Helen, and he agreed. That's when he said he'd speak to Hayley and to the HR department at Cowan McCauley to see if they had another phone number or an address for her.'

'But Hayley didn't remember ever having met Helen?'

'No. And Cowan McCauley wouldn't give anything away. I've looked on social media. But you know, Helen Jones – there are hundreds of them. Dan said that it probably wasn't even her real name.'

Sarah eyes me as she finishes typing. She had clearly been thinking the same.

'The thing is, Tate,' she begins, pushing her laptop away from her and resting her arms on the tabletop. She hesitates, frowning, but I know what she's thinking: she's thinking that I can't prove any of this. I can't prove Helen exists, and I can't prove that my feelings for Dan were ever reciprocated. I can't even prove to her that Dan and I ever had this telephone conversation. Not unless I know something about the police investigation that I couldn't otherwise know.

'Maddy's phone,' I say quickly. 'He told me about Maddy's phone. It smashed when she fell from the roof, but the police told him they'd recovered the data.'

Sarah looks interested. 'And? What did they find?'

'There were text messages and calls in her log. Messages between her and Dan – messages he knew about, of course.

"What do you want to do about dinner?" "Won't be late." That kind of thing. Messages earlier that day to Kay – Emily's best mate's mum – to tell her that Emily had been grounded and that they had confiscated her phone. There was school stuff, emails to teachers. Messages to friends. But there was nothing between Maddy and anyone that referred to a meeting at the office that night.'

Sarah sits back, thinking about this. 'So, how do they know she was meeting anyone? Where did the police get that from?'

'Dan's statement. It was what Maddy told *him* before she went out.' I pre-empt her next question. 'He'd noticed that she was getting messages from someone before she left the house – and replying to them. He said she seemed distracted. Tense. Wound up. When he asked her who she was talking to, she just said, "It's work stuff," and shut herself in the bathroom. But he said that when he thought about it, there was no sound on the phone she was using. She had it on silent, which wasn't normal for her. He could always hear when she got a message, usually. She had the same notification sounds as him.'

'So . . . ?'

'So, in hindsight, he now thinks Maddy was using another phone. He said that Emily's phone was always on silent. She was always secretive about who she was talking to and when.'

'So Dan thinks Maddy was using Emily's phone . . .'

I nod.

'. . . and pretending to be Emily?'

'That's what we're thinking,' I agree. 'We don't know for sure, obviously. But Dan had confiscated Emily's phone the previous evening and now it's missing. Dan and Emily searched the house for it the next day. They searched high and low. They couldn't find it anywhere.'

'Has Dan told the police this?'

'Yes, of course. But the only phone recovered at the scene was Maddy's iPhone. Emily's was a Samsung Galaxy S10. The police searched the area for it, but no Samsung was found. Not on the roof. Not on the ground. Not anywhere.'

Sarah nods and types this up. I wait for her to finish.

'So presumably they've tried tracking it?'

'It's switched off. It's been switched off since that evening – from round about the same time Maddy died.'

Sarah's eyes flicker up to meet mine. 'You know that for sure?'

I shrug. 'That's what the police told Dan.'

'So,' she says slowly, 'either it ran out of charge at that point, which would have been highly coincidental, or . . .'

'Or whoever killed Maddy took the phone from her and turned it off.'

'But the police will know if it was in the building before it was turned off. They'll have been able to cell-site it.'

'They haven't told Dan about that,' I say. 'But I guess we'll find out soon enough.'

Sarah types some more.

'Obviously they're going to say it was me,' I tell her. 'That I took the phone and chucked it in the Thames or something.'

'But you didn't.'

'No,' I say firmly. 'I didn't. Because I wasn't the person who went to meet Maddy that night.'

Sarah thinks about this for a minute. 'So, you think that

Helen had somehow befriended Emily, which is how she had her phone number? And Maddy found out and went to meet her?'

'Maybe,' I say. 'That's where I'm lost. Dan too. We don't know what happened from there. But if the police could only find Helen, check *her* phone . . .' I trail off. 'Even if she's deleted the messages, they can track where she was at the time Maddy fell. Right?'

'So long as she had her phone with her. And so long as it was turned on,' Sarah agrees.

'And if it wasn't?'

She shrugs. 'It can still provide a picture, if it cell-sites somewhere and is then turned off at a critical point.'

'Good,' I say, pleased.

Sarah sits back, surveying the screen of her laptop for a moment. 'OK,' she says finally. 'I'll seek further disclosure regarding the phone work they've done. And I'll ask why they're refusing to show us the CCTV. They must have viewed it by now, so they're hiding something.'

I open my mouth to speak and shut it again.

There's a knock on the door. We both look up. The door opens. It's DC Gallagher, the detective who spoke to me in the witness room on the evening Maddy died.

'How much longer do you need?'

'Let me speak to my client,' Sarah says.

DC Gallagher shuts the door.

Sarah turns back to face me. 'It might be good to find out a little more of what they've got before we go any further.'

I nod. This sounds good to me.

'They'll drip-feed it, of course,' Sarah continues. 'There will be more than one interview. There could be several. But my advice to you hasn't changed. No comment, Tate. Let's put them to proof.' She pauses. 'Which means that they have to prove you killed Maddy. You don't have to prove that you didn't. So let's see what their witnesses are saying, shall we?'

10

WITNESS STATEMENT

Criminal Procedure Rules r. 16.2; Criminal Justice
Act 1967, S.9; Magistrates' Court Act 1980, s.5B

STATEMENT OF: Jeremy Allen Seager

AGE IF UNDER 18: +18 yrs (if over 18 insert 'over 18')

OCCUPATION: CEO

This statement (consisting of 5 page(s) signed by me) is true to the best of my knowledge and belief and I make it knowing that, if it is tendered in evidence, I shall be liable to prosecution if I have wilfully stated in it anything which I know to be false, or do not believe to be true.

WITNESS SIGNATURE: J.A. Seager   **DATE:** 12/12/2022

I am the above-named person. Most people know me as Jerry. I am the chief executive officer of the London branch of Le Crédit Privé Français, a leading international bank, known by the acronym CPF. Our London offices are situated on levels twelve to nineteen of 225 Eastcheap, EC1, which I shall refer to as '225'. 225 is a high-rise commercial office block housing several different companies. The block is managed by East-cheap Property Management (EPM) and they have a contract with a security company called Sky Guardians Security (SGS).

On Saturday 10th December at just after 11 p.m., I was at home watching TV with my wife, Sharon. We were just about to get ready to go to bed when I received a phone call from Dan Blakely. Dan is an employee at CPF and I also consider him to be a friend. He has been head of information systems at the bank for the past twelve years and was recently promoted to the board as director of operations. He is, in my opinion, excellent at his job.

Dan apologised for calling so late. He sounded very shaken and upset and I asked him if he was OK. He said that he wasn't OK and told me that his wife Maddy had died. He said she had gone out earlier that evening to meet someone unknown to him. He had then been called by the police to say that a woman had fallen to her death from the roof terrace of our workplace and that they believed it to be Maddy. The police believed that Maddy had arranged to meet someone at 225 as she had Dan's security pass in her coat pocket and had used it to gain access. He said that the police were treating her death as suspicious as she had been attacked before falling from the roof. The police therefore believed she had been pushed.

I was extremely shocked and upset at this news as I had got to know Maddy over the years that Dan had worked at the bank and Sharon and I were very fond of her and their daughter, Emily. We had been invited to dinner at their house numerous times. Dan told me that he had already been to the mortuary at Southwark St Martin's Hospital and made a positive identification of Maddy's body. He had asked the senior investigating officer if the police had viewed the CCTV from 225 and if they had any leads as to who might have been on the roof terrace with Maddy before she fell. The officer had told him that they didn't have any leads as yet, but that the security guard on duty had been instructed to preserve the CCTV footage and that they would send someone to view it in the morning. Dan expressed his concerns to me about this as both Dan and I have had issues with the security company in the past and had raised these more than once with Jamie Hopkins, head of the block management company, EPM. During the week there are usually two doormen from SGS on duty but at the weekend there is usually only one, and Dan didn't think that the particular doorman on duty that night was sufficiently trained to be able to export the footage onto a removable storage device. Dan told me that he had therefore decided to go straight from the mortuary to 225 to check the footage had been properly preserved and to export it himself, if necessary, before any mistakes could be made.

I am not particularly knowledgeable regarding video security systems, but Dan is very experienced in this regard and has made me aware that mistakes can happen. For instance, the cameras have motion detection to save on storage space and so often switch on and off and therefore don't record everything, so it can be hard to find an 'event', with the result that it can then be overlooked or overwritten. Also, the footage often records on a loop and if the operative is inexperienced, they can accidentally reset it to start recording again, so that, again, it overwrites. On this occasion, Dan told me that his instincts had been correct and that the security guard on duty, Kevin Prescott, was not sufficiently trained to replay the recording, let alone produce copies for the police. He also noted that the time on the system was inaccurate as it was still set at BST rather than GMT as it should have been.

Dan told me that he acted swiftly to try to retrieve the data but that the relevant period had already been overwritten. He informed me that there was no coverage whatsoever of the inside of the building at the time Maddy died. Dan also discovered that the cameras in the stairwell and lower-ground-floor corridor were not functioning. They appeared to have been turned off, along with the camera that pointed at the exit to the car park at the rear. He was completely distraught about this and told me that he held SGS fully responsible. He asked me to take it up with Jamie Hopkins of EPM. I agreed that I would do so straight away. Dan Blakely is highly experienced and I trust him fully in every respect, and have compete faith in him professionally. If Dan was unable to recover the missing footage, then I'm confident that no one else will be able to do so. It is clearly lost and if Dan holds SGS responsible for this error, I will support him fully on this point.

I also feel it important to mention that at the office Christmas party on Friday, the day before Maddy died, I mislaid my SGS security pass. The last time I used it was when I entered the building to go up to the bar for the party at around 7 p.m. When I looked for it in my coat pocket sometime before I left the party at around midnight, it was gone. There was a lot of alcohol drunk that night and I didn't think anything of it at the time. I assumed that it must have fallen out of my pocket and that another staff member had picked it up in error, confusing it for their own. If it didn't turn up on Monday, the normal procedure would be to report it lost and get a replacement. But after Dan phoned and told me about what had happened to Maddy, it occurred to me that it might have been stolen rather than lost. In hindsight, I remember something occurring when I was outside on the roof terrace in the smoking area on the evening of the party. It was not long after I'd had my turn on the karaoke. I put my coat on and went outside for a cigarette. There was no one else out there except one of the agency staff. I didn't know her name at the time and I asked her who she was. She told me that her name was Tate Kinsella. She made a point of talking to me and began flirting with me. She got up very close to me and tried to kiss me. I remember this because I rebuffed her and she wasn't very happy about it. It was after that that I discovered my SGS pass had gone.

I fully support the police with their enquiries and am willing to attend court if necessary.

SIGNED: J.A. Seager   **DATE:** 12/12/2022

11

Monday, 19 December

The interview room is warm and airless. When DC Gallagher
has finished reading Jerry's statement, she looks up and gives
me a long, penetrating stare.

'OK, Tate,' she says. 'Tell us about the security pass.'

I turn to look at Sarah, who's sitting next to me. She inclines
her head and gives it a quick shake.

'No comment,' I say, although I want to answer the question. I remember flirting with Jerry on the roof terrace that
evening. It was just a stupid joke; it didn't mean anything, and
I wasn't at all upset about it. I didn't even think it worth men-
tioning to Sarah. I had nothing to do with his security pass
going missing that night. I want to tell the police this, but I
know I must listen to my lawyer. She's experienced. She knows
what she's doing. This is my first police interview. Sarah, on
the other hand, has done this a million times.

'Do you remember speaking to Jerry Seager?' I'm asked.

'No comment.'

'What did he say to you?'

'No comment,' I repeat.

'Did you flirt with him?'

'No comment.'

'Maybe you don't remember. Were you drunk?'

'No comment,' I say again.

'Or did you flirt with him deliberately?' asks DC Gallagher. 'Did you try to kiss him so that you could get up close to him and steal his security pass?'

'Do you have any evidence that my client stole it?' Sarah jumps in quickly.

DC Gallagher looks across at her.

'There were . . . what?' Sarah continues. 'Over a hundred people at the party that night?'

DC Gallagher ignores her and looks back at me.

'Where was Jerry's coat when he wasn't wearing it?' Sarah persists.

'I'm asking the questions,' DC Gallagher retorts.

'But only the ones that suit you.'

'Did you take Jerry's pass from his coat pocket?' DC Gallagher asks me, ignoring Sarah.

'No comment,' I reply.

'What did you do with the missing pass, Tate?'

'No comment.'

'How did you steal it?'

'No comment.'

'*When* did you steal it?'

'No comment.'

'Who did you give it to?'

'No comment.'

'Did you keep it and use it to get into the building?' she asks me. 'On the night that Maddy Blakely died?'

'No.'

Sarah shakes her head at me.

'Comment,' I add.

DC Gallagher looks irritated. 'Did you use it to let anyone else into the building?'

'No comment.'

'What about . . .' She scans her notes. 'Helen?' she asks. 'Helen Jones?'

Sarah raises her eyes. She's interested – as am I.

'You gave a statement saying that there was someone with you that night,' DC Gallagher reads from the page in front of her. 'That you let them into the building. A woman named "Helen Jones". Did you give Jerry Seager's pass to Helen Jones, Tate?'

'No comment.'

DC Gallagher sits back in her seat and smiles. 'No. You didn't. Because there was no one with you that night.'

Sarah shoots me a warning glance.

'The thing is, Tate, we've checked out what you said in your statement, and you see . . . what you've told us doesn't make sense. We haven't been able to find any trace of Helen Jones.' She enunciates the name acerbically, as if I've made up something ridiculous. 'There's no one of that name living in the mansion block you pointed out in Kenrick Place. Cowan McCauley have no record of a Helen Jones ever having worked for them. And Hayley Allbright's never met anyone of that name.' She looks up at me. 'How do you explain that?'

I heave a sigh.

DC Gallagher leans forward, clearly encouraged by my expression. 'The truth is, you left the party on your own on the Friday night, didn't you, Tate? And on the Saturday, you came back to 225 Eastcheap – alone. Again.' She pauses for effect. 'There was no one with you on either occasion, was there, Tate?'

'No comment.'

'The truth is that there is no Helen Jones. The truth is that you were acting alone. The truth is that you were obsessed with Maddy Blakely's husband. Isn't that right, Tate?'

I close my eyes to shut her out.

DC Gallagher waits until I open them again, then gazes at me for a long moment before pulling out another sheet of paper from a file on the table in front of her. 'We have a statement here from Dan Blakely's PA, Hayley Allbright. Hayley likes you. She says she's never had a problem with you either personally or professionally. But she mentions that she believed you were obsessed with Dan Blakely. She says that she often caught you watching him.'

I look down at my hands and pick at the cuticle of my thumb.

'Hayley says,' DC Gallagher continues, 'Dan told her that, on one occasion, some personal items – his diary, a family photo in a silver frame – had gone missing from his desk.' She peers up at me. 'Did you steal those items from Dan Blakely's desk, Tate? Did you take his things?'

'You don't have to answer that,' Sarah intervenes sharply.

DC Gallagher lowers her eyes and continues to read. 'Hayley says that on one occasion in late August, she dropped off some papers to Dan at home and saw you hiding behind a bush in his garden. And on another occasion in early September, she met him at a restaurant in Soho for a business lunch before driving him to the airport for an overseas trip. When they came out of the restaurant, she saw your green Corsa outside, parked across the street. She doesn't think Dan noticed your car and she didn't mention it because she didn't want to worry him, but she saw you, Tate. She saw you, sitting in the driver's seat. She saw you trying to slide down so that she didn't see you.' DC Gallagher looks up at me. 'Have you been stalking Dan Blakely, Tate?'

'Again, you don't have to answer that,' says Sarah. 'You haven't been arrested for theft or stalking. So maybe DC Gallagher would like to get to the point.'

'Are you in love with him?' asks the other officer, DC Heaton, speaking for the first time. 'Tate, are you in love with Dan Blakely?'

I bite my lip.

'Must be tough,' she continues gently. 'Loving someone who you know, deep down, won't ever love you back. Dan has a daughter, doesn't he? A daughter he thinks the world of. He would never give up his wife and his daughter and his beautiful home to live in an apartment and be a part-time dad.'

I shrug.

'What was that, Tate?' DC Gallagher pounces.

Sarah reaches across under the table and places her hand on mine. She squeezes it and looks at me sympathetically while moving her head from side to side.

'No comment,' I say.

'That must have made you feel pretty desperate,' says DC Heaton.

DC Gallagher slides Hayley's statement into the back of her notepad. 'So desperate,' she agrees with her colleague, 'that when you saw an opportunity to take Jerry Seager's pass out of his coat pocket at the party, you hatched a plan, and the following day you carried it out. You got a taxi, alone,' she emphasises, 'from your address to 225 Eastcheap, where you'd arranged to meet Maddy Blakely on the roof terrace in the early evening of Saturday. And you used Jerry Seager's pass to get in.'

I glance at Sarah again. She's frowning, uncertain. She's wondering why – if I had gone to 225 innocently, to find an earring, as I'd told her I had – I would need to use someone else's security pass.

DC Gallagher notices Sarah's expression. Her own is one of mild pleasure. 'Your client hasn't explained to you, has she?'

'Explained what?' Sarah asks coolly.

DC Gallagher smiles. 'That you need a security pass to move around the building inside 225 Eastcheap. You need a pass to go everywhere. From corridors and stairwells to access the offices on every floor.'

'Yes. I'm aware of that,' Sarah says guardedly.

'And has she told you that there is a record of everyone coming in and out, via all the various places they swipe?'

Sarah looks at me. I nod guiltily. After a moment, she shrugs. 'I'd have figured that to be the case.'

'Well, Tate was in the building,' DC Gallagher says. 'She gave a statement in which she puts herself in the building that evening, in the lift, in the stairwell, and – crucially – on the roof terrace. She admits she was on the roof terrace soon after Maddy Blakely fell.'

'Yes,' says Sarah. 'We know that already. What's your point?'

'Tate's a temporary staff member,' DC Gallagher explains, with exaggerated patience. 'Or *was*. And as such – and I have had this confirmed by multiple sources – as a temporary, junior staff member, Tate has never been issued with a security pass.'

12

WITNESS STATEMENT

Criminal Procedure Rules r. 16.2; Criminal Justice
Act 1967, S.9; Magistrates' Court Act 1980, s.5B

STATEMENT OF: Kevin Prescott

AGE IF UNDER 18: +18 yrs (if over 18 insert 'over 18')

OCCUPATION: Security Officer

This statement (consisting of 8 page(s) signed by me) is true to the best of my knowledge and belief and I make it knowing that, if it is tendered in evidence, I shall be liable to prosecution if I have wilfully stated in it anything which I know to be false, or do not believe to be true.

WITNESS SIGNATURE: K. Prescott   **DATE:** 11/12/2022

I am the above-named person. I am employed as a security officer by a company called Sky Guardians Security. I am currently contracted to work as a doorman at 225 Eastcheap, a multi-office tower block in Central London which is home to a number of different companies. I am an experienced doorman and although my background is in entertainment security, I have worked in a commercial office environment for the last four contracts and the procedure for getting in and out of the building has been reasonably similar every time. Permanent staff members are given a security pass with their name on it and a photo, taken on their first day of work. You need a security pass to get in through the turnstile on the ground floor at the entrance and also to get from the lift and stairwells to the offices on the different floors. The pass then has to be either renewed at regular intervals or handed in when a staff member's employment ends.

Different companies have different policies, but none of the companies at 225 Eastcheap give out security passes to temporary agency staff. Temporary staff members can enter the building through the external doors without a pass, as can any visitors, but every day, when they come in, they first need to come to the security desk and sign the visitors' book. They would then be issued with a visitor card on a lanyard and we would phone up to the relevant company, who would send someone down to meet them. We would then let them through the turnstile on the ground floor and they would be escorted upstairs.

The turnstile on the ground floor has a solid perspex screen which draws back when you swipe your pass at the reader. Although a staff member would be able to buzz or swipe a visitor or temporary staff member through the doors to the offices on the floors upstairs, it would be impossible for anyone to get through the ground-floor turnstile without their own security pass. It is also impossible for more than one person at a time to get through the turnstile or to 'swipe' someone else in. You have to have your own pass to get through the turnstile, just as you do at the tube station, for instance. There is one other entrance to the building, which is at lower ground level and backs onto Greystone Way. This is the entrance to the underground car park and only staff members with a permanent pass can enter or exit this way. These measures, combined with a good-quality video surveillance system, provide a very high level of security. I would say that it's impossible for anyone who doesn't work in the building to gain access – unless, of course, someone has unauthorised use of another staff member's security pass.

For this reason, I don't always monitor who is going in and out through the turnstile or the car park entrance, especially at the weekends, when I work alone. As I can't be in two places at once, I prefer to stay in the office and monitor the whole building live via the camera surveillance system. But I have other duties too, including touring the building at regular intervals, and I can't watch the cameras live during every minute of my shift. At six o'clock on a Saturday, I would not expect many staff members to be in the building anyway. And at weekends, staff members are asked to contact us in advance to let us know that they will be in. I had not been informed that anyone would be in the building and so wasn't expecting anyone to be there that night. Therefore, if anyone I didn't know came in, I would have assumed they were there with the cleaners. But as long as they had used a security pass, I would not usually have searched or questioned them.

On the evening of Saturday 10th December, I was on duty at 225 Eastcheap as usual. At approximately 7.15 p.m., I was seated in the office, which is in the corner to the left of the desk as you go in. I was watching the security cameras when a woman came into the building through the revolving doors into the lobby. She had long, dark, wavy hair and a red coat. She was in her mid to late thirties, I would say. She walked over and was waiting by the front desk and so I got up and walked out into the lobby to meet her. She asked me for directions to St Katharine Docks near Tower Bridge and I gave them to her. She asked if she could use the toilet and I explained that the toilets are located by the stairwells inside the turnstile and that only staff members were allowed through. She pleaded with me for a moment, saying she was desperate, but I told her that I couldn't let her in. She then seemed to forget about needing the toilet. She told me she was going to a party at the Docks, but had got lost. She showed me the location on her phone and I pointed out which route to take. She smiled and said thank you, then she told me she liked a man in uniform and asked what time I finished work. I told her I wouldn't be finished until the early hours of the morning. At that point, I was not comfortable with the way the conversation was going and I tried to get her to leave. I said something like, 'You'll be tucked up in bed by then.' At this, she leaned close to me and said, 'You could always come and join me there later if you like.' I then told her that she needed to go as I had to get back to work. She continued flirting with me, so I talked to her for a moment longer and then showed her to the door.

This conversation definitely happened on Saturday night, the tenth. I know that because of what happened next. I noticed through the glass windows in the foyer that there was a lot of commotion outside. I could see that cars were backing up in the street and people were getting out of them and running across the road. I ushered the woman out of the building and locked the revolving doors. I could immediately see that someone had been injured. There was a woman lying on the pavement and a small crowd was around her, maybe four or five people. Someone was kneeling down, trying to give her first aid. Someone else was standing next to her on the phone to the emergency services. I was informed that an ambulance was on its way. I immediately took charge of the situation and asked everyone to step back. Other security officers arrived to assist from some of the nearby shops and bars. We worked together to secure the scene. We asked the pedestrians to move away and we directed the traffic to reverse back into Turn Again Lane and out onto Greystone Way.

I did not see where the woman with dark hair who had come into the building went. However, I was at one point approached by a female member of the public who asked for my help. The woman who approached me was in her sixties, perhaps, and had short grey hair and glasses. She was gripping the arm of another woman, who was of medium build, mid to late thirties, with long fair hair and wearing a beige puffa jacket. The older woman told me that the younger woman was a witness to what had happened inside the building, that she had been with the woman who had fallen and was trying to leave the scene. I told the younger woman that she had to stay and talk to the police.

I took her arm and she tried to shrug me off. She then started screaming at me to let go. I told her that if she stayed right there and didn't move, I would let go of her arm. She agreed that she would. I then kept her in my sight until the police arrived and I pointed her out to them. I saw them take her away in a police car. I have since been told that she is a temporary staff member at CPF, one of the companies at 225 Eastcheap, which operates on levels twelve to nineteen. I'm told that her name is Tate Kinsella. I don't remember having seen her before, but I work the evening and weekend shifts and don't tend to see many of the staff that work there during the day. However, I can confirm that I have checked the records for the past four months, that she has worked there and that there is no record of a security pass having been issued in that name.

The police at the scene later told me that the woman who fell from the roof had died. They said they were not yet sure what kind of investigation this was and asked me to preserve the CCTV footage for that time period, which I did. I did not immediately check the footage myself as I know there are no security cameras on the roof. Also, as I mentioned, while I know and recognise some of the staff that work at the US law firms who tend to work during weekday evenings, I don't know many of the day staff from the bank and might not have been able to recognise them in any event. However, I was not concerned with this as I knew that there were no visitors inside the building and that all staff present at the time of the incident would be traceable and identifiable from both the footage and from the log of their movements using their employee security passes.

In respect of the CCTV footage, I consider myself to be suitably trained to operate the surveillance systems and also to produce copies of the footage for the police as needed. However, I had spoken to my superior at SGS and we had agreed that, given the nature and seriousness of the incident that evening, I would leave it until the morning so he could come down and do it himself. I did not at any stage attempt to play it back or produce copies for the police. As far as I'm aware, the time and date on the system were correct. I did not turn off the cameras on the ground and lower ground floors or in the car park, nor am I aware of them having been turned off.

Later that evening, at some time after 10 p.m., I was in the office when a man arrived. I know him to be Daniel Blakely, who is the head of IT at CPF. He made me aware that it was his wife who had fallen from the roof earlier that evening and he asked to see the CCTV footage of the relevant period. I told him that I couldn't show it to him as the police had asked me to preserve it and I didn't want to interfere with their investigation. I can confirm that there was a disagreement between us, but I do not wish to say anything further about this. Dan Blakely is a grieving man whose wife had just died in terrible circumstances and I do not wish to make matters any worse for him than they already are.

Further to the above, I can confirm that I was also on duty on the evening of Friday 9th December. I was on the desk all evening, checking passes. I do not remember any ex-staff member coming into the building and asking to be let up to the party. In any event, I would never let someone into the building if they did not have a security pass. They would first have to sign the visitors' book and someone from the company would have to come down to collect them. I have checked the visitors' book for the evening of Friday 9th December and can confirm that no one who didn't work there had signed in. This is what I would have expected as the party was for staff only and there were no guests invited.

This statement is true to the best of my knowledge and belief. I am willing to attend court if necessary.

SIGNED: K. Prescott   **DATE:** 11/12/2022

13

Monday, 19 December

Sarah follows me into the consultation room, closes the door and leans up against it. I slide into my usual seat on the bench at the table and watch her silently.

'So, what was that?' Sarah continues to stand in the doorway, frowning at me, hugging her laptop to her chest defensively, as if she's not sure whether to stay or go.

I put my head in my hands. 'I'm sorry.'

'Why?' She looks back at me, her expression incredulous, as I look up again. 'Why would you not tell me that temps don't get a security pass? And why wouldn't you realise that the police would know that?'

'I had a security pass,' I mutter.

'It just wasn't yours.'

I look at her for a moment, thinking hard.

'I'm trying to help you, Tate,' she says firmly. 'That's what I'm here for. But I can't represent you properly if I'm the only person in the room who doesn't know the most basic of facts.'

'I'm sorry,' I say again.

'You do realise,' she persists, 'that the police will have a record of every pass used in the building that evening. They haven't told us whose yet, but it's fairly obvious that Jerry Seager's is going to be one of them.'

'I didn't take Jerry's pass,' I tell her.

'So whose did you use?'

I hesitate. 'Temp One.'

'*Temp One?*'

'It's a . . . a contractor's pass,' I say. 'It's registered as "Temp One".'

'The security guard said temps don't get given passes.'

'Contract staff get given them. Cleaners, construction workers, anyone who needs one. If the bosses ask, they give them out. It's not as cut and dried as Kevin says.'

'But the passes have photos. Names.'

'The permanent ones do.'

She watches me for a moment. 'Who gave it to you?'

'Dan,' I confess. 'About a month before . . . before it happened. He gave it to me so that I could get in and out for hospital appointments without having to go through security every time.'

'Hospital appointments?'

'It's . . . just a heart palpitation thing. It's not important.'

'And there will be a record of it?'

I look up. 'Of what?'

'That someone used the Temp One pass that night?'

'Absolutely. Yes.'

'So why didn't you just tell them that? Tell *me* that!'

'I shouldn't have used it,' I explain. 'Not at the weekend. I thought if I told anyone, I'd get Dan into trouble.'

'More trouble than you're already in?'

'Look, I told them . . . you . . . that I was in the building,' I point out. 'I thought that was enough. I knew I was going to have to explain what I was doing there. I didn't know I'd need to explain how I got in.'

'OK, but when Jerry Seager's pass went missing . . .'

'I didn't know it had gone missing!'

Sarah hesitates. 'Didn't you?'

'No!' I say emphatically. 'This is the first I've heard of it. And whoever took it out of his coat pocket that night, it definitely wasn't me! He wasn't even wearing his coat when he came out onto the terrace.'

'He's lying?'

'Not lying, no. But he's mistaken. He was drunk. Everyone was. He was in his shirtsleeves. He was hot.'

'And did you try to kiss him?'

'Not that I remember. But I could have done. I remember talking to him, flirting with him. Like I said, we'd all drunk a lot. I was missing Dan. I may have said something to Jerry that he took the wrong way. And then Hayley's found out I was in the building the night Maddy died and – oh, wait – suddenly she's remembered all this stuff about me!'

'It's not true?'

'No!' I hesitate. 'OK, so I did take the photograph. I was cleaning his desk and I accidentally knocked it off. I was too embarrassed to tell Dan, so I thought I'd just take it to get the glass replaced and put it back before he noticed.'

'And what about the diary?'

I stare at the table in front of me. 'He was working from

home a lot around that time. I just wanted to make a note of all the board meetings so that I knew when he would be in. I was going to put it back.'

'Did you stalk him?'

'Definitely not! Hayley doesn't know we were in a relationship,' I explain. 'She's seen a few things and got the wrong end of the stick.'

'So when she saw you at his house that time . . .'

'It was *her* I was hiding from, not him! Same as the time outside the restaurant. We'd agreed I'd take him to the airport, then *she* offered. He couldn't tell her he already had a lift, that I was waiting outside. I didn't know she was going to be there, so I hid.'

Sarah eyes me thoughtfully. 'What about Helen? Everything you told me—'

'Is true!' I insist. 'She was there at the party. Someone had to have let her in. And she phoned me the next day, like I told you. We got a cab together. She told me she'd lost her earring, that she'd lost her job at Cowan McCauley. Right up until we got into the building, everything's true. Except that . . . except that – obviously – I didn't swipe her in.'

'No,' she says. 'Because apparently that's not even possible!'

I look up at her penitently.

'Did you even try?'

I shake my head. 'I left her in the lobby. It was like you said: I didn't know her. I didn't feel comfortable. She gave me a description of the earring and I left her there and went in to look for it on my own.'

She makes a persevering face.

'I didn't know the passes only let in one person. I made a mistake.'

'You didn't make a *mistake*, Tate. You lied,' Sarah reprimands me. 'You lied to the police, and once you do that, *that's* when they start to build a case against you. The moment you get caught out in a lie, it casts doubt on *everything else* you say.'

'I swear to God,' I plead, my eyes filling with tears. 'It wasn't me who killed Maddy! Whoever was up there on the roof with her when she fell – it wasn't me!'

'So, why lie?'

'I panicked! And once I'd said it, I didn't know how to go back.'

She waits for me.

'When I found out that it was Maddy who'd died,' I explain, 'I knew I was in big trouble. I was in the building. I was having an affair with her husband. The police were bound to find that out, sooner or later. I knew straight away that this would put the spotlight on me.'

'But you told me you didn't find out that it was Maddy until later?'

I put my head in my hands. Teardrops plop onto the table-top. I use my sleeve to wipe them away. After a moment, I feel the table move. Sarah slides onto the bench opposite me and places her laptop on the table, shrugging her bag from her shoulder and dropping it to the floor.

'When did you know it was Maddy?' she asks me softly.

'I saw her shoe,' I sob. 'I was in the police car and I saw her shoe.'

She opens her laptop, still looking at me.

'It was a trainer. A white trainer,' I continue. 'They picked it up and put it in an evidence bag right in front of me. I was sitting there, looking through the windscreen of the police car at it, and it suddenly hit me: Helen was wearing heels. Slingbacks. Red slingbacks with killer heels. She was all dressed up, as if we were going out for the evening. But this wasn't a slingback. It was a white trainer. And so I remember thinking, "That isn't right." And then . . . and then I remembered that the bag I'd seen hanging on the railing was a . . . well, it looked like a Gucci. Pink and grey. It looked familiar, but it wasn't Helen's. And I kept asking myself: Where have I seen that bag before?'

Sarah waits.

'And then it came to me in a flash: Maddy. She'd come into the office a few weeks earlier. She'd come in to see Dan and she was carrying that bag. I liked it and I asked her whose it was and she said, "Mine," and I laughed and said, "I meant which designer?" and she said, "That one who makes all the fake designer handbags. The name escapes me," and I laughed again.' I look up at her. 'It was Maddy's bag. And it was Maddy's shoe.'

Sarah nods. 'So, when you told me that you found out at the police station that it was Maddy, that wasn't true either.'

I hang my head. 'I knew I was in serious trouble. I needed them – you – to believe that there was someone else there in the building besides me. I swear, I was going to tell them the truth. When the police arrived, I still thought it was Helen who had fallen. I thought she'd got into the building somehow and . . . you know. That's what I thought had happened. But then . . . then I saw the shoe.' I close my eyes. 'And I freaked out. I threw up with the shock. And when the cop started asking me questions, I just carried on as if I still thought it was Helen. Afterwards, I wanted to come clean, but I knew I'd be in even more trouble. I knew how it would look.'

'Well, in all honesty, it doesn't look that great now, Tate,' Sarah says. 'You've been caught out in a lie about what happened inside the building. And witnesses say they had to stop you leaving the scene.'

'They misunderstood!' I protest. 'I was trying to get to her . . . to Helen. At that point, I still thought it was Helen. They had to hold me back because I was trying to get closer to her, not because I was trying to run away. If I'd known then that it was Maddy . . . If I'd done anything wrong, why would I even tell the police I had been in the building?'

'Arguably,' she says, 'at that point, you still thought there would be CCTV.'

I fall silent, looking back at her. 'What are you saying?'

There's a further silence and then she says, 'I'm saying that the police might wonder if you had something to do with what happened to the CCTV.'

'No!' I protest again in horror. 'When would I have done that? How would I have done that? How would I even know how to reset it?'

She's silent, still.

I look at her and begin to cry again. 'I didn't kill Maddy. You have to believe me.'

'It doesn't matter what I believe, Tate,' Sarah tells me. 'It will come down to what the police can prove. At the moment, the case against you is largely circumstantial, but what you say to the police can make all the difference. If a suspect lies about what happened at a crime scene, the police and – more importantly – the jury are going to want to ask themselves why.'

'But there was someone else in the building!' I protest. 'There had to be. How can I have been using both Temp One *and* Jerry Seager's security pass?'

'You're sure about this?' Sarah asks me. 'That there will be a record of a pass for Temp One inside the building?'

'They'll find Temp One there,' I insist. 'I promise you. Someone else had to be using Jerry's pass.' I run my tongue over my dry lips. 'And I think it was Helen.'

'Helen,' she repeats.

'Yes.' I lean towards her. 'Helen. She was at the office party. She had loads of opportunity to steal it. In fact, she could have stolen a hundred security passes that evening. It was probably completely random that it was Jerry's – all of our coats were hanging up on hooks near the bar. Anyone could have stolen it, obviously, but everyone else at the party on the Friday worked there and already had a pass. The only other person I saw in the building on the Saturday was Helen. And now it looks as though the security guard saw her too!'

Sarah nods, as if she was expecting this. 'So, that was Helen? The member of the public who came into reception and flirted with the security guard?'

'Dressed up in her long red coat and slingbacks,' I agree. 'All ready for a party at the Docks. Except that she wasn't going to a party at the Docks. Because she came to the building in a taxi to look for an earring with me.'

Sarah moves away from me slightly. 'But if Helen was in reception talking to the security guard when Maddy fell, how could she have been the one who pushed her off the roof of the building?'

'She couldn't,' I say. 'But isn't it a bit convenient that she distracted the guard at the exact same moment that Maddy fell?'

Her eyes fix on mine.

'The security guy is lying,' I say. 'He wasn't trying to get rid of her. He was flirting back with her. All that stuff about "You'll be tucked up in bed by then . . ."'

'It doesn't sound like the sort of thing you say when you want someone to go away,' she agrees.

'So, if he lied about that, then maybe he's lied about every-thing. Maybe he *did* let her in to use the toilet. Or maybe she sneaked in with Jerry's pass. Either way, he took his eye off the ball and is covering his tracks. That's what I think. Maybe what really happened is that she sneaked in after I did and took the lift up to the roof. And then, when the security guy realised that he'd let a complete stranger into the building and someone had died, he went into the office and destroyed the CCTV to cover his back.'

Sarah looks at me thoughtfully for a moment. 'It's an inter-esting theory,' she says finally.

'But?'

'But it's just that. A theory,' she says. 'Without any evidence that's what happened, it's not something we can realistically put forward as a defence.'

I drop my head, study my fingernails. 'So what happens now?'

'My advice doesn't change, Tate. You made a statement denying you saw Maddy that night. You told them about Helen. Now you continue to exercise your right to silence. We go back in, find out what else they've got and take it from there.'

'OK,' I agree.

She stands up. 'I'll get some water.'

The door opens and I hear movement outside. I sit with my head in my hands and wait. A minute later, she returns with two plastic cups and places them on the table in front of me. She closes her laptop, then picks up her bag and coat. 'Ready?' she says.

I nod.

'Feeling OK?' she asks me.

'Yep.' My tone is decisive.

But my gut twists a little as I follow her out of the door and down the corridor to the interview room. I really am sorry about all the lies I've told her. After all, she's working so hard for me.

14

The second interview is over two hours long. The third is closer to three. The questions are interminable. How well did I know Maddy? How did I lure her to the building? What was I wearing? What colour are my eyes? What did I have for breakfast that morning? What did I watch on TV? But no phone, forensic or CCTV evidence is produced. Sarah's questions about Emily's phone are either ignored or deflected. Little more is revealed.

'Shouldn't I have told them,' I ask Sarah between interviews, 'that I had nothing to do with Jerry's security pass?'

'Not unless they can prove that you *did* have anything to do with it,' she tells me. 'They have to prove it. You don't have to *dis*prove it. Like I said before, the law says it's on them, not on you. Jerry Seager was far from certain at what point during the evening his pass went missing, and right now, they haven't come up with any evidence that says it was you.'

'But if I'm innocent . . .'

'If you're innocent, then they won't be able to prove that

you took it. As you said, if your pass – Temp One – is also detected as being inside the building, there had to be someone else inside too, and without the CCTV they will have no way of knowing for sure if either of those passholders was you.'

Frustrated by my silence, the two detectives stretch the third interview out until way after midnight, pausing at length between questions and appearing wounded by my 'No comment' responses, as if they were deserving of a confession or, at the very least, a different reply. Eventually, DC Gallagher looks at the clock on the wall and says she's ending the interview. She presses a button and ejects the DVD discs one by one, puts them back in their cases, then seals them up with a large sticky label on which she's written my name and the time and date in thick black marker pen. She and DC Heaton walk us all back to the custody area and disappear through a side door.

'It's going to CPS,' Sarah tells me back in the consultation room. 'That means they've finished interviewing you for now. They'll send off your file to a lawyer, who'll make a decision in the next few hours as to what happens next.'

I ask anxiously, 'And what will that be?'

'Well,' she says. 'If they don't have enough evidence to charge you, they'll bail you.'

'And if they do have enough evidence?'

'Then it will be a charge and . . .' – she hesitates – '. . . a remand.'

My heart thumps. 'Remand?'

'You'll be taken to the magistrates' court and then to the crown court. It's there that we can apply for bail.'

'And would we get it?'

'Bail in murder cases is rare,' she says, 'but let's take this one step at a time. They may not have enough evidence to charge you. Or,' she says, watching my expression, 'they might . . . and we can deal with it. Whatever happens, we'll deal with it. In the meantime, stay strong and try and get some rest.'

I say goodbye to her and am led back to my cell, where I lie down on the narrow bed, dazed and exhausted by the day's events. I close my eyes, but the coldness of my toes, the detergent odour of the thin plastic mattress, the banging of cell doors by the other inmates – none of this is conducive to sleep. Instead, I watch the shadows move across the ceiling and listen to my neighbours shouting to each other, the steady pounding of fist and foot against metal almost lulling me to sleep after a while. But every time it goes quiet, the banging starts up again and each time my heart starts thumping with it. And then, for the millionth time, I see Maddy falling, her arms flailing wildly as she plummets from the roof and sails through the air before thudding like a sack to the ground.

Hours later, after the banging and shouting stop, I'm still awake and thinking in the dark when the door rattles and opens. A shaft of bright light enters the cell. I quickly lift my hand to shield my eyes.

'Up you get,' says the custody assistant.

My heart flickers. 'What time is it?'

'Five fifteen.'

I swing my legs to the ground and am led along the corridor of cells into the custody area and up to the desk. I stand there for a moment, blinking in the glare and curling my toes to mitigate the strange sensation of the cold, hard lino beneath my paper shoes. After a moment, the desk sergeant stops typing, looks up and tells me to listen carefully.

'I'm releasing you on bail,' he tells me.

The tension drops from my body. My knees buckle slightly and I clutch the edge of the desk.

'With a number of conditions,' he continues, glancing at me over the top of his computer monitor. 'If you have a problem with any of the conditions, we'll get your lawyer on the phone.'

'OK,' I say.

'One,' he announces. 'You are to live and sleep at your home address: Flat 312, Park East, Sussex Gardens. Two. You're to have no contact with the following people: Daniel Blakely, Jerry Seager, Kevin Prescott, Hayley Allbright, Sharon Seager—'

'Sharon Seager?' I query. 'Jerry's wife? Why?'

'She's a prosecution witness,' he informs me. 'No contact, direct or indirect. That includes all forms of electronic communication, including social media. Do you have a problem with that?'

'No. I just don't understand what she has to do with the case against me.'

'Three,' the desk sergeant continues, ignoring my question. 'You're not to enter 225 Eastcheap, EC1.'

'Not a problem,' I agree.

'And four. You're not to go to 57 Packington Street, Islington.'

Dan's address.

He points to an electronic signature pad in front of me and

hands me a pen. 'Sign here, please.' He then pushes a large plastic bag towards me containing the few belongings I came with. 'Oh. And your sister called.'

I look up sharply. 'Which one?'

He peers at his screen. 'Fern.'

I groan.

'She wanted to know if you were OK. We told her you were fine and that you'd be on your way home soon.'

'OK, thank you.'

It's pitch-black and cold outside. I'm still wearing just the tracksuit the police gave me; they've given me back my purse, but I've no coat or phone. I walk briskly until I get my bearings, then head for the tube station, where the first trains of the day are running. I get on the Hammersmith and City Line to Paddington and then walk the short distance home. It's still early and the street is empty and silent, the windows of my block unlit. I enter the building, grateful that my neighbours aren't up yet to see me skulking home in a police tracksuit. Getting bail – avoiding the remand wing of the nearest women's prison – is a colossal relief and one that I honestly wasn't expecting. Things could have gone a whole lot worse for me, I know.

I push my key into the lock and open the door. The flat is warm. There's no sign of George. I check her food bowls. They're almost full, but the food is fresh, which means she's been here. I breathe yet another sigh of relief. I scribble a quick note to say thank you, run up two flights and push it under my neighbour's door. I then go back down and take a long, hot shower, scrubbing every inch of my hair and body, even though my wrists are swollen from the handcuffs and aching like mad. I pull on a pair of clean pyjamas and throw the police tracksuit into a bin liner. In the bedroom, I fold and cut two pieces of Tubigrip and tug one gently over each wrist. I then swallow a couple of painkillers and lower my aching body into bed. For a few delicious moments, as I drift into sleep, I allow myself to savour the buzzing, electrical silence, the soft scent of my clean pillow, the sensation of the crisp cotton sheets against my legs. As if from far away, I hear the clatter of George's cat flap and I allow myself a small moment of elation or, at least, something that stretches way beyond relief. George is home. *I'm home.* I've been so, so lucky. So goddamned lucky. But I mustn't get ahead of myself. I need to stay focused. This is just the beginning. I am in absolutely no doubt that the most perilous step in all of this is yet to come.

PART THREE

PART THREE

15

Tuesday, 20 December

It's just after seven thirty in the evening when my sister Fern arrives. I'm sitting on the sofa with George, eating pizza. I flick on the TV. It's *EastEnders*. I turn the volume up loud before going out to the hall to let her in.

'Why didn't you call me?' she says as soon as the door swings open. She pushes past me, her trademark Chanel pervading the hallway as she tugs off her Armani riding boots, one by one, and marches into my living room.

'Hello, Fern,' I say to the empty hallway. 'Nice to see you. Why don't you come in?'

Josh, my nephew, grins and steps in after her. He's fifteen and tall – over six feet – but gangly and awkward with it. I can tell he likes girls, but also finds them excruciating. As a member of the unspeakable sex, I'm conscious that hugging him might be too intimate, so I tap my cheek instead. In response, he taps his own cheek, then moves his head playfully as I reach up on tiptoes to kiss him. I step backwards and trip over Fern's boots and Josh lets out a chuckle. I laugh too. It feels good; a release. I realise that I haven't laughed in a while.

'Nice fringe,' I remark. 'It's new, isn't it?'

He nods. 'I'm growing it.'

'Great,' I say. 'It'll be the perfect place to keep your head lice.'

'Yeah. You want some?' He steps forward, shaking his thick, curly fringe at me. I duck, dodging him, and we laugh again.

Fern appears back in the hallway and glares at us, tiny but fearsome in her stockinged feet. Her long blonde hair is swept back underneath an Alice band that makes her forehead appear much larger than I'd remembered. She unhooks and shrugs off the cape-poncho-blanket thing she's wearing and hands it to me. It's soft and expensive. I look around for somewhere safe to put it, imagining Fern's face when she sees the cat snuggling into it, her claws tugging at the threads.

'Oh, give it here,' Fern says sharply and snatches it back from me. She struts off into the living room again. Josh kicks off his trainers and we follow her inside.

Josh's eyes land on the pizza.

'Want some?' I pick up the plate and hold it out to him.

He takes a slice and sits down on the sofa.

Fern has her hands over her ears. 'For crying out loud,' she shouts. 'Do something about this racket!'

I pick up the TV remote from the coffee table and turn down the sound.

'Off, Tate. Turn it off,' she snaps. 'We need to talk. I can't believe you watch this rubbish anyway.'

'I like to keep up with what's happening in the soaps,' I say. 'You never know.'

'You never know *what*?'

I shrug.

Josh says, through a mouthful of pizza, 'She needs to know what's going on in case she gets a part.'

I smile at him gratefully, though I know this will infuriate Fern.

'How can you even think about that?' she asks me. 'You've just been arrested by the police and you're sitting here, eating pizza and watching TV, like nothing has even happened!'

'I have to eat, Fern,' I say. 'It's just pizza.'

'You can order yourself a pizza,' she points out, 'but you can't pick up the phone?'

'The police took my phone.'

'Don't give me that, Tate. You're allowed a call from the police station.'

'Yes – *a* call. You're only allowed one.'

'So, who did you call?' she asks huffily. 'Because Blair and Heath didn't know anything about it. And Skye only found out when she phoned your office and they told her that you don't work there any more! And then finding out you'd been *arrested*. Honestly! I nearly fell over when Skye told me. The trouble you've put us to. But no, not a thought for anyone else. This is so freaking typical of you.'

'My neighbour,' I say.

Her brows snap together. 'What?'

'I called my neighbour. I needed her to look after George.'

Fern continues to look puzzled.

'That's the cat, Mum,' Josh says.

'Well then, after you got out,' Fern says. 'And don't tell me

115

you only just got home because I phoned the police station at lunchtime and they told me you'd left hours ago!'

'They took my phone,' I remind her.

Momentarily defeated, Fern lowers herself down onto the pouffe near the window and places her cape-poncho-blanket across her lap. 'So, what did you do?' she asks, after a moment. 'The police wouldn't tell us anything.'

'They're not allowed to.'

'Why on earth not?'

'I don't know. Data protection? I might not have wanted you to know,' I say provocatively. 'I might have thought it wasn't any of your business.'

Fern's face tightens. 'Is that what you think? That it's none of my business?'

I exhale loudly and sink down onto the sofa next to Josh. 'I'm not saying that.'

Fern tugs at the gold chain around her neck with a manicured fingernail and straightens the collar of her blouse. 'So, what was it then?' she asks finally. 'Did you steal something?'

'No, Fern. I didn't steal anything.'

'Then what?' she asks. 'What did you do?'

'I didn't do anything,' I tell her. 'I've been framed. I've been set up. A woman fell from the roof of the building where I work.'

Josh gapes at me. They both do.

'The office was closed,' I explain. 'It happened at the weekend, last weekend. She was attacked with a broken bottle. They think she was pushed.'

'Oh my freaking word,' Fern whispers. 'And they think it was you?'

I nod. 'I was in the building when it happened.'

'Why? What were you doing there?'

'Long story. But I didn't attack her and I didn't push her.'

'So who did?' Fern looks frightened.

'I don't know,' I say. 'But it wasn't me.'

'Is she dead?' Josh asks.

'She fell from the twenty-fifth floor,' I say. 'You don't survive that.'

Fern puts her hand to her mouth. 'Oh, my goodness! The poor woman. Did you know her?'

'A little,' I say. 'Not well.'

'But why were you in the building?' Fern asks. 'And what was the woman doing on the roof?'

'It's a roof terrace,' I explain. 'They think she went there to meet someone. They think she went to meet me. But she didn't. I wasn't there when she fell.'

'And this happened when?'

'The Saturday before last.'

'So . . . why were you in the office on a Saturday? I thought you were just an office junior or something?'

'I got a phone call,' I explain. 'From a woman I met at a party there the night before.' I tell the story again about Helen and the earring, the taxi journey to the building, losing Helen inside.

Fern looks at me intently. 'And that's all they have against you? That you were somewhere inside the building when she fell?'

'Pretty much,' I say, neglecting to mention my romantic involvement with the victim's husband, my misdirection of the investigation, my lies to the police. 'It's all circumstantial.'

Fern continues to look at me for a moment, taking it in. I can't tell if she's on my side or not. It's almost as if she wants to be, is trying to be. I sense it could go either way.

But then there's a noise out in the hallway, a clinking sound in the kitchen. We all hear it.

Fern's head jerks towards the door. 'What was that?'

'Nothing,' I say quickly.

'There's somebody in your flat.'

'It's nothing. It's no one.'

The front door closes.

Fern leaps up, walks over to the door and peers out into the hallway. 'Someone just left your flat,' she says accusingly. 'What's going on, Tate? Who was that?'

'It's my neighbour,' I tell her. 'She needed to use the bathroom.'

'Why would your neighbour need to use your bathroom? Why can't she use her own bathroom?'

I hesitate. 'It's the . . . the plumbing,' I say. 'It's . . . fucked.'

Josh laughs. Fern winces. She hates bad language.

'Sorry,' I say. 'I don't know the word for when your plumbing is . . . buggered.'

Josh laughs again.

Fern sits back down. 'Something's going on with you, Tate. Something's not right. You're on bail for . . .' She trails off. 'What are you on bail for?'

'Murder.'

Her face falls, as if this is a revelation. She says softly, as if to herself, 'My God. And yet . . . you don't seem to be taking this seriously – at all!'

'Give me a break, Fern.' I put my face in my hands. 'I *am* taking it seriously. But I've had the week from hell. I'm relieved to have got bail. I'm tired and I just need a break from all the misery. That's all.'

'So is this the same neighbour you called from the police station?'

'Yes,' I nod through my fingers.

'And who is she to you?'

'My neighbour.'

'But—'

'She's just a neighbour – a friend.'

'So why wouldn't she come in and say hello before she left?'

'I don't know,' I say despairingly. 'Maybe she was in a hurry.'

She looks at me for a moment. 'You're up to something. I can tell.'

'Fern, please,' I say. 'I'm begging you. I've had hours and hours of questioning. I'm not sure how much more of this I can take.'

The room falls silent. 'Right,' Fern says. 'Well, we need to get you a lawyer, don't we?'

I look up. 'I already have one.'

'Not a legal aid lawyer,' she says. 'A proper lawyer.'

'She *is* a proper lawyer,' I say. 'She's great. It's thanks to her that I got bail.'

'So what's she doing right now, then?'

I sigh. 'I don't know. Eating pizza. Watching *EastEnders*. Having a nice, relaxing evening, if she's lucky, having spent the best part of the last twenty-four hours locked up with me, getting our buttocks numbed to buggery on cold, hard chairs in a police interview room.'

'Yeuch!' Josh grimaces, presumably at the thought of my buttocks.

'There's nothing we can do now,' I tell them both. 'I just need to wait.'

Fern frowns. 'You can't just rest on your laurels, you know.'

I let out a snort of laughter.

'This is not a joke, Tate!'

'Sorry,' I mutter. 'I thought "laurels" was your euphemism for buttocks. You know, like how you say "freaking" instead of "fucking".'

Josh laughs.

'Just stop talking,' says Fern in a worn-out voice.

I do as I'm told.

'You're on bail,' she continues, after a moment. 'All that means is that they don't have enough evidence against you – yet. Which means they're out looking for it right now. Which means, you need to prepare your defence.'

'It doesn't work like that. You don't get legal aid until they charge you.'

'Then you have to pay.'

I shrug. 'I don't have any money. You know that.'

'I know you don't.' She looks at me resignedly. 'I'm going to help you out. Give me your lawyer's phone number. If she's as good as you say, she can make this go away.'

I look back at her, shocked. 'Are you serious? You're offering to pay for a lawyer for me?'

'Yes,' she says, 'I'm offering to pay for a lawyer for you. And there's no need to be like that.'

'I'm sorry, but I don't understand. Why would you want to do this for me?'

'Because you need help and I'm your big sister. Whatever you think, I've always been here for you.'

I almost want to laugh again. This interest in me and my welfare is unprecedented. Fern has never given me money. Over the past twenty years, she's barely given me the time of day. But as I look back at her, I realise she's close to tears.

'I'm sorry,' I say finally. 'If you really mean it, then that's incredibly generous of you.'

Fern opens her handbag, takes out a compact mirror and dabs at each eye with a forefinger before snapping it shut. 'It's not going to be a free ride, Tate. I'm flat out at the moment. It's my busiest time of year and I could do with some help at Scott Street. I'll have to put you in the kitchen,' she says. 'Given your . . . situation, I can't risk having you front of house.'

'You want *me* to work in your hotel?' I ask, stunned.

'You need a job, don't you?'

'Yes,' I admit.

'Well, who else is going to take you on right now? You'd have to tell them you're on bail and . . . and what you're on bail for. You'd have to, Tate,' she insists, as I open my mouth to protest. 'And don't worry. I'll pay you. As well as paying your legal costs.'

'Fern—'

'But there's a catch.'

My eyes meet hers.

'I want to sit in on every meeting you have with your solicitor.'

'There's no need for that,' I protest.

'Yes, there is.'

I groan. 'Why?'

'Because you need me,' she says. 'And I need to keep an eye on you. And if I'm going to keep an eye on you, I need to know what's going on.'

I look at her, thinking it through. 'That's got to be the worst deal ever,' I point out. 'For you, I mean. A lawyer will be expensive. You can get staff from an agency. Why would you want me?'

'Because you're in trouble, Tate.' Fern closes her eyes for a moment and breathes in deeply. 'You're *lost*. Even *I* can see that.'

I glance across at Josh, embarrassed at the turn the conversation has taken, but he just grins and says, 'I'm going to be working at Scott Street over Christmas too. Come on, Tay-Tay. It'll be fun.'

His old baby name for me makes my heart flip a little. I look across at Fern, who, like Josh, is now smiling faintly, encouragingly, back at me.

'OK. Thank you,' I agree.

When they've gone, I go into the bedroom, pull my new phone out from under my pillow and take it off mute. I tap out a message. Sorry about that. She never comes to see me. Typical.

Back comes the reply. Did she know it was me?

No. But she heard you leave.

Sorry. Tried to be quiet.

It's OK.

What did she want?

She knows I got arrested. She wants to pay for a lawyer. She wants to sit in on all of the meetings.

Are you serious?

Yeah. But don't worry, I'll deal with it.

We'll talk about it tomorrow. You must be exhausted.

I am.

Get some sleep.

Yeah. Speak tomorrow. Thanks for sorting out the phone.

Least I could do, Tee. Must have been a nightmare. Some kisses are tapped out.

One for the team, I type, and send some kisses back.

16

My day at Fern's hotel begins at eight after the breakfast shift has got under way. My role is to unstack the trays that Josh and the other waiters bring me and to sort the dirty crockery and cutlery into plastic crates before rinsing them off with a dish hose. I then push the crates onto a conveyor belt where they are moved through a machine and blasted with scalding water, ready for one of us to unstack onto rows of stainless-steel shelving after they've emerged on the other side, steaming hot, dry and shiny. I've done worse jobs – such is the lot of a resting actress – but lifting the crockery and the crates makes my wrists ache. The dish hose has a fierce splashback effect so that every time I taser a stubborn puddle of Béarnaise sauce or caked-on tiramisu, I end up with small particles of it on my neck, in my hair and – if I'm not careful to shut it – in my mouth.

But, in counterpoint to the bleakness that has brought me here, I'm made to feel welcome by the kitchen staff, whose cheerful banter and song – along with the Christmas music playing through the speakers – keeps me from sliding into introspection. The restaurant is busy and the time flies by.

My first appointment with Sarah is booked for 4 p.m. on the Thursday. When Fern pushes open the swing door to the kitchen, I'm momentarily surprised to see her, even though the arches of my feet are telling me that my shift must be over by now.

'Come on then,' she says, holding the door open for me.

Fern's wearing an expensive navy blue suit and matching stilettos and her hair is wound up in a stylish French knot. I – by contrast – am wearing trainers and jeans and a plastic apron and my hair is a straggly mess. I'm well used to feeling like the pauper to Fern's princess whenever she is around me, but seeing her here now, like this, dressed up and in charge of everything – including me – reminds me acutely of how far she's come. We both grew up on a council estate in Lewisham. My parents were poor and we had very little. But for my brothers and sisters this was the springboard from which they would fly high. My brother Blair sold his company at the right time and, to a degree, got lucky, but Fern has worked exceptionally hard, I realise, and has achieved so much. As I follow her through the softly carpeted dining room, where Josh and two other staff members are hoovering and laying tables for dinner, instead of being envious and resentful of Fern's achievements as I have in the past, I feel a sudden, intense pride in her. I realise that it's a far nicer feeling to have.

The reception area is vast and open, the wooden floor gleaming. The same Christmas music is playing and there is a huge tree standing floor to ceiling in the corner, beautifully adorned with silver baubles, turquoise ribbon and fairy lights. I follow Fern's gaze past the clusters of soft seating and tables to a huge open fireplace where Sarah is seated. When she sees us, she closes her laptop, then gets up from the sofa, reaches for her bag and crosses the room. Fern directs us towards the lift and we take it up to the fifth floor, where Fern's office is.

'Thanks for coming,' says Fern to Sarah as we follow her down the corridor. 'I'm so busy right now that this is easier for us. We really appreciate this, don't we, Tate?'

'Yes. Thanks. It's good of you to come,' I agree.

Fern opens the door to her office. The room is large and luxurious, the furnishings expensive – flock wallpaper, a thick, plush carpet, a solid oak desk next to a sash window overlooking the garden, green leather wingback armchairs beside a log fire. Fern offers up her desk chair to Sarah and arranges seats for us opposite. I sink down into mine and glance at my sister, who's plucking a pen out of a penholder and pulling a notepad from a pile on the corner of the desk. I feel guilty for taking her money but, at the same time, wary. She's going to tackle this with the same earnestness she brings to everything she does. If things were different, I would be glad to have her on my side.

'OK,' Sarah says, opening her laptop. 'The first thing we need to think about is whether we want to ask for a second post-mortem.'

My gut twists. 'No,' I say quickly.

Fern raises an eyebrow.

'It's standard procedure,' Sarah says. 'To get our own expert to establish the cause of death. To be sure we're happy with the police coroner's findings.'

'We know why she died. She fell from a roof. Twenty-five floors. She had a heart attack.'

'Even so,' says Sarah. 'There might have been something else, some incidental finding or other medical issue that's important.'

'No,' I say again. 'I can't do that to Dan, to Emily. I can't be the reason they can't bury her.' A lump rises in my throat and I swallow it down. 'It would be cruel to have her cut open again,' I say. 'I want her to rest.'

Fern looks unsure. 'Tate, do you not think it's—'

'No.' I'm not going to be moved on this. 'There's no question as to why she died; that's not the issue here. The issue is that I wasn't on the roof with her. I didn't attack her with a broken bottle and I didn't push her off the roof. Whatever her injuries, I wasn't the reason she died.'

'That is true,' Fern says, nodding, turning to Sarah. 'The issue is who did it. And from what Tate has told me, they don't seem to have any real evidence against her. She was there in the building, but . . . so what? They can't prove Tate did this – because she didn't.' She looks across the desk at Sarah. 'Right?'

I shoot Fern a grateful glance, touched by her faith in me. I envy her innocence as she sits there, legs crossed, her pen poised, her notebook open on her lap.

'The problem we have,' says Sarah, 'is that Tate is the only person the police have in the building at the time of death. They have no CCTV and no other witnesses. They're not required to disclose anything more to me at this stage, but I think we can safely assume that – other than the ones we know about – there were no more CPF passes used inside the building that night. And they'd need some kind of evidence or other grounds for suspicion to go after anyone else.'

'So, basically, they want Tate for this?' Fern asks.

'It's looking that way.'

'And how likely is it that she'll be charged?'

'It's difficult to say at the moment. The forensics will be key.'

'But we know that Tate was on the roof, that she drank from the wine bottle the night before, smoked cigarettes.'

'They'll be looking at other things too,' Sarah says. 'Fibres on clothing, for example. Fibres from other people on the victim. And, of course, blood and glass.'

'But Tate walked on the roof after it happened,' Fern points out. 'There's going to be glass on her shoes. There's bound to be.'

'That's right. And that will be our defence. What will be trickier is if there's glass or blood on the rest of her clothing. Her jumper. Her coat. Her jeans.'

Fern shrugs. 'But there won't be, will there?'

'There could be,' Sarah warns. 'Small shards of glass can travel surprisingly far. Then there's blood. If Tate touched anything – the railing, for instance – or leaned against it, there's a chance of a transfer.'

'But if that's the case, we can explain that too, right?'

'We'll try. But our explanation is . . .' Sarah hesitates. 'Open to question. We only have Tate's word that she went up onto the roof *after* Maddy died.'

Fern's brow knits as she considers this. 'You mean, they might not believe her?'

'It's something we have to consider,' Sarah agrees. 'Especially if the account that's been given to the police appears to have . . .' – she glances at me – '. . . inconsistencies.'

'What inconsistencies?' Fern asks sharply.

Sarah looks awkward.

I moisten my lips. 'I lied to the police,' I tell Fern. 'About Helen. About swiping her into the building. I didn't swipe her into the building. I left her in the lobby. I have no idea where she went after that.'

Fern looks horrified.

'She got into the building, Fern,' I say. 'I know she did.'

'So why lie about it?'

'Because I needed the police to believe that there was someone in the building besides me.'

'Why would you need to do that if you're innocent?'

I take a breath. 'Because I knew they'd come after me, as soon as they found out . . .'

'Found out what?' Fern asks.

I clear my throat. 'They think I was fixated on Maddy's husband. Dan, my boss,' I tell her. 'You know. Like . . . a crush.'

'And were you?'

'No. But . . .' I sigh. 'We were having an affair.'

'What?' Fern asks, incredulous. 'Are you serious?'

'Yes. And so . . .' I clear my throat again. 'I had a motive. A good reason for wanting his wife dead.'

Fern stares at me.

'I didn't do it, Fern,' I remind her.

'But why . . .' Her voice is reduced to a whisper. 'Why didn't you tell me this before?'

'Because of how it looks, obviously,' I say. 'And because I'm ashamed.'

Fern continues to stare at me as if I'm someone she's never seen before.

'I didn't kill anyone,' I say again, more gently. 'There was someone else there besides me that night. Helen. She got inside the building somehow. I'm sure of it.'

I can see Fern's inner turmoil. She desperately wants to believe in me – I'm her little sister; I'm not a killer. But she can't ignore the way it looks. Sarah and I sit in silence while she gazes at the page of her notebook, at all the notes she wrote there when she thought I was just somebody's fall guy. Now I'm the prime suspect – and with good reason. But I'm still her sister. Eventually, she looks up again and shoots me a weak smile. She turns to Sarah, swallows and says, 'What's the plan, then? What do we do?'

Sarah nods, relieved. 'Like I said, the forensics will be key.'

'No,' Fern says. 'We can't sit around waiting for the forensics to prove Tate could have done this. We need to get ahead. We need to find this Helen. We need to prove that she was there too, that she could have got into the building and that she lied to the security guard.' She licks a fingertip and flicks over the page of her notebook, reading from a list she's made. 'We need to find out her true identity, because, I mean, Helen Jones – well, that's clearly not her real name, is it? We need to talk to the taxi company. And, most of all, we need to get CCTV from the nearby offices, shops and bars.'

Sarah looks pensive. 'We can do that, for sure,' she says finally. 'We can spend lots of time hunting for footage. But even if it exists, it's not guaranteed that anyone will let us see it. And even if we do get ourselves some images . . . then what? It won't prove that the woman we know as Helen Jones was anything but a random member of the public who went into the building and asked for directions from the security guard. I suggest we come at it from a different angle.'

I lift my head. 'What angle?'

'We ask ourselves why. Why would Helen lure you to the building? Why kill Maddy?'

I shrug. 'Because she was crazy? Because she was depressed? Because she wanted to help me?'

Fern looks dubious. 'You're saying she killed your . . . your . . . love rival, then disappeared, leaving you to take the blame? How would that help you?'

'It wouldn't,' Sarah agrees. 'So maybe we're looking at something a little more . . . tangible than that.'

'Like what?' I ask warily.

'Well, I've been thinking about how she told you on the roof that night that she'd fucked up everything. Something about a relationship that had gone wrong and how it was all her fault.'

I nod. 'Yes.'

'And then she showed all this interest in your relationship with Dan,' Sarah continues. 'She kept asking about him, talking about Maddy and where she worked, about Maddy having everything and . . . and you having nothing.' She inhales and looks at me quizzically. 'But maybe she was the one who had nothing. Until she met you, that is.'

I take a breath, feeling Fern's stillness beside me.

'I know you might not want to hear this, Tate, but . . .' Sarah pauses, then says empathetically but firmly, 'is there any chance that Helen's messed-up relationship was with Dan?'

I look at her, aghast. 'You think . . . you think Dan and Helen were in a relationship? *Dan and Helen?*'

'I'm sorry,' she says. 'I know it's not something you'd want to think about. But if I didn't mention it, I wouldn't be doing my job.'

Fern looks sideways at me, waiting. I can feel her sympathy. I look up at the ceiling, blinking back tears.

'Oh my God,' Fern murmurs. 'She saw you coming.'

'*What?*' I turn to face her, frowning.

'Think about it, Tate.' Fern speaks quickly. 'She snuck into the office party, because that's where Dan worked. She was desperate, suicidal. She decided to kill herself there to make some kind of statement to him. But then she met you and when you told her that *you* were in a relationship with him, she came up with a better idea: to get Maddy up to the roof and push her off and frame you. That way she'd have both of you out of the picture, leaving the field clear for her to win Dan back.'

'Or maybe she knew about you and Dan already,' Sarah suggests. 'And deliberately targeted you, from the start.'

Fern's eyes widen. 'Maybe you were meant to go up to the roof to find Helen the night of the party. Maybe she was waiting for you to come up and talk her down. She deliberately handed you the wine bottle so that your DNA would be on it. She was already setting you up.' She stops, pieces it together. 'That's how she knew the name of Dan's PA. That's how she knew so much about Maddy. She was in a relationship with him. Of course she was!' She turns to Sarah. 'We need to talk to Dan . . . right?'

I feel my mouth open, but I say nothing. I wait.

'No.' Sarah shakes her head. 'We can't. Dan's a prosecution witness. One of Tate's bail conditions is not to approach him. It could land her in jail.'

'So what do we do?' Fern asks.

'I'm thinking we tail him,' Sarah says, turning to me. 'If you agree, that is.'

'You mean . . . Dan?' I am thrown by this.

She nods. 'It's perfectly legal.'

'But why?'

'Because if we're right that you're not the only person who has feelings for him . . . if Helen – or whoever it was that killed Maddy – did so for the same reason that the police think *you* did . . .'

'Because she's in love with him?'

'Yes. If that's the case, then that person is highly likely – one way or another – to still be around. Around him, I mean,' Sarah adds.

I pause, thinking. I take a breath. 'So, she, Helen—'

'Or whoever.'

'—or whoever,' I agree, 'would either be stalking him, watching him, following him. Or . . .'

Sarah and Fern both look at me sympathetically.

'. . . or she could be with him,' I say, inhaling deeply. 'She could still be seeing him. Meeting up with him. In a relationship with him, even.'

'Yes,' Sarah says. 'I'm sorry, but it makes sense, doesn't it? My idea is that if we put a tail on *him*, it should in turn lead us to *her*.'

*

I wait until I am well away from the hotel and have crossed Kensington Road into Hyde Park. The night is dark and crisp, the sky above starless and black. I stop on the path, under the trees. I can hear the hum of machinery and the screams of fairground rides from Winter Wonderland echoing in the distance. I pull my phone out of my pocket, open my call history and tap the number at the top.

'The strategy is to look for Helen Jones,' I say, my heart pumping. 'Get a private investigator on it.'

'That's OK, isn't it?' comes the reply. 'I mean . . . they're not going to find her.'

'I know,' I agree, 'but . . . they might find you.'

A pause. 'How?'

'I don't know. But Sarah wants to put a tail on Dan. So we need to be careful. Play it safe. Calls but no texts, right? From now on. Calls only.'

'Got it.'

I shiver in the breeze and start walking again.

'You still there?'

'Yeah. Just need to keep walking.'

'It's fine, Tee. Don't get paranoid.'

'I think I'm still tired.'

'It's not surprising. You've been through a lot. But it's all going to be fine. I promise you. We're here for you.'

'Both of you?'

'One hundred per cent.'

'OK.'

'Trust in it, Tee. You can do this. *We* can do this. Together.'

17

We wait. It's a long wait; just over six weeks. The trauma of my arrest has left me hyper-alert, hyper-aware of my surroundings. Or paranoid. Is there a difference? I don't know, but I'm permanently on edge. I start to feel as though I'm being watched as I leave my flat and walk to get the bus in the morning. It's only a few stops from Edgware Road to Scott Street, but each time the bus shudders to a halt and the doors slide open, I expect to see Gallagher and Heaton waiting on the pavement, ready to step aboard and flash their badges at the driver before handcuffing me and dragging me back to my police cell again.

I spend Christmas Day at Fern's. My entire family is there: my parents, my brothers and sisters and their children. Fern and Josh keep my secret and my parents and siblings know nothing about my bail status and the real reason behind my arrest. They all think it was a simple misunderstanding over an employment matter that I'm now helping the police with. This was Fern's idea. I know she hated lying to my mother, but she also wanted to protect her and let her enjoy Christmas. Luckily for both of us, the police strategy is to keep the investigation under wraps for the time being and not to leak it to the press. So we eat turkey and mince pies and play board games and bicker as if everything is normal. It feels safe and warm and comforting in Fern's living room with my family all around me, but I know this is just an illusion. I'm not safe, not yet.

My job at the hotel keeps me occupied, thankfully, and the New Year comes quickly. Business tails off in early January, but Fern wants to use the lull for an early spring clean. I need the work and I need to keep busy, so I go along with her suggestion. To my surprise, Fern's not afraid to get her hands dirty, and as we polish cutlery and tables, scrub floors and sweep out fireplaces together, all the things I've disliked about my big sister for the past two decades I now see as strengths. I no longer see the showy, self-important businesswoman who pitches up at family gatherings, who swans about my parents' house talking on her phone and barking out orders. Instead, I take comfort in her competence, in her fortitude. She's tiny – five feet nothing – but indomitable with it. It's as if the police can't get me when I'm inside the hotel with her, and even though I know deep down that she couldn't prevent me from being arrested again, I'm reassured by her presence. This job is the only thing that stops me from holing up in my flat, where agoraphobia could easily take root. I can see how these things begin.

I don't show my sister my fear, though. That would involve opening up to her and I can't do that. Instead, I'm flippant and dismissive of my situation in her presence. I laugh as she chastises me for some inappropriate joke I've just made, then sucks in her cheeks to stifle a smile. But I cry most evenings as I walk back home across the park or wait at the bus stop. I cry for Maddy, who has somehow become muddled up in my head with my sister. I realise how close to the surface everything feels right now, and how I still have everything to gain, as well as everything to lose.

February arrives. The forensics have been fast-tracked and finally Maddy's body is released by the coroner. Her funeral takes place on a cool, crisp morning under a pale, bright winter sky. I imagine the flowers, the coffin, the hymns inside the church, the procession to the graveside. I imagine Dan in a dark suit and overcoat, his arm slung protectively around his daughter, freshly dug earth piled up on the grass behind them, Heaton and Gallagher standing silently on the path nearby. I don't know that there'll be a police presence, of course, but cops always come to funerals on TV, so maybe they'll come looking for me. I imagine them in their belted coats and dark trousers, respectful but observant, their eyes scanning the horse chestnuts and fir trees that border the burial ground.

Three days later, in the second week of February, I finally get the phone call I've been waiting for. I know what it is as soon as the phone rings. My legs are numb with trepidation, my stomach weak. The next part has begun.

18

The forensics came back negative. The neck of the wine bottle used to kill Maddy has no trace of my DNA on it and the cigarette butts aren't mine. There's no glass on my trainers, no blood or fibres from Maddy on my coat or any of my jumpers. There's no trace of me under Maddy's fingernails or on her clothing. There's no other evidence to connect me with Maddy's death. I'm being released from police bail.

Fern has ordered a bottle of champagne from the bar downstairs. She answers the knock at the door and shows the barman in. He places a tray with three champagne flutes on the tabletop, pops the cork and sets the ice bucket down near the comfy seats by the fireplace.

When he's gone, Fern picks up the bottle, pours the champagne, hands us each a glass, then inhales deeply. 'So, that's it?' she says. 'It's all over?'

'That's it,' Sarah agrees. 'Unless any new evidence comes to light, of course.'

Fern looks sceptical. 'But that's not going to happen, is it?'

'That's just something I have to advise you,' Sarah tells her, looking at me.

Fern gives me a lopsided smile. 'It's so weird, Tate. There's literally no evidence of you. It's like you were never there!'

'I know,' I say. 'Obviously, I spotted the glass on the ground and so I walked carefully around it. And they didn't take my shoes until nine days later, of course. And I always just assumed the broken wine bottle was the same one we left there. But it can't have been, can it?' I lift my eyes to meet Sarah's.

'No,' she agrees. 'It can't have been.'

'Are you sure you *were* there, Tate?' Fern smiles.

She's joking, but it makes me uneasy. 'The Temp One security pass was used inside the building,' I remind them both quickly. This has been confirmed by EPM, the block management company, and Dan has now told the police that he remembers loaning it to me.

'Right.' Fern nods. 'And if you were using the Temp One pass, you'd have no need to steal Jerry's.'

'Exactly.'

'Which,' she says, raising her glass, 'is one more reason why my little sister is innocent. To Tate, who is innocent!'

Sarah raises her glass and I feel myself flush. I'm a little embarrassed, but at the same time am touched that my sister is so clearly over the moon for me.

'I wonder who did steal Jerry's pass, though?' Fern asks.

'That's the million-dollar question,' I say.

Fern gazes expectantly back and forth between me and Sarah, then shrugs her shoulders. 'Well . . . never mind. It's excellent news. In fact, it's freaking amazing. I just don't know what to say, except, thank you, Sarah.'

'Yes. Thank you, Sarah,' I echo. My eyes well up and my voice breaks a little. 'And thank you both for believing in me.'

Fern scrutinises me for a moment, then puts down her champagne glass, comes over to where I'm standing and wraps her arms around me. 'Come on, silly,' she says. 'Of course we believed in you.'

I look over her shoulder at Sarah, who says, 'Congratulations, Tate. It's a great result.' But her tone is flat and there's something brittle about her smile.

Fern lets go of me and begins asking Sarah questions. She's asking about the tail that Sarah put on Dan and if anyone has been seen with him, and Sarah is telling her no. Fern's asking if we'll be told when they catch the person who killed Maddy, because she really wants to see them nailed after everything they've put me through. Sarah's saying that we won't find that out unless someone is charged. I nod coolly as they speak, but my insides are roiling. *Something is wrong*, is what I'm thinking. Sarah knows something. What does she know?

Then Fern's phone rings and she pulls it out of her pocket. 'Oh God,' she groans. 'I'm sorry. I'm going to have to take this. Enjoy the champagne. Go drink it downstairs. Have some food. Have what you want. I'll settle the bill later. It's on me.'

Sarah leans down, glass in hand, gathers up her coat and laptop bag, then opens the door and steps outside. I do the same, grabbing the bottle of champagne as I go. We walk down the corridor to the lift together, in silence. Sarah presses the button and we wait a moment or two.

'So, what's wrong?' I ask finally, under my breath.

'What do you mean?'

'There's something wrong,' I say. 'What is it?'

'No,' she says, smiling tightly. 'Nothing's wrong.'

'So, that's really it?' I ask. 'The end of the investigation against me?'

Sarah says brightly, 'Yes. That's it. All done.'

'And when you talked about further evidence coming to light,' I persist, 'you don't . . . know anything more? Anything you haven't told me, I mean?'

She shakes her head. 'No. It's all good. Unless there's something worrying you?'

I hesitate. 'No. There's nothing.'

The lift door slides open and we step inside.

'So, do you want to go to the bar?' I ask quickly, as the door slides shut again. 'It seems a shame to waste the champagne. And actually . . . I still have some questions, if you don't mind?'

She looks at me. 'Sure.'

We descend in silence, side by side. When the door opens, she follows me out and across the lobby into the bar. It's decorated in oak and mahogany, with light grey walls, sleek floors, soft lighting. It's four in the afternoon and it's almost empty. I can see the same barman who brought us the champagne and I catch his eye. He nods, acknowledges who we are, that we have drinks already. We choose a table on a podium, near the window in the lounge area, the furthest away from the bar. I slide into my seat, placing the champagne bottle and my glass on the tabletop. Sarah pulls out a chair opposite me and puts her laptop on the floor beside her.

'So, you had some questions?'

'Just one or two things,' I say. I don't really know quite what it is I want to ask her, but I do know that I don't want her to leave just yet. 'Could you tell me again exactly what the police told you?'

Sarah eyes me carefully, then says, 'I think you know more than I do, don't you?'

A flicker of fear makes me lose myself for a moment. 'Why would you say that?'

'Don't you think I'm the one who should be asking why?'

'Why . . . what?'

'Why would you tell me . . .' she begins, then stops herself. 'Why would you let me . . . the police, your sister – everyone – think that you killed Maddy?'

'I told you I *didn't* kill Maddy,' I correct her.

'Yes,' she agrees. 'That's what you told me. But, at the same time, you did a really great job of making sure that everyone – including me – would suspect that you did.'

I look hard at her, waiting. Thinking. Time stands still. 'What makes you say that?' I ask again.

'A few things.'

'Like what?' I press her, then ask more gently, 'What is it you think you know?'

'When I checked your custody record, it showed that you'd given the police your neighbour at number 316 as your nomination, the one phone call you were allowed. You needed her to feed your cat, that's what you said. The name on the custody record is Clare. No surname. Just a phone number.'

'That's right,' I say. 'Stupid of me, but in the stress of the moment I just couldn't remember her last name.'

'You also told me,' Sarah continues, 'that Dan had been upset with you for swiping a complete stranger into the building. But it wasn't possible to swipe anyone else into the building and Dan would have known that. So why would he have been upset with you? He wouldn't have believed you. He'd have called you out on it.'

I take another sip of my drink, trying to appear casual. But my hand is trembling and I have to put the glass back down.

'And then there's the office party. The police say – and you agreed – that you met Jerry Seager and flirted with him outside on the smoking terrace soon after he'd finished his turn on the karaoke. But you also told me that he was still singing when you left the bar and climbed up the outer fire escape and found Helen on the roof. You told me that you were with her for the rest of the evening. So that doesn't fit with you meeting Jerry when you did.'

It's all explainable. Timing. That's all. Just timing.

'And then there's the PI I've had tailing Dan, who's come up with absolutely nothing. So, my PI took it upon himself to observe your building instead.'

My stomach turns. My feelings of being watched were real. I wasn't just being paranoid. There really was someone there.

'And what he *did* see was a woman with long, dark, wavy hair coming out of the flat two floors up from yours and getting into the driver's seat of your car. She had the keys to your Corsa. She drove your Corsa. She returned in your Corsa.' Sarah pauses. 'He saw you together.'

I gaze at her, my heart racing.

'So I figured that your call from the police station asking your neighbour to feed your cat was in fact also a tip-off to the person who was living there to let them know you'd been arrested. And I'm guessing that person is the same woman who walked into the lobby at 225 and distracted Kevin, the security guard, while Maddy was pushed from the roof?'

Sarah waits a moment, looking up at me, but I can't speak. I suddenly feel winded. Punched in the gut.

'He took photos.' She opens her bag and removes a file, then pulls out a sheet with a series of still images on it and slides it across the table towards me. I take it, but I don't need to look at it. I already know what – and who – I'm going to see. I know that Sarah is halfway there already, and that it's only a matter of time before she works out the rest.

I close my eyes and inwardly curse Fern. Bloody Fern, insisting on paying Sarah to continue representing me. But then, on the other hand . . . I look up at her. She's been so calm, so reassuring. I find her presence so comforting. It would be such a huge, *massive* relief to get it all out of my head and into her safe, capable hands.

'You can't tell anyone,' I say, thinking quickly. 'You told me that. That was the first thing you told me. You told me that you had a duty of confidentiality towards me.'

Sarah's mouth sets in a hard line, but her eyes are gentle. 'Absolutely,' she says. 'That's right. I do.'

'And you still aren't allowed to tell anyone what I tell you. Even now?'

'No. So long as we're talking about the past – about what you've done in the past – and not what you're about to do.'

'What do you mean?'

'Are you about to tell me that you are going to commit a crime? Are you about to involve me in something that's yet to happen?'

I think hard. 'No.'

'Then I can't tell anyone. It's completely confidential.'

'Are you sure?'

'I'm sure.'

I take a breath. 'I told you what I told you because I needed to . . . to . . .'

'Test it?' she offers.

I nod. 'Yes. Exactly that. I needed the police to believe it. And so I needed you to believe it too. If I'd told you the truth, you'd have given me different advice. I needed the interview to pan out naturally. You know. According to plan.'

Sarah brings her glass to her lips and swallows. 'And what was the plan?'

I hesitate. 'This really won't go any further?'

She shakes her head. 'No. It won't. It can't.'

'And even when you're no longer my lawyer . . . you still can't tell anyone?'

'No,' she says firmly.

'Even if I've done something . . . something *very* wrong? You're still not allowed to. Even then?'

She puts her glass back down on the table. 'Correct.'

I think about this for a moment. 'And other people? Are

they protected too? You can't tell anyone what I tell you about them?'

'I have to act in your best interests, so, no. I can't repeat what you tell me in confidence. Even if it's about someone other than you.'

'And what if I choose not to tell you? What then?'

'Nothing. You don't have to tell me. But I probably won't be able to act for you any more.'

'Do I need you to?' I ask. 'Do I still need a lawyer?'

Sarah looks me in the eye. 'Maybe not. Maybe not for Maddy's murder. But . . . if you've done something wrong – if you've broken the law – then it's possible that you might.'

This is what I wanted to be sure about. From the moment Sarah told me that the police weren't going to charge me, I'd known I wasn't quite ready to let her go. 'And if I tell you something different from what I already told you, will you have to stop acting for me?' I ask.

'It depends.'

'On what?'

'On a few things. But first, on your reasons.'

I reach for my glass, play with the stem, then look up at the ceiling. 'OK,' I say finally, in a whisper. 'OK, I'll tell you. I'll tell you everything.'

PART FOUR

19

Nine months earlier

Maddy stood at the sink in her kitchen, stacking the dishwasher. It was mid-afternoon and the sun had climbed high over the apple trees, bathing the room in a dancing yellow light. It was almost ten years since they'd moved from their small house in Archway to this beautiful Victorian end-of-terrace in Islington, but still, every day, when Maddy came downstairs and walked through the door, she would see her kitchen with fresh new eyes. She loved everything about it, from the marble worktops and oak floors to the sunlit view onto the mature, south-facing garden. She hadn't thought they could afford it and hadn't dared to fall in love with it. It wasn't until Dan came home smiling and said he'd put in an offer that she'd realised quite how well he was doing at the bank.

It was theirs within six weeks. It needed work, but not much. She'd been the one to paint the walls and strip and varnish the doors, to pick out the rugs, blinds and lampshades. Decorating wasn't really Dan's forte, and he was too busy with work in any event, but she hadn't minded. It was the most beautiful home she'd ever lived in and she had been more than happy to be the one to make it their own.

A gentle breeze drifted through the open patio doors as Maddy took an empty saucepan from the hob and placed it into the rack. The dishwasher still wasn't full, so she walked down the hallway, looking left into the living room and right into the study, then headed upstairs and pushed open Emily's bedroom door. It was dark, as usual, and stuffy. Maddy rolled up the blind to let in some light and air. She glanced around the room hopelessly. The freshly washed and ironed clothes she'd placed on Emily's bed yesterday morning were now in a heap on the floor, tangled up amongst all the dirty ones. On every available surface – bedside table, desk, chest of drawers – were crisp and biscuit packets, empty sweet wrappers and lolly sticks. Bowls and spoons. That's where all the bowls and spoons had gone! She picked them up, stacked them, then pulled the waste-paper basket out from under the desk, gathering up all the wrappers and cramming them into it, pressing them down.

Her hand brushed something hard. Glass. She pulled it out and looked at the label. It was an empty vodka bottle. A litre bottle. Maddy's pulse quickened. Was her fourteen-year-old daughter drinking vodka alone in her bedroom? If not, where? And why was the empty bottle in Emily's bin?

Maddy scooped everything up and took it downstairs and into the kitchen, where she stacked the bowls and spoons into the dishwasher and switched it on. She sorted the contents of the waste-paper basket into the waste and recycling bins, then pushed the vodka bottle under the sink, behind the food-waste caddy. She didn't want to worry Dan until she'd spoken to

Emily about it. But she was worried. She had thought that everything was getting better. After all, when was the last time Emily had come home smelling of alcohol? Not for a while.

Not since . . .

Maddy's heart skipped a beat as the memory of that awful night came back to haunt her, the night that Emily hadn't come home. She and Dan had been frantic as the hours had ticked on with no sign of their daughter and no response from her phone. Ten, then eleven o'clock had come and gone, then midnight. At one, they'd called the police. An officer had arrived and had sat in the lamplight in the living room asking questions about Emily's friendship group, questions that hadn't brought the police any closer to finding her, because all her usual friends – including her best friend, Rosie – were safely at home.

The night had seemed to last for ever. Emily had finally turned up at dawn, drunk and apologetic, mortified to find a police officer in their house. Maddy still didn't know where her daughter had been that night; Emily had refused to discuss it, other than to say that she'd been with a group of friends from school and that they'd met some other kids from her year and there had been alcohol and she hadn't realised how strong it was and she'd lost all track of time.

Maddy shut down the memory. It didn't matter where Emily had been that night; she'd been OK, hadn't she? And nothing had happened since to give Maddy and Dan any real cause for concern. There would be an explanation for the empty vodka bottle; maybe it had been there from the time before. There was no reason to worry. She looked up at the clock. Her daughter would be home soon and everything would be fine.

Maddy suddenly felt dizzy. She grabbed hold of the work-top and steadied herself for a few seconds before walking carefully over to her favourite wingback chair near the patio doors and sitting down. After a moment, she felt a little better. She turned to look out at the garden, at the trees, which were beginning to blossom, the buds swelling and opening. Pretty white flowers now covered the jasmine they'd planted at the foot of the pergola in the hope that it would eventually climb up and obscure the beam at the front, which was on upside down. Maddy smiled to herself at the memory. She'd wanted somewhere shaded to sit and so Dan had ordered the pergola online last summer. He'd spent hours putting it together with his friend Jeff, but it had been a hot day and they'd had a few beers. The pergola was more than a little wonky and when Maddy looked at it, it appeared to be moving very slightly.

He wasn't very practical, it was true, but Dan was a good husband and father. He often had to work long hours at the bank, but he was always there for her and Emily, had always been there for them. Whatever was going on at work, she knew that they came first. Ambitious as he was, it was their daughter who Dan was most proud of.

They'd both wanted children passionately, she and Dan. It was almost the first conversation they'd had. They'd met through mutual friends, Jeff and Caz, who'd thrown a dinner party with the sole purpose of introducing them to each other, which might have been awkward and embarrassing, but wasn't. Dan had been a perfect dinner guest, breaking the ice with a joke or two and then, as the wine began to flow, asking every-one about themselves. *Which four famous people would you invite to a dinner party? What advice would you go back and give your twenty-year-old self?* He'd listened intently to the answers Maddy had given (Maya Angelou and Charlotte Brontë had been on her list, but Maddy couldn't remember who else). She'd said that she would advise herself to go with her instincts, be more spontaneous. When it was his turn, Dan had thought hard for several moments, throwing out several names, then changing his mind. He'd then asked if they'd mind waiting while he went back and advised himself to be more decisive and everyone had laughed because the joke had been spontaneous and sincere, rather than staged and corny, and Maddy couldn't take her eyes off his smile.

After dinner, their hosts had got up to clear the dishes, then disappeared 'to check on the children' and Maddy and Dan had sat at the kitchen table and talked for over an hour. They had the same taste in music. Both preferred white wine over red. Dan had told Maddy that he'd been an only child and – he said – a lonely child. He longed for a big family of his own. Maddy, too, had been an only child and she felt the same way. At the end of the evening, they'd shared a taxi home. They'd only been together three months when he'd proposed to her, reminding her with a grin that she'd wanted to be more spontaneous, but Maddy hadn't hesitated to say yes. She'd known that he was the one.

Maddy had miscarried twice before she'd finally fallen pregnant with Emily. Both she and Dan were elated when, the third time, Maddy had managed to go full term. But after Emily, there were more miscarriages and they'd eventually had to accept that she was going to be an only child, just as they had been. Emily had been an easy baby, a delightful toddler and a loving child. The terrible twos hadn't been that terrible. It was when Emily turned twelve, somewhere in that summer between Years 7 and 8, that she'd become the teenager Maddy had heard other friends talk about. 'You've got all this to come,' Caz had warned her when her own daughter, Katy, had flounced out of a room, screaming at her mother that she 'couldn't wait to get out of this hellhole'. Maddy hadn't believed Caz, until now.

It wasn't *all* the time, though; it wasn't relentless. It was just that you never knew what mood Emily was going to be in. Maddy remembered Caz telling her that with Katy – who was now in her twenties and perfectly lovely – she would 'dip a toe in in the morning to see if she was going to be a shark or a shellfish' and if it was the former, she'd say as little as possible until the hormonal wave had passed. It was the hormones, those difficult hormones. And it wasn't easy being a teenager these days, with social media there to highlight her every fault and failing, to compare her looks, her body and her mind to those of someone happier, thinner and more popular. It was a tough, new, very different world that her daughter inhabited, she knew.

Maddy heard the front door open. Emily's voice called out, 'Mum!'

'In here, love.'

The kitchen door burst open. 'Mum, guess what?' Emily was beaming. 'My English teacher told us the results of our end-of-year exams and guess what? I got an eight!'

Maddy stood up, pleased. 'An eight? Really? That's fantastic, Em! Well done!'

Emily beamed. 'I know. And my history tutor said we'd get the results back on Monday, but she said that no one had done badly.'

'I'm so thrilled, Em.'

'Me too.' Emily paused. 'So, can I go to the lido, Mum?'

'What? When?'

'Now. Everyone's going.'

Maddy hesitated. 'Who's "everyone"?'

'It's just the usual crowd, Mum. You don't have to ask me every time.'

'Just tell me some names, so I know whose parents to call in an emergency.'

'What emergency? We're just going to the pool, Mum. Please don't make it a thing.'

'Well, I guess I know where you'll be,' Maddy conceded. 'So, OK.'

Emily's face lit up momentarily, then looked stricken. 'What am I going to wear? I don't have anything!'

'You have a swimsuit, don't you?'

'Mum! That thing! It's way too small for me. And anyway, it's babyish. It has frills on it.'

'I've got a swimsuit,' Maddy said. 'It should fit you.'

'Mum! Everyone's going and I'll be the only one looking like an idiot.'

Maddy sighed. She didn't think her swimsuit was idiotic, but what did she know?

'I need to buy something!'

'OK. Well . . . I'll give you some money. You'll find something down at the Angel and you can get a bus from there.'

'Mum!' Tears formed in the corners of Emily's eyes. 'The Angel's in the opposite direction. By the time I've walked down there, found something I like and got a bus to Parliament Hill, everyone will have gone home!'

Maddy took a breath, walked over to the patio doors and locked them, then took her car keys from a basket on the work-top. 'Come on.'

Emily's eyes widened. 'You'll take me?'

Maddy smiled. 'I'll stop in Bromfield Street and you can run into H&M. If you're quick, we'll beat the traffic and you can be at the lido in an hour.'

Emily beamed and flung her arms around her mother, kissing her cheek. 'Thank you, Mum. I love you! You're the best mum ever!'

Maddy smiled. 'Go and grab a towel and some sunscreen and whatever else you'll need while I find my handbag.'

'OK.' Emily nodded excitedly and ran upstairs.

Maddy found her handbag on a chair in the study. Was she weak, a pushover? She wasn't sure, but she wanted her daughter to be happy. Safe, yes. But happy too. She'd only be young once.

She waited at the foot of the stairs. Emily was still rooting around in her bedroom, no doubt throwing more clothes on the floor, but never mind. You have to pick your battles, Maddy told herself. She thought about that for a moment longer, then walked back into the kitchen, took out the empty vodka bottle from behind the food caddy under the sink and threw it into the recycling bin.

20

Early June, and I'd been invited to a school reunion. I'd read the invitation, my mind numb with dread: a reunion of a school I hated – what good could possibly come of this? A room full of people I didn't know any more. Married people with kids and careers and businesses and successful lives. And me in the worst possible place my ex-classmates could find me. Pushing forty and still single. Childless. Qualified for nothing but my stalled acting career.

My instinct was to delete the message. Instead, I spent a week ruminating, looking at everyone's profiles on Facebook, flip-flopping from accepting to declining, from curiosity to shame and back again. In the end, I knew I had to go. I couldn't bear the thought of hiding out at home, inconspicuous in my absence. Forgotten. Unseen. I'm an actress now, I figured. I've done some stuff. My life may have stalled a bit lately, but if anyone can blag their way through the evening, it should be me.

So, there I was, my stomach in knots as I pushed open the door to the Pig and Whistle in Soho, where Tracy Carnegie, organised as ever, had summoned us all that night. I arrived late and flustered, disappointed by what I was wearing, having had to put aside the ensemble I'd planned (my favourite dress, matching new shoes I'd ordered too late online) and find a replacement at the eleventh hour. My second choice of outfit was smart but understated: jeans, boots and a blue silk shirt. I was too covered up for the warm evening and I'd had to tie up my long fair hair – my best feature – to hide the grey roots that, in my panic and deliberations over my outfit, I'd left myself insufficient time to touch up.

As bad luck would have it, the first person I saw was Annabel Mercer. Annabel bloody Mercer. The class bully and my nemesis. She was standing near the bar with Kayla Crossley and Caroline Bolton, although it took me a moment to recognise everyone. Kayla, in a little black dress, had aged well over the twenty years since I'd last seen her, her bobbed dark hair and pink lipstick just the same as she used to wear in school. Annabel looked glamorous – tall, slim and angular, with fashionably cropped bleached-white hair, her shoulder blades protruding elegantly from a long and expensive-looking low-backed dress. Caroline, in a glittery, bosom-revealing tank top, was glossy and voluptuous. She'd put on weight, but, like everyone else, was chatting away confidently, seemingly quite comfortable in her additional skin.

As I wavered uncertainly in the doorway, Kayla lifted her head and smiled at me, a genuine smile of pleasure, it seemed, which gave me courage. I smiled back. She waved me over and, in a single beat, it was too late to change my mind and reverse out again.

As I approached, Annabel followed Kayla's gaze and looked round.

'Oh my God. It's Tate Kinsella!' she exclaimed. 'Jesus Christ. Look at *you*.' Her tone was disparaging – intentionally so, of course, just as it had always been. I stepped back, looking for an opportunity to escape, but Kayla took my arm, drawing me closer. Reaching behind Caroline, she grabbed a glass of Prosecco from a tray on the bar and pressed it into my hand.

'It's so good to see you, Tate,' Kayla said. 'How are you? What have you been up to?'

'Me? Oh, well . . . not a lot,' I answered truthfully, caught off guard by being thrown so abruptly into the spotlight.

'I think you're being a teeny bit modest here,' smiled Kayla. 'I saw your profile on Facebook. You're an actress.'

'What have you been in?' asked Caroline. 'Anything we'd know?'

I hesitated, feeling blindsided. Annabel was looking at me intently, her eyes narrowed. Kayla was smiling warmly. Caroline took a slug of Prosecco. They were all waiting. I had the stage.

'Oh, this and that,' I said. 'Theatre, mainly. A bit of TV.'

'TV! Wow. Like what?' Kayla pressed me.

'Oh, you know,' I said. 'The usual. I don't want to brag.'

'Oh, come on! Tell us. *EastEnders? Corrie?*'

I'd done neither. What if they found out? 'Well, there was an ad you might have seen,' I said. 'Carpet Palace? I was the woman on the flying carpet. The one that flew through the window and landed in that couple's living room?'

They looked back at me blankly.

'Oh ... wait. Yeah!' Kayla said kindly. 'I know the one you mean. Was it ... like ... a few years ago now?'

'Ten,' I admitted. 'But you know, that's my ... erm ... well, that's the one everyone remembers.'

'I don't,' said Annabel.

'I never watch the ads,' said Caroline. 'You don't have time when you've got kids. "Ad break" means get up and sort the kids out. Have you got kids, Tate? Are you married?'

'No. No kids,' I said jovially. 'Just my cat.'

Annabel let out a snort of laughter. 'Crazy cat lady! That's perfect! Just what I'd have guessed.'

I gave a false little laugh, although I was feeling far from light-hearted. 'I have *one* cat,' I objected, 'and she doesn't define who I am. And, you know,' I continued, *'crazy cat lady* ... I mean, what is that? It's a pejorative term invented by men for women who don't want to have sex with them. Which, as women' – I wagged a finger playfully – 'we really shouldn't buy into, you know?'

I was met with more blank faces.

'And besides, that's not me anyway. Because I'm not lonely and I have sex. I mean, I'm not ... you know. Lonely.'

I'd said it twice. *Sex. Sex.* I'd told them I had sex. The second I'd said it, I knew that I'd just given Annabel the opening she'd been waiting for.

'We remember,' she said pointedly.

A smirk of recognition had also spread across Caroline's slightly pudgy features.

'Wait. What do we remember?' Kayla asked.

'That Tate likes sex,' Annabel said.

Caroline literally doubled up with laughter, tipping forward so that she had to steady herself by grabbing Annabel's arm.

Kayla looked uncomfortable. 'It's OK, Tate . . .' she began. 'No one thinks—'

'I have a boyfriend,' I blurted out.

Caroline stopped laughing and looked at me with interest. 'Your status says you're single.'

I smiled back, unnerved. How much did they know about me? Had they seen my showreel? Had they *all* been looking me up?

'I keep it quiet,' I said quickly. 'For professional reasons.'

Annabel narrowed her eyes.

'What reasons?' Caroline frowned.

'Is he an actor?' Kayla asked. 'Oh my God. Are you dating someone famous?'

Yes. This was good. I lowered my eyes, fixing them on my Prosecco glass, and flashed them an enigmatic smile.

'Oh my God. You are! Who is he?' Kayla pressed me.

'Sorry.' I shook my head, still smiling. 'I can't say.'

'Oh, come on! We won't tell anyone. We promise.'

I laughed. 'I can't!'

'Give us a clue,' Caroline persisted. 'Is he British or American?'

I hesitated. 'British.'

Fuck. American. Why didn't I say American? That would have been a *much* bigger, better void to lose a boyfriend in.

But it was too late. Annabel was looking at me disbelievingly. I felt myself flushing and lifted my arm, running my sleeve across my forehead to wipe away the beads of perspiration that were gathering on my brow.

'So, what are you in at the moment?' Kayla was asking me, but Annabel's expression had thrown me and I couldn't think straight.

I ran my tongue over the roof of my mouth. It was dry. I needed a drink of water. I glanced towards the bar, but the staff were all serving down the other end. I took a slurp of Prosecco instead. 'I'm . . . resting at the moment.'

'*Resting?*'

'It means she hasn't got a job,' said Annabel.

'No, I . . . I do,' I corrected her. 'I temp during the . . . the . . . well, whenever I'm not acting.'

'Do you?' Caroline asked, her eyes incredulous.

Oh God. Wrong answer. 'You know,' I mumble. 'Pay the bills.'

'Doesn't your famous boyfriend help you out?'

Oh, fuck. Fuck. *Fuck.* 'Never,' I say. 'I always pay my own way.' But my hand was trembling visibly.

'Careful,' said Annabel. 'You're spilling your free drink.'

Kayla reached out and steadied my glass. I stepped back and smeared the puddle of Prosecco under the toe of my boot.

'Sorry. Is there a kitty somewhere? Do we need to . . . are we meant to chip in?'

'Here, kitty, kitty,' Annabel said under her breath and Caroline snorted. Even Kayla was smiling this time.

'Don't worry. We're just teasing,' said Caroline. 'The Prosecco is on me.'

'Oh. Thank you,' I said. 'I'll have to get you one after—'

'No need,' Caroline cut in.

'So, what about you?' I asked her, because I felt that's where we were heading. 'What do *you* do?'

'I'm a marketing manager for a big engineering firm,' Caroline said proudly. 'And I'm a mum of three boys. Nathan's ten, Kurt's seven and Callum is five.' She paused. 'I don't really need to work, to be honest. My husband is a company director and our home is paid for, but I'm like you, Tate, I like my independence.' Her eyes sparkled. 'It's good to keep your hand in, isn't it? Have your own income?'

'Absolutely,' I agreed. I turned to Kayla. 'And you?'

'I'm a mum too,' she said. 'I have two girls. They're older, they're both at uni. I run my own interior design company.'

'Wow. That must be fun. You get to—'

'And Annabel's a producer,' said Caroline, cutting in again. She cleared her throat. 'She might know your boyfriend.'

My legs weakened underneath me. I turned to Annabel. 'What do you . . . what do you produce?'

'Movies,' she said loftily. 'I work for a production and distribution company in Paris.' But her voice was bored. She knew I was a fake. She was barely looking at me.

My heart sank. Annabel Mercer was a film producer! She was a successful bloody film producer. This was just so . . . so unfair. This was so far from fair. My first instincts had been right. I shouldn't have come. I'd messed up the minute I opened my mouth.

'Are you OK, Tate?' Kayla asked me. 'You seem a little . . . distant.'

'I'm fine,' I said. 'I just need the loo. I'll catch up with you in a bit.'

I weaved my way through the crowd in the bar towards the sign that directed me to the toilets. Over in the far corner, in a huddle, I could see several others from my year, some of the people from my core subject sets, and some of the girls from my A-level classes who had always been perfectly nice to me. I hesitated, contemplating joining them, but I just couldn't face talking myself up to anyone else. I needed a cigarette. So, I headed out of the door, looking for the smoking area. I went up a flight of stairs to where the toilets were, but then I saw a sign leading to a terrace and I went up another flight.

The terrace was on the top floor. I pushed open a door. It was empty and there was no view, just a rooftop with a load of chimney stacks looking onto more chimney tops and another terrace on the adjacent building. The cool, fresh air was a relief. I lit a cigarette and breathed in deeply for a moment. Then I stepped forward, moving a little nearer to the edge of the building, curious to see how close I could get to it, what the view was like down to the street below. I gripped the railing that bordered the terrace and peered over, feeling my stomach somersault as I looked down.

And then, to my right, out of the corner of my eye, I saw her. A woman with dark, wavy hair. She'd climbed up and was sitting on the ledge of the wall, her legs dangling in mid-air.

'Hey,' I called out. 'I . . . I don't think you should be sitting there. It's not safe. You could easily fall.'

She turned her head slightly towards me.

I stepped closer. 'Oh my God,' I said. 'Are you . . . Is that . . . Helen? My God. *Helen!* What are you doing up there?'

21

My voice echoed in the still night air. 'Helen?' I said again. 'Where you're sitting, it's . . . it's not safe. You could fall.'

She turned her head. 'Can you leave me alone, please?'

'I don't think I should.'

'I just want to . . . I need a minute.'

'And then you'll come down?'

She shook her head.

I felt myself shiver. 'If you're thinking about jumping . . . please don't.'

She didn't answer.

'You might not kill yourself,' I said. 'You can't be sure. Not from this height. You might just be horribly maimed. Paralysed. Spend the rest of your life in a wheelchair with Annabel Mercer pushing you around. You know, like Rhonda in *Muriel's Wedding*.'

She let out a strangled cry, a half sob, half laugh.

'Come on,' I said gently. 'Things can't be that bad.'

'Oh yeah? You wanna bet?' She picked up a bottle of wine

that was on the wall next to her, tipped back her head and took a long slug.

'Do you want to talk about it?'

She shook her head. 'There's nothing to say. I've fucked up everything. I've really, *royally* fucked up.'

'How have you fucked up?'

I saw her inch towards the edge.

'Look,' I said quickly. 'My life's a complete car wreck. I should be the one jumping.'

She didn't answer.

'Seriously. I'm an out-of-work-actress-slash-office-temp-slash-dogsbody. I live on my own with a cat. And instead of making up some great, undetectable shit about myself down there, like I should have done, I've just gone and told a stupid pack of lies and shown everyone what a bloody loser I am.'

'What did you tell them?'

'That I'm dating a famous actor.'

'Are you?'

'No. I don't even have a boyfriend.'

'Everyone is so fucking successful,' she said. 'I don't know why the fuck I came.'

'Me neither. But trust me. You won't find a bigger loser here than me.'

She didn't argue, which hurt a little, but at least her balance was now weighted towards me, rather than towards the edge of the wall. 'What have you been in, then?' she asked.

'What?'

'You said you're an actress.'

I shrugged. 'One advert. Years ago. Carpet Palace? I was the woman on the flying carpet that flew into that couple's living room?'

She didn't reply.

'No,' I sighed. 'That's it, really. I haven't had any decent work in years. I'm twenty-one grand in debt and I'm not qualified to do anything except act. Actually, that's not true. I have OCR Level Two typing, but my speed sucks and I have RSI. So I do a lot of photocopying. And scanning. And shredding. Which' – I was aware that I was gabbling – 'will be really useful as research if I ever get a part as an insanely bored office temp. But in the meantime, it's totally, insanely fucking boring. And guess what? My brothers and sisters are all married with kids and they're all, like, multimillionaires.'

She turned to face me. 'Really?'

I nodded. 'Yep. Every one of them. They all have the big house, the nice car, the designer clothes, the expensive holidays.' I paused. 'They're living the dream. And then there's me.'

'Here.' Helen stretched out her arm and offered me the wine bottle. I stepped forward and took it from her. 'Are they really *millionaires*?'

'They really are.' I took a slug of wine. 'I'm not kidding. Every one of them. Fern – you remember Fern? She owns a chain of hotels. And Blair floated his company on the stock market before the crash and pocketed fifty million. He went from being rich to super rich overnight.'

'If they're so rich, why don't they help you pay off your debts?'

'They all got together and came to an agreement that they

wouldn't do that. They think I need to get my shit together, learn to help myself.'

She nodded slowly. 'Nice.'

My phone bleeped.

'Your famous boyfriend?' she asked sardonically.

I smiled. 'Amazon. Delivery tomorrow.'

'What have you ordered?'

'Shoes,' I said.

She started to cry.

'It's a bit late, to be honest,' I said. 'I wanted them for tonight.'

She cried harder.

'Hey.' I moved closer.

'I had a boyfriend,' she sobbed. 'I had a *fiancé*. I had a home. And . . . and then I went and fucked everything up.'

'Helen, come down,' I pleaded. 'Let's go somewhere. We can talk about it.'

She didn't answer. We stayed like that for a moment, her teetering on the edge of the wall and me watching her in silence. I didn't want to blow it by saying the wrong thing.

'What happened to you, Hel?' I asked her finally. 'You left school so suddenly.'

'We moved,' she murmured. 'To Shropshire. Shrewsbury.'

'Shrewsbury?'

She sniffed. 'My dad got a new job.'

'Just like that? I mean . . . you were at school on the Friday. And then you just weren't there on the Monday.'

'I didn't know it was my last day,' she said. 'My parents didn't tell me until afterwards that I wasn't coming back.'

'Was it because of . . . Did you tell them?' I hesitated. 'About . . .'

She shook her head, a sudden, startling movement. 'No. But I was pretty messed up. I think they just thought it would be good for all of us to have a new start.'

I swallowed hard. 'I was pretty messed up too.'

Helen looked up at me. Her face was pained, strained, her eyes glazed over with tears.

'I tried to find you,' I told her. 'Later, I mean. Online.'

She sniffed. 'I don't do social media.'

'I don't blame you,' I said. 'After . . . after everything.'

We fell silent. A breeze lifted the corner of her skirt and she pushed it down, held it there. A pause, then she wiped her eyes. 'Can I have one of your cigarettes?'

'Sure.' I quickly pulled the packet out of my bag and held it out to her.

She reached for the pack. 'I can't quite . . . Can you move closer?'

'Come down,' I begged her. 'Please, Hel. Where do you live? Maybe we can share a cab home, or . . . or we could go and find a bar or something. We can catch up. Talk about old times. I mean . . . just talk. About anything you want.'

She considered this for a moment and then, to my surprise, she turned, gripped the railing and swung her legs over the wall and jumped down.

I quickly moved next to her, positioning myself between her and the wall. I tapped out a cigarette, passed it to her, lit it for her and then held out the wine bottle. She took it, breathed out a plume of smoke, took a slug of wine and leaned back against the chimney top.

'So, it's really you.' She looked at me sideways. 'Tee McGee.' She said this in a phony, comedy voice and her mouth curved into a smile.

'Jones. Helen Jones,' I said in a James Bond voice. 'The one and only.'

She snorted and passed the wine bottle back to me, then put the cigarette to her lips, letting out another plume of smoke. 'We had some fun, didn't we?' she said. 'I mean . . . before . . .'

'We were badass,' I agreed. 'Badass. Do you remember when you stole those ice lollies? You put them in your jeans pockets and then the shopkeeper stopped you and started questioning you, but you couldn't speak . . .'

'. . . because my arse was so frigging cold.'

I threw my head back, laughing. 'I mean . . . fancy stealing ice lollies!'

'It was hot!' she protested, smiling. 'I wanted an ice lolly. And I wasn't wearing jeans,' she corrected me. 'They were flimsy shorts, made of, like . . . next to nothing. My arse was completely frozen. It was torture.'

We laughed again, then fell silent. We were both thinking about her flimsy shorts, thinking about all the other things that happened that summer, how our friendship had frozen in time like those ice lollies, then melted away under the sun.

'He's married. Did you know that?' she said. 'He has a wife and a daughter. He works for a bank in the City. He's some big shot there.'

I felt my gut searing. 'I saw that too. I mean . . . it was a while ago, but . . . yeah. I looked him up.'

She started to cry again. 'Why do some people just breeze through life, getting everything? Why do some people have to fight so hard just to stay sane? Just to stay alive?' Her sobs turned into huge, racking gulps. 'God! Why do I have to fuck *everything* up?'

She leaned into me, putting her head on my shoulder, so I put my arms around her and hugged her tight. 'Come on,' I said into her hair. 'Let's call a cab. In the morning, when you've had a good night's sleep, things will look different.'

'I don't think so.'

'You're drunk. Things always look better when—'

'No!' She shook her head vehemently. 'No, they don't. They won't. I've been kicked out of my apartment. I have to get out by the end of the week.'

'What? Why?'

'Because I lost my job and I couldn't pay the rent.'

'Why did you lose your job?'

'I had too much time off. I was . . .' She stifled a sob. 'I was sick.'

'You were sick?'

She nodded.

'Well, couldn't you just explain that?'

She hesitated. 'No,' she said.

'So, what will you do?' I asked. 'Where will you go?'

She shrugged her shoulders.

I thought about this for a minute. 'Well, that's it, then. It's settled. You're coming to stay with me.'

'I can't ask that of you.'

'Yes,' I said firmly, excitedly. 'Yes, you can.'

She looked back at me for a moment to see if I meant it and then a grin began to form on her face. 'Are you serious?'

I grinned back at her. 'Deadly serious. Come home with me tonight and then tomorrow we'll go and pick up all your stuff.'

'Oh my God, Tate.' She started to cry in earnest again. 'Oh my God, I would love that! Are you sure you have room?'

'I'll make room. I'll absolutely bloody make room!'

'Oh my God, I can't believe it. I can't believe I've found you again.' She flung her arms around me.

Tears sprang to my own eyes too as I hugged her. 'And I can't believe I've found you, Hel. I thought I'd lost you for ever. You're the best friend I ever had!'

'I've missed you so much, Tee! I love you so much!'

I held her tight. 'I've missed you so much too, Hel,' I whispered into her hair. 'And I love you too.'

She pulled away from me and reached into her pocket for a tissue, then blew her nose hard, and we both burst out laughing at how loud it was. 'Whatever's happened, Hel,' I said, 'we'll make it better. I promise you.'

22

Maddy closed her eyes. They felt grainy and her head ached. She was tired, but she had wanted to get the edits she'd been working on finished before she started dinner. Get an early night. She rubbed her temples and looked back at her computer screen, but it was no good. The lines of words were blurring around the edges and moving on the page.

The front door slammed. 'Hello,' Dan called out cheerfully from the hallway.

'In here,' she called back.

Dan appeared in the doorway of the study and saw her bleary eyes. 'Still working? You look exhausted, Mads.'

'I'm going to stop now.' Maddy closed the document and switched off her monitor.

'Where's Emily?'

'She's not home yet.'

Dan frowned and looked at his watch. 'It's gone seven.'

'I know.'

'Have you called her?'

'She messaged earlier and said she was going to Rosie's after school to do homework. I told her she needed to be back for dinner.'

'I'll call her.' Dan reached for his phone.

Maddy followed him into the kitchen, unhooked an apron from the back of the door and slipped it over her head, tying it at the waist. She fetched onions and carrots from the refrigerator drawer, pushing them over the countertop towards her husband, who was standing at the breakfast bar, phone to one ear, shrugging off his jacket and loosening his tie.

'Straight to voicemail.' He put his phone on the worktop and sat down, frowning.

'Maybe she's in a dead zone.' The phrase sounded ominous. Maddy added, 'On her way home.'

'Maybe.'

Maddy handed Dan a knife. 'For the carrots,' she clarified, smiling, but she, too, was worrying just a little now.

'Why don't you message Kay?'

'Yeah. I'll do that.' Maddy put a pan on the stove and filled the kettle to boil water for the spaghetti, then picked up her phone and opened the messaging app. She tapped out a message, then opened the fridge and took out a bottle of chilled white wine. Taking two glasses from the cupboard, she unscrewed the bottle and poured them a glass each. She placed one on the worktop in front of Dan.

Her phone bleeped. She picked it up.

'What did she say?'

'Emily's not there. She hasn't been there.' Maddy looked

up at Dan, feeling the same apprehension that she could see on his face. 'I'll get Kay to ask Rosie where she is.'

Maddy tapped out another message, then took a bunch of spaghetti out of the packet, snapped it in two and dropped it into the pan. The answer came back a few minutes later: Sorry Maddy, Rosie doesn't know. They went to the shops after school and then Rosie came home.

'She doesn't know,' Maddy said to Dan.

Dan pursed his lips. 'So she lied.'

'Looks that way.'

Maddy tapped out a message to Emily: Where are you? But there was no reply.

She made a marinara sauce and they sat down to dinner. As they ate, she told Dan about the vodka bottle.

'So, here we go again,' he said, sighing.

'I suppose so.' Maddy sighed too.

They waited, watching the clock. At ten forty-five the front door opened. Maddy's heart leaped with relief. She followed Dan out to the hallway, where Emily was standing, looking shamefaced, kicking off her shoes.

'I'm sorry,' she said quickly.

'Where have you been?' Dan demanded.

'I missed the bus.'

'The bus from where?' Maddy protested. 'You said you were going to Rosie's.'

'I know. I know. I'm sorry.'

'Emily, it's nearly eleven o'clock. You didn't answer any of our calls or messages. And you've lied to us. You weren't at Rosie's.'

'I didn't lie. There was a change of plan. My phone was only on two per cent, so I didn't want to use it up. And then it died.'

'Where have you been?'

'I met some of my friends at the park and we were talking and I lost track of time.'

'Have you been drinking?'

'No!'

'Where did you get vodka?' Dan asked her.

Emily looked irritated. 'What are you on about?'

'Your mum found an empty bottle of vodka in the waste-paper bin in your bedroom.'

'Oh, for God's sake!' Emily said. 'That's been there ages and it's not even mine.'

'Then whose is it?'

'No one's.'

'Did you drink it?' Dan pressed her.

'I can't remember. Some of it, maybe. It ended up in my bag, that's all, and so I put it in the bin.'

'Right. That's it!' Dan said. 'You're grounded.'

'Dad! I told you!' Emily wailed. 'It's been there ages.'

'It's nearly eleven o'clock. You were supposed to be home for dinner, and you didn't even have the consideration to let us know where you were.'

'I told you, my phone died!'

'So, who are these friends you've been hanging around with?' Dan said. 'I want to know their names.'

'Here we go again. That's all you care about! Seriously. You never stop going on about it. It's your problem, not mine, if you don't like my friends.'

'Em,' said Maddy. 'We don't *know* your friends. *That's* the problem. And of course we care. You're out with these people all the time and you're out until late and we have no idea who they are or where you are.'

'You don't need to know them! They're my friends, not yours! You can't stop me having friends just because you don't know their parents.'

'You wanna bet?' said Dan.

'Aargh!' Emily screamed. 'I hate you!'

'Right. That's it. Give me your phone.'

'Dad, no!'

'Give it to me!'

Emily placed her phone into her father's hand, burst into tears and ran up the stairs.

Dan looked at the phone, then walked back into the kitchen and put it on charge. He sat down at the worktop and put his head in his hands. 'What did we do?' he asked plaintively. 'Where did we go wrong?'

'We didn't. It's just . . . it's a phase. We'll get through it.'

'But it's not getting any better. It's getting worse, Mads. We need to do something about it.'

'What can we do?' asked Maddy. 'Except be there for her. There's nothing else we can do.'

Dan heaved a sigh, then looked across at his daughter's confiscated phone, which was lying on the glossy worktop. As they sat in silence, the phone powered into life and a message flashed up. Dan pulled the phone towards him, peering at it. Maddy turned it a little so that they could both see it.

Please don't be mad at me, the message said. There was no contact name beside it – just a red heart.

Dan and Maddy looked at each other. The phone lit up again and another message flashed in front of them. It's only because you are so amazing. So beautiful.

Dan bristled in his seat, his back stiffening, his face clouding. He watched the phone, waiting for the next message, his eyes transfixed.

But I can wait.

Dan's head shot up. 'The little shit. He's trying to have sex with my daughter!' he exclaimed.

'You don't know that—' Maddy began.

'Maddy!' He gave her a *Wake up!* face. ' "I can wait." There's only one thing that can mean. Right. That's it!' Dan leaped out of his seat and marched towards the door.

'Dan, stop!' Maddy pleaded. 'Wait. This isn't going to work. She won't tell you anything. If you confront her like this, the mood she's in, she'll just shut down even further.'

'You want me to ignore it?'

'What choice do we have, Dan? She's going to have boyfriends.'

'She's fourteen! She's underage!'

'But it's what happens, isn't it? Boys are going to try.'

'So, you condone this?'

'No,' Maddy sighed. 'Of course I don't. But this isn't the way to tackle it. When she's calmed down, I'll go upstairs. I'll remind her that boys will want to . . .' She looked at her husband's widening eyes. 'To try,' she said carefully, 'but that she doesn't have to let them. Let me handle it. She's not going to tell you anything if you go storming up there now, laying down the law. She might even . . . go.' The thought made Maddy's heart rate quicken.

Dan gazed at Maddy for a moment, then his shoulders slouched in defeat. He walked back to the breakfast bar and sat down, fixing his tired, red-rimmed eyes on the phone. He watched it, waiting, but, to Maddy's immense relief, the owner of the red heart had taken Emily's silence as her answer, for now.

23

We didn't go straight home after the Pig and Whistle. We went for a drink somewhere in Soho. I can't remember where, exactly – we were pretty wasted by the time we left. I remember going down some steps into a bar that looked like a wine cellar, with exposed stone walls and wooden kegs for tables, and I remember ordering a cold bottle of rosé, which came in a silver ice bucket with glasses the size of small goldfish bowls. We sat on high stools up at the bar. There were tea lights all along the bar top. Helen was wearing a beautiful pair of diamond earrings, which were twinkling and shimmering in the flickering light.

So, yes, Helen existed. She *exists*. Her real name was – *is* – Helen Milocewska. Her mother is English, her father Polish. We became friends at school in the autumn of Year 8, when she was moved up to my set for English and, for a while, we were inseparable. She was one of the prettiest, cleverest girls in our year group and I was honoured that she'd singled me out. As it turned out, we had loads in common. We loved books and movies and plays and she loved reading them aloud, as did

I. We thought up ideas for 'screenplays' and before long we were writing them. We assigned ourselves parts and performed them together on the cracked concrete site of an old disused bomb shelter at the back of the school field.

For two long, hot summers we saw each other every day. During the second summer, when we were fourteen, we started shoplifting and that's when we decided we needed fake names in case we got caught. Helen had done some research. She said we needed to keep our first names. It's what undercover cops do – you probably know that. It's in case someone they know calls out to them in the street: 'Hey, Helen!' 'Hey, Tee.' (I hated my Christian name, hated how unusual it was, had already started telling people that my real name was Tina and insisting that everyone called me 'Tee'.) So, in our own little fictional world, and to anyone who didn't know us, she became Helen Jones and I became Tee McGee.

Thankfully, we were never arrested, so we didn't need the fake names. We didn't even shoplift for very long. In fact, I think that time with the ice lollies might even have been the last time, because Helen so nearly got caught. We weren't that badass really; we were just searching for a bit of drama. We lost our nerve sometime after that. But the fake names stuck. They were 'our thing'; they were part of the glue that held us together, until we were pulled apart.

But we didn't talk about that, that night in the Soho wine cellar. I wanted to know what Helen had done – or thought she'd done – that was so terrible she'd contemplated jumping from a roof. She told me she didn't think she'd really wanted to end her life, but – both literally and metaphorically – she couldn't seem to stop herself from teetering on rooftops, from living life close to the edge. Losing her job was just one more thing in a long line of things. Crap always found her, she said. When anything good came along, she didn't know what to do with it. She didn't know how to just be happy, to allow a bright future for herself. If there was no drama, then she would create it. She'd engineer fights with her fiancé, Matt. She'd push him away in ways that she hated herself for. And when he kept coming back, refusing to let her sabotage the relationship, she'd made sure she did the unforgivable: she decided to terminate her pregnancy.

When she confessed, told Matt what she'd done, she'd known it would be the end of their relationship. As for the baby, she didn't know why she'd done what she'd done except that her gran had died recently and she'd become scared of the future. She now bitterly regretted the termination. It was the first thing she thought of when she woke in the morning and the last thing on her mind when she fell asleep at night. That and Matt's accusing silence. For three weeks he'd avoided her, slept on the sofa, eaten at work. Finally, she'd moved out of the beautiful home she'd shared with him and into a tiny, soulless studio flat.

Then there was her job. She'd taken a lot of time off work due to pregnancy sickness that she couldn't tell anyone about, so when she was hauled into the HR office, she couldn't give an explanation or a fit note. Her work had been below par, she said, in any event. She hadn't been able to focus. She was pining for her grandmother. She missed Matt. She missed her baby. She felt the greatest of guilt about all of it. There was simply nothing good left in her life.

She didn't know what had made her go to the school reunion

that night. One last attempt to recapture something from her past life, maybe? Or the fact that she knew it had a roof terrace she could jump from? She wasn't entirely sure. But she told me later that meeting me again had made her feel as if there was still something out there, something left. My appearance on the roof terrace, my concern for her and my offer of a place to stay were enough to reignite whatever spark had been extinguished inside her. It had given her something to cling on to, she said.

This in turn made me feel good. I was fortified by her presence. She'd been my soulmate and I'd been bereft when I lost her, but here she was, back in my life again. Overwhelmingly, I wanted to fix things for her. I know, I know. Trying to fix someone who's broken is never the answer to your problems. Read any self-help book and it will tell you that this is not the path to redemption, that you have to begin and end with yourself. But in this case, nothing could have been truer. My past and Helen's were intertwined in a way I'd barely allowed myself to remember until now. And so, a spark was lit inside me too.

But I'm jumping ahead. That night was about saving Helen. We went to the bar and then she came back to my place and I made us cheese on toast and we made a plan for her to get out of her miserable studio flat and bring her things to mine the following day. And then she went to sleep on a fold-out bed behind the sofa in my living room and I ate some more cheese on toast and then I went to bed.

So no one lost their life that weekend. Or an earring. Helen still has both earrings. They are so pretty. They twinkle and shimmer every time they catch the light.

24

Maddy stood in line in the post office, feeling hot and uncomfortable. She'd woken with the now familiar black cloud forming above her eyes and it was building, growing thicker, like a storm brewing in her head. She tugged off her sweat top and pulled her water bottle out of her bag and took a few sips. She needed to stay hydrated. But she knew what was coming. First the cloud, soon the storm – or worse, the hurricane.

She needed a plan. If she walked up to the supermarket on the corner, she could buy a few things for dinner and be back home in bed with her heated beanbag and her sleep headphones before her headache became unbearable. Emily wasn't due home from school for a few hours yet. She could sleep it off. It would be OK.

She heaved a sigh at the prospect of yet another day wasted, but she'd feel a little better once she'd slept. She'd be more productive then – and besides, she knew there was no way when she was feeling like this that she was going to be able to look at a screen.

Maddy reached the front of the queue, handed over a package, bought stamps, then pushed open the glass door of the post office into the street. As she walked down to the Tesco Express on the corner, her phone rang. She pulled it out of her pocket to look at it and, as she did so, she felt a hard thwack against the right-hand side of her body. Her bag fell from her shoulder, her phone clattered onto the pavement and she landed on the ground with a thud.

It took her a moment to realise what had happened. She'd walked into a pole! No, not a pole; she'd walked into a bloody traffic light! She quickly pulled herself to her feet, embarrassed, holding up a hand to thank the couple who were now hurrying over to help.

'It's all right.' She forced a smile and leaned down to pick up her phone and her bag. 'I'm not hurt.'

'Are you sure?' the woman asked her, looking doubtful.

'Honestly. Thank you anyway. You're very kind, but I'm fine.'

'So long as you're sure,' said the woman. The man nodded his agreement and they both carried on up the street.

But Maddy wasn't fine. She wasn't even OK. She'd grazed her hand and her leg was throbbing. She was hurt and sore and in pain. She felt an unexpected surge of anger as she watched the couple walk away. The little shits! Not the couple. It was those bloody kids that Emily was hanging around with. They were the cause of all this.

Last night, while Dan cleared up the dinner things, Maddy had gone upstairs to talk to Emily. She'd taken her up some spaghetti and sauce as a peace offering and they'd had the

185

conversation, the one about the boyfriend. Emily had clammed up initially, angry that she and Dan had been reading her messages. Maddy had explained that they had been worried but hadn't meant to pry.

'I'm not stupid, Mum,' Emily had told her. 'I know I don't have to do anything. If you've read the messages, you should know that.'

'But the next time—'

'There won't be a next time. I'm not having sex, Mum.'

'OK, but . . . but maybe we should talk about it?'

'What is there to talk about?'

'You know. Sex.'

'I don't need to talk to you about that,' Emily had said scornfully. 'We learn all that stuff at school.'

'But if there *is* anything you're worried about, you know you can talk to me, don't you?'

'There's nothing to talk about. I'm not having sex, all right? Please just leave me alone.'

Maddy had left it there. She'd felt reassured and had, in turn, reassured Dan – or tried to. She'd known that he still wasn't happy, but Emily was her own person, she'd pointed out. She'd never allow herself to be pressured into anything. She'd be more likely to tell the guy to fuck off. And that's what had happened, hadn't it, by the look of things? Dan had reluctantly accepted this. But as Maddy was brushing her teeth, finally about to go to bed, Kay had messaged Maddy to say that Rosie had let slip that one of the group had a 'whip'.

It's modern-day slang for wheels, Kay had explained. She'd followed it with a second message to say that Rosie had insisted that the friend with the car was someone on the fringes of the group, nothing for her parents to be concerned about. But Kay *was* concerned and Maddy was too, although for Kay's benefit she'd pretended not to be. Out of the two of them, it was definitely more likely to be Emily leading Rosie astray and Maddy often felt the weight of this silent accusation; she didn't want to fuel it with her own anxiety. But it was easier for Kay. Rosie was more compliant, more likely to listen to her parents and – not to be down on Rosie – she was . . . plainer. And . . . bigger. Emily was – by anyone's standards – beautiful. She was charismatic, independent-minded – and, well, more mature-looking than Rosie. Maddy felt mean for thinking it, but there was far less likelihood of Rosie having that same draw for the opposite sex.

Of course, it didn't mean that the car owner was giving the girls lifts anywhere; nor, of course, did it mean that he was the suspected Lothario behind the red heart. But if he was old enough to drive, then he had to be at least seventeen and too old to be hanging around with a pair of fourteen-year-old girls. Maddy sighed. She wouldn't tell Dan, not yet. But she'd known the instant she read Kay's message that this was going to be yet another sleepless night.

Like most nights, she'd initially fallen into a deep sleep, with the help of some headache tablets, but she'd woken again an hour or two later with the feeling that something was wrong. Had she heard the front door open? She knew it was unlikely, but since that time when Emily had stayed out all night, she couldn't take it for granted that her daughter was still safely tucked up in bed. Even though it had only happened the once, it was as though she couldn't move on from it. She couldn't get the what-ifs out of her head.

So, last night – as most nights – her mind had swum up out of her drowsy body and nudged it into wakefulness. She'd pushed back the covers and padded down the landing, hyper-vigilant, alert now the way she'd been when Emily was a baby with bronchiolitis or croup. She'd gently turned the handle and crept into her daughter's room, her eyes searching in the darkness for the body-shaped lump under the duvet. She'd listened for the sound of her daughter's breathing until she was certain. And then – only then – could she go back to bed.

She had to do this. She had to endure it; she had to go through this pathetic routine, night after night, because experience had taught her that if she didn't, she'd just lie awake anyway, torturing herself. She would run through all the possibilities, and, really, they were endless: Emily had got a call and sneaked out. Dan had got up for water and put the chain on. Emily had tried to get back in; neither she nor Dan had heard her. Or worse: Emily was out getting drunk somewhere; she was in trouble. And now: she was a passenger in a car and the driver had been drinking; there had been an accident. There was about to be a knock at the door from the police.

And so it went on. Every new prospect was increasingly alarming, increasingly unbearable. And Maddy couldn't even comfort herself with the thought that she was being ridiculous, that this was just her imagination going wild, because these things happened, didn't they? They happened to people and they happened to children. They happened every day to other parents. So why not to her?

She sighed now and looked down at her phone. It seemed OK. Not broken, anyway, thankfully. She pushed it into her pocket, took out a tissue and cleaned the broken skin on the heel of her hand, removing a small piece of grit. *Meanwhile, gritting her teeth* . . . She thought about that for a moment. *Hmm. Grit and determination. Better. I could use that*, she realised. *I'd have to play with it. But* . . .

A small glimmer of hope rose inside her, as it always did when she thought about the book she wanted to write, the book that she was so close to finding the time for. It wouldn't be long. *This, too, shall pass.* And then she would write a deep, heartfelt story about the joy *and* the pain of motherhood. She'd have a ton of material. Ha! Write what you know, they say, and she knew all right.

So, none of this was wasted, was it? Not one single experience or emotion. This difficult time of her life would be over and some good would come of it and other parents would find comfort and inspiration in her words. Everybody knew that parenting a teenager wasn't easy and they'd see that they, too, could get through it, because this was just a phase, right?

But what if it wasn't? Maddy drew a long, shaky breath as she picked up her bag and walked carefully, cautiously on up the street. It had been going on for months now, on and off, the overstepping of boundaries, the staying out late. And now Emily had a boyfriend she couldn't even talk to her mum about. Maddy felt hurt by this; she had been so close to her own mother, had shared everything. Was she herself that unapproachable? Or was there a very good reason why Emily didn't want her parents to meet these new friends? What if she was being brainwashed? She'd read books, seen documentaries, read articles and stories about teenagers who'd been lost to cults or suicide pacts. Or worse.

She couldn't actually imagine what would be worse than losing her daughter, but it would come to her at 3 a.m., she knew. Maddy knew that anything was possible when you had a child. Your worst fears could so easily become reality. You saw it in the news all the time. Those parents who appeared on TV. Poor, brave, heartbroken men and women who'd gone public to warn all the other parents. 'Be careful! Stay alert! Stay *awake*!'

So, last night she'd stayed awake longer, opened the door wider, moved closer. Her daughter always slept so soundly, so silently, submerged under the sheets, stiff and still like an Egyptian mummy. She'd always slept that way, often not moving for hours. When she was younger, Maddy used to worry that she'd died in her sleep. She didn't worry about that any more. Her worries had mutated. Her daughter dying in her sleep was somehow much less frightening than all of the other dangers that could befall her. Maddy knew each time her daughter stepped outside the front door that this could be it – the time she didn't come back home again.

Now, she picked up a basket near to the entrance of the supermarket, then moved round the shop, selecting olives, cheese, fish and vegetables, avocados, nuts. She yawned out loud as she stood in line at the checkout, then glanced round, embarrassed, to see if anyone had overheard. The man in the queue behind her was smiling. Normally, she was quite friendly and would have smiled back, would probably even have got chatting. It was the writer in her. She liked people, liked finding out about them, swapping stories. But she didn't seem to be feeling like that lately. Everyone was annoying her. She looked away, down at her basket instead.

A moment later, she reached the checkout and began to pile her goods onto the counter. She'd selected some nice, healthy food. But food wasn't the only thing that mattered, was it? What did that book say – the one they'd just published at work, the one about sleep? The message was clear: a good seven to eight hours of sleep was just as important for your health as your diet. It was crucial, in fact. It was when your body repaired itself, when cells regenerated, when memories were formed. No wonder she was forgetting things lately. And the stress . . . well, that wasn't good either, was it? It was so bad for the body. What was the point of eating well and making sure she got enough exercise if she was going to spend half the night lying awake, worrying about Emily?

The cloud over her eyes thickened as she held out her store loyalty card for the guy on the checkout to scan. She paid for the food and walked home. As she walked up the path and into the house, her phone rang again. She realised then that she'd completely forgotten someone had been trying to call. She pulled it out and saw there had been several missed calls, all from Dan. She pushed the slider across.

'Where were you?' he asked, his voice agitated. 'I've been trying to call you.'

'I'm sorry,' she said. 'I fell over and hurt my arm. And then—'

'You fell over? Where? What happened?'

'It's nothing. I just slipped.'

'Where?'

'Union Road, near Tesco. In the street.'

'Are you OK?'

'I'm fine. Just tired. I've got a bad head again. It's made me a bit foggy.'

A pause. 'Right,' he said decisively. 'I'm on my way home.'

'Don't be daft, Dan. You can't just leave the office in the middle of the day. I told you. I'm OK. I just need to go back to bed for a bit.'

'Wait! Just . . . wait, can you? I'm on my way. I'll be half an hour, tops.'

'Why? What's going on?'

There was a brief moment of silence and then, 'I'm sorry, Mads. You're not going to like this,' he said.

25

I woke early, but as there was no sound from the living room, I stayed in bed for a while. When I got up, Helen was still asleep, so I tiptoed about, made tea and toast and got back into bed again. I was still tired and I had a bit of a headache from all the wine we'd drunk the night before. But I was feeling positive and excited. My flat was small and it would be a squeeze, but the thought of having Helen living here with me was really lifting my spirits. I'd been on my own for too long.

When Helen woke, we took a walk through Hyde Park, along the Serpentine. The morning was warm and the sun already high in the sky. She told me that she was feeling a little better and was ready to collect a few things. We drove in my Corsa the short distance back to her flat near Baker Street, where I left her for a bit. We agreed that she'd call me again when she'd had a bath and finished packing. It would be around six, she said. I'd go and collect her as soon as she was ready. In the meantime, I'd go out for groceries, I suggested. I'd cook a nice meal.

'Don't go to any trouble,' she said.

'It's no trouble,' I told her. 'I'm happy to.'

In the end, we settled on a takeout and some hair of the dog – a bottle of rosé from the supermarket next to the Chinese takeaway at the end of my road. I offered to help her put her furniture into storage the next day, but she said she didn't have any. Most of her larger belongings were at her fiancé's and she said they could stay there. She said that what she didn't need or I didn't have room for could go in a box for the charity shop.

When I got home, I cleaned the bathroom, washed the dishes, hoovered the flat and emptied the bins. I pulled out Helen's bed, rearranging its position a few times, fed George and sat back down on the sofa to wait. It was still only four o'clock. I contemplated answering a few emails, sending off my CV for a few acting jobs, but I was still feeling a little weary and a bit hungover. I looked round for my phone, then realised it must still be in my bag, so I walked into the hallway and picked it up from the floor where I'd dropped it and rooted around inside. My hand touched something hard, cold, metallic. I pulled it out. It was a can of Fanta that Helen had bought me on the way to the park earlier that morning – one for each of us, along with a pack of fruit pastilles from a newsagent on the Edgware Road.

As I groped around in the inside pocket of my bag for my phone, I also found the half-eaten pack of sweets. She must have stuffed them there as we sat on the bench by the lake. I smiled to myself. It was so Helen. Such a familiar gesture. When we were younger, I'd often found her half-finished packs of food and cans of drink in my bag. And she had such a sweet tooth; we both had back then. Like typical teenagers, we were addicted to sweets and fizzy drinks. Nowadays, I tried not to eat sugary foods because, unlike Helen, who was still whippet-thin, I had to think of the calories. I hadn't had a can of Fanta or a fruit pastille for years.

But maybe the sugar would pick me up a little. I walked into the living room, placed my phone and the sweets on the table and then sat back on the sofa and pulled back the ring pull with a satisfying fizz and a tinny snap. Next, I tore a sugar-coated fruit pastille out of the silvery paper and popped it into my mouth, which was instantly flooded with flavour. Orange. No, lime. That sweet and sour, tangy taste. It was so weird. It was taking me right back, back to the hot, heady days when Helen and I had hung out together drinking pop and eating sweets in the arcade at the shops near the Lanes. Or that second summer, sitting on the creaky old swings at the park we'd called 'the Rec'.

He's married. He has a wife and a daughter. Helen's words came to me from nowhere.

My heart beat faster.

He works for a bank in the City. He's some big shot there.

I slowly placed the can on the coffee table. We'd talked about him more, I was sure of it, but we'd drunk a lot of wine and I couldn't quite remember everything that had been said.

I reached out, pulling my laptop towards me. I'd looked him up just the once, a few years ago, but I'd had to close down the webpage soon after I'd found him because the thought of him existing, continuing to exist – having an actual life, a *good* life – was making me feel physically sick. I felt just as sick now as I opened up the browser and tapped in his name.

Up came the page of results. The words 'Corporate Banking', 'Individual Banking', 'Wealth Management' leaped out at me before my eyes moved down, and there he was again, smiling back at me. No room for doubt; this was him. Even though I hadn't seen his face for nearly twenty-five years, it was as familiar to me as if it were yesterday. It was as handsome and as heartbreaking and as sickening as I remembered. It was everything I was afraid of and everything I'd tried to forget.

I clicked on the arrow and across the series of images – smiling, warm, glowing images. With a group of colleagues, stepping up onto a podium to receive an award. Shaking hands in a suit and tie. Clutching a pink-boxed bottle of Laurent-Perrier. He must be in his late forties now, but he'd changed very little. He was still stunningly good-looking, with a full head of thick fair hair and the same disarming smile. And then, as I scrolled, I came across a family shot. His arm around a woman – a beautiful woman – the other around a teenaged girl. He was happy. He had a happy life. The anger rose within me like bile.

I pushed the laptop away from me onto the sofa and ran to the bathroom and threw up into the toilet I'd just bleached. Afterwards, I leaned back against the bath and closed my eyes. The bathroom was cold and the floor was hard, but I didn't have the strength to move. So I curled up on the bath-mat and, with my eyes closed, I remembered. I remembered how it happened, how it started, that very first day he'd walked into the Rec. There had been a few of us there. Helen and I were on the swings and the boys – Sid Cole, Tommy Dougherty, Tony Letch – were sat on the grass by the roundabout with their bikes. It was the summer holidays and we were bored. I remembered the hot sun beating down on us as he came through the gate and sauntered over, said he was looking for a missing dog or something, but then ended up staying to chat. He'd lit a cigarette and Sid had asked if he could have one. And he'd smiled that smile of his and flipped Sid the pack.

He asked us what we were doing. Tommy told him that they'd planned to cycle up to the waste ground behind the old depot, but that he had a puncture. And so he'd lowered himself onto his haunches, cigarette hanging out of his mouth, and he'd pumped up the tyre, got Tommy to take the bike for a spin around the Rec. He then told Tommy that it was no good, that he would need a puncture kit. He had one, though. He had some kind of garage or lock-up near the depot. Said he'd help Tommy fix it if he liked, take them all up there, drop them up at the waste ground afterwards. He said his van was parked up just outside the Rec and that he could put their bikes in the back.

The boys had looked at each other in silence, their eyes locking. He shrugged. He was going that way anyway. Take it or leave it, he told them. It was up to them. He started to walk off. The boys quickly clambered to their feet and asked him to wait. And then, as they'd pushed their bikes towards him, he'd turned, looked up at me and Helen and asked us if we wanted to come along too.

Helen jumped off the swing. My parents would kill me, going off with a stranger in his van like this, but I didn't want to look like a loser. Everyone else was going. How would it look if I said no? And besides, the thrill of doing something grown-up – something extraordinary, something different – was irresistible. So what if we didn't know the guy? There were five of us and only one of him. Although they were only fifteen, Tommy and Sid were both over six feet tall. Tony was stocky. He played rugby. They weren't weaklings. And anyway, this man seemed completely normal. It would be fine and my parents didn't need to know.

So I followed Helen across the Rec. The boys had looked put out then, clearly wanting it to be a 'boys only' outing, but they didn't say much except to nudge each other and tell each other in hushed tones to 'act cool' as they pushed their bikes out of the park gates and lifted them into his van. Tommy and Sid sat up front with him and the rest of us climbed into the back with the bikes. Not strictly legal, he told us, so keep your heads down. But that just made it even more of an adventure. The thrill of doing something we shouldn't was a draw like no other.

On the way he stopped at a garage and he bought a load of cans of Fanta and Coke and a whole stash of sweets, crisps, chocolate bars and cakes. There was enough for everyone and plenty to spare. He put the bag in the middle and told us to help ourselves.

And then we had the best time ever, eating and drinking, sitting in the sunshine outside his lock-up, splashing each other with the hose he used to clean his van and riding the bikes up and down and doing wheelies. We stayed there all afternoon. It had been a long, boring summer and we'd had nothing to do but go to the Spar and sit on the wall outside and bicker, or go to the Rec and sit on the swings and bicker there instead. But here was something different, *someone* different, someone to look up to. He taught Sid and Tommy how to fix the puncture. He then showed them how to find their way around a car engine. He had an amazing music collection and told us to find some tracks to play while they worked. So Helen and I sat up in the front of the van, drinking Fanta and playing music on his sound system, choosing our favourite tracks with pride, as if we were DJs. When we played a song everyone loved and got a thumbs-up or a steady nod of the head in time with the music, we enjoyed the feeling that gave us. We cranked up the volume and blared it out.

I'd never sat in the front of a van before. I'd never sat in a vehicle that didn't also have my own or somebody else's parent in it. I'd never sat so high up. We felt so grown-up, so cool, sitting there in the front seats on our own like that. At one point, he asked me to slide across into the driver's seat, turn the key in the ignition and switch on the engine. When I put my foot on the pedal and revved the engine as requested, he looked up from behind the bonnet and winked at me and I felt myself light up inside like the sun.

We sat there all afternoon, eating and drinking, high on sugar and sunshine, occasionally tooting on the horn, enjoying how that made him look up and laugh. I watched his fair head as it moved around underneath the bonnet and my heart began to ache in this strange, alien way. He was so handsome, so commanding. He made the boys look like . . . boys. Stupid boys. Which they were, of course, fawning all over him like a bunch of idiots, trying to be like him, trying to look cool. But I secretly understood it. The attention he gave us – all of us – was intoxicating. He was like no one I'd ever known.

Later, as the sun went down, he said the boys could leave their bikes in the lock-up if they wanted and come back for them tomorrow, that he would give us all a lift home. Everyone got in, but we didn't go anywhere for a while. There was a mattress in the back and the boys stretched out on it and he got out a bottle of vodka and passed it round and we all just lay back and chilled and listened to music and the boys smoked and we drank and we all just hung out in his van.

It was a magical afternoon and a magical evening. There was an energy about him, and he was a grown-up, which made *us* feel grown-up too. He had money and transport, and in that lay freedom for all of us. He had alcohol as well, which tasted rubbish at first, but when I mixed it with Fanta or Coke it wasn't so bad. And the feeling I got from it was like no other; all my insecurities, all the arguments with my parents, the envy I felt towards my siblings . . . the warm glow from the vodka just wiped it all away. It made me feel confident. It made the music sound so amazing. It made us all laugh and laugh. It was warm and it was heady and it was such good fun.

The boys went back to get their bikes the next day, but Helen and I weren't invited. Instead, we went to the Rec, hoping he'd come back. A few days later, when the boys were there, he came for us again and we all went out. And before long, it became a regular thing. We didn't do much. He just picked us all up and we hung out at the lock-up or went for drives, drank vodka and smoked. We listened to music and we sang. He had a great voice. He could sing, *really* sing. He sang lead vocals in a band, he told us. He promised he'd take us all to his next gig. He was funny and clever and so, so handsome and I fell for him, hook, line and sinker. He was my first true love and the feeling was the most intense I'd ever known.

But Helen liked him too, and she was way prettier than me. He soon made it clear that he liked her back. Before too long, she was sitting up front with him and they were talking in hushed tones together and he was putting his arm around her and his hand on her knee and making sure that she was the very last one to be driven home. I was eaten up inside with jealousy. It was torture watching them together; being dropped off at the end of my road and having to get out of the van and leave them alone. I felt pathetic, in the way, but I kept going out with them all because I loved him and I had to see him; I had to be with him – even though it was Helen he wanted, not me.

And then a miracle happened. One day, he dumped Helen for me. All of a sudden, he was done with her and it was me he wanted instead. He'd been with the wrong girl all along, he told me, and had only just realised. I was delirious with happiness. For the first time in my life I felt noticed. So Helen was hurt and jealous. What could I do? He didn't want her; he wanted me. I'd never known happiness like it and there was no way I was going to give it up. Besides, Helen was so pretty, she'd soon find someone else. I'd spent ample time watching from the sidelines while boys fawned all over her. I deserved this. She needed to get over herself.

So, for a blissful few weeks, while Helen sulked in the back of the van, I sat up front next to him and was showered with attention. I enjoyed the elevated status that this, in turn, gave me within the group, but when I was finally alone with him, when he put his arms around me and kissed me, it was all I'd ever wanted.

Or so I told myself. In truth, it was the kind of attention that scared me a little, and when we'd dropped everyone else off, when we started to take longer to get back to my street, when, one evening, we pulled up in a quiet, dark road, I was afraid. I so badly wanted him to kiss me, and when he did, I was in seventh heaven. But when his hands wandered under my T-shirt, I didn't like it. I flinched and asked him to stop. I wasn't ready for this, I told him. That was fine, he smiled, the first time, and the next. But the time after that, as he stroked my back, I felt my bra coming off and before I could say anything, he was lifting my T-shirt up and over my head. I froze. I whimpered. I begged him to stop. Just a cuddle, he said. A kiss and a cuddle with our tops off. Under the blanket on the mattress in the back of his van.

But he wanted more than that, of course, and after a while I could see he was getting frustrated, that I was going to lose him. I was desperate, so desperate to keep him, that I eventually did what he wanted. When it happened, finally, it was cold and clinical. It was not what I'd expected, and it hurt in more ways than one.

And then it was over for me too, just like it had been for Helen. Just like that, he stopped coming to the Rec. And when I walked my broken heart the five miles to the lock-up one Sunday to find him, there was no mistaking the coldness in his voice, the look of disdain in his eyes as he told me I shouldn't have come.

It was over. All that was left was the hurt and the guilt and the shame. The boys were angry with us when he stopped coming for us. They called us a pair of slappers and told us we'd ruined their fun.

And then the rumours started. At the Rec, in school, everywhere we went. At school, as word got round, the girls sniggered behind their hands or stopped talking when we entered a classroom, while the boys made a play for us, tried it on with us both. And Helen let them. That's where it took her from that point on.

This was what I remembered on that cold bathroom floor as I waited for Helen. I remembered it all as I lay there with my heart pounding so hard I thought it would beat its way right out of my chest. But what I was remembering now wasn't the version the kids at school had told us all those years ago, the version that I'd told myself, the version that had lived on silently inside me, the one where Helen and I were dirty and loose and undesirable and to blame.

The version I was remembering was the true one, the one that made me want to punch a hole in the bathroom door. The one that made me want to find him and yank every thick blond hair out of his smug, smiling head. It made me want to pick up a knife and thrust it into him, and to twist and twist it with all my might into the cold cavity in his chest where his heart should have been.

26

Maddy sat at the breakfast bar in the kitchen, swiping through the screenshots Dan had taken of the messages on Emily's phone. When she reached the end, she felt dizzy. She got up from her stool, walked across the kitchen to her chair by the window and lowered herself into it.

Dan followed and crouched down in front of her. 'Are you OK?' he asked.

Maddy looked up anxiously. 'You hacked her phone?'

'I didn't hack it. I . . . intercepted a few more messages, that's all.'

'She's not going to be happy. I promised her we wouldn't.'

'Mads!' he objected. 'Does it matter? Our fourteen-year-old daughter's being groomed by a bloody paedophile!'

Maddy winced. 'You don't know that, Dan.'

'I do,' he said defiantly, standing up. 'I bloody well do know that!'

'We don't know how old he is.'

'Mads, wise up,' he said angrily. 'Those messages. It's

pretty fucking obvious that he's not a fucking pupil at St Mary's!'

Maddy knew this had to be true. Apart from anything else, if this . . . this *person* were a pupil at Emily's school, she would have been able to warn him that her parents had taken her phone; he wouldn't continue to send messages declaring his love for her, pleading with her to reply.

'I know,' she agreed. 'But . . . but if he's, like, seventeen or something, would the police consider him a paedophile?'

'Seventeen?' Dan frowned at her. 'You think he's seventeen? Or . . . you *know* he's seventeen?'

'I don't know anything about him,' Maddy said, closing her eyes. 'I just know that—' She stopped and corrected herself. 'I just *knew* that one of their group had a car.'

Dan's features hardened. 'When did you find that out?'

'Rosie let it slip to Kay last night.'

'And you didn't think to tell me?'

'I was going to. But you'd grounded Em anyway by then. I wanted to talk to her first.'

'So, what else did Kay say?'

'Just that one of their group of friends had a "whip". It means wheels,' she added, seeing Dan's expression. 'And you know, the way Rosie was talking, it was . . . well, it was just like it was someone on the periphery of their group. I don't know why, but I figured he was still a teenager.'

'But he's older than that, Mads. It's obvious.' Dan picked up his phone from the countertop and scrolled through the screenshots, reading out loud: '"Don't be mad at me, please, Em. You're all I think about. When you're sixteen we'll be together. We'll go somewhere where no one knows us." Think about it, Mads. Why would they have to go somewhere where no one knows them?'

Maddy didn't need to think about it; this was the message that scared her the most. Was Emily really planning to run away from home? *We'll go somewhere where no one knows us.* Of course, this *could* just be the romantic fantasy of a besotted teenage boy. But it could equally be the devious scheme of a fully grown man.

'I'm telling you, Mads, that's no seventeen-year-old talking.' His face suddenly crumpled up. He looked as if he was about to cry.

Maddy got up from her chair and reached out to comfort him. 'She said they hadn't . . . that they weren't . . .' she began tentatively. 'I believe her, Dan.'

'Mads,' he said, a sob catching in his throat. 'We can't trust her.'

'I'll talk to her,' Maddy said.

'You've already talked to her. She had the chance to tell you the truth and she chose not to.'

'I'll tell her that what he's doing is illegal. She may not realise that what he's asking is wrong.'

'She's fourteen. She's not stupid.'

'She's not stupid, but . . . but she's immature. She may act tough, streetwise, like she knows everything. But really, she's still just a child.'

'Exactly. And he's an adult.' Dan rubbed his eyes. 'Why else would she need to keep him a secret? Why else would she save him into her contacts like that, with no name, not even an initial?'

'Just a single red heart.' Maddy looked through the patio doors into the garden, where a pair of pigeons were cooing and necking on the pergola above the garden furniture. If she or Dan didn't go out and chase them away, there would be bird shit all over her lovely cushions. But it seemed trivial in this context. That shit would wash off; this wouldn't. This was not going to go away.

'What do we do? Do we call the police?' she asked.

'They won't do anything. The texts aren't enough to prove anything. They might talk to Emily, but she'll lie and then she'll warn him. We need to find out more.' Dan had clearly thought this through. 'We need to find out who he is.'

'How?'

He eyed her carefully. 'You could call him, Mads,' he said. 'Withhold your number. Or call from another phone.'

'And say what?' Maddy protested.

'Just tell him some kind of bullshit. You're good at that.'

'Good at lying?' she asked indignantly.

'Pretending. Coming up with ideas. It's the writer in you.'

For a moment, Maddy felt flattered that he was taking her writing ambitions seriously. 'What would I say?'

'I don't know. Pretend to be . . . from the tax office or something. You only need to find out one thing about him. That's all we need, Mads. Something to go on. Just a clue.'

Maddy thought about this. 'What if it's not his real phone number? What if it's, like . . . a . . . a burner or something?'

'A burner?'

'You know.' Maddy inhaled deeply. She knew this would

upset him, but it had to be said. 'A phone that he uses . . . just for her.'

Dan looked angry for a second, but then he nodded and sank down onto the bar stool. 'And then we really *would* tip him off.'

He fell silent. Maddy stroked his back, then moved into the kitchen to switch on the kettle. The pounding that had started at the top of her head was grinding its way into her temples. She desperately needed to go upstairs and lie down.

The sound of the front door opening made them both jump. Dan reached out and switched off the phone as Emily walked into the kitchen. Maddy swung round and looked across the room at her daughter, seeing her objectively, the way a man might see her: long legs under a short pleated skirt, knee-high socks, black school blazer and burgundy tie. She looked at her daughter's beautiful long fair hair and her full lips and imagined not seeing her again. She tried her hardest not to cry.

Emily saw this and swallowed. 'I'm sorry,' she said.

'What are you sorry for?' Dan asked her, rising from his seat.

'For being a twat.'

Dan and Maddy looked at each other.

'And for going off on one. I really am sorry.'

'OK,' Maddy said. 'It's OK.'

'So, can I have my phone back?'

Maddy sighed. 'We need to talk to you,' she said abruptly.

Dan shot her a warning look.

Maddy gazed back at him helplessly. He took a breath, then nodded. They'd run out of options. What else could they do?

'Some more messages came up, Em,' said Maddy, noticing the change in her daughter's expression. 'And before you say anything, we looked at them because we had to. We're your parents and we've got every reason to be worried.'

'Worried?' said Emily sharply. 'What about?'

'This . . . person you're seeing,' Maddy began. 'The one sending you the messages. We have reason to believe—'

'How old is he?' Dan jumped in.

Emily looked caught out. 'Why are you asking me that?'

'How old is he?' Dan repeated.

'He's . . . What's Rosie said?' Emily demanded angrily.

'That he's old enough to drive,' Maddy told her, although this wasn't strictly what Rosie had said.

But it was enough to call their daughter's bluff. A flush crept up Emily's neck. 'OK, so he's a little bit older than me,' she admitted.

'How old?' Dan pressed her.

'I don't know.'

Dan looked at Maddy and shook his head cynically.

'You don't know how old he is?' Maddy frowned.

'He didn't say.'

'What are we talking about, Em?' Maddy asked. 'Do you think he's older than twenty?'

Emily looked uncomfortable. 'No.' She shrugged. 'I think he's . . . like, eighteen?'

Dan stepped closer to her. 'Who is he?' he demanded.

'Just a friend of a friend.'

'*What* friend of *what* friend?'

'Brody,' she said. 'He's his cousin.'

'Who the hell is Brody?'

'For God's sake, Dad . . .' Emily flung her arms in the air.

'He's just a friend. And it doesn't matter anyway, because it's over. We had an argument and it's over. So it's irrelevant. I'm not going to see him again.'

Dan looked disbelieving. 'So why is he still sending you messages?'

'I don't know, do I? Ask him!'

Dan nodded and picked up her phone as if about to call the number.

'No!' Emily screamed out, reaching for the phone. 'Don't you dare!'

'Why not?'

'Because you'll shame me, that's why! If you call him, he'll think I care! He'll think I want to get back with him.'

'OK,' said Maddy. 'Dad's not going to call him. Right, Dan?' She looked up at him, placing her hands on the worktop to steady herself. Her headache had become unbearable.

Dan said, 'I think we should call the police.'

'What? You've got to be kidding me!'

'You're fourteen. You're underage, Em. It's illegal.'

'Nothing's happened!' Emily's voice was shrill. 'He hasn't done anything!'

'Are you sure about that?'

'If you call the police, I swear . . . I swear I'll walk out of here and I'll never come back!' Emily lowered her voice, as if in a sinister warning to them both. 'I mean it. If you call the police, you'll never see me again!'

Maddy wanted to plead with her daughter, to reassure her, but as she opened her mouth to speak, she felt herself slipping, sliding, as the worktop fell away, out of her grasp. There was a heavy, painful thump against her shoulder and then everything went black.

When she came to, she was on the floor near the breakfast bar, a cushion under her head. Emily was kneeling beside her, sobbing. 'Mum,' she cried, seeing Maddy's eyes opening. 'Mum, I'm sorry. Please be OK.'

'I am OK, love,' she murmured. 'I just fainted.'

Emily wiped her eyes and looked over to her father, who was hovering nearby on the phone. 'Dad!' she called to him.

When he saw Maddy's eyes were open, Dan dropped down beside her. 'Mads? Can you hear me? Don't worry, love. I'm calling an ambulance.'

'You don't need to do that,' Maddy told him. 'I just fainted. I don't need an ambulance.'

'I'm sorry, I'm sorry,' Em was saying, over and over. 'I'll end it with him, properly. I promise, Mum. I'll show you. Dad, give me the phone.'

'Em, not now,' Dan said. 'Give Mum a chance to—' He stopped, apologised to the call handler and ended the call. He stroked Maddy's hair away from her face.

'But I can prove it to you,' Emily was arguing. 'Give me the phone and I'll show you.'

Maddy nodded at her husband and said, 'Give her the phone.'

Dan looked uncertain, but got up, fetched the phone and handed it to Emily. He helped Maddy up and walked her over to the chair by the window.

'There,' Emily said triumphantly, tapping out a message and holding up her screen to them both. 'Look. I've told him.' She pushed the phone up close. It's over, said her message.

I don't want to see you any more. Don't contact me again. 'And . . . send.' Emily tapped the arrow next to the message and showed her parents the double tick that showed it had been delivered. 'It's over, Mum. You don't need to worry any more, I promise you. I'll never see him again.'

27

By six thirty, Helen had unpacked and was having a bath. I went out for the food and wine. When I got back, Helen was out of the bathroom. I opened one of the bottles of wine I'd bought from the supermarket next to the Chinese takeaway, poured two glasses, then dished up the food: chicken chow mein for her, and kung pao prawns and egg fried rice for me.

'Cheers,' I said, raising my glass to her as we sat opposite each other, either side of the tiny table in the corner of my living room. It wasn't quite the ambience of the Soho wine cellar, but I'd cleared the table of its usual clutter and lit two tall, slim red candles. In the half-light, Helen's features looked pale, almost ghoulish, behind the strands of wet hair framing her narrow face.

'To us,' she said. 'To finding each other again.'

'Yeah,' I smiled. 'I'm so glad I went to the reunion. I so nearly didn't.'

'Me neither.'

'And,' I added gently, 'I'm so, so glad I came up to the roof terrace when I did.'

'Must have been fate,' she smiled.

'That and fags,' I smiled back. 'And shame. God. I bet Annabel Mercer was glad *she* went. She'd have loved every minute. I can't believe what an idiot I made of myself.'

'Forget it,' Helen said, gathering up a forkful of noodles. 'They always were such nasty little bitches.'

'They've a lot to answer for,' I said.

She heaved a long sigh. 'I guess we gave them a lot to talk about.'

I caught her eye and shook my head. 'No. *We* didn't.'

'Well, *I* did, then.'

'No,' I said again. 'That's not what I meant. I meant that it wasn't our fault. We didn't do anything wrong – either of us.' I paused. 'Except that I betrayed you,' I said sadly.

'You didn't betray me.'

I looked her in the eye. 'Well, I wasn't a very good friend, was I? After what he did to you.'

She put her fork down, reached out and took hold of my hand across the table. 'Tee, don't beat yourself up about that. You were fourteen. You didn't know. And besides, I went with him when I knew you liked him too, didn't I?'

'I just thought he'd dumped you,' I said. 'I thought . . .'

'I know,' she said soothingly. 'I know what you thought. It's OK, Tee.'

'So that wasn't why we stopped being friends?'

'No,' she insisted. 'The bullying was part of the reason I left school, but never you. I wanted to say goodbye to you, but my dad had to start his new job sooner than expected and . . . we just left. It happened very suddenly and my parents didn't warn me. But I promise, it wasn't anything to do with you.'

I swallowed, shamefaced. 'I thought he was going to be my boyfriend.'

Helen's face softened. 'I know. I know you did, Tee. I thought the same thing. He tricked us both.'

' "When you're sixteen, we'll be together." Is that what he told you?'

She nodded.

I shook my head. 'I was so blind. I thought it was love.'

'Me too. He was so handsome. He was so charming. And when he looked at you, it was as if the whole world had melted away and there was no one else there, except you.'

'And then afterwards,' I said, the anger rising inside me, 'he wouldn't even look at you, right? Just drove you home and told you to get out of the van.'

She nodded again.

'And that's all he was after,' I said. 'From either of us. That's all he came for.'

She looked back at me in silence.

'And we blamed ourselves,' I continued. 'We thought it was something we'd done.'

'I thought I wasn't good enough for him,' she confessed. 'I thought he'd lost interest because I wasn't . . . you know. Enough.'

'Enough?'

'In the sack.'

It all suddenly clicked. 'Is that why you . . . why you felt you had to have sex with other men?'

'I guess.'

I thought about this. 'I just thought it was because I was boring,' I told her. 'And unattractive. I just thought he'd woken up to reality, that he'd finally realised I wasn't anything special after all.'

'You were beautiful, Tee,' she said. 'You were lovely.'

'I wasn't beautiful,' I corrected her. '*You* were beautiful. But whatever good points I had, I didn't see them, especially not after that.'

She put down her glass and we were silent for a moment.

'But it wasn't about us, was it?' I said. '*You* were beautiful and he still did it to you. And it's taken me all this time to realise that he did the exact same thing to you.' I shook my head again. 'I should have realised. I should have stuck by you. Instead, I let him divide us. If only I'd stuck by you, listened to you when you tried to warn me about him, we could have done something, couldn't we?'

'Like what?' She frowned.

'Gone to the police.'

'And said what?'

'That he was a child abuser, Helen.'

She flinched. 'I know we were underage,' she said. 'But . . . but he didn't *make* us do it, did he?'

'He exploited us. He set out to have sex with us. Both of us. In turn. One by one. He groomed us.'

'*Groomed*? That's online, isn't it?'

'Not necessarily.'

She stared back at me in silence.

'Don't you see?' I persisted. 'He never cared about the boys, about helping them with their bikes and stuff. They were just his way in, his way of normalising what he was about to do, his way of gaining our trust. If he'd walked up to us in the park and asked us if we wanted to get in his van with him and go for a ride, we'd have called him a pervert and told him to fuck off.'

'But *grooming*?' Helen said, frowning. 'That wasn't even a thing back then, was it?'

'No,' I agreed. 'It was just what blokes did. They tried it on. And *we*,' I added, my heart flipping with the anger and the pain, 'we were just the dirty little slags that let them.'

Helen winced.

'Except that we weren't,' I continued, my heart beating against my ribcage. 'Because we were children and he was an adult, and because he tricked us and he used us. We didn't know what he was doing. But now we do. And it's called grooming.' I picked up my phone, tapped a web page and held it up for her. 'Grooming: it's "befriending and gaining the trust of a vulnerable person so that you can exploit them for sex".'

'But ...' she said, thinking it through, 'was it really? I mean, he seemed genuinely interested ... you know? At first he did, anyway.'

'It's a common way in,' I explained. 'That's what it says here. "Feigning romantic interest". It's what they do. It's what *he* did. We would never have had sex with him if we'd known that was all he wanted. Right?'

'No, of course not. But ... I mean ... blokes do that to

women all the time, don't they? And to be fair, women do it to men too.'

'Sometimes,' I agreed. 'But it doesn't leave men with the same black mark on their reputation, the same deep feelings of self-loathing. And anyway,' I added, 'it's usually because a man has done it to her first.'

Helen looked at me thoughtfully, then lowered her eyes.

'Men are competitive,' I said. 'They have to make girls "easy" in order to devalue each other's conquests. And that's why the laws are there, so that you're old enough to be able to handle it emotionally if it happens to you.' I paused. 'So that you're not at an age where it's going to rip up your life and tear it into a thousand pieces.'

I could see tears forming in Helen's eyes.

'He exploited us, Hel,' I persisted. 'He used us. Both of us. And as soon as we gave him what he wanted, the challenge was over. In his eyes, he'd won a prize that was no longer worth having. We were soiled goods. He wanted *good* girls. Nice little fourteen-year-old virgins. But we didn't know that,' I continued. 'We were too young to know that, and so we blamed ourselves. And you know what? He was banking on that. He was banking on being able to make us feel the same level of repulsion towards ourselves that he now felt towards us. Because that's how men like him see women. Except we weren't women. We were girls.'

'OK, but this was . . . what? Twenty-five years ago now?'

'It was still against the law, Hel. Even then. We could have . . . we *should* have gone to the police. And we didn't. But you know what?' I leaned forward. 'It's not too late. We can do it now.'

'What? Are you kidding me?'

'No. I'm serious.'

She looked uncertain. 'Will the police even care? I mean . . . we said yes to him, Tee. We let him have sex with us. It's not like he raped us, is it?'

'It doesn't matter. It was a criminal offence. Even back then. You could go to jail for it.'

Helen frowned. 'Would he still go to jail for it now? After all this time?'

'I don't know for sure,' I confessed. 'But people do, don't they? Look at all these historic cases. Jeffrey Epstein. Max Clifford. It's in the news all the time.'

'But that's different,' she said. 'Surely? Those victims were forced. Or at least, they didn't want it to happen.'

'*I* didn't want it to happen, Hel. Did you?'

Helen thought about this for a moment. 'No. No, I didn't. Not like that.'

'Me neither,' I told her. 'I loved him and I didn't want to lose him. But I didn't have sex with him because I wanted to. I did it because he kept asking me and then he wasn't asking any more, he was just doing it. And when I stopped him from doing it, he accused me of leading him on. I did it because I couldn't bear the thought of him turning his back on me. He said he'd bought me stuff and taken me places and that I owed him, and I believed him when he said that. Why wouldn't I believe what he told me? He was a grown-up and I was a child.'

She nodded, swallowed. 'It was the same for me.'

I picked up my wine glass and took a long sip, looked at her, waited.

'I knew it was against the law,' she murmured. 'I knew he shouldn't have . . . we shouldn't have . . . because we were underage, you know? But I thought that . . . I thought that law was for . . . well, for rapists. Men who forced themselves on you. And . . . and older men. I mean . . . well, he wasn't that much older than us . . . was he?'

'I've checked,' I told her. 'He's forty-eight now. That would have made him twenty-four at the time. He was old enough to know that it was illegal to have sex with us.'

'So how did he think he was going to get away with it?'

'He *did* get away with, Hel!' I said. 'He's got away with it for nearly twenty-five years!'

'I just mean . . .'

'Because that's the way the world was then,' I told her. 'And still is, to a degree. If a woman had sex and then got dumped, she was a slapper. If a man had sex and moved on to someone else, he was a stud. Someone to look up to. "He's got a way with women", that's what they'd say. Except that we weren't women. We were girls.'

'It was so cold,' Helen said softly, tears beginning to run down her cheeks. 'It was like you said. It was cold and . . . and rough.'

'Same,' I said. 'It made me feel like I was nothing.'

'A piece of meat.'

I nodded.

'But I'd said yes to that, apparently.'

'But you didn't,' I said. 'Not to that.'

We fell silent.

'He didn't even tell me not to tell anyone,' I said, after a moment.

'Me neither.'

I shook my head. 'He was *that* confident when he told us to get out of the van and go home and stop calling him that we would hate ourselves too much to tell anyone. And he was right. That's exactly what happened. Until all the kids at school found out, of course, called us slags and made it our fault. And then, no matter how hard you try, it creeps back in, over and over, and makes you hate yourself again, over and over, for the rest of your life.'

Helen sniffed and wiped her tears away with her sleeve.

I took hold of her hand across the tabletop. 'It's the kind of thing that stays with you. Makes you sabotage your life, Hel.'

She swallowed and licked another teardrop from the corner of her mouth. 'I keep on going for the bad guys,' she said. 'It's like I'm repeating what happened, trying to make it turn out differently the next time.'

'Definition of madness,' I smiled.

She smiled back weakly. I got up and fetched a fresh paper towel from the kitchen, handed it to her, then crouched down, wrapped my arms around her and laid my head on her shoulder.

'You said he didn't *make* you,' I said.

She sniffed, nodded.

'Well, he did. He did make you. He formed you. You were gullible, malleable, young and in love. You'd have done anything he wanted. He *made* you into someone who would have sex with him and then into someone who would have sex with anyone else who asked you after that. Because once he'd taken what he wanted and spat you out, there was nothing left of you, the original you. Don't you see? He took the good bits of you and he mangled them up and then he threw the rest of you away.'

She nodded, unable to speak.

'You weren't who you were going to be yet. You didn't have a chance to be who you should have been. He came along and changed all that.'

She nodded again.

'And so now' – I got up from my crouching position, walked back round the table and sat down in my seat in front of her – 'we're going to find him and we are going to get you – the old you and the old me – back.'

28

We didn't have to find him, of course, or even look for him. Jeremy Allen Seager was exactly where he had always been: hiding in plain sight. Not that he'd ever hidden from us, nor would it have crossed his mind to do so; we were no threat to him and his comfortable existence. We were just the dirty little slags he'd disposed of when he was a good-looking man in his twenties who sang in a band by night, while by day he worked his way up at the bank.

He called himself Jem in those days. He lived in Lewisham and messed around with car engines at a lock-up at weekends, but I remembered he'd had a good job because he always had money and he never stayed out too late on a weekday night. He'd told us that he was going places, that he was going to be rich one day, and now, as the CEO of a leading international bank in the City, he was never going to hide his light under a bushel. The online images I'd seen of him on a podium with his wife and daughter were the first of many that Helen and I would pore over in the days to come.

He'd come a long way and he was proud of it, as his beaming face and interviews in the business media made abundantly clear. No doubt he still saw himself as a bit of a rock star and he still had the looks to carry it off. He may have worked hard to get where he was, but life had been kind to him, and it made me sick to my stomach. My own father, who had worked a manual job as a builder, was bald at thirty and could barely bend due to the slipped discs in his back, but there were no signs of wear and tear on Jerry Seager's face or his body. He looked like the cat that had got the cream in every photo and I didn't doubt for one moment that it wasn't an act.

The wear and tear was there on Helen's face, though. I looked up at her as she stared at the online images, her face pale, her knuckles white as they gripped the seat of the sofa underneath her. The wear and tear had devastated my best friend's life. And while that bastard had been climbing his way up the corporate ladder, I, too, had been left with an open wound that I'd spent my life hiding in a corner licking like a frightened little mouse. But I was no longer a mouse; I was a lion. I was a ticking time bomb ready to explode.

29

A door slammed in the distance. Maddy opened her eyes, turned her head slowly towards the clock on the bedside table and squinted at the luminous numbers. Oh my God. It was four fifteen. Four fifteen in the afternoon! A whole day wasted. A whole day with the work piling up, washing and shopping to do and the kitchen a mess. And now here was Emily, home from school. She opened her eyes fully. The smallest slither of sunlight was seeping under the blind. It hurt her eyes, but she kept them open. She needed to pull herself together, get up, go down and say hello to her daughter, find out about her day. Emily was below her in the kitchen now, opening cupboard doors and slamming them shut. Every slam of a cupboard door felt as though it was her head that was being slapped.

'Mum!' Emily's voice called up the stairs.

Maddy propped herself up onto one elbow and squinted across the room. She no longer felt nauseous, but she felt weak and she could feel the pain still hovering in the back of her head and down her neck. She needed to go carefully. She hadn't eaten all day, she realised, and she didn't want to faint again. She still had the bruise from when her head had hit the floor. She inched over towards the edge of the bed and lowered a foot onto the rug. The gentle weave hugged her toes. It felt good, solid, safe and warm. Maddy closed her eyes, drew a deep breath and slid her feet back and forth. If she could just stay like this for a minute or two in the quiet, still, empty room, then . . .

'Mum!' Emily called again.

'Coming,' Maddy croaked. She trod tentatively over the creaking floorboards towards the bedroom door and opened it, screwing her eyes up tight against the glare of the sun that was streaming through the landing window, casting a square of light onto the carpet outside the door.

Emily was halfway up the stairs. 'Mum, can I—' She broke off, taking in the sight of her mother, and her face fell. 'Why aren't you dressed?' she asked.

Maddy glanced down at her bare legs, at her knickers and skimpy top, and grabbed a towel that was hanging over the banister to dry. 'I was just going to have a bath,' she said shakily. 'Did you have a good day?'

'Have you been in bed?'

'Just a nap,' Maddy lied.

'Why?' Emily asked, a tiny flicker of fear crossing her face. 'What's wrong with you, Mum?'

'Nothing,' Maddy said reassuringly. 'I just didn't sleep well last night. I'm feeling much better now. What is it you want, love?'

'There's no milk. I just wanted to ask what there was to eat. Rosie's here,' she added. 'But it's OK. We can go to the shop.'

'Wait . . .' Maddy racked her brain. There wasn't much in, she knew. 'I think there might be some pizzas in the freezer,' she suggested brightly. 'I'll come down and have a look.'

'It's OK, Mum,' Emily said. 'Don't worry.'

But Maddy did worry. Ever since she'd fainted, Emily's demeanour towards her had changed. She was still just as secretive, just as unreachable, but she'd dialled down the teenage tantrums, the arguments, the challenging behaviour. Maddy almost missed it. She knew that it wasn't the normal run of things for her daughter to be creeping around her like this.

'Honestly, Em. I'm fine. Just give me a minute.' She turned and walked back into her room to dress.

But a moment later, Emily was at the foot of the stairs again, calling her. 'Mum! We're going out.'

'Wait. Where are you going?' Maddy pulled a sundress over her head and stepped back out onto the landing. 'What about your pizza?'

'It'll take too long. Don't worry. We'll get something out.'

'But you don't have any money,' Maddy protested.

'Yes, I do.'

'Where did you get it?'

A pause. 'Rosie's got some.'

'But—'

'Come on, let's go,' Emily was saying to Rosie, who was hovering out of sight. She turned the latch on the front door and stepped outside.

'Em, wait,' Maddy called, leaning over the banister, clutching at it. She still felt light-headed. 'Dad will be leaving the office soon. I'll call him. I'll ask him to pick something up on the way home.'

'It's OK, Mum,' Emily said, irritation creeping into her voice. 'I told you. We're going out.'

Maddy watched despairingly as Rosie shuffled into view and bolted out of the door. Maddy heard it slam shut and the house fell silent. Where were they going, she wondered, she and Rosie? To the shop to buy a load of sugary treats of zero nutritional value, no doubt. But after that?

She sighed and walked into the bathroom, turned on the bath taps and sat down in her favourite wicker chair to wait for the bath to run. The rush of water into the tub was soothing. She placed a cold flannel over her forehead and rested the back of her head against the soft pile of towels on the shelf behind her, letting them take the weight of her skull. She closed her eyes and imagined the pressure of the water pushing her thoughts away down the plughole. But moments later, as she stepped out of her underwear into the steamy water and sank down under the bubbles, the chatter in her head started up again.

Emily had told them the relationship with this cousin of Brody's was over and Maddy wanted to trust her daughter, but she couldn't help but worry. For a start, Emily never seemed to need money; she rarely asked her parents for it and neither she nor Rosie had part-time jobs. Yet Maddy had found packs of sweets, biscuits, crisps and fizzy drinks in her bedroom on numerous occasions. She hadn't found alcohol again, thank goodness, but two days ago she'd found a bottle of vape juice in the top drawer of Emily's desk. She'd challenged Emily about it and Emily had sworn it wasn't hers. It was Brody's, she'd said; his parents were getting suspicious and so he'd asked her to look after it for him. Maddy had accepted her explanation and it had gone the next day, but it didn't stop her backsliding into doubt and suspicion. It didn't stop her lying awake at night.

She hadn't told Dan about the vape juice, nor had she voiced her suspicions about where Emily was getting her money from. It would lead to a big confrontation, and Maddy knew that this would only drive Emily further away from them. She, at least, still had an open line of communication with their daughter, albeit, at times, a tenuous one. Although Emily's attachment to her mother had in recent months been expressed, for the most part, through challenges and arguments, Maddy knew this was all part of Emily still needing her, whereas she could tell that Emily felt smothered by her father's love and, in truth, Maddy could understand that. Dan just didn't seem to get that their daughter wasn't ten any more.

Was that what this was, though? The realisation seeped into her as she sank deeper into the scalding water. Maybe it would have been better for Emily if there had been another child to take the weight of her father's love. Working from home as she had done since Emily was born, Maddy had been the one to hand down the discipline while Dan worked his way up at the bank. She'd enabled Dan to play 'good cop' to her 'bad cop' so that when he came home he could be the fun parent, the one to give Emily nothing but love, never a cross word, never a frown. Now, though, in contrast, Dan was almost too hard on Emily. He couldn't let go, didn't know when to back off, and

Emily reacted angrily to any form of discipline from him. So maybe this was a reaction to the intensity of Dan's feelings for her? Maybe this boyfriend was Emily's way of breaking away from him – from them. Which meant that there was still every chance that he might lure her back.

Maddy stepped out of the bath and put a towel around her head, careful not to wrap it too tight and set the headache off again, then brushed her teeth and went into the bedroom to get dressed. As she did so, she heard the front door open. She felt herself tense up. Emily? Or Dan?

Dan's voice called out to her and she felt a twinge of disappointment. She was glad he was home, of course she was, but she knew she wouldn't be able to unwind and let the aftereffects of the headache wear off until her daughter was safely back in the house.

30

Helen opened the door and came into the living room. She'd heard my phone ring, and she waited for me to finish the call.

'Don't tell me. You've got work.' She half smiled, half frowned.

'I'm sorry,' I said. 'It's just typical. But I could really use the money. Besides, you know what it's like when you're temping. If you say no, you're the last person they call the next time.'

'It's OK. Of course you have to take it. But what do we do about today?'

I hesitated. 'Could you . . . would you go, Hel? And then I'll go at the weekend.'

She looked upset. 'You want me to go to the police station by myself?'

'I'll go too. First thing on Saturday,' I promised.

'Why can't I wait and go on Saturday with you?'

'Because . . .' I looked into her eyes, pleading with her. 'Because we have an appointment and one of us needs to be there. If neither of us turns up today the police might not take us seriously.'

'They might not take us seriously anyway.'

'Why wouldn't they? He committed an offence, Hel. And they gave us an appointment, didn't they?'

Helen didn't look convinced.

'The sooner we get things moving the better,' I said gently. 'If you go today, then it's happening. It's started. They might even want to talk to me tonight. And then he might even get arrested tomorrow! Just imagine him being arrested.' I felt excited. 'Think of him being handcuffed. Locked up in a prison cell.'

'I know,' Helen said. 'That does feel good, but . . .'

'But you're scared. I get that. I am too. But we have to be brave, Hel.'

'I'd rather we went together.' She sank down onto the sofa and heaved a sigh. 'It was a long time ago,' she said. 'What if they don't believe us?'

'Then we'll track down Sid and Tommy. And Tony Letch. We'll give the police their names and they'll have to give a statement.'

'Can they do that? Force someone?'

'I think so.'

'But you're not sure?'

'Not completely,' I admitted. 'But I'll check. And anyway, it doesn't matter. There are two of us. They'll have to believe us if we're both saying the same thing.' I looked down at the time on my phone. I needed to get to work. I hadn't washed or brushed my teeth yet. I needed to pack some lunch and find something to wear.

Helen's face softened. 'Go on,' she said. 'Go and get ready.'

'And you'll go?'

She pursed her lips and nodded. I smiled gratefully at her, then leaped up off the sofa to go to the bathroom. I turned in the doorway. 'You have a driver's licence, right?'

'Yes.'

'Take my car,' I said. 'I don't need it today. I'll call my insurance company in my lunch break and get you added to the policy. And then you can use it whenever you like.'

'Really?' I saw her eyes light up.

'Absolutely. Why don't you use it to pick up the rest of your stuff later? Take your time, go to Matt's and drop off some stuff there. Whatever you want to do – it's all fine.'

'Wow. I really appreciate that, Tee,' she said. 'And I'll keep the appointment. I promise. I'll go.'

'Great. It'll be much quicker in the car. And if you park in the multistorey on King Street, it's only a five-minute walk from there.'

'OK.'

I hesitated in the doorway.

'I won't let you down, Tee,' she said. '*Us* down.'

'I'll be thinking of you,' I said. 'All day.'

I power-walked to Lancaster Gate and down to the Central Line. The law firm I was going to be working for had its main offices on Cannon Street, not far from London Bridge. As luck would have it, the tube pulled in just as I arrived and I got to work on time. I was greeted with a quick induction and a long schedule of printing and scanning demands from the firm's many associates. My job was to print off all the letters and their multiple attachments and put them into envelopes, ready to go out in the post.

The work was monotonous, but, on the plus side, the printer was situated on a landing on the fifth floor next to a huge floor-to-ceiling window with an amazing view out across the Thames. In the distance was the South Bank, with Borough Market, Southwark Cathedral and the Clink, the old prison, now a museum, which I'd visited on a boring, wet Sunday the previous year. As I looked out across the water, I remembered the ghoulish expressions on the faces of the prisoners whose heads had been chopped off and stuck on spikes. While I worked, I entertained myself by imagining the look on *his* face as the police knocked on his door, arrested him and marched him off to the slammer. I imagined his eyes bulging out of their sockets with the same expression of fear and surprise.

Helen's appointment was at two. At around three, I sneaked off to the toilet and tried calling her, but there was no answer. There was no reply either to any of the messages I sent. When five o'clock came, I hurried down the stairs and out of the doors, and headed for Bank, where I got onto a crowded tube train. By six, I was walking up the street to my flat. My stomach turned in anticipation as I saw that my car was sitting outside in a different parking spot, facing the other way. This had to mean that Helen had been to the police station and was now back home again.

I pushed my key into the lock and opened the door, kicked off my shoes and walked into the living room. Helen was sitting on the sofa in silence, hugging her knees. George appeared through the cat flap and mewed at my legs, but I couldn't take my eyes off Helen. Something was wrong.

'What happened?' I asked, sitting opposite her.

'Nothing,' she said.

'What do you mean, "nothing"?'

'They can't do anything.'

'The police?'

She nodded.

'But . . . why?'

'It was too long ago.'

'No, it wasn't!' I cried out. 'They prosecute these things all the time. Old stuff, stuff that happened in the eighties and nineties. You hear about it on the news, victims reporting rapes after twenty years because they've been too afraid to come forward—'

'Rapes, yes. This wasn't rape.'

'I know, but . . .' I blinked at her uncomprehendingly. 'It was still a criminal offence.'

'It doesn't matter. It wasn't rape. He didn't force us.'

'We were underage. He didn't have to!'

'We were over thirteen. It's not rape if you're over thirteen. If you were over thirteen and he didn't force you, there's a law. You had to report it within a year of it happening. So that's it. We're too late.'

'That can't be right.'

'It is.'

'But—'

'Tate.' Her voice was sharp, angry. 'It's the fucking law, all right?'

'OK, but—'

'You don't believe me?'

'Of course I do. I just . . .'

'Just what?'

'I just wondered if you'd . . . you know . . .' I looked up at her. 'Told them everything?'

She looked back at me, her eyes blazing. 'You want to know what I told them?' she hissed. 'You want me to go over it all *again*?'

'You don't have to tell me,' I said quickly. 'I just wondered . . .'

'Yes, Tate,' she said abruptly. 'The answer to your question is yes, I told them everything. Every single detail. I had to.' She let out an outlandish, high-pitched cackle. 'I gave them a blow-by-blow account, you could say.'

'Hel . . . it's OK.'

She leaned forward. 'I told them how I let a man fuck me when I was still just a schoolgirl. I told them *where* it hap-pened, *how* it happened, but – no – that wasn't enough. They wanted me to be more explicit, and so I had to use words like "penis" and "vagina". I had to use words like "come" and "mouth". And "fucking sore"!'

'Helen,' I pleaded. 'Please. Stop.'

'To a stranger, Tate!' Tears sprang to her eyes. 'I had to say all those intimate, disgusting things to a complete stranger!'

'I'm sorry, Hel . . .'

'They made me go through everything in graphic detail. Over and over.' Her voice broke up into sobs. 'It was like it was happening all over again!'

'Oh, Hel . . .'

'And then, when they were finally satisfied, they got me to sit in a room by myself for *two whole hours*. Two hours I sat there, replaying it all in my head. Remembering how disgusting it was, how humiliated, how filthy, how *used* I felt when he got me onto my hands and knees, naked, in the back of his van, and fucked me like I was a dog!'

'I'm sorry. I'm so sorry, Hel . . .'

'I told them all that!' She groaned out loud, as if in physical pain. 'And then they came back *two hours* later and told me they weren't going to do anything! I went through all of that for nothing! For nothing! And all I wish now is that I'd listened to myself instead of listening to you. Why did I listen to you?' She put her head against her knees. Her hair fell down over them and I reached out to smooth it back, but she smacked my hand away.

'I'm sorry, Hel,' I said, in tears myself. 'I'm so sorry that I didn't come with you. I'm so sorry you went through all of that alone. I've let you down – again!'

She didn't look up. 'I felt better when I was just fucking my life up.'

At least you had a life to fuck up, I thought. 'I've never even had a boyfriend,' I blurted out.

She looked up slowly then, her eyes tired, her cheeks crimson, streaked with tears. 'What, never?'

I swallowed. 'No.'

'Why not?'

I shrugged. 'I've just never . . . not since . . . not since him.'

'You've never had . . .' She trailed off. '*Anyone?*'

I took a deep breath and shook my head.

She waited.

'There were men who liked me,' I said. 'There was one who I knew *really* liked me. And he was nice. But I got scared. The thought of being that close to someone, it . . . it made me run the other way.'

'Are you gay?' she asked.

I shrugged. 'I don't know. I don't think so. I like men. I think about them. I enjoy their company, but then, when something starts to happen, I . . . I always make an excuse.'

'Because of him?'

'I don't know. I just can't seem to trust anyone. I feel safer on my own. But at the same time, I'm lonely. It's like I can't win. I want someone. But I can't bear to be touched that way.'

She looked at me, saying nothing.

'He did those things to me too,' I said finally. 'You know . . . making me give him oral sex and . . . making me . . . you know, touch myself . . . while he watched and . . . moving me into different positions and the . . . you know, from behind.' My voice sounded reedy and odd as I stumbled over the vocabulary, trying to find the language. It was as though I was fourteen again, trying to find the words for something that had happened to me that I didn't fully understand. It hadn't been anything really terrible that he'd done to me, but it *was* terrible because I'd been fourteen and because there was no love there and because it had been and felt so *fucking* cold. 'It was like I was auditioning for a job as a porn star,' I said. 'Acting out some kind of role to please him. It felt alien, bizarre . . . like it wasn't even me. Afterwards I felt disgusted with myself because I'd *let* him. I blamed myself; how could I have *let* him? But I know now that I was just trying to pass an audition to be his girlfriend, not to be a porn star. I didn't want to do those things. It wasn't me!'

Helen nodded. 'I know. Nor me.'

'I felt sick when I looked him up again,' I told her. 'I *was* sick. I didn't want to remember it all – I wanted to bury it. And I never wanted to put you through any of this. But I've tried – and you've tried – to just get over it and . . . and we can't, Hel! And once you know that, you can't *un*-know it. We have to do something. We can't just sit back and let him continue to fuck up our lives.'

Helen wiped her eyes, twisted her body to face me and put her feet down on the floor.

'I'm not having it,' I said, anger rising inside me. I brought my fist down heavily on the arm of the chair. I screamed out loud, 'I'm not having it! I'm not fucking having it!'

Helen looked alarmed.

'I'm not going to let them dismiss what happened to us for a second time!'

'So, what are you going to do?' she asked.

'I'm going to find him. I'm going to make him pay.'

Her eyes widened. 'How?'

I said, 'I'm not sure. I need to think. But you did all that for me – for us – and now it's my turn. If they're not going to do anything about it, then I will.'

31

I take a breath, reach for my glass. We've drunk the last of the champagne. It's five in the afternoon and I feel like an alcoholic as well as a whore as Sarah asks, 'Do you want another drink?'

Helen was right. Saying those things out loud to a complete stranger feels debasing, degrading. It makes me feel *less*, somehow. *Damaged*. Doesn't that mean 'flawed', 'less valuable'? Less datable? *Damaged*. It's ironic, I reflect, how that word – with all its negative connotations – is used to describe the person who has been broken instead of the person who smashed them up.

So, yes, I do want another drink. 'I'll get it,' I say.

'No.' She puts her hand out, touches mine. 'Please. Let me.'

She catches the waiter's eye and he comes straight over. He brings a glass of Sauvignon and some salted peanuts. Sarah has a soda and lime.

'The police were right,' Sarah says, when the waiter has gone. 'Because this happened to you in the 1990s it would fall under the old 1956 Sexual Offences Act. It set a twelve-month time limit for fourteen- and fifteen-year-old female victims to report acts of unlawful sex. It's an anomaly which hasn't been put right by the new law, even though there's now no time limit to report the equivalent offence.'

'So, if it happened now . . .'

'If it happened now, he'd be guilty of grooming, abuse of trust and sexual activity with a child under sixteen. He could get up to fourteen years in prison.'

I already know this, of course. I looked it up.

She adds, 'The police used to get round it by prosecuting it as indecent assault instead, which had no time limit. But a 2004 House of Lords case closed down that avenue.'

'So no one cares,' I say.

'It's unjust, I agree. There are academics and lawyers who agree too.'

'But no one cares enough to fight it and change the law.'

'It's way up at the tip of a very big iceberg,' Sarah says. 'The whole system is in crisis. The prosecution of sexual assaults on women is at an all-time low.'

I survey her in silence, feeling both vindicated and aggrieved at the same time.

'So you got a job at the bank, at CPF?' she asks. 'Am I right?'

'Yes.'

'Working for Dan?'

'Yes.'

'And was that just by chance? Working for him, I mean?'

'Yes.'

'And the relationship between you . . .'

'There wasn't one.'

'So the affair . . . it was never real?'

'No.'

'What about Helen?'

'What about her?'

'Did he ever have a relationship with her?'

I snort a laugh. 'No.'

'So why . . . ?' I can see her mind whirring.

'It was all part of the plan. Well,' I correct myself, 'not the original plan.'

'And what was that?'

'To bring in a wrecking ball, to demolish Jerry's nice, comfortable life. To gain the friendship and trust of his colleagues, then stand up at a company meeting, ask him if he remembered me, announce what he did. Tell his wife and daughter. Make him regret that he ever walked into the Rec that day and met me and Helen.'

'But you didn't do any of that?'

'No.' I lick my lips. 'The plan changed.'

'How? Why?'

'I met Maddy.'

She raises an eyebrow. 'You knew Maddy?'

I nod. My heart feels heavy, though it's a relief to tell her. 'Maddy was my friend,' I say.

PART FIVE

PART FIVE

32

Getting a job at CPF wasn't too difficult. I had a few things in my favour, including A-level French. It was early July and the summer holidays were looming, the time when most companies were short-staffed – or about to be – and might need an office dogsbody. I made it clear in my application that I was willing to do pretty much anything I was asked. I would stuff envelopes and deliver the post, unjam the photocopier and make the tea. I'd set out chairs for meetings, run errands for the PAs. I was presentable, hard-working and ultimately ambitious, though not averse to taking orders from colleagues younger than me. I wanted to become a bilingual secretary, I told them, specialising in international finance, but I knew that I would have to start at the bottom; I first needed to improve both my typing speed and my French. That said – I made it clear – it was good enough to translate simple letters and answer the phone to the overseas partners and associates, an advantage that – for the paygrade I was seeking – was enough to get them to notice me.

They had nothing permanent right now, they responded,

but they liked my application. Could I come in and meet them? I agreed readily and – although I'd applied directly, speculatively – gave them almost nothing to lose by suggesting that, subject to the interview, of course, they try me out on a temporary basis through the agency.

While I waited for them to find a convenient date to meet, I brushed up on my French. I read French novels, watched French movies on Netflix. I'd spent a few summers in France as a teenager and soon it all came flooding back. I watched YouTube tutorials and learned banking terminology in both English and French. By the day of the interview, I was as prepared as I would ever be.

I arrived early. I'd had my hair styled and was wearing my best suit. As I went through the doors into the building, signed in with security, then ascended in the lift to the nineteenth level, my nerves started to get the better of me. But my interviewers were friendly and when the lead – one of the partners – began the interview with '*Bonjour. Comment ça va?*' I quickly rose to the challenge and responded confidently. In the conversation that ensued, I even managed to make a joke about assets and liabilities that made the same partner smile and shake my hand warmly at the end when I stood up to leave.

When the agency called to say that CPF had an opening for me on a 'temporary but potentially long-term' basis, Helen and I celebrated with a bottle of Laurent-Perrier. I handed a glass to her and grinned mischievously.

'What?' Helen grinned back at me.

And so again I showed her the online photo of our nemesis standing on a podium, receiving a boxed bottle of the same champagne. We clinked glasses and – after we'd drunk the champagne and followed it with a second bottle of something less expensive – she confessed to being both impressed and a little shocked by how calm and calculated I could be. I'd achieved the goal I'd set for myself through sheer grit and determination, she said.

'Not talent?' I asked. After all, I'd just auditioned for and landed the biggest acting role of my career.

'Talent. Of course,' she agreed, and told me that she couldn't have done what I'd done. I think from that point on, she really started to believe in me.

That same week, my neighbour two floors up, Clare Henry, told us that she'd been offered a job teaching English abroad. She asked if Helen might want to look after her flat for her for a year or so while she was away overseas. It was perfect timing. Helen was now working for an estate agent in Bloomsbury and could afford the rent, and while we didn't want to lose each other's company, the makeshift bed in my living room had just started to become a little challenging for us both in terms of the lack of space and privacy.

So, it was a double celebration that evening and I marked it with a promise to Helen that justice – no matter how rough – would be done. We spent the evening thinking up new and different acts of revenge against Jerry, including having Helen turn up at an office party and seduce him, handcuff him, tie him up naked and dangle him from a desk. But we knew that wasn't going to cut it; it was far too trivial. He needed to be exposed in a far more insidious way for the kind of man he really was.

I started my new job in the first week of August, but I didn't finally meet Jerry until two weeks later. I found out from one of the secretaries that he was on holiday in the South of France with his family and I took the opportunity of offering to clear out some boxes from his office, making sure to have a poke around while I was there. His room was big, around twenty square metres, with plush carpets and a view of St Paul's. There was a three-seater couch big enough to sleep on along one wall, and in the corner a cabinet housing a compact fridge and a Nespresso machine. Next to it was a tray with mugs, tea, coffee, large lumps of crystal sugar and small packets of Italian biscuits. It was exactly like a hotel room and the thought hit me like a thunderbolt: did he bring young girls here?

Too risky, maybe. But, for the very first time, I realised that Helen and I might not have been the only ones. I'd been so full of self-loathing, convinced that what had happened was *our* fault, mine and Helen's – that what *he'd* done was acceptable and what *we'd* done was not – that this possibility hadn't even entered my mind.

My gut twisted as my eyes scanned his desk and landed on a photo of his wife and daughter. There were several more photos, all portraying him as the epitome of the loving family man. But a leopard doesn't change its spots, does it? And even though he was now in his late forties, he was still good-looking and presumably just as charming. And now, of course, he had the additional allure of status, money and power. Was he still preying on young girls, even now? If so, then what I was doing was wholly defensible. Maybe I could catch him at it, nail him, send him to prison, even if it was too late for any kind of legal retribution for Helen and me.

The idea was thrilling. Did he still have a van? I wondered. I recalled his story about how he was in a band and how he needed the van to lug their gear around. I'd seen the large black cases that housed a drum kit in the lock-up a few times, but I'd only ever seen a mattress in the back of the van. Somewhere to sleep after gigs in far-flung cities, he'd told us. But I wondered, now, if the band was just his cover story; whether he was, in fact – even then – a premeditative, serial paedophile.

On the Sunday night before the Monday he was due to return to the office, I couldn't sleep. All those weeks and months when, as a schoolgirl, I'd lain awake mourning him, fantasising about what it would be like to see him, to talk to him again. And now – finally – it was about to happen. Of course, he'd never recognise me. I was now a thirty-eight-year-old woman named Tate Kinsella. The last time he'd seen me I'd been a freckled fourteen-year-old named Tee McGee. But even if he did remember, that would just add to the fun, wouldn't it? He'd be alarmed. Scared, even. He'd wonder if my presence at the firm was anything more than sheer coincidence, but he wouldn't be able to do anything about it. How could he?

But as it turned out, when I did bump into him, he barely even acknowledged my existence. I'd been nothing to him, while he'd been everything to me. I was far too average-looking, too junior in the firm – but too old, no doubt, I reflected bitterly – to be of any interest to him. No matter. I'd use that to my advantage, make it my business to keep my ears open and my eyes peeled. I'd find every scrap of dirt on him. There was no hurry, I decided. I'd take my time. Revenge is a dish best served cold, as they say, and I wanted it to be as cold as it could be.

33

They say you can tell what kind of a person someone is by the way they talk to waiters. I don't think anyone has ever said that about office temps, but after a few weeks of working at CPF, I'd begun to apply the analogy. I hadn't got anywhere close to building up the degree of friendship and trust amongst my colleagues that I'd envisaged when I'd come up with my master plan. Although no one was exactly rude to me, the associates were, for the most part, too self-absorbed, and the secretaries too busy, to invest in what they no doubt perceived was only going to be a short-term acquaintance. Beyond the scope of giving me orders and thanking me for my phone messages, very little attention was paid to me and I'd begun to feel somewhat invisible, so when Maddy walked into the office and we struck up a conversation, I was more than ready for a bit of company.

I liked her immediately. She was unlike the other wives of the partners and managers. She was gentle, modest – self-effacing, even – and beautiful, in a natural, make-up-free, slightly scatter-brained way. That's how it first appeared to me, anyway. It was a hot day at the end of August. I was the only staff member on the floor, having been left to answer the phones while the few staff that weren't away on holiday went to a departmental meeting. I looked up as she came in. She was around my height, five feet six or seven, and she was wearing a blue and white floral dress. Her bare legs were pale and she had on white trainers, no socks. Her streaky-blonde hair hung loose and a little untidily around her shoulders, exposing (as I observed when she came closer) a few dark roots and more than a touch of grey. She opened the door to Dan's office and poked her head inside before turning round and noticing me.

'Are you looking for Dan?' I asked her.

'Yes. Have you seen him?'

'He's in a meeting upstairs,' I said. 'Up on the eighteenth. Is it urgent? Shall I call him?'

'No. No.' She waved her hand dismissively. 'I'm just his wife.' Then she smiled at what she'd said and pulled a world-weary expression. 'I'm no one important. I'm just a wife!'

'That's OK,' I smiled back. 'I'm just a temp. The office junior. I'm genuinely insignificant.'

She laughed and walked over to where I was sitting and held out her hand. I took it. 'I'm Maddy,' she said.

'I'm Tate.'

She looked at me carefully.

'Like Kate, but with a T,' I clarified.

'Like the art gallery?'

'That's it.'

She nodded, then frowned. 'Is that crap? Like the art gallery. Does everyone say that?'

'No, they don't. And I don't mind anyway. It's a stupid name.'

She wrinkled her nose. 'I like it. It's strong. Solid. Fearless.'

'Wow,' I said. 'I hope I can live up to all of that!'

She pulled a desk chair towards her and sat down opposite me. She blew her fringe up, away from her face, and took a few deep breaths, her chest rising and falling heavily. Her eyes, I noticed, had dark shadows underneath. It had been a blistering day and, in spite of the air con in the building, I felt her exhaustion. The previous night had been sweltering and uncomfortable, and tonight would be the same.

'Ridiculous, isn't it?' I said. 'The heat.'

'Unnecessary,' she agreed, contorting her features as if to imply that someone had made a poor managerial decision. 'Completely unnecessary.'

I laughed and she relaxed her expression, her eyes twinkling back at me. She dropped her bag onto the floor beside her. It was lovely: large and shiny, a top-handled bucket bag in a pretty pink and grey. Designer, no doubt. Had to be.

'I like your bag,' I said.

'Thank you.'

'Whose is it?'

She looked confused. 'Mine.'

'I meant which designer?'

'Oh. Erm . . .' She frowned. 'That one who makes all the fake designer handbags? The name escapes me.'

I laughed again and she grinned back at me.

'Can I get you a drink?' I offered. 'A tea or a coffee?'

'Some water would be great.' But as I slid my chair back,

she pushed herself to her feet. 'Water cooler,' she said. 'I know where it is.'

'I can get it,' I protested.

'No,' she said firmly. 'I can guarantee you do enough running around after this lot. You're not going to run around after me.'

'I don't mind.'

'I know you don't. But I'll go. Do you want some?'

She seemed determined not to trouble me, so I told her that I did. I watched as she went across the room and into the corridor, leaving her handbag on the floor opposite me. Ridiculously, I felt befriended. She was so nice. So kind and attentive. She was quite literally the only person I'd met since I'd worked at the bank with whom I'd felt any kind of connection. And she'd trusted me with her bag, hadn't she?

The phone rang and I answered it. It was one of the finance directors from our Paris Saint-Georges branch in the 9th Arrondissement. He wanted to speak to our head of funds. I explained that she was in the meeting upstairs, but I'd pass on a message. I'd just put the phone down when I heard an almighty bang. I looked up and over to the glass double doors to the corridor. They appeared to be streaked with water. I could just about make out Maddy's blue and white floral dress, motionless behind the glass.

I leaped out of my seat and ran into the corridor. Maddy was standing in front of me, looking dazed and confused. There were two empty plastic cups on the floor.

'What happened?' I asked, looking from Maddy to the glass doors.

'I'm so stupid,' Maddy said. 'I thought I'd left the doors open.'

'You walked right into them?'

She nodded.

'Oh my God. Are you hurt?'

She lifted one hand and rubbed her temple. 'I'm OK. Don't worry. I didn't realise . . . What an idiot.'

'Not at all. Could have happened to anyone,' I told her, although secretly I was uncertain how. The glass along this wall was expansive and always spotlessly clean, but the doors had frosted white circles dotted along the rim and big silver handles that you couldn't really miss. 'Come and sit down,' I said, reaching out my hand to her. 'I'll get some more water, then I'll call security. Get someone to clear this up.'

'No!' Maddy said abruptly. 'Please. Don't call anyone. I'll do it. Just tell me where I can find a cloth.'

'You don't need to do it,' I argued. 'No one's going to ask what happened. It's just a bit of water. No one's going to care.'

'I know, but . . . please?' She lifted her eyes to meet mine. 'Please don't tell anyone. I feel so clumsy. So embarrassed.'

'But why?' I frowned.

'I don't want to worry Dan. I haven't been too well lately,' she confessed, her eyes locking on to mine. 'So . . . please. Can we just . . . keep this between us?'

'Absolutely,' I agreed. I leaned down and picked up the cups. 'Come on,' I said. 'I'll clear it up. If anyone comes, I'll say it was me. That's what I get for wearing heels I can't walk in,' I added, and shook my head sagely, as if with the benefit of hindsight.

Maddy's eyes moved down to my ballerinas and then back up at me.

'I changed out of them after I tripped,' I said. 'Obviously.'

The hint of a smile appeared at the corner of her mouth and she looked at me silently, gratefully.

'Come on,' I coaxed her, and she allowed me to usher her back to the seat near my desk. I went back out to the toilets, fetched a wad of paper towels and wiped the water from the glass as best I could. I then fetched some more water from the cooler, went back inside and handed Maddy a cup.

She thanked me and took it, one hand still on her temple.

'Have you got a bump?' I asked her.

'A little one,' she smiled. She gave her head one last rub and dropped her hand into her lap. 'But I'm OK.' She paused. 'I get migraines. I get . . . dizzy. Double vision.'

'You should tell Dan.'

'He already knows.'

'I mean . . . about today. Just to be safe. You shouldn't go home on your own.'

'I'll be fine. Look, I was just walking too fast and . . . Don't worry. I'll go carefully.'

I nodded.

'Thank you, though. I appreciate your concern.' She moistened her lips and said, 'Dan's about to be promoted, to the board of directors.'

'I heard,' I smiled. 'Congratulations.'

'Thank you. The thing is, this wouldn't look good for him.'

'What wouldn't?' I asked, confused.

'You know. My headaches.'

'But—'

'He wouldn't want his colleagues to know that he has any . . . issues in his personal life.'

'Really?' I frowned.

She nodded. 'Yes.'

This sounded ridiculous to me, not to mention discriminatory, but what did I know? She would have a far better insight into the workings of the company than me.

'So, I'll tell him later.' Her eyes were still on mine. 'In private. If that's OK?'

'Well, of course it is,' I agreed.

She smiled. 'Thanks, Tate. And I'm sorry to have interrupted your day.'

'You haven't interrupted anything. I've literally got nothing to do except answer the phones if they ring.'

She looked at me curiously for a second. 'I hope you don't mind me asking, but . . . how come you're doing this job?'

'I know,' I sighed. 'It's a job for a twenty-year-old, not an old woman like me.'

'You're not *old*,' she objected. 'But you *are* bright. Too bright to be answering the phones and making tea.'

I was flattered, pleased it was so immediately apparent that there was a little bit more to me. I quickly embarked on my fake story, the one about my ambitions at the bank, about my willingness to learn, my poor typing speed, my fledgling French. But I noticed that her smile had faded. She was sitting there in silence, her eyes fixed rather disconcertingly on me. I couldn't see any holes in the story I'd just given, but her reaction – or lack of one – was unsettling me. Had Dan maybe twigged that I was here under false pretences and sent his friendly wife into the office to interrogate me?

I stopped talking and waited, but still she didn't speak. She just sat there, her dark, shadowy eyes fixed on me.

And then they moved. Her eyes, that is. First they looked up at the ceiling, then away to her left. Then her mouth curved up into a strange, ethereal smile. And then she fell sideways, crashed to the floor and her body began to shake uncontrollably.

34

I dropped down onto the floor beside Maddy, put my hand on her arm and talked to her in a soothing voice. I told her that she was going to be OK, but the jerking of her limbs and the froth at the corners of her mouth were really scaring me. I stood up shakily and scanned my desk for my phone. Maddy hadn't wanted to cause a fuss. She – and presumably Dan too – hadn't wanted his colleagues to know that she was unwell, but this was an emergency, wasn't it? I had to call for an ambulance, surely?

I looked over at the double doors to the corridor outside, willing Dan to come back in from the meeting and take this decision away from me. Should I call upstairs for him, I wondered – make up some excuse to call him out from the meeting without anyone else twigging? But there wasn't time for all that. This was serious. I needed to call 999 immediately.

The call handler asked me a series of questions, then gave me a set of instructions. Don't move her, don't put anything in her mouth. No fingers, no water. Just stay with her and talk to her until the paramedics arrive. I did as I was told and put my phone on speaker and laid it on the floor next to me. After a minute or two, Maddy stopped shaking and her eyes came back into focus. I moved her onto her side as instructed and she let out a deep sigh and lay silent and still, her eyes looking up at me. The paramedics arrived soon afterwards, two of them – a man and a woman – followed by someone from security who stood guard at the door so that when the rest of the staff started to filter down from the meeting they were quickly turned away – everyone except Dan, that is, who spoke briefly in a hushed tone with the security guard, then hurried over and knelt down beside his wife. Maddy was now crying and saying, 'I'm sorry,' repeatedly. Dan stroked her damp hair away from her face and told her not to worry, but I could tell by the way they were with each other that there was something else behind her concern that hadn't been shared with me.

We were all still at floor level behind the desk, out of sight of both the security guard and the other staff members who'd appeared at the door. An idea suddenly came to me. 'Does anyone know that it's Maddy who's unwell?' I asked Dan.

He looked up at me enquiringly.

'She didn't want anyone to know she was sick,' I said. 'But does anyone know for sure that the ambulance wasn't called for me?'

'I don't think so,' he said.

I turned to the paramedics. 'What did you tell the security staff when you came in?'

They hadn't told them anything. All the door security staff knew was that an ambulance had been called to level fourteen and that approximately thirty minutes earlier Maddy, who was well known to them, had been issued a visitor pass and allowed up onto the floor with me.

'So, let me go with her,' I said to Dan. 'In the ambulance.'

Dan's eyes widened. 'You mean . . . ?'

'We'll make it appear as if it's me who's unwell and that Maddy's just going to the hospital with me. It's nearly five,' I said. 'Everyone will be going home soon anyway. We wait for a bit, then we both walk out. We get into the lift. And for anyone left in the building, we make it look as though it's Maddy who's supporting me.'

Dan turned to the paramedic. 'Can my wife walk?'

She'd need a little time to recover, they said. But after that she should be fine to go down in the lift with me.

Dan turned to Maddy. 'What do you think?'

'Yes,' she said. 'Yes. That's perfect.'

So that's what we did. We waited a while and then, when Maddy was ready, we walked out into the corridor, past the security guard, the five of us, me and Maddy in a huddle together. I played my part well – walking with a slow, frail gait and pulling the most pained of faces – and we all got into the lift. We went down into the lobby, past a few curious faces and through the revolving door into the street. I climbed up into the waiting ambulance with Maddy and the paramedics got in too. As soon as they'd shut the door, I sat back out of the way and waited while they attended to Maddy, attaching monitors to check her oxygen levels, her temperature and her pulse.

When they asked her if she'd ever had a seizure before, she glanced over at me before replying that she had. I heard her say softly, 'I have an underlying health condition.' The male paramedic looked from Maddy to me and back again, then got out of the ambulance and shut the door. A few minutes later, the door opened again and he got back in and did some more checks on Maddy, then told us that Dan had gone to pick up their daughter and that they were going to take Maddy home.

'Do you have to be anywhere?' Maddy asked me.

'No.'

'Come too, then,' she said. 'Please. Come home with me.'

'Sure. Of course,' I agreed.

The paramedics asked us to fasten our seatbelts and then they got into the front of the ambulance and we moved off along Eastcheap.

'How are you feeling?' I asked Maddy.

'A little spaced out.' She looked up at me with tired eyes. 'Thank you. Thank you for what you did.'

'It was nothing,' I said. 'No trouble at all.'

She studied me for a moment, sizing me up. 'You're a really good actress,' she said. 'I thought you were about to keel over at one point.'

I couldn't help myself. 'I am actually a trained actress,' I confided. 'No one at CPF knows.'

'Well, that explains it,' she said. 'You're very talented.'

I flushed with pride, grateful that, for once, I'd been able to show what I was capable of without having to prove my worth with a list of my TV and film credits. 'Thank you. No plans to give up my day job, though.'

She smiled and said that I should keep going, that I really had something. I asked her what she did. She told me that she was an editor for a publishing house. 'I also have an idea for a novel of my own,' she said shyly.

'What's it about?' I asked.

'Typical first novel, I suppose, based on myself. A middle-aged woman with a fourteen-year-old daughter. Actually, she's just turned fifteen.'

'What happens?'

She hesitated. 'I don't know why I'm telling you this. I'll never write it.'

'Don't give up on your dream,' I urged her.

Her eyes flickered up to meet mine and she looked as though she was about to say something, but appeared to change her mind.

'I could help you,' I offered, feeling excited at the thought of doing something creative. 'My friend Helen and I used to write screenplays all the time when we were in school. Not real ones, obviously. But we loved writing them and acting them out.'

'A screenplay,' she mused, smiling faintly. 'Now there's an idea.'

I grinned. 'I'll help you write it, then I'll star in it. I'll play you. I could play you, right?'

'Absolutely.' She smiled and gave me a curious look, sizing me up, then said, 'You're a good person, Tate.'

'So are you,' I replied.

Maddy's eyes twinkled at me for a moment, then she closed them, laid her head back against the seat and a minute later she was asleep.

35

The ambulance turned right at the Angel and drove along Upper Street, past Islington Green. We turned into a tree-lined street and then into another and stopped outside a Victorian terraced house fronted by wrought-iron railings and tall, dense bushes that concealed its small front garden. I followed Maddy and the paramedics down a narrow path and through a front door with a stained-glass panel, then down a traditional tiled and corniced hallway into a glossy modern kitchen-diner at the back. Once satisfied that Maddy was comfortable, the paramedics left. I insisted that I put the kettle on while Maddy remained seated in the armchair near the patio doors leading out to the garden. She agreed and closed her eyes as I found my way around the kitchen, opening and shutting drawers and cupboards until I'd found spoons, teabags and cups.

'Maddy,' I said gently when I'd made the tea, 'do you want to be in bed?'

She opened her eyes. 'Will you come and sit with me?' she murmured.

'Of course.'

'Then, yes,' she said. 'That would be good.'

I followed her up the stairs with our mugs of tea. In the bedroom, she flicked on a lamp and undressed while I placed our drinks on the bedside table and, at Maddy's suggestion, lifted a light tub chair from the corner of the room and brought it closer to the bed. Maddy got under the covers and let out a satisfied sigh and a moment later she was dozing again. I sat and drank my tea, taking in the room – duck-egg-blue voile panel curtains, a dark oak dresser, wooden floorboards – and checking my phone. There was a message from Helen asking me if I wanted to go out for dinner. I told her that something had come up and asked if she could feed George for me. I then checked the news and answered an email. When I looked up, Maddy's eyes were open again.

'How are you feeling?' I asked.

'Better,' she said. 'A little concussed. And a little ashamed.'

'You've nothing to be ashamed of.'

She propped herself up a little, taking a plump white pillow from the other side of the bed and drawing it under her head. 'The seizures. I haven't had that many,' she said. 'I don't really know what to expect.'

'Lots of people have seizures,' I said. 'Why on earth should that reflect negatively on Dan?'

She reached for her tea and sipped it. It was probably lukewarm by now. I rose from my seat, about to offer to go downstairs and make another one, but she put her hand out, indicating for me to sit back down.

'It's not the bank,' she said.

'What do you mean?'

'It's not Dan's job that we're concerned about.' She put her mug back down on the bedside table. 'It's Emily. Our daughter.'

I looked at her enquiringly.

'We don't want her to know that I'm . . . that I'm this unwell.'

I nodded.

'I have a brain tumour,' she said.

'Oh my God,' I said, shocked. 'I'm so sorry. 'Is it . . . ? Can they . . . ?'

'No.' Her eyes swam with tears and she blinked them away. 'They can't operate. It's a stage four glioblastoma. It's the most aggressive form of brain tumour there is. The prognosis isn't good.'

I blinked back my own tears and swallowed. 'So, what are they going to do?'

'They'll keep trying to shrink it,' she said, 'but the treatment is mostly palliative.' Tears shimmered in her eyes again. 'They've given me from three to eighteen months to live.'

I gazed back at her, feeling awful, not knowing what to say.

She wiped her eyes. 'Emily doesn't know. She mustn't know.'

'OK,' I said.

'She thinks it's just migraines. She's at a difficult age. She's just started her GCSE year and . . . and we've had some problems with her lately.' She looked up at me. 'Do you have kids?'

'No, but I have nieces and nephews,' I said. 'One of them is fifteen. He's always lovely to me, but I hear he gives his mum a hard time.'

'It's normal,' she said. 'At that age. We know that. And normal is good. Normal is what we want. We don't want to put her life on hold. We don't want to mess up her education. Dan and I talked it through and we both felt we'd rather pretend that everything's OK for as long as we can.'

'But she'll spend less time with you, won't she?' I pointed out. 'I mean, less time than she would if she knew.'

Maddy's lower lip trembled. 'What fifteen-year-old would want to hang out with her dying mother just waiting for it to happen?'

'It would be tough,' I agreed.

'I'd rather spend less time with her than . . . than . . .'

'It's OK,' I said. 'I understand.'

I didn't have kids. What did I know? But my expression must have said otherwise, because Maddy continued to explain. 'We think she was seeing someone,' she said. 'Someone . . . wrong for her. Someone . . .' She hesitated. 'Older than her. We never found out who he was. But she told us it was over and we want it to stay that way. When the time comes, we'll break it to her, but until then we don't want to stop her living her life as normal. And we definitely don't want to give her anything to go running to *him* about.'

I was touched, if a little surprised, that she'd shared all this with me, but I guessed it had been hard for her, keeping this a secret and having no one to talk to but Dan. He would have his own burden to carry, his own pain to deal with, and maybe it was easier to talk to a stranger for whom she had no responsibility, no feelings to consider. So, instead of telling her that she needn't explain, that it was none of my business, that I couldn't even begin to think what I'd do in her situation, I told her that I thought I would do the same.

She leaned in closer to me. 'We really can't tell anyone at the bank,' she said resolutely. 'Dan's boss, Jerry, and his wife Sharon are friends of ours. They've been to our house and met Emily numerous times. They have a daughter the same age and it might slip out, and you know, kids all talk online these days. Every child knows someone who knows someone else. So we decided it would be safer to keep it simple and just not tell anyone at all.'

'So literally no one else knows? Not even your parents?'

'Both my parents died,' she said. 'My mum had a brain tumour too and . . . and my dad had early-onset Parkinson's.' She sighed. 'My chances weren't the best . . . I've always known that. So, yes. It's just me and Dan . . . And now you, of course.'

'Look, I won't breathe a word, I promise. I have no friends at the bank. There's no one for me to tell.'

'I guessed.' She blushed. 'I didn't mean . . .'

'I know what you meant,' I said soothingly. 'And you're right. I'm just the office temp. No one is interested in anything I have to say. But, just for the record, I'd never have talked about what happened today.'

'I know,' she said. 'I like you, Tate. I feel I can trust you.'

'I like you too,' I said. 'And you *can* trust me.'

She gave a thin smile, and then we heard the front door opening and the sound of voices in the hallway below. Maddy put a finger to her lips. We sat in silence, listening – we could hear Dan's deep, low voice first, the words themselves muffled, and then the higher-pitched, argumentative tone of their daughter. Dan's reply, again reassuring, soft, low, and then the sound of Emily thundering up the stairs, but then – as she appeared to remember what her father had just told her – the footsteps on the landing fading and her bedroom door gently closing shut.

Maddy turned to me. 'Believe it or not, that's Emily on a good day,' she whispered, and we both grinned.

'I was the worst teenager ever,' I said. And then a strange, unsettling semblance of a thought popped into my head.

The door opened and Dan came into the bedroom, shutting the door behind him again.

I stood up. 'I'll go now,' I whispered to Maddy. 'Save explaining to Emily who I am and why I'm sitting in her mother's bedroom.'

'Thanks, Tate. I really appreciate you looking after Maddy,' Dan said, under his breath.

'It's no problem,' I said. 'I'm feeling a lot better now after my funny turn.'

He smiled. 'So do you think you'll be well enough for work tomorrow, or will you need a day off?'

The agency didn't pay me if I didn't work, but I doubted he'd realise that. 'Don't worry. I'll be there,' I whispered.

'Can I offer you a lift home?'

'No. Stay with Maddy,' I insisted. I turned to say goodbye to her, then spontaneously leaned forward and hugged her instead. Maddy hugged me back – which no doubt surprised her husband – and then I followed him down the stairs and he showed me out of the front door.

It was eight o'clock and just getting dark outside, which caught me by surprise. It had been such a hot summer's day and the air was still thick, yet the nights were now drawing in. As I walked down the path and neared the gate to the street, I stopped to consider which route home was best. I'd just plumped for walking down to the Angel and getting a bus along Pentonville Road when a car rounded the corner and a pair of headlights shone in my eyes. The vehicle pulled up on the other side of the road and a face looked up from the driver's seat. At first, the windows were deep in shadow and I couldn't see in, but then the car door opened, a light blinked on and a woman stepped out and looked straight towards me. Hayley. It was Hayley from work. What was she doing here? Whatever it was, I couldn't let her see me. I was supposed to be ill. Why would I have come back to Dan and Maddy's house? I should be in hospital or at home.

As she peered into Dan and Maddy's front garden, I made a split-second decision and dived into a bush. My arms were bare and the branches were rigid and unforgiving, but I wriggled my way in further and listened carefully to the sound of Hayley's footsteps, her high heels click-clacking across the road and up the path. A moment later, the footsteps stopped and I heard the doorbell ring. In one swift movement, I dived back out onto the grass. I clambered to my feet and then ran like the wind towards the gate and out onto the street.

36

It wasn't long before I made the connection. I was in the office the following morning, walking back from the kitchen with two mugs of coffee. I'd offered to make one for Hayley in the hope that we might then strike up a conversation, one that would encourage her to reveal what she'd seen – or not seen – the previous night. *Had* she seen me in Dan and Maddy's garden? I thought she had, but I couldn't be sure. Had she mentioned anything to Dan when he'd answered the door to her, and if so, had he made an excuse for my presence that I didn't yet know about? If only he were here, we'd be able to confer, get our stories straight, but it was nearly lunchtime and he still hadn't got in.

I stopped outside his room and glanced in through the door, which was slightly ajar. His chair was still tucked in neatly behind his desk. I scanned the desk for his laptop but it was empty, save for the usual clutter: a pen holder full of pens, a small desk fan, a thick, black leather-bound diary, the inevitable family photograph. My eyes shifted to the silver-framed snapshot of a smiling Maddy and a teenage girl with kohl-ringed eyes and long blonde hair. Emily, I presumed. I squinted to get a better look at her and that's when I remembered what Maddy had told me. *We think she was seeing someone . . . someone older than her. We never found out who he was.*

No one seemed to be looking my way, so I nudged the door open wider with my foot and stepped inside, inching closer to Dan's desk, still clutching the hot mugs of coffee, holding them steady so that I didn't splash any liquid onto the deep, plush carpet under my feet. My throat tightened as I got a better look at the photograph: Maddy, all lit up and laughing, taken pre-diagnosis, no doubt. She was leaning in lovingly towards her daughter, whose own smile, in contrast, was tight and tolerant. Emily had that paradoxical air of both belligerence and extreme vulnerability that many adolescents seem to project.

She was pretty. Shockingly pretty. Big blue eyes with long, dark lashes, a dainty, upturned nose, full lips and thick, shiny hair. Young men would definitely look twice. But she was only fifteen. And Maddy was dying. Maddy was soon going to leave her teenage daughter without a mother. Tears sprang to my eyes as I thought about Josh and how Fern might feel if she knew that she was going to die and leave him behind. She would be petrified of leaving Josh alone in the world. Well, not alone; he'd have his dad, of course, but she'd want to be certain before she died that all her affairs were in order, that her husband was free from worry, that Josh was OK and safe from harm.

A lump rose to my throat as I imagined myself promising Fern on her deathbed that I would look after Josh for her. But who would look out for Maddy's daughter? Dan would have to continue to keep a roof over their heads and he worked long hours. Would Jerry be supportive of him? I wondered. Jerry was more than Dan's boss, he was a friend of the family; that's what Maddy had told me. *They've been to our house and met Emily numerous times.* And then the thought struck me so suddenly I felt I'd been punched: Jerry Seager. What if Jerry Seager was the older man Emily had been seeing? What if Jerry Seager had been grooming Emily for sex, just as he'd groomed Helen and me?

The thought was chilling – sickening. Maddy had said that Emily's relationship with this older man was over – but was it really? From what I knew of Jerry, he wouldn't give up until he'd got what he wanted, and a beautiful young girl like Emily would be exactly who he'd want.

I made myself breathe deeply and evenly, then turned and slipped out of the room. For a split second, I noticed Hayley watching me, but she quickly averted her eyes and tilted her head back towards her computer screen, making a play of being engrossed in her work. When I walked over and placed her coffee mug on her desk, she looked up blankly, feigning surprise at seeing me standing there. But then her eyes moved to my bare arms and I realised what she was looking at. I felt myself flush. My skin was lightly scratched from my hideout in the bushes. I knew the marks were visible, but although we'd had some rain overnight, it was still too warm and muggy to put on a cardigan.

'My cat,' I said. 'I had to worm her. She hates it. She always scratches me.'

Hayley's forehead creased and she looked at her coffee as if she wasn't sure whether to drink it or not.

'I've washed my hands since then, don't worry,' I told her.

'Oh. Yeah,' she said awkwardly. 'I wasn't thinking that.' She reached out for the coffee cup and took a tentative sip.

'Do you know where Dan is?' I asked her, as casually as I could.

'He's working from home today.'

I took a mouthful of coffee. 'I need him to sign something,' I said. 'Have you got his mobile number?'

'Sorry, I'm not allowed to give it out. What do you need signed?'

'Oh. Just my timesheet. From the agency.'

'I can sign those.'

'Can you?'

'Yeah.' She smiled. 'No problem.'

'OK,' I said. 'I'll dig it out.'

'Are you OK, then? After yesterday?'

'Yeah,' I said. 'I think it was just the heat.'

Her brows drew together. 'Should you be here?'

'I'm OK. The ambulance was just a precaution. They said my blood pressure was low and . . . I do faint sometimes. It's happened before.'

'Well, don't do anything too strenuous.' She flashed me a weak smile. I thanked her and went back to my desk.

I set about translating a letter to one of the Paris Saint-Georges directors, which Dan had asked me to have a go at. It was my least favourite way of translating: from English into French. The vocabulary was complex and specialised and I found myself looking up every other word. After I'd constructed a few very amateur sentences, I found myself staring at my computer, thinking instead about Emily and about Jerry. I knew my hunch was a strong one, but there was no way I could dump all of this on Maddy until I was certain, so I opened up the browser on my computer and typed Emily's name into the search engine. I scanned the first page of results. She'd kept her social media profiles private – sensible girl – but it didn't take me long to find out which school she went to, thanks to a school newsletter – unintentionally published, no doubt – naming her as one of several students to have been invited to have hot chocolate with the head. The newsletter was two years old, but the school catchment area took in Dan and Maddy's street. There was no accompanying photo, but the name (Emily Blakely – not unusual, but not that common either) and the location of the school both told me that this was her.

At some point before lunch, Hayley went out to run an errand for Dan. My Google search had brought up nothing else, so I stood up and pulled my bag over my shoulder and strode purposefully from the room. When I got to Dan's office, though, I slowed my pace and looked cautiously to my left and right. A couple of heads were bowed over paper files. Two or three of my colleagues were talking in the small kitchen. Others were sitting silently at their desks and staring at their screens. No one appeared to be paying any attention to me.

I sidled into Dan's room and rooted around inside my bag for my phone for a moment before realising, with annoyance, that I'd left it in my desk drawer. I had no camera. But it didn't matter. I quickly picked up the silver-framed photograph. Dan wouldn't miss it, not today. My eyes then landed on the black leather desk diary. I picked that up too and slid it into my bag along with the photograph. Checking that the coast was clear, I slipped out of the room again, went back to my desk, took my phone out of my drawer, then told one of the secretaries that I had a hospital appointment which I'd already cleared with Hayley. I fired off a quick email to Hayley to tell her that I wasn't feeling that well after all, and was going to the doctor.

I had a little time to play with before the school day ended, and so I walked to London Bridge and caught the bus north to Islington. I got off at the Angel and walked west towards Emily's school. I stood behind a car a few feet back from the gates. I wasn't completely confident about being able to identify Emily amongst hundreds of identically dressed teenage girls, but it didn't matter. This was just a practice run. I knew she wasn't going to Jerry; not this time.

As the students began to filter out in small groups, heads bowed together, talking quietly or laughing and shouting to one another, jostling and pushing, I took one last look at the photo and slipped it back into my bag. I studied each group of females, one by one, immediately filtering out anyone who wasn't Emily before turning my attention to the next group.

And then I saw her. She was with another shorter, stockier girl with a neat brown bob. They were on their phones, walking side by side, occasionally glancing up and watching with disdain as a schoolbag got thrown into the road or a football bounced or someone screamed or was slide tackled. They walked in the direction of Upper Street and turned the corner to head north towards Islington Green. I crossed the road and walked in the opposite direction for a moment before turning round and following her home.

37

'Wait,' Sarah says. 'How did you know that she wasn't going to him?'

I smile a little proudly. 'I had Dan's diary, didn't I? I knew where *he* was. And he and Jerry were very often in conference together, so I made a note of all the board meetings and all the directors' lunches they were going to, and after that I made sure I always had one eye on the door to his office. If Jerry left early for any reason I didn't know about, I'd phone Helen, who was on standby.'

'And Helen would follow him?'

I shake my head. 'Not him. It was easier to track Emily. Safer, too. As soon as he left the office, I'd phone Helen. She had my car – she needed it for her job, so I let her use it. She'd invent a last-minute house viewing or say that a genuine one had taken longer. I would phone her and she would hotfoot it to the school or to Maddy's house, depending on what time it was. She'd wait for Emily and follow her. Emily had a fairly regular pattern. She usually went to the shops on Union Road, to Rosie's house, or home. When I finished work, I'd go and meet Helen wherever she was and we'd stake Emily out for the rest of the evening until we were confident that she'd gone to bed. Her bedroom was at the front of the house, so you could see the lights go off. Once, she stayed at Rosie's house. A few times, at the weekend, we lost her. But mostly, she was at home.'

Sarah nods. 'And Emily didn't know Helen, of course.'

'Or me.'

'And she didn't know your car.'

'No,' I agree. 'So, even if she did notice us, it was unlikely she'd pay us much attention, or think anything of it. And we were very careful. We always kept our distance and kept the lights off in the car. Besides, I knew that if I was right about this – if we were going to see her and Jerry together – it was going to happen before too long.'

'And it did.' Sarah scrutinises me, waiting. 'Right?'

I nod. 'He hasn't changed. He's still the same filthy pervert that he's always been.' My voice breaks with emotion as I speak about him the way I should always have done – with anger, with contempt, with the disgust and repulsion that I'd swallowed whole when I was too young to know that it belonged to him instead of to me.

'And you told Maddy.'

'Yes.'

'How did she take it?'

I sigh, my heart heavy at the memory. 'As you'd expect,' I say. 'Except—'

'Except?' Sarah raised an eyebrow.

'Except,' I say, 'her idea of how to stop him was way, way better than mine. It was tragic. It was scary. But it was the best.'

38

September had arrived and the weather had cooled. Maddy's back garden was a mixed palette of forest green, lime and faded yellow where the grass had been scorched by the sun. The garden furniture on the patio had been tucked away for the winter inside thick canvas hoods. Helen and I sat awkwardly side by side at the table in her kitchen while Maddy made a pot of coffee and, when it was ready, splashed it into the waiting cups. I noticed how clumsily she did this, how she struggled to fit the jug back onto the hotplate, how her hands trembled as she walked over with the coffee mugs and placed them on the table in front of us. I wasn't sure if this was the shock of what we'd just told her or the effect of her illness, but seeing her looking this vulnerable was making me feel like a real bitch for what we'd just done.

In the end, it had been Helen who had witnessed it, Helen who had the evidence on her phone. Maddy would no doubt want to hear about it from her, we'd decided, and I'd expected some resistance, some disbelief or denial. At first, that's what I'd thought we were dealing with when Maddy had taken the phone from Helen and stared and stared at the video. 'But Jerry doesn't have a van,' she'd murmured, uncomprehending. 'Where would he get a van from? Why would he have a van?'

'Maybe he hired it,' I'd suggested.

Maddy had lifted her dazed eyes to meet mine. She looked as though she'd been slapped.

'I'm so sorry,' I'd said. The last time I'd felt this way was when I'd told a friend at drama school – the first real friend I'd had after Helen – that her boyfriend was cheating on her. Her reaction was to blame me, as if I was enjoying what I'd just told her, and she'd never spoken to me again. I'd vowed after that to stay out of other people's business. But this was different. How could we not tell Maddy what was happening to her daughter? What other choice did we have?

Maddy slid into her seat and fixed her eyes on her coffee cup. 'How did you know?'

'I saw Emily with him,' Helen answered her, looking confused. She nodded at her phone.

'I don't mean that.' She turned to Helen. 'I mean, how did you know to follow them? How did you know that this was happening?'

Helen and I looked at each other. Helen gave an almost imperceptible nod.

'Because he did it to us too.' My heart thudded like a drum as I spoke the words out loud.

For a moment, Maddy seemed unable to grasp this. 'He did it to you?'

I swallowed. I could feel Helen stiffen beside me. 'When

we were the same age as Emily, he had sex with us both. Not together,' I added quickly. 'Helen first. And then me.'

And then I told her everything. How he'd cheated his way into our lives. How he'd befriended us and charmed us and made us feel like grown-ups, how he'd bought us sweets and drinks and vodka and had romanced us with music and – when we were giddy with love and tipsy on alcohol – how he'd guilt-tripped us into having sex with him on a mattress in the back of his van.

Maddy's eyes grew wider and wider as I spoke and then she clapped her hand to her mouth. 'Excuse me,' she mumbled. Her chair screeched back and she ran out of the kitchen, her hip colliding with a kitchen unit as she went. We could hear the door to the downstairs cloakroom in the hallway slam shut, then the loud noise of vomiting.

'Do you think we should go and see if she's all right?' Helen said.

I got up and went out into the hallway and Helen followed me. 'Maddy,' I called through the closed door to the cloak-room. 'Are you OK? Can we get you anything?'

There was no answer for a moment. Finally, the door opened and Maddy stepped out, looking pale and gaunt. 'It's OK,' she said, wiping her mouth. 'I'll be all right in a second.'

She walked carefully back into the kitchen, with us following, and collapsed into an armchair by the window. 'I like the idea of coffee,' she murmured, 'but I can't seem to stomach it any more.'

'It's probably the shock too. Can I get you some water?' I asked.

She nodded, and so I fetched a glass from the cupboard,

filled it at the kitchen tap and handed it to Maddy, then sank onto a bar stool at the kitchen counter. Helen pulled out a stool and sat down next to me. Maddy slowly sipped from the glass and breathed several long, deep breaths. Then she placed the glass on the coffee table beside her, swallowed hard and looked from Helen to me.

'So, did you tell anyone?'

'About what he did?' I asked.

She nodded.

'At the time . . . no,' I said. 'For years, I tried not to think about him. And then I met up with Helen again.'

I looked at Helen, who said, in a tiny voice, 'We blamed ourselves, you see.'

Maddy made a gulping sound.

'Until we talked about it,' I said. 'And that's when we decided to do something.'

'You went to the police?'

'Helen did. But they said they couldn't do anything.' I told her the reasons why.

'But . . .' Maddy sniffed. 'All those cases . . . I mean, Max Clifford . . .'

'That was different,' I said. 'They didn't want him to do it; he just did it. But we consented. We were . . .' I swallowed, hating the word, '. . . willing. So, with us, it wasn't rape. It wasn't even indecent assault. It was underage sex. The only sexual offence with a time limit,' I added bitterly.

Maddy looked thoughtfully back at me and then her expression changed. 'And so that's why you're working at the bank?'

I nodded.

'You got a job there . . . on purpose?'

'Yeah. I wanted to expose him. Dig a bit first, perhaps. Find something out.'

'And now you have,' she said flatly.

'I'm sorry,' I said again.

'Don't be.' She gave a thin smile. 'I'm glad you did what you did.'

I straightened up on my stool. 'So, will you go to the police?'

Maddy's expression was one of bewilderment, as if she hadn't considered this.

'The law's changed now,' I said, talking quickly. 'Well, I'm sure you know that. He can get up to fourteen years in prison. This time, they'll take it seriously.'

She laid her head back against the chair, her words blurring a little as she murmured, 'We'd have to be able to prove it, though. We'd have to have evidence.'

'We *have* evidence,' I said, confused. 'On Helen's phone.'

'You have evidence of a hug. Of Emily getting into a van with him. But that's all. It could be innocent.'

I thought for a moment. 'We'd need Emily on board, obviously.'

'And what if she isn't on board?'

'Well . . .' I said, floundering a little. 'I guess you'll want to talk to her first.'

Maddy turned her head to look out into the garden.

'Do *you* believe he's abusing her?' I pressed her.

'Or trying to,' Helen said kindly.

Maddy looked from Helen to me. 'I don't *believe* it,' she said, her voice quivering. 'I *know* it. But he's manipulated her, hasn't he? She'll protect him. She'll lie for him. She won't turn him in.'

I frowned. 'Do you know that for sure?'

Maddy put her head in her hands and we waited. 'No,' she said finally. 'But we've been here before.'

'Before?'

'A few months ago. I told you she was seeing someone. Someone too old for her. We'd found messages between them. On her phone.'

'You read them?' I said eagerly. 'What did they say?'

'That she was special. That she was amazing.' She gulped, fighting back tears again. 'That when she was sixteen they'd be together.'

Helen and I looked at each other.

'And that they'd go somewhere, just the two of them, some-where where no one knew them.'

I saw Helen bite her lip. It had been Jerry.

'And what did Emily say?'

'She lied,' Maddy said. 'She lied about everything.' Her eyes flickered around the kitchen, as if seeing it for the very first time. 'To think . . .' she said, 'to think that I had him in my house! To think that I . . .' – her voice shook – '. . . cooked food for him. Poured wine for him. All this time . . .' She started sobbing, then, really sobbing. 'I just can't . . . I just can't . . .'

I crouched down beside her, put my arms around her and held her while she cried. After she'd stopped shaking, I let go of her. 'Why don't you just call the police?' I said soothingly. 'Let them deal with it. Let them gather the evidence.'

'Gather the evidence?' Maddy lifted her head, her eyes

wide. 'You're talking about it like it's going to be some big investigation. But it's Emily. Just Emily!'

'You have the phone number. The messages . . .'

'That wasn't Jerry's real phone number!' she cried out. 'Why would he use his registered phone number?'

'Oh,' I said, realising.

'Without Emily, they won't be able to prove a thing. And even if she *does* agree to talk to them, it's going to be . . .' She shook her head. 'Horrendous!'

'That's true,' Helen chipped in.

I glanced up at Helen, frowning.

'Well, she'll have to go through what I did, won't she?' she said. 'All those humiliating questions.'

'But for a reason,' I said. 'It will go somewhere this time.'

'Yeah,' Maddy huffed. 'To a courtroom, where she'll get asked all the same humiliating questions before some clever lawyer rips her to shreds. It will all turn into a long-drawn-out bloody nightmare. And what if it's too late by then?'

'Too late for what?'

But I'd realised what she'd meant as soon as I said it.

Her eyes sparked with desperation, with rage. 'I'm dying, Tate!' she wailed, the agony inside her spilling out like blood. 'Do you think this is how I want to spend my final weeks or months with my family? With police and lawyers and social workers coming in and out of my house? Going to court hearings and seeing him watching us, and not just him – all of our nosy neighbours, all the school mums sitting in the public gallery. Coming home and watching Emily eaten up inside with the hurt and the guilt and the shame of what she's done?'

'What *she's* done? Don't you mean what *he's* done?'

'But she'll blame herself, won't she?' Maddy flung her arms up. 'Like you did. And that's assuming she even realises that there's any blame to be had. But even if she does – when she does – we're still going to be a million miles away from him being locked up for this. It could take months and months – even years – for it to get to trial. I might not even live long enough to . . . to . . . to see my daughter through to the . . . through to the . . .' She let out a sob. 'To the end.'

I felt awful. In an instant, I saw it from her point of view. 'God, Maddy. I'm sorry. I've been so insensitive.'

'There'll be no way back,' she whispered. 'Once we start this, there'll be no way back. I need time to think. I need to work out how to handle this.'

'Of course,' I said. 'Of course you do.'

Helen leaned forward. 'We're here for you.'

'We really are,' I agreed. 'Every step of the way. We'll support you, whatever you decide to do.'

Maddy nodded, then closed her eyes and leaned back against her seat again. 'Sorry,' she murmured. 'I have to . . . I have to rest my head a minute.'

We waited, but she didn't move a muscle, just lay still, her head tilted up at the ceiling, her eyes shut.

After a few minutes, Helen looked at me and whispered softly, 'Is she asleep? Should we go?'

Maddy lifted her head then, and looked directly at Helen. Tears fell down her cheeks as she stuttered and stumbled over her words. 'I just don't think I'm going to have that long.'

39

The alarm going off sounded like a train whistle blowing in Maddy's ear. She reached out and pressed the switch to silence it and instantly felt her stomach rise up. She was coming to expect it now, the nausea. For the last three mornings it had been there before she'd even woken, stirring inside her like an omen, the association it brought with it making her heart sink to its bottommost depths. The last time she'd felt this sick in the mornings was when she'd been pregnant with Emily, but there had been something wonderful to come out of that. She'd been able to count off the weeks until the sickness would pass, until the foetus inside her grew into a beautiful baby, the baby she'd always wanted. Now, the tumour felt like an evil invader that would cause her to suffer until it finally killed her. She wanted to cry with the unfairness, the wretchedness, the utter pointlessness of it all.

She'd had a fitful night, filled with mixed-up dreams and waking thoughts about Emily, and had finally fallen into a deep sleep in the early hours of the morning. At some point she'd heard Dan leave. She closed her eyes and lay still, hoping to quell the nausea, but instead began to think about everything she'd learned the day before, about the messages, the hug, the van. She began replaying Emily's entire childhood over in her head, this new information superimposed onto every scene so that she now saw it in a sickening new light. She saw it clearly now: the extra attention Jerry had always paid to her beautiful daughter. The way he'd hugged her, sometimes lingering just a little too long. The way he'd stood transfixed in the doorway during the water fight in the garden that she'd had with Rosie when she was ten or eleven, as they ran around squealing in their swimsuits. And then there was that time at the dinner table a year ago, maybe, when he'd asked Em if she had a boyfriend – how amused he'd been when Em had flushed bright pink and lowered her eyes.

Maddy's stomach tugged. The sickness wasn't going to abate; she was going to have to get up and get it over with. She pulled back her duvet and got out of bed, moved across the room and opened her bedroom door. The house was silent. Emily was still in bed. She moved quickly across the landing and into the bathroom, where she switched on the radio, turned it up loud, lifted the toilet seat, kneeled down on the rug and threw up as quietly as she could. The radio was tuned to Radio 3 and a piano concerto was playing, the notes tinkling higher and higher into a feverish pitch that made her head feel as though it was going to explode. As soon as she was sure she'd finished throwing up, she reached out and snapped it off.

'Mum!' Emily was outside the door, her voice high-pitched with indignation. 'I'm trying to talk to you!'

Maddy quickly flushed the toilet, stood up and opened a window. Grabbing her toothbrush, she squeezed toothpaste onto it, put it into her mouth and then opened the door.

Emily was standing in her pyjamas, scowling. 'The radio was really loud, Mum. You woke me up!'

'I'm sorry, darling. Do you need the bathroom?' Maddy said, her mouth full of toothpaste.

'Yes, but . . . why did you have to have it up so loud?'

Maddy flicked on the toothbrush, which started whirring noisily, drowning out her daughter. She spat in the sink and put her toothbrush back in the holder. 'It's all yours,' she smiled. 'You having a shower?'

'Yes, but . . .'

'Toast in fifteen, then?' Maddy stepped out, sidling past her daughter, who was refusing to budge.

Emily looked momentarily confused. 'OK,' she said, then went into the bathroom and shut the door.

Maddy walked shakily back into her room and pulled on a T-shirt and a pair of sweatpants. She'd long ago become adept at changing the subject whenever Emily confronted her with one of her numerous transgressions. *Keep your centre of gravity*, Maddy had read in a parenting book that she'd been editing before she got ill. *Don't allow yourself to be buffeted by the moods of your teen.* But since her diagnosis, changing the subject had become her modus operandi. Dan had often joked that Emily had the attention span of a gnat, which, on occasions like this, definitely worked to Maddy's advantage. She wasn't one hundred per cent certain that Emily hadn't heard her being sick, but, if she had, something would have kicked off on social media and eclipsed any of her curiosity by the time she'd got dressed and come downstairs.

The parenting book didn't give any advice, though, about what to do if you suspected, but couldn't prove, that your teen was being sexually abused by your husband's boss. That was her problem, and hers alone. The thought of talking to Dan about this filled her with dread; there was no knowing how he would react. Well, there was: he'd storm straight round to Jerry's house and beat the crap out of him – that's what he'd do. And then he'd get arrested and sent to prison. He'd lose his job and, in all likelihood, his career. And then there was Emily, who'd said the previous time, 'For God's sake . . . We had an argument and it's over . . . Nothing happened,' before threatening, 'If you call the police, you'll never see me again.'

Maddy believed her. She would never forget that night, the night when Emily hadn't come home. It had been the longest night of her life. If she had to compare it, it had been worse than the night she'd spent after being told she had a terminal brain tumour. But now she had that to contend with too, and she couldn't bear the thought of losing her daughter as well. Nothing was worth the risk of that happening again.

If they never saw *him* again, that would solve the problem, Maddy mused. She wondered if there was a way to make this happen, if there was some agreement that could be made whereby he got to leave the country or something in exchange for her silence. But she immediately felt ashamed for thinking this. It would bring a conclusion for her family, maybe, but there would be other young girls to think about.

That was it. She was calling the police. She had to, of course she did. She finished dressing, then headed across the landing and down the stairs. She could hear Emily getting out of the shower now. She'd see her off to school, then get straight on the phone. But by the time she'd boiled the kettle, set her tea to brew, taken the bread out of its wrapper and popped it into the toaster, she was having second thoughts again. What would the police actually do? Would they head straight to the bank at Eastcheap, march into the office and arrest Jerry with nothing but Maddy's word to go on? Surely they'd need some evidence? Surely they'd need a statement from Emily first? Her heart leaped. Christ! What if they went to talk to her at school?

'Mum? What are you doing?'

Maddy jumped up from where she'd been leaning on the kitchen counter. 'Hi, love. Right. Toast and jam, is it?'

'Erm, yeah. Delayed reaction,' Emily said. 'I took it out of the toaster like five minutes ago.'

'Five minutes!' Maddy snorted a laugh. 'You've only just walked into the kitchen!'

'Errr . . . no,' Emily said, grabbing the toast and spreading butter over it quickly to prove her point. 'I walked into the kitchen five minutes ago. You were standing there, daydreaming as usual, which is why you didn't see me. You're never with it, Mum. You're always thinking about something else.'

Maddy reached up into the cupboard and took out the jam, passed it to her daughter, then reached for a teaspoon. 'Em . . .' she began.

Emily picked up her plate of toast and walked over to the table. She already had her earbuds in and was staring at her phone.

OK, Maddy, she sighed to herself, fetching the milk from the fridge. You're going to have to talk to her. 'Em, put your phone down, please. I need to talk you,' she said – but only in her head. She cast her mind back to the last time, to the conversation that had taken place. What was the point of even going there? Emily was only going to lie again, then make more threats about leaving home if Maddy went to the police. And then she'd tip him off, of course. He'd have plenty of time to get ready with all his excuses and reasons and alibis, and in the meantime, Emily, true to current form, would ensure that Maddy thought *she* was the unreasonable one.

Maddy watched her daughter as she sat at the table with her back to her mother, pushing a piece of toast into her mouth and scrolling up and down on her phone. She longed to stroke that mane of beautiful blonde hair, lift it up, tuck it to one side and wrap her arms around her. She longed to reassure her, tell her that they were in this together and that they'd work something out. But she knew this was unrealistic. Emily was trying to break *away* from her, not get closer. That's what all the cattiness, the arguments, the confrontations with Maddy were about. Maddy knew that it was completely natural, that Emily was still desperately attached to her mother, but was trying so hard not to be. Deep down, she was frightened of being cast out into the world to fend for herself. She needed her mother more than she would ever let on.

But Maddy *was* going to leave her, wasn't she? And then it would just be the two of them: Emily and Dan. Dan would have to keep working. Emily was going to have to grow up fast. *But not like this, not like this, not like this!*

Her head was now throbbing. Maddy bore it until Emily had left for school, then went upstairs, took a headache pill and climbed back into bed. Just for an hour, she told herself. After that, she needed to get to the hospital for her radiotherapy appointment. She'd insisted Dan go to work as normal, that she'd go through the treatment by herself. After all, it was going to be relentless; every weekday, initially, for several weeks. And now that she knew what was going on, it was doubly important to keep her illness a secret.

She took a breath and tried to relax. As much as it tore her to pieces to think about what Jerry might do to her daughter – what he might have already done – she had to think ahead to the outcome and, at the moment, all she could see in the distance was a screaming argument, threats, slamming doors and apologetic police officers shrugging their shoulders as Emily yelled at her. *For God's sake, Mum! It was nothing! It was just a hug! What the fuck have you done?*

Even if Emily broke down and admitted everything, things didn't look much brighter. The press wouldn't be allowed to publish her name, but word would get out. Rumours would spread. It would be all round her school, passed on by the parents, who were worse than the kids for gossip. And then she'd be *that* girl. For the rest of her life, whenever anyone heard Emily's name or walked past her in the street, that would be the first thing they'd think about her. She'd never be able to fully get over it. She'd never be allowed to forget.

But if it got Jerry off the streets, it had to be done, didn't it? Maddy lifted her phone from the bedside table. Her heart thumping, she propped herself up on a couple of pillows and tapped the phone icon, ready to dial. But then she paused. How long would he get? Tate had said 'up to fourteen years', but what did that actually mean?

Her heart still thumping, she opened the browser, did a search for solicitors' firms in London and found a criminal law firm in Warren Street with good reviews. She dialled the main number and asked to speak to someone who could give her some advice.

'I'll just put you through. Is this for yourself?' the receptionist asked.

'No. It's for my husband,' Maddy said. 'He's in trouble. The police want to talk to him.'

'No problem.' The phone clicked and another voice answered. It was a man. He told her his name – Stephen – and asked for Maddy's.

'Angie,' she lied.

'OK, Angie. How can I help?'

'My husband has . . . my husband is . . .' She faltered. 'Is this confidential? At the moment, I'm really just after a bit of . . . erm . . . speculative advice.'

'Totally confidential,' Stephen said. 'I'm not allowed to tell anyone what you say to me. Besides which, you don't have to tell me your surname. Let's just have a chat. Let's see if I can help.'

Maddy breathed out, reassured. 'It's my husband,' she said. 'He's been . . . he's been seeing a fourteen-year-old girl.'

'As in sleeping with her?'

'Yes.'

'He's told you this?'

'Yes,' Maddy said again, feeling a flush of shame at the thought of Dan doing such a thing, not to mention her supposed complicity. 'He wants to know if the police can prove it. And if they can, he wants to know what sentence he could get.'

'Could I talk to him?'

'He's scared to speak to anyone,' Maddy said. 'He asked me to call you just to ask a couple of questions before he hands himself in to the police.'

'OK. Well, I'm afraid I can't go into any detail with you. I'd need to speak to him. But I can give you some general guidance based on what you tell me.'

'OK. I'd appreciate that. Thanks.'

'Do the police have a statement from the girl?'

Maddy hesitated. 'No,' she said.

'Are they likely to get one?'

Maddy hesitated again. 'No, it seems she's not willing.'

'So how do the police know about this?'

'Her mother has found messages and . . . and she's seen them together and has told the police. But the girl won't give a statement. So we don't know what will happen next.'

'OK,' Stephen said. 'Well, the police can prosecute any crime without a victim statement if there is good evidence from other sources – the mother, the phone messages and suchlike. But without the victim, it would be a much weaker case. I don't think I can tell you much more than that without knowing the specific facts. And for that, I'd need to talk to your husband.'

'OK.' Maddy cleared her throat. 'I'm so sorry. I don't want to waste your time, so can I just ask . . . if he's convicted, what sentence he would get?'

'Again, it depends what he's charged with, and all the facts of the case, but if you get him to give me a call, I can go through it with him. In the meantime, if you do a search online for something called the Crown Court Sentencing Guidelines, you'll find a list of all the offences, all the aggravating and mitigating features. For sexual activity with a child of fourteen, there's a starting point of five years.'

'Five years,' Maddy repeated, falling silent.

'Yes,' Stephen said, misinterpreting the dismay in her voice and softening his own to reassure her. 'But, of course, he'd only serve half. If he got five years, he'd be out in two and a half.'

Maddy went cold. Two and a half years. Was that all? Her head started to buzz. She vaguely remembered thanking Stephen and the conversation must have ended there, but her mind had already jogged on ahead two and a half years to the moment when Jerry walked out of prison and back into Emily's life again. A life with *him* in it, but no Maddy – the thought was horrific. But that was the reality. She'd almost certainly no longer be there.

Or would she? She might survive longer than predicted. But what kind of life would it be? She felt hot tears creep into the corners of her eyes and roll down her cheeks at the memory of her mother. Maddy couldn't think of her without being reminded of the indignity and pain she'd suffered in her final months. She imagined spending another year – another two – feeling the way she was feeling right now, with this low, dull, sometimes unbearable pain coursing through her head. The nausea, the throwing up, the brain fog. And it could get worse, much worse. Early-onset vascular dementia was common with her type of tumour, as was paralysis. She could become bed-bound, useless, a burden, her life reduced to nothing but rounds of chemotherapy. And how long could she hide it from Emily? Not for long. The reality was that it could be a slow, upsetting deterioration. She could use up the best years of Emily's life.

Maddy forced herself to slow her breathing and swiped her phone to check the exact time of her hospital appointment, but as she did so, her phone slipped out of her hand and dropped to the floor. She leaned down to pick it up and felt a sudden, shooting pain down the back of her head. She screamed out loud and fell sideways onto the bed, clutching her head in her palms and drawing her knees up to her chest. She stayed like that, massaging the back of her skull, until the pain abated a little, then reached out and tugged the duvet back over her. *I can't take this any more,* she told herself, knowing deep in her core that this was true. *I just can't take any more of this. What the hell am I going to do?*

And then, like a wish from a genie, it came to her. She felt goosebumps as the idea slowly dawned on her. There *was* a way. She didn't have to be a burden – or a victim. She still had control over her own destiny. She wasn't yet at the stage her mother had got to, when it was already too late, when it had all been taken out of her hands. Her spirits lifted instantly; there was hope. She knew she could survive another day, another week, another month or more of this pain so long as she got to be in the driving seat, the one in control. She punched the pillow hard with all the strength she could muster. *Thump.* Fuck the tumour. *Thump*. And fuck *him* too! She was going to survive a little longer, but on *her* terms – not theirs.

She took a deep breath, in and out, and let her shoulders drop, feeling the enormous flood of relief and clarity that comes with having made a momentous, life-changing decision, like the decision to leave a job you hate, or an unhappy marriage. It was the feeling she'd had after she and Dan had decided to stop trying for a second baby, immediately releasing themselves from the perpetual cycle of hope and anguish that had taken over their lives. It was that *knowing* in your heart of hearts – because of the way you feel after you've made it – that the decision is not just the right one; it's the only one.

In a moment, she was going to take another headache pill and then she was going to rest, truly rest, for a while. And then she was going to get up and get herself to her radiotherapy appointment. Her treatment would shrink the tumour, keep things at bay for a little while. She had time. She would have long enough for what she wanted to do.

40

Maddy slept for an hour – a deep, dreamless sleep. At midnight, her phone under her pillow vibrated and nudged her awake. After a moment of confusion, she remembered why she'd woken and sat up, focused now. She pushed back the covers, padded down the landing and crept into her daughter's bedroom. She looked at the bed, searching in the darkness for the body-shaped lump under the duvet. She listened for the sound of Emily's breathing, just as she had done so many times before. As her eyes adjusted to the darkness, she scanned the floor to make sure that there was nothing in her path – a stray gym bag or a trainer she could trip over – then she tiptoed to the window and rolled back the blind to let in a little light. Maddy knew from experience that this wouldn't disturb her daughter, that it would take a hurricane or an earthquake to wake Emily within the first few hours of the night. In the morning, too, it had been hard to rouse her at times. There had been more arguments than Maddy cared to remember about Emily still being in bed fifteen minutes before she was due to leave for school.

But for once, she was really grateful that her daughter was such a sound sleeper. The biggest issue for Maddy right now was her poor coordination, which could quite literally trip her up. She had to go carefully, slowly, and think through every step, tell her muscles what to do and give them time to react. She moved slowly back towards the bed, her heart thumping and her fingers trembling a little as she reached for her daughter's phone. It was face down, on charge, on the bedside table as usual. Maddy picked it up, pulled out the cable and switched it on, then glanced across at Emily, whose head was tilted back on the pillow, her mouth gaping slightly, her forehead furrowed as though in concentration, as if she were watching a movie and trying to make sense of the plot.

Maddy hovered in the half-light, leaning forward, making sure to keep her balance, and held the phone out towards Emily's upturned hand. She inched the phone gently forward until it was touching Emily's fingertip. A second later, she felt a small nudge and the phone lit up. Yes! Her heart skipped a beat. She'd done it. She was in.

She turned the phone round to face her and was instantly unsettled. Emily's home page was a photo of her and Rosie, arm in arm, their tongues pushed out playfully towards the person behind the camera. Emily was wearing her new bikini and in the background Maddy recognised the lido, the open-air swimming pool at Parliament Hill. Maddy had taken her there that day; she'd trusted her. She hadn't pressed her as to who else would be there. *It's just the usual crowd, Mum. You don't have to ask me every time.* But who was that behind the camera, getting a good eyeful of her daughter's beautiful, slim, semi-naked body and that of her shorter, fuller-figured friend?

The thought made her stomach turn. Keeping her thumb on the phone screen, she tiptoed back over towards the window, where she lowered the blind before stepping carefully out of the door. She crept downstairs and into the kitchen, where she sat at the counter and pulled open her laptop. She now had access to the stored passwords to all of Emily's social media accounts. Even without the phone nearby, she would have access to the web-based message logs. She opened the messaging app's web page in her browser, tapped the matching icon on Emily's home page, selected 'link a device' from the three-button menu in the top right-hand corner and, when the camera appeared, pointed the phone up to the QR code displayed on the web browser page.

She waited as Emily's messages loaded. And there he was: the red heart. Right at the top, her top caller, her most frequent contact, above Rosie even. Maddy wanted to weep as she scrolled up through the weeks and months of messages, through the jokes, the banter, the flirting that made it patently obvious they were far more to each other than was natural, that there was nothing innocent about the hug outside the van. The texts were the stuff of a romantic relationship that was heading towards intimacy but – Maddy realised, with enormous relief – still didn't appear to have got there. He was still trying, oh so hard: showering her with praise and adoration, doing her bidding, picking her up and taking her places, buying her food, sweets and alcohol. He was the perfect listener, never passing judgement, only occasionally offering the odd snippet of helpful advice during her many tales of woe about all the shit (as she referred to it) in her life.

Maddy skimmed over those messages, not wanting to be hurt by anything said about her by her daughter in a moment of anger. Instead, she focused on the sexual references. I'm sorry. We don't have to do anything. Not until you're ready. And then, in the next breath: You're just so beautiful, so amazing, so gorgeous, it's so hard to keep my hands off you. Can you understand that? I want you so badly, Em. You're all I think about from first thing in the morning until I go to sleep at night.

These were the messages that Maddy zoomed in on, the ones that lit and stoked the fire inside her, the ones that strengthened her resolve to go through with this, no matter what. Before this, she'd just had the things she'd been told about him coupled with a hug captured on camera and a handful of messages. But now she could see it for herself: the unnatural obsession, the lust, the sickening urges. And the betrayal of his relationship with Dan to get to her. It was all there on her computer screen.

Maddy had never wanted to harm anyone before. She'd always been so level-headed, so law-abiding, so reasonable and forgiving. Hatred was anathema to her; she'd never seen the point in such a negative emotion. But now she did. She felt the anger rising within her as, mentally, she launched herself at him, grabbing fistfuls of his hair, gouging at his cheeks with her fingernails. The feeling was electric. She now understood the power of vengeance and the energy it gave.

But she also knew that this fire inside her was going to burn her, too, if she let it. She needed to find a way to separate and switch off her emotions so that she could plan this thing, but at the same time look at her daughter and feel nothing but love in the treasured moments they had left together. She needed to be detached, forensic about it, like a career thief planning a heist or . . . or a novelist or screenwriter writing a story. Her heart flipped. That was it.

It was the only way for her to get through it. This would be her story, the one she'd always wanted to write.

41

Maddy phoned me two days later and asked me to meet her at the hospital. I was in the office when my mobile rang and her name flashed up.

'I have a plan,' she said. 'Come and meet me. Tell them you're not well, that you need to go to the hospital. Then come to UCH. That's where I am. Meet me in the radiotherapy unit.'

I did a quick Google search for *low blood pressure fainting serious*, then walked over to Hayley's desk and told her that a cancellation appointment had come up at UCH for treatment I'd been waiting for and that I needed to get there straight away.

'God. It sounds serious.' She frowned. 'I thought you'd just fainted?'

'It's all to do with my blood pressure,' I said. 'They did tests. They think it's my heart.'

'God,' said Hayley again. She eyed me with genuine concern. 'I hope you're OK?'

'I have a hole in my heart,' I lied. 'I was born with it.' There had been a girl at school who had been born with a hole in her heart. She'd very occasionally skipped school for treatment, but otherwise didn't really seem to have any problems, so it seemed like a credible condition for me to adopt.

'Oh my gosh,' Hayley said. 'I'm sorry. Do you have a pacemaker?'

'Not yet,' I said. 'But they might be giving me one.'

That didn't sound particularly credible, and I immediately wished I hadn't said it, but Hayley didn't seem to notice. 'We should do a health and safety risk assessment,' she said.

'Sure,' I agreed. 'But if I'm going to make the appointment, I just need to . . .' I nodded towards the door '. . . go. If that's OK?'

'Of course,' she said. 'I'll let Dan know.'

I booked a cab as I walked to the lift and it turned up quickly and took me to the hospital, where Maddy was waiting for me on a bench in the foyer of the oncology centre, looking pale and drained but somehow uplifted at the same time. I bought sweet chai teas and two cinnamon buns from the hospital café and we went out and sat on a bench in a small courtyard under an ornamental willow tree, sipping from the cardboard cups and licking sugar from our lips while Maddy told me what she had in mind.

I thought it was a joke at first, because she seemed so upbeat.

'It's the perfect building,' she said. 'Not only does he work there – he's got an office with a sofa and a fridge and everything, so it's the obvious place. But it's a hundred metres high. Three hundred feet. That's just about optimal, apparently. It's pretty much the perfect height.'

'The perfect height for . . . ?' I began warily.

'It's the optimal height,' she said matter-of-factly, blowing over the rim of her paper cup, 'if you want a guarantee that you won't survive the fall, but at the same time you don't want too much time to think about it on the way down.'

A lump formed in my throat. It was as though she was talking me through the plot of a TV thriller rather than something that was actually going to happen in real life. But I quickly realised that she was serious, that she had been thinking of nothing else since I'd seen her last.

'Maddy,' I whispered. 'You don't mean this. This isn't right. There must be another way.'

'No.' She was gentle, but firm. 'There *is* no other way, Tate. I've been over it and over it in my head. And I'm going to die sooner or later anyway.'

'You might have years left yet,' I said. 'You might be OK.'

'Tate . . .' She shook her head and – after a moment's hesitation – reached out and took my hand. 'I'm in pain so much of the time.'

'But that's just the treatment, isn't it? It will be over soon.'

'No. There's only so much treatment you can have. It's only delaying the inevitable. It's no way to live. And it's only going to get worse.'

'But Emily wouldn't want this.'

'You're right. She wouldn't. But she's going to lose me anyway. I'm her mother and I know what's best for her; it's my job to look out for her. Trust me, there's no other way of doing this that is going to end with my daughter being able to grieve like a normal person and then get on with the rest of her life.'

'So, your life for hers,' I said.

'Yes,' she agreed. 'But my life is no life. So for me, it's a no-brainer.' A pause. 'I'm sorry, but we don't have to be down-hearted. This way, I get to have control over my own destiny. And I now have a purpose. My life won't have been for nothing. I still get to leave my mark on the world.'

'I do get that,' I said.

'So will you hear me out?'

I nodded again and listened while she told me her idea for 'our script', as she kept calling it. It was just an outline, she said. She needed my help – mine and Helen's – to write, rehearse and perform it. It would be the most important story we'd ever write, she told me, and between the three of us we could fine-tune it to the point of perfection to ensure that nothing could go wrong.

I called another cab, took her home and helped her into bed. She was silent on the way back, closing her eyes and breathing deeply. I could tell she was in pain, but she looked peaceful. Happier than I'd ever seen her, in fact.

I thought about it for two days, mulling it over. It was grim, but it was a solution. It was the potential sentence that convinced me in the end. Two and a half years! This was not justice for Emily, nor for what Jerry had done to me and to Helen – and to who knew how many other girls after that. He was a serial abuser. He was evil. He needed to be stopped. But what if we talked Emily into going to court and giving evidence against him and then he called her a liar – and a jury believed him? Maddy was right. The thought of destroying Emily's spirit, her life, her reputation, only to see him walk free at the end of it all, was just too horrific to bear.

After work on the Friday, Helen and I picked up Margheritas and grissini sticks from Pizza Union in King's Cross and drove to Maddy's. Dan had left that afternoon for a conference in Paris, and Emily was staying the night at Rosie's, so we had the house to ourselves. We arranged ourselves at the kitchen table with plates of pizza, notepaper and pens. Maddy had her laptop open in front of her and had created a document entitled '*A Mother's Love* : WIP. First Draft'.

Helen was on board, but nervous. 'What if we get caught?' she asked.

I said, 'We'll just have to make sure that we don't.'

'But what if we do?'

'Look. Right now, we're just writing a story. A script,' Maddy said. 'It could be pure fiction. And honestly, you don't have to be involved in any more than that. You don't have to do anything you don't want to do.'

'And what about Tate?'

'She doesn't have to do anything either.'

'Well, I will,' I said resolutely. 'I'll do anything you need.'

Maddy shot me a look of gratitude.

'Don't worry, Hel,' I said. 'You can have a bit part. A minor role. Maddy and I will star.'

Maddy gave me another warm smile and we settled down to write. Helen's only role, for now, we decided, would be to continue to keep Emily under surveillance. This was at Maddy's request and there was nothing illegal about it. After all, she'd be acting in the prevention of a crime. And of the three of us, she was best placed to do this; Emily didn't yet know her, or my car, and Helen's job gave her enough flexibility to get away from work at the end of the school day. Whenever there was a plan for her and Jerry to be alone together, we would conspire to ensure that something would happen to prevent it. Something or other would crop up to bring Emily home early or, alternatively, to prevent her from going out in the first place. This was a benefit, not a threat, we figured. The frustration he'd feel at this – the wait for his prize – would only serve to ensure that, when the time came, he'd be sufficiently hooked.

'Any sign of her getting into a vehicle with him or otherwise being alone with him, you call me. I'll make sure they're interrupted,' Maddy told us.

'What about Dan?' I asked.

Maddy's fingers continued to tap the keyboard.

'What if he finds out?'

'How's he going to find out?'

'I don't know,' I said. 'Maybe because Hayley watches my every move. I'm sure she thinks I've got the hots for him.'

Maddy stopped typing and looked up at me, intrigued. 'Does she?'

'Well, yeah. I mean, first she sees me lurking in your garden. And then the next day she sees me go into his office. I'm not sure if she noticed his diary and the photo were gone, but she doesn't miss very much.'

Maddy snorted. 'Sounds like *she's* the one who has the hots for him.'

'I know, right?'

'OK,' Maddy said, nodding sagely. 'So, let's use it. Let's make it work for us.'

When I looked baffled, she said, 'I've edited enough books to know that every potential threat to the plot is an opportunity in disguise.'

'Plot.' Helen shivered and shook her head.

'What?' I smiled.

'Well, it sounds so . . . *Macbeth*. Like we're the Three Witches.'

I grinned. 'Fair is foul and foul is fair.'

Maddy chuckled.

'So, when shall we three meet again?' I said.

'Tuesday? Upon the heath?' Maddy quipped back.

'A bit cold,' I said. 'How about my place? Or Helen's – Clare Henry's. That would be perfect. Nobody will come looking for any of us there.'

Helen looked uncomfortable.

'Are you not OK with this, Hel?' I asked her gently.

She sighed. 'I just . . .' She looked from me to Maddy and back again. 'I want to do it. I really want to stop him from hurting Emily. From hurting anyone ever again.'

'But?'

'It's not just a script, is it? It's a . . . a conspiracy. To . . . to commit a crime. If we get caught, we could go to prison for a very long time.'

'We won't,' said Maddy. 'Between us, we'll make sure of it. That's why I need your help.'

In order to conceal her illness, Maddy had taken a sabbatical 'to work on a creative idea'. 'I've realised that if I don't do it now, I never will,' she'd told her employer, which was entirely true.

We wrote together, any opportunity we got. Pretending to everyone at the office that they were my own, I went with Maddy to her hospital appointments, or met her there with Helen after we'd both finished work. The ideas kept coming, the obstacles got raised, the plot holes got addressed. We found that any obstacle is better dealt with head-on; better to bring it out into the open and throw the ideas around until you find a solution. We discovered that there's always an answer if you open your mind wide enough.

Helen's apprehension was soon outweighed by her love of the creative process. She turned out to be an excellent researcher, looking into the legal and medical aspects. That the tumour would show up on the medical records was a problem, she said, and we spent an entire week discussing this. We knew the direction we were going, the objective we wanted to achieve, and we never lost sight of that. Maddy didn't want to waste a single moment and even when she was drained from the radiation and sick from the chemo, we would collect her in the car and take her to Helen's flat, where we would work late into the night. Maddy would doze on the couch whenever she needed to. I would look up as she fell silent, then pull her laptop round to face me and take over the typing. She would occasionally stir and prop herself up on the cushions to chip in with ideas or directions before drifting back off again.

At the office, I watched Jerry, observed his habits, his routines, who came in and out of his room. In late November, I managed to invite myself along to an evening in the bar with

Hayley and some of the other secretaries, where I made sure to sit strategically facing him, clocking the cigarettes he went outside for and watching what and how much he drank. On a Saturday in early December, we had our dress rehearsal, only I played Maddy's part for her. I went in through the entrance in the basement car park, letting myself in through the gate wearing Dan's coat, with Dan's pass, bypassing the cameras in the lift by heading past the gym and up the stairwell and onto the roof. Meanwhile, Helen hovered near the entrance, peering through the glass, ready to enter the minute that Kevin, the weekend security guard, stepped out into the foyer. But he remained in his office the whole time, watching *Strictly* with his feet up on the desk and a giant bag of popcorn in his lap.

The preparation took us a little over two months. Soon it would be the evening of the office Christmas party.

We were ready. It was time.

PART SIX

42

Friday, 9 December

I weaved my way through the crowded room towards the glass door that led out on to the terrace. Spirits were high and the Christmas karaoke was in full swing. Dan and Hayley had just done a not-too-shoddy Elton John and Kiki Dee. Now, *he* was up, singing an Elvis number, pulling open his shirt buttons and gyrating his hips. He could sing, all right. He still had that voice, the one that had melted my heart all those years ago. He still had the floppy fringe and the big brown eyes that had held mine as if they would never let me go. But it had all been an act, just like this one, and I cringed as I watched him. He'd no doubt only picked an Elvis song as an excuse to bare his chest and thrust his groin at the female interns. It made me feel sick.

On the other hand, it was just what I needed. I'd hovered nearby, watching, waiting for my moment as he chugged Chablis straight from the bottle – his 'big man' thing, his way of telling everyone that he was the CEO of the bank and that expensive wine was just like water to someone as successful as him. As Dan and Hayley each sang their last 'I won't go breaking your heart' and handed back their microphones to the compère, he started his warm-up, flexing his shoulders and rotating his neck. He set the bottle down on a nearby table, then stepped into the spotlight, grabbing the microphone from its stand. The bar was crowded, all eyes were on him and his lewd performance, the male associates guffawing and doubling up with laughter, the females grinning politely but no doubt wanting to knee him hard in the groin. Nobody noticed as I moved in on the bottle, lifting it swiftly from the table and drawing it up into the bell sleeve of my green silk maxi dress, where I concealed it quickly, my hand encased in a super-clear vinyl glove.

As I reached the door, I spotted several people from my department congregating in the smoking area outside. I stopped short and crept back into the shadows behind the coats at the corner of the bar. When I was sure no one was looking in my direction, I went outside into the cold night air and round the corner, where, carefully clutching the bottle, I climbed up the narrow fire escape to the upper level of the roof terrace. When I got to the top, I set the bottle down for a moment and caught my breath.

The view was better here, but nobody ever came up this far. There was no heat, little lighting and no seating, and the fire escape was narrow and awkward to climb. I picked up the bottle again and moved nearer to the wall, trying not to think about the sheer drop beyond the railing, plunging down to the street below. I felt my knees weaken, but drew closer to the edge until I reached the railing that bordered the building. Holding it tight, I bent down behind one of the angled skylights and tucked the bottle through a gap between the skylight and the wall.

I took off my vinyl glove and pushed it into my handbag,

which was strapped across my body, then headed back down the fire escape to the terrace below. The group of associates from my department had dispersed and gone back inside. I moved into the smoking area and sat down at a table under the awning. It was pleasantly lit, with pretty lights strung along a trellis and a tall outdoor kerosene patio heater shaped like a Christmas tree, which let out a warm amber glow. After a short while, two secretaries from the eighteenth came out, wobbling in their high heels and shivering in their thin party dresses. They smiled at me and lit their cigarettes, spoke in hushed tones while they smoked them, then left.

A few more people came and went. Eventually, he came. Jerry. He was drunk and sweating, his shirt buttons still open. He stuck a cigarette in his mouth and flicked his lighter, lifted an arm and wiped his forehead with a rolled-up sleeve. He spotted me and eyed me curiously for a moment. I could tell he was trying to remember who I was.

'Want one?' he offered, swaying a little.

I shook my head. 'Just put one out.'

'So . . . who are you?' he asked, scowling.

'Tate,' I told him.

'Pardon?' he said rudely, loudly.

'My name's Tate.'

'Kate?'

'Tate,' I repeated. 'With a T.' I moistened my lips. 'Tee,' I said again, and watched his face as I enunciated the letter, unable to resist seeing if it lit a spark of recognition. But my name meant nothing. *I* had meant nothing.

'*Tate?*' he sneered.

317

'Yes.'

'Do you have a gallery?' he asked, then snorted happily.

'Funny,' I said, without smiling.

'I'd like to see it,' he grinned.

'Would you?' I stood up.

He looked a little taken aback.

I gave him my most salacious pout, took the hem of my skirt between my thumb and forefinger and slid it up my leg a little before stopping. Back down I went. Up again. Would I? Wouldn't I? But I wasn't smiling. I wasn't friendly.

'I know your sort,' he said, sounding frightened.

'My sort?'

'Prick-tease.'

No personal pronouns. He was very drunk.

'Oh,' I said. 'So, I'm a tease?'

'Yeah.'

'And you're a prick.' This time I was smiling.

His jaw dropped. He glared at me for a moment, then took one last drag of his cigarette and dropped it on the ground.

'You're history,' he tried to say, but it came out as 'ristry'. He turned round and headed back through the glass door into the bar.

When I was certain he'd gone, I took a fresh vinyl glove out of the packet in my handbag. I pulled it on, then leaned down and picked up the cigarette butt with a finger and thumb and folded it into my palm. I climbed back up the fire escape and onto the roof with it and dropped it onto the ground with two others. I had enough now, I figured. All had gone smoothly. My evening's work was done.

43

It was pitch-black outside her living-room window, but it wasn't time yet. Maddy swallowed a couple of headache pills, then lay back on the sofa and dozed lightly for a while. When she woke, the pressure inside her skull had eased a little, but had been replaced by a lingering sadness. She knew this was to be expected, but she also didn't doubt herself for a second. All the planning, all the preparation that had gone into this moment had given her plenty of opportunity for reflection and, honestly, she was ready. She felt ready. Everything was coming together. She just needed to stay strong.

She pushed her hand under the cushion behind her head and pulled out Emily's phone. She'd bought a new Samsung and a supermarket SIM card, one that wouldn't activate, at least not without money. The plan had been to swap the SIM out for Emily's and for Maddy to use the new phone. But she no longer needed to do this, and it was better this way; in the end, it had all happened so organically, so perfectly. Not that she'd enjoyed seeing her husband and daughter fighting, but when Dan had grounded Emily and confiscated her phone, Maddy had felt a sense of ease about all of it, that it was all happening the way it was meant to. Emily's phone could simply go missing from the kitchen cabinet where Dan had put it. Most importantly, at the crucial time, both Emily and Dan would be safely at home.

After Dan had left for the office party, Maddy had gone upstairs to comfort her crying daughter. The argument with Dan had been over something trivial – Emily's attitude, her lippiness – which would all be forgotten in twenty-four hours' time. Emily would need her father more than ever, but in the meantime, this was Maddy's chance to be there for her. She'd taken up some hot chocolate, tapped on the door, and asked if she could come in.

'I hate him,' Emily had moaned, lying on her bed and wiping her tear-and-kohl-streaked eyes. 'He's the worst father in the world.'

Maddy had placed the cocoa on the bedside table and sat down next to her.

'He loves you, Em.'

'Well, he's got a funny way of showing it.'

'You'll understand when you have your own children,' Maddy said, but the thought of Emily's children unexpectedly made her cry.

'Mum!' Emily had looked startled then, and sat up, wrapping her arms around her mother. 'Don't cry, Mum,' she'd said. 'It's all right. Me and Dad will be OK.'

'I know. I know you will.' Maddy wiped away her tears and kissed her daughter. She hadn't intended for Emily to wind up comforting her, but she'd been glad of the opportunity to hold her in her arms, to stroke her hair, without giving anything away. 'You're growing up, Em,' she'd said, 'and that's hard for your dad, because in his head you'll always be his little girl. That may seem annoying now, but one day you'll look back and treasure it. Never forget that he loves you and will never stop loving you, no matter what. And neither will I.'

'What's it like when you have children?' Emily had asked her. 'Do you love them as much as you love your parents?'

'Oh, Em.' Maddy had wanted to laugh. 'It's a love like no other. I can't begin to tell you. You love them more.'

'I can't imagine loving anyone more than I love my parents,' Emily had said matter-of-factly, and Maddy's heart had swelled and broken and swelled again.

They'd lain back on Emily's bed then, playing games.

'Which four famous people would you invite to dinner?' Maddy had asked.

Emily had replied confidently, 'Marcus Aurelius, Rosa Parks, Greta Thunberg and Adolf Hitler.'

'Adolf Hitler!' Maddy had gasped. 'Why Adolf Hitler?'

'So that I could ask him *why*,' Emily said, 'and then me and the others would change his mind and change history and save the lives of all those millions of poor Jews.'

'And what if he wouldn't listen?'

'Then he wouldn't get a very nice pudding, would he?'

Emily had said this in a clipped, sinister, upper-class English voice, like a 1940s movie villain. She'd done it so perfectly that Maddy had laughed out loud. She told Emily what a good actress she was and Emily had asked, 'Do you really think so?' and Maddy had said that she really did. Emily had looked pleased and said, shyly, that she'd thought about joining the school drama club, but she didn't know if she was any good. Maddy had said that she really was, insisting that she wouldn't have said it if she didn't mean it, and Emily had looked even more pleased and said that maybe she would give it a go.

Maddy fought back tears now, as she thought about her amazing daughter, about everything that she already was, and everything she could yet be. She was doing this for Emily – and not just Emily. She was doing it for who knew how many other young girls Jerry had already harmed or would go on to harm in the future. In the next twenty-four hours, things would begin rolling towards their conclusion. Before too long, Emily would be free to live the life she'd been destined to live and Maddy would be able to rest in peace, knowing that she'd played her part, setting things in motion, all ready for Tate to take the next step. So long as she got this next bit right, they had him, she was certain of it. It would bring closure for her, for Tate, for Helen, for Emily – an end to all the hurt, all the pain.

She checked the time on the phone. Midnight. Emily would be asleep by now. Maddy swung her legs off the sofa and tip-toed upstairs, turned the door handle to Emily's room and crept inside. As she'd done last time, she carefully stepped over to the window and rolled up the blind to let in a little light. She moved towards the bed again. Emily was on her back, her mouth ajar, her hair cascading over the pillow and framing her face like a halo. Maddy took in her daughter's beautiful features: the long, thick lashes, the upturned nose, the gentle ridges that led from her nostrils to her bow-shaped upper lip, her soft, velvety cheek with its youthful, unblemished skin. Hot, silent tears came then. She ached and ached to lean forward and plant a kiss on that cheek, the cheek that she'd nuzzled her face into when Emily was a baby.

Instead, she held the phone out and, for the final time, found her way in.

44

Saturday, 10 December

So, this was the day. It had begun like any other December day with a slight frost, iced-over rainwater in the buckets by the greenhouse, crows on the lawn pecking at the last of the autumn apples that nobody had bothered to pick this year. For weeks, Maddy had watched them slowly ripen, then, one by one, drop from the tree to the ground. There were hundreds of them. Normally Dan would have picked them up and whacked them into the bushes with a tennis racket. This year he hadn't bothered to do that either, but Maddy thought they looked beautiful, like a crochet blanket or a vast ball pit of red, gold and yellow stretching across one whole corner of the garden and reflecting the light of the bright winter sun.

Now, it was mid-afternoon and the light was fading. Maddy was sitting in her favourite chair by the patio doors in the kitchen, listening intently to the argument that Dan and Emily were having on the landing upstairs.

'I haven't got it!' Emily was yelling. 'You took it off me.'

'Yes,' said Dan. 'And now it's not where I left it!'

'I haven't got it!' Emily pleaded. 'I don't know how many times you want me to say it.'

'Well, where is it, then?'

'I don't know!'

A pause.

'If you've lost it—'

'I haven't lost it. Why would I have lost it?'

'I don't know.' Emily's voice was sullen. 'But you were the last one to have it. Maybe you took it with you when you went out last night.'

Another pause.

'You owe me a phone, Dad.'

'I'll try ringing it.'

'It won't ring. I left it on silent.'

'Emily, if you've got it and you're lying to me—'

'Oh my God! First you ground me for no reason and now this. I swear, it's like every day you're deliberately trying to start an argument.'

A laugh. Dan's voice saying, 'Ring, ring. Yes? Hello, Mr Kettle. It's the pot here. You're black!'

'Oh, shut up, Dad. You're not funny. And where are you phoning from? The twentieth century?'

'Pardon?'

'Phones don't go "ring, ring" any more. You're such a fucking dinosaur.'

'Stop swearing, Em. You're always swearing.' Dan sounded tired.

'And you're always being a fucking idiot.'

'I mean it. Stop.'

'What are you going to do? You can't ground me if I'm already grounded!'

'Don't push me, Em. If you swear one more time . . .'

'I'm already a prisoner in this house! I might as well actually do something to deserve being locked up!'

The sound of a door slamming. Silence. Dan's feet on the stairs.

'I don't think she's got it,' he said, coming into the kitchen and scratching his head. 'But it's really odd.'

'It will turn up.' Maddy turned her head towards the window to the garden.

Dan walked over and crouched down in front of her, wrapped his arms around her and held her tight.

Maddy looked out over his shoulder at the fading light and remembered how much they'd loved this garden. In the summer, when Emily was small, there had been a paddling pool under the apple trees. She could see it now: Emily splashing and jumping in and out of the water, Dan standing on the patio with an apron on, tending to the barbeque. She could feel the summer heat on her shoulders and arms as she sat on the lounger, calling to Emily to come to her, a bottle of sun cream in one hand and an open book on her knee.

They were good memories. Ones to treasure. The three of them together, happy. Memories for Dan and Emily to hold on to.

She felt for the phone in her pocket, curling her fingers around it. 'Need the toilet,' she murmured.

Dan abruptly let go of her, anticipating a bout of sickness.

She gave him a gentle smile and walked out of the kitchen

and into the downstairs cloakroom, bolting the door behind her and pulling down the toilet lid. As she lowered herself onto the seat, she slid the phone out of her pocket and switched it on. She took a breath. It was time, right? And Emily and Dan had set the mood so perfectly. Why not stay with that feeling and run with it? Sink into it, feel it. Become Emily.

Maddy tapped in the new passcode she'd created the previous night when she'd turned off the phone's location services and changed the security settings. She opened the messaging app and brought up the latest message from Emily. Jerry hadn't yet responded, which was a little perturbing; he was normally as keen as mustard. But there had been the office party last night and he had no doubt been hungover all day. He'd be in debt to his wife and trying to play the good husband. But he'd be low in mood, too, and now in need of a pickup, perhaps?

Slowly, her fingers shaking, she began to type. Please can you come and get me, my dad is doing my head in. Can't take it anymore. Got to get out of here.

And . . . send. Maddy drew in a sharp breath and waited. Within moments she could see the ellipsis moving and the word *typing*. And then came the reply. Hold tight, baby. Today's not the best. I'll get some time off tomorrow.

Maddy breathed in and out, then typed: I can't wait until tomorrow. If I don't get out of here then somethings going to happen.

The reply was swift. What do you mean?

You said you loved me, Maddy typed.

I do, baby, the message came back. You know I do.

So why cant we just go somewhere?

It's not that simple.

It can be if you want it to be.

Em, you're scaring me.

Well, I'm not scared.

A pause. Don't do anything hasty. Think about it.

Maddy typed: You said we could go somewhere where no one knows us.

When you're sixteen, I said. When no one can stop us.

Cant wait till then.

'Mads?' Dan's voice came through the door. 'You all right in there?'

Maddy turned the phone off and pushed it into her pocket. She stood up and pressed the flush to the toilet, washed her hands and opened the door.

'You OK, love?' Dan asked.

She nodded. 'Yes. I think I'll just go upstairs and lie down for a bit.'

Upstairs, Maddy crawled into bed, fully clothed, and took the phone out of her pocket again. There were two more messages. Em, wait. I can get out in an hour or so. I'll phone you then. OK? And when she hadn't replied: Please tell me you're not going to do anything rash.

Maddy waited, counting the minutes as she put herself in Emily's position mentally, packed herself a bag and climbed out of the bedroom window onto the porch outside. In her head, she dropped to the ground and jogged to the end of the street and round the corner, then out onto Upper Street and down to the Green. The number 43 bus would be waiting. Two minutes to board it. She looked at the phone.

Please don't blank me. Let's talk about this.

Maddy shifted onto her side so that she was facing the wall. I've left, she typed. I've done it. I don't have any money. Can you book me a hotel?

A slight delay and then, Where are you?

Maddy typed. On a bus.

Which bus?

Tell me the name of the hotel and I'll go there.

He replied, I cant book a hotel with a credit card, baby. It will leave a trail.

I need somewhere to stay, Maddy typed. I'm not going home.

I can meet you with the van in an hour.

I'm not sleeping in the van, she told him. I need somewhere proper. Why can't we get a hotel together. You can pay with cash.

A pause. Together?

Yeah. If you like.

Maddy imagined his face as he read this. The dark, filthy thoughts that would run through his mind.

You sure bout this? came his reply, a moment later.

Maddy took a breath. Yeah. I'm sure.

Another pause. Maddy could almost feel his excitement.

And then, as she'd expected. We cant go to a hotel, baby. You're 15, I'm 48. It just wouldn't look right.

Brilliant, Maddy thought to herself. Bloody brilliant. Not only had she steered him in the right direction, but his self-acknowledged perversion was there on the phone in black and white.

Your office, then. Just for tonight. You told me you have a sofa and a fridge and everything. We can go there. Maddy waited nervously now, anticipating his objections, feeling his dilemma. His office: it would be the ultimate prize. He could persuade her to let him fuck her on his desk and then he could think about it with a grin on his face every single day after that.

I'm not sure, baby, came his reply. It's a bit risky. But he wanted it, of course he did.

You don't have to do anything. I've got my dad's security pass. I know how to get in, Maddy typed.

What are you doing with his security pass?!!

I took it so I could stay at the office if I couldn't get hold of you. I'll let myself in through the car park entrance. No one needs to know.

There are cameras, Em. Security!

I'm wearing Dad's coat. I'll put the hood up. Maddy took a long, deep breath. I'm going there. You can come or not, it's up to you.

She switched the phone off then, pushed it under her pillow and closed her eyes. She lay still for a moment, imagining his reaction as he figured out his next move. Soon, she'd get up, she'd say goodbye to this room, to this house, to her husband. She'd make her excuse and then she'd go to her darling daughter and say her goodbyes for the very last time. A tear slid out of her eye but she quickly wiped it away. There was no time for sentimentality. Sentimentality wouldn't lock that filthy bastard up for life. She was going to die anyway. This way, it would be over quickly and the pain would be fleeting, finite, far more bearable than the relentless drip, drip, drip of pain and discomfort that was eating away at her now.

For the millionth time, she saw herself falling. She'd dreamed about it, but she never felt the landing. There was never a landing. There was just the wonderful release, the sensation of floating away into the air, carried on a breeze up into the sky and out through space, where she would soon be at one with the universe. She'd get to see her parents again; the thought was uplifting. And Dan and Em, in turn, would join her when their lives had been lived and their time had come. There would be a family reunion to look forward to in the future, she really believed that. There was nothing to be sorry about. It would all be worthwhile. She just had to do this first. It would be her final gift to Emily and Dan.

There was a small vibration from underneath the pillow, which made her jump, then she remembered: the burner phone. She pulled it out and read the message. Hey. How's it going?

She replied, All good. I think I've caught him!

Really?

Tell you in a minute.

She pulled out Emily's phone, checked it. There was a string of messages, telling her how to get into the office building without anyone from security seeing her, how to avoid the cameras on the way up. He seemed desperate. Maddy read through them, skimming them until she got to the last one. She smiled to herself as she read it.

I'll meet you there as soon as I can.

45

I pause for breath, take a sip of my drink. I finished the wine ages ago, and Sarah and I are both drinking tap water from the jug on the table. I've been too engrossed in my story and Sarah has been listening too intently for either of us to want to stop and call the waiter over. Now Sarah picks up the water jug and tops up my glass.

'So the plan was to get Jerry onto the roof terrace, where Maddy would then throw herself off it and fall to her death, but make it look as though Jerry was responsible. So, framing him for her murder instead? Am I right?'

I nod.

'And the injury to her head? It was from the bottle you left there?'

'She was meant to scratch him,' I say. 'To get his DNA underneath her fingernails. My idea was to put the bottle there for the police to find, along with the cigarette butts . . .'

'To put him firmly on the rooftop.'

'Exactly. In case he tried to say afterwards that they'd had their tussle somewhere else in the building, that he'd never been on the roof with her. That he had had nothing to do with the fall.'

Sarah looks at me. 'She broke the bottle and hit herself with it? Is that what you're saying?'

'She must have done, to make the attack look as realistic, as serious, as she could.'

'That's a big thing to do.' Sarah frowns. 'To hit yourself over the head with a broken bottle.'

'I agree,' I say. 'But there was a lot at stake.'

I pick up the empty peanut packet and begin to fold the foil into a concertina against the tabletop. Sarah watches me. I am aware that she's thinking it through, step by step. There'd be a post-mortem, an inquest even. Maddy's tumour would show up on a brain scan. Jerry's defence team would get disclosure of the medical records. The tumour would support Jerry's prospective defence. His defence would be the truth, of course: that Maddy had known she was dying and, realising that her death was likely to be drawn-out and unpleasant, already had a good reason for wanting to bring her life to an early end. 'She killed herself and framed me' might be a ludicrous defence in any other circumstance, but the presence of the tumour might well persuade the police – or the Crown Prosecution Service, or a jury – to accept his explanation that Maddy had decided to take him down with her, that she'd entrapped him by luring him to the building and throwing herself off.

Of course, if this were his defence, then he'd have to ascribe a motive to Maddy. He'd have to admit that she'd discovered his unhealthy sexual interest in her teenage daughter – and there would be plenty of evidence of that on Emily's phone. But given a choice between a couple of years for grooming or a life sentence for murder, he'd take the former, right? It would be a case of damage limitation; he'd be out of prison before too long. Meanwhile, the police might go looking for Maddy's co-conspirators. Our plan could fail or go horribly wrong.

Unless . . .

I glance up at Sarah and watch as her eyes widen with recognition. She's there. She's thinking what we had begun thinking: what if he believed he'd got away with it? With everything? After all, a conviction for a sex offence would put him on the sex offenders register. Everyone would know him as a paedophile. He'd get his head kicked in in prison, his wife would leave him, his daughter would shun him. The police would have one eye on him and his whereabouts for ever after. His life would be a shipwreck – not quite the shipwreck that we wanted for him, but he'd want to avoid being caught if he could. So, if that opportunity presented itself, what would he do? What would anyone in his situation do – if they could?

Sarah picks up her glass and looks me in the eye as she lifts it to her lips. 'Go on.'

Around me the hotel staff are laying tables for dinner. A waiter is hovering nearby. I smile to acknowledge him and he steps forwards. 'Good evening. Will you be eating, ladies?' he asks us.

I turn to Sarah.

'I could eat something,' she admits. 'We could share some starters, maybe?'

'Good idea,' I agree.

The waiter brings menus and we order some more wine and a sharing platter of bread, olives, cheese and seafood. I wonder briefly whether Fern will come down, ask what we're discussing and insist on joining us. If that happens, I'll have to make up something. But I'm getting pretty good at that.

I break off a piece of bread. Sarah is looking at me, waiting.

'Do you remember what you told me about getting caught out in a lie?' I ask.

She nods.

'You said that's when they start to build a case against you. That once you've lied to the police, it casts doubt on everything else you say.'

'It's the worst thing you can do,' Sarah agrees. 'You're better off saying nothing at all.'

'But that can hurt you too, right?'

'It can do, yes, but the police like it better when you trip yourself up. They like to lull you into a false sense of security to get you talking and in order to do that, they'll hold certain things back.'

'They let you dig an escape hole for yourself,' I say. 'One that they can later push you into.'

'Exactly.'

'And then, when it's big enough to bury you in . . .'

There's no need for me to finish that sentence. She looks at me for a long, thoughtful moment. 'Wasn't it terribly risky, though?' she asks finally. 'What you did?'

'Yes,' I say. 'It was.'

'Why, then? Why put yourself in the building? On the roof?'

'We needed to divert their attention away from Jerry.'

'But why destroy the CCTV, the one thing that could have proved your innocence?'

'We couldn't let the police see it. We had to give Jerry a chance to escape.'

'So Dan *did* destroy it?'

'No,' I jump in quickly.

'He just pitched up at the right moment and discovered it had been accidentally deleted?'

I nod. I open my mouth to speak, but close it again.

Sarah picks up her napkin and wipes the corner of her mouth. 'And then there's all the other tech stuff,' she muses. 'The phone hacking, the security system. Maddy knowing how to get in past the cameras without the security guy seeing her.'

'Jerry told her how.'

Sarah's eyes travel up to meet mine. 'But this was such a massive and horrid decision for Maddy. Are you really telling me that she did all this – plotted all this with you and Helen – without telling her husband a thing? She loved him. Right?'

'Of course she did.'

'And yet . . . she left the house and jumped to her death without him knowing it was going to happen? Without saying a proper goodbye?'

'She had to,' I insist. 'If she'd told him, he wouldn't have let her go through with it. She knew that. He'd confront Jerry, beat the crap out of him. It would ruin everything. And besides, she didn't want to make him an accomplice to . . . to what we did. She couldn't involve him. He had to stay clean . . . in the clear. For Emily. He's all she has.'

Sarah eyes me. 'So Maddy hit herself over the head with the wine bottle that Jerry had been drinking out of?'

I nod.

'Then – concussed, no doubt, and bleeding profusely – she picked herself up off the ground and threw herself over the edge?'

I wince at Sarah's words, but nod again.

Sarah falls silent for a moment. 'So, how *did* she get past security?'

I shrug. 'Like I said, she went in through the underground car park entrance and avoided the lift.'

'And bypassed every single camera?'

'We put covers over the lenses.'

'Who did that?' Sarah persists. 'Who put covers over the lenses?'

I gaze back at her. 'We knew what we were doing. We researched it. We worked it all out.'

'And Kevin from security didn't notice that someone was putting covers over the lenses?'

'Like I said, he wasn't particularly vigilant.'

'But what if he had been? You'd have to get to the camera without being seen in the first place, so what if he'd seen you and gone up to investigate?'

'He didn't, though.'

'But you couldn't be sure he wouldn't, could you?'

I shake my head reluctantly, uneasily.

Her eyes cloud with doubt. 'And the time on the hard drive? Who reset it? Or was that just luck too?'

'Lots of mistakes can happen with CCTV,' I tell her,

sidestepping her question. 'It often has the time or date set wrong or goes on a loop and gets overwritten before it's retrieved.' I hesitate, then concede, 'I guess it was luck, though.'

She gives me a look – a look that tells me I've been rumbled.

There's no point in pretending any longer.

'You told me you can't tell anyone else what I tell you in confidence,' I say quickly.

She nods. 'That's right.'

'Even if they're not your client?'

'Not unless you tell me to.'

I take a deep breath. 'There was someone else there that night,' I say slowly. 'But I need to know for sure that they can't be arrested. I can't let that happen.' I let my hands drop onto the table. 'It's someone who . . .' I hesitate. 'Who has a bright future ahead of them.'

'If I told someone about this person and this person got arrested, they'd tell the truth and then the police would find out about you, too. Right?'

I nod anxiously.

'So, I can't tell anyone about them. How can I? I have to act in your best interests at all times.'

I meet her eyes. 'Are you sure?'

'Yes,' she says firmly. 'I'm sure.'

I exhale with relief. 'I'm sorry. Everything I've told you is true, except that . . . except that Hayley was the one who reset the time on the CCTV and turned off the downstairs cameras.'

'*Hayley?*' I can see the surprise in Sarah's eyes.

I nod. 'She'd worked for Dan for twelve years. She knew

pretty much everything he knew about the building, about the security systems.'

'You're telling me that Hayley was in on it?' She hesitates. '*All* of it?'

I look back at Sarah in silence, knowing that whatever I say next could – in the wrong hands – have the direst of consequences. But I want to tell her the truth now – the whole truth. She's sharp. She's switched on. I can tell by the questions she's asking that if there's anything we've overlooked, she'll see it. It's the question that's been playing on my mind since the day the police arrested me. Are we really going to pull this off?

46

Six months earlier

I stood in Dan's office, still clutching the hot mugs of coffee, holding them steady so that I didn't splash any liquid onto the thick, plush carpet under my feet. My throat tightened as I got a better look at the photograph on his desk: Maddy, all lit up and laughing, leaning in lovingly towards her beautiful daughter. And in a crashing, bruising moment, as I recalled the conversation I'd had with Maddy in her bedroom the previous day, it came to me: what if Jerry Seager was the older man Emily had been seeing? What if Jerry Seager had been grooming Emily for sex, just as he'd groomed Helen and me?

I made myself breathe deeply and evenly for a moment, then turned and slipped out of the room. For a split second, I noticed Hayley watching me, but she quickly averted her eyes and tilted her head back towards her computer. I walked over and placed her coffee mug on her desk. She thanked me without looking up, keeping her eyes fixed firmly on her computer screen.

'Do you know where Dan is?' I asked her, as casually as I could. I lifted my own mug and peered at her over the rim.

'He's working from home today.'

I took a mouthful of coffee. 'I need him to sign something. Have you got his mobile number?'

'Sorry, I'm not allowed to give it out,' she said, still looking straight ahead at her screen. 'What do you need signed?'

'Oh. Just my timesheet. From the agency.'

'I can sign those.'

'Can you?'

'Yeah. No problem.'

'OK,' I said. 'I'll dig it out.'

'Are you OK?' she asked. 'After yesterday?' But her voice was flat and unfriendly and she was still gazing ahead at her screen as she spoke.

'Yeah,' I said. 'I think it was just the heat.'

'Should you be here?' Again, unfriendly. No eye contact. Did she know that I was lying to her?

'I'm OK,' I murmured. 'The ambulance was just a precaution. They said my blood pressure was low and . . . I do faint sometimes. It's happened before.'

She turned so that her back was now towards me. She clearly wanted us to finish the conversation and for me to go away.

'Hayley . . .' I began, intending to just come out with it and make up some excuse for hiding in Dan's garden.

She hesitated, then moved her chair very slightly back towards me. I waited until she lifted her head to look at me. It was only then that I noticed her eyes were shimmering with tears.

'Hayley?' I said softly. 'Are you OK?'

She bit her lip and nodded.

'What's wrong?'

She looked around the room for a second to make sure no one was watching. 'I can't talk . . .' she croaked back. 'Someone will see.' A tear leaked out of the corner of her eye and trickled down her cheek and into her mouth. She licked it away.

I reached out and touched her arm. 'I'll meet you in the toilets,' I whispered. 'I'll go now. Wait a few minutes, then follow me. OK?'

She nodded, swallowing hard. I put my coffee mug down on her desk and walked away, out through the glass doors and into the corridor. I pushed open the door to the female toilets, where I checked all three cubicles were empty, then leaned against a basin and waited. A few moments later, Hayley entered.

'There's no one else here,' I reassured her. 'And if anyone comes in, just go into a cubicle and wait until they've gone.'

She nodded, looking a little uncomfortable, but grateful too.

'What's happened, Hayley?' I asked her gently. 'Has someone upset you?'

Her eyes met mine and she started sobbing, her shoulders shaking.

I reached out and put my arms around her. 'Please. Tell me what's happened,' I said after a moment. 'You can talk to me. I promise you, I won't breathe a word.'

'It's Jerry,' she sobbed.

I felt myself stiffen. 'What about him?'

She pulled away and wiped her eyes. 'He's just bawled me out, in front of a client.'

I looked at her, aghast. 'What for?'

'He thought I'd asked the secretaries to prioritise some of my typing over a report he'd told them was urgent. He summoned me up to the bar, where he was meeting his client, and yelled at me in front of everyone, including the bar staff. He'd totally got it wrong, but he didn't wait for me to explain.'

'The bully,' I said angrily. 'Showing off in front of the client.'

'He's always doing it,' she sobbed.

'He's done this before?'

She nodded. 'He's always talking down to me.'

'Is it just you?' I asked. 'Or . . . is he like that with other people?'

She looked as if she was about to say something, then appeared to change her mind. She caught sight of herself in the mirror. 'Oh God,' she wailed. 'Look at me. I'm a wreck. Everyone's going to notice that I've been crying. They'll see the minute I walk back into the office.'

I shrugged. 'Don't go back then. Let's go out.'

'What? Where?'

'It's nearly lunchtime anyway,' I said. 'Dan's not here and Jerry's in his meeting. I'll go back in, grab both of our bags and make some excuse to Maria. No one will miss you. And Dan always calls your mobile, right? He'll be able to get hold of you if he needs you.'

She nodded slowly.

'Go down to the lobby before anyone sees you,' I insisted. 'I won't be far behind. We'll get a coffee somewhere. OK?'

Hayley agreed, so I poked my head out of the toilet door, then walked across the corridor and called the lift. When it arrived, I ushered Hayley inside. 'I'll meet you by the Monument,' I said as the lift door slid shut. 'I'll be five minutes behind you.'

I walked back into the office and over to my desk, where I pulled my bag over my shoulder and strode purposefully across the room. No one appeared to be paying any attention to me. As I passed Dan's office, I stopped and sidled in, then, realising I'd left my phone in my desk drawer, quickly picked up the silver-framed photograph of Maddy and Emily. My eyes then landed on the black leather desk diary. I picked that up too and slid both into my bag. Checking that the coast was clear, I slipped out of the room again, went back to my desk and took my phone from the drawer. I then went over to Hayley's desk, grabbed her bag and pushed it underneath my own, calling to Maria that I was going to a hospital appointment and that I'd squared it with Hayley, who had gone to run an errand for Dan before lunch.

I met Hayley by the Monument, as arranged. We bought a coffee from Pret, then walked south towards London Bridge and down the steps to the Thames. We chose a bench on the wharf and sat there, sipping our drinks and watching the boats glide through the sparkling, sunlit water before disappearing into the shadow under the bridge.

'He tried to have sex with me,' Hayley said abruptly.

I felt a shockwave run through me. 'Jerry?'

She nodded.

I placed my cup on the wall beside me. 'When?'

'A few months ago.' She sniffed. 'I mean, he'd been making dirty comments to me at office parties for years, but he does that to everyone. Maria told me that he once said something really crude to her about the wine bottle he was holding and where he wanted to put it.' She saw my face. 'Disgusting, right? But everyone just put it down to him getting out of control when he'd had too much to drink. I'd never let it bother me. I mean, we're in a male-dominated industry. Even in this day and age you hear about that kind of behaviour all the time. But I never expected . . .' She swallowed.

'What?' I pressed her.

'He began stopping at my desk to talk to me, complimenting me on my hair or what I was wearing. Then he started asking me personal questions about my sex life, which I really didn't like, but I didn't feel confident enough to tell anyone, or to tell him to stop. I mean, he's the CEO of the bank. He could fire me in an instant. So, I mostly managed to ignore it. But then one day after work . . .'

She stopped and looked down at her coffee cup and I could see her hand was shaking. I reached out and took the cup from her, placing it on the wall next to mine.

'He waited until everyone had left,' she continued. 'I was the last one there – or I thought I was. I had some contracts I had to finish for Dan. When he came out, I was surprised to see him. Next thing I know, he's calling me into his office, asking me to sit down on his sofa. And then he said that I was wasting my talents working for Dan. He said he wanted me to be his PA. It would be a big promotion. I'd have to work hard, go on business trips with him and work long hours, he said, but he could see that I had what it took to go all the way.'

'So what did you say?'

'I didn't want to work for him.' Her mouth set in a hard line. 'I knew what he wanted. I knew what he meant when he said *all the way*. So I just said that I was happy working for Dan. And then . . .' She closed her eyes and took a breath. 'Then he locked the door and turned down the blinds, and he came over to where I was sitting and he sat down next to me . . . and he put his hand on my shoulder. So I reached up and took it off. And then he got angry. He told me I'd been leading him on.'

I continued to look at her, aghast. 'What did he do to you, Hayley?'

'He . . .' She started to sob again. 'He said, "I've given you a lot of breaks here, given you a lot of opportunities. I think you owe me. Are we understanding each other here, Hayley?" And then he moved his hand down and he put it on my . . . on my . . .' she stuttered, 'on my breast. He . . . he squeezed it.'

I touched her hand. 'It's OK,' I said. 'It's OK.'

'And so I pulled his hand off and . . . and I got up off the sofa. He got up too and put his arms around me, so I pushed him off and then he came at me again, so I slapped him. He didn't like that.' She shook her head, trying to get rid of the memory. 'He got really, really angry. He grabbed hold of me and he pushed me up against the desk.'

'God, Hayley! He didn't . . . ?'

She stifled a sob. 'I thought he was going to. But he stopped.' She turned her eyes to meet mine. Tears ran down her cheeks. 'He let go of me and then he told me to fuck off out of his room. He was leaning over me and spit came out of his mouth as he said it. He was so close that it landed on my face. My legs had turned to jelly, but I somehow managed to get to the door and unlock it, and then he looked across at me and he said that it was a little too early in my career to start making waves. I told him I didn't understand. And he said, "Oh, I think you do." And then he said, "Shut the door on your way out." So I did. I ran out of the office and all the way to the tube station and I got the tube and then I ran from the tube station all the way home.'

I shook my head. 'And you've never told anyone this?'

'You heard what he said to me, Tate.'

'Has anything happened since?'

She shook her head. 'He mostly ignores me. He makes a point of talking to other people as if I'm not even there. Sometimes he makes sarcastic comments and talks down to me. Occasionally, he shouts at me, like today. It's obvious to everyone in the office that he doesn't like me, but no one knows the real reason. He bad-mouths me to people and makes out that it's me, tells people that I'm lazy and stupid. I've thought about leaving, but—'

'No!' I said indignantly. 'Why should you?'

She shrugged. 'I'm ready for a career move, to be honest. I've worked for Dan for twelve years and I've learned a lot, but I'm keen to move out of PA work and into IT.'

'You'd be so good at that,' I told her enthusiastically. 'You're really good at all that tech stuff. Why don't you just do it?'

She exhaled deeply. 'Jerry's the only one who's allowed to give out references and I'm scared that if I go somewhere new he'd do something to mess things up for me.'

'You really think he would?'

'I don't doubt it for a moment,' she said. 'One of the secretaries who used to work here told me that he takes it very personally when anyone leaves the bank.'

I studied her face for a moment, then turned to look up at a flock of gulls that had been wheeling around in my eyeline, eventually settling on the surface of the water. I thought about everything Hayley had just told me, and about the hunch I'd had when I was standing in Dan's office. I didn't know for sure that he had harmed Maddy's daughter, but I'd been right about one thing: Jerry was a predator. What kind of world was it that would cut short the life of someone good like Maddy and yet allow someone like him to go on living the life he wanted, to go on *doing* what he wanted . . . *taking* what he wanted?

'Hayley . . .' I began. I stopped, thinking about how much I was able to tell her. I shifted around on the bench so that I was sitting square to her. 'Hayley,' I said, 'I'm going to tell you something that's going to shock you.'

She blinked. 'Is it anything to do with you being in Dan's garden last night?'

'In a way, yes,' I answered her truthfully, relieved that this was now out in the open. 'But that's something I can't talk about at the moment. I hope you can just take my word for it that I had a very good reason for being there.'

She hesitated, looking puzzled for a moment, then faked a smile. 'It's none of my business, is it?'

'It's not what you think,' I reassured her. 'I made a promise to someone and I have to keep it. But what you told me about Jerry . . . Well, you're not the only one, Hayley. He did it to me too. Only he *did* manage to have sex with me.'

Her mouth fell open. 'Are you serious?'

I nod.

'*When?*'

'When I was fourteen. He did it to my friend Helen too.'

She looked first horrified, then puzzled. 'Oh my God,' she breathed. 'You were *fourteen*! So he . . . he raped you?'

I shook my head. 'It wasn't rape. It was underage sex. But there's a law and . . . and we're now out of time to prosecute him for what he did to us.'

Her eyes sparked with rage. 'But you were children!'

I nodded.

'So . . . so is that why you're here? Did you get the job at the bank *on purpose*?'

I nodded again. 'The police wouldn't do anything about what he did to us – it was too long ago – and so I wanted to find him and . . .'

She eyed me. 'And what?'

I told her about my plan – my initial plan: to destroy his life, to tell his wife and daughter, to stand up at a meeting and tell all his staff and colleagues exactly who he was and what he'd done. But then I'd started to have doubts about my ability to pull it off. I hadn't made any friends at the bank. What if no one believed me? Meanwhile, I'd begun to suspect that Helen and I weren't his only victims. I just needed some evidence, I told Hayley – and then he could still be prosecuted. It only took one person to make a complaint against him, I said, for other young women and girls to come forward. That's how it often happened, I said. If one woman was brave enough, others might then speak up. There was strength in numbers, I reminded her, and I was convinced that there were going to be others. I didn't mention Emily to Hayley at this point, because I couldn't prove it yet. I also knew that Maddy should be the person I talked to first.

But, like Maddy, Hayley feared the repercussions. It was her word against Jerry's, she said. He hadn't raped her, had he? She had no physical evidence and even if a jury believed her, word would get around. She'd be viewed across the City as an upstart, a troublemaker, a bitter, litigious man-hater. Jerry was right: no one would want to employ her. It would be the end of her career.

What could I say? So we left it there. I promised to keep Hayley's secret, as I'd promised to keep Maddy's. Hayley touched up her puffy eyes with concealer and went back to the office, and even though she knew that there was nothing wrong with my heart and that the hospital appointments were a front for something else that I was up to, she signed my timesheet and I took the rest of the afternoon off. I took the photograph of Emily down to St Mary's Academy and followed her home and for two weeks Helen and I kept her under surveillance until we had the evidence we needed, which we then took to Maddy, who before long came up with her plan.

But I wasn't lying when I said that Hayley had been watching my every move. I could tell she was curious about what I was doing when I wasn't in the office. She knew it had something to do with me hiding in Dan's garden, and she suspected that it also had something to do with the diary and the photograph of his wife and daughter that Dan had mentioned to her were missing from his desk. And all the while, she was getting angry – as angry as Maddy and Helen and I were – about what Jerry was getting away with. As I said to Helen, once you know it, you can't *un-know* it. The spark that had been lit inside us had been lit inside her too.

47

It was lunchtime on the Saturday of the weekend that Dan was away in Paris. We were sitting round the kitchen table at Maddy's, writing, when there was a knock at the front door. We looked at each other in silence. Emily had phoned just an hour ago to ask if she could stay another night at Rosie's and Dan wasn't due back until the following day. Maddy got up and went to answer it. When she returned, Hayley was with her. As she came into the kitchen, Hayley looked momentarily taken aback at the sight of me and Helen. She stood there for a moment, her eyes flickering back and forth between us – the Three Witches – and then she said, 'I'm sorry. I'm sorry to interrupt.'

Maddy smiled. 'Don't be silly. Would you like a cup of coffee? Or tea?'

A flush crept up Hayley's neck as she hovered awkwardly in the doorway. She told Maddy that she was fine, thank you, then – after a moment's hesitation – looked across the table at me. 'Can we talk?' she asked.

I got up out of my seat and Maddy opened a patio door to the garden so that Hayley and I could step outside. She closed it behind us. The garden furniture had been tucked away and so we stood on the patio and looked out at the garden, at the blanket of red, green and golden apples spread across the grass. As I watched the crows pecking away, unperturbed by our presence, Hayley glanced back over her shoulder through the glass doors.

'Maddy looks very thin,' she said. 'And tired.'

'Yes,' I agreed.

'And is that your friend?'

'Yes,' I said. 'That's Helen.'

She continued to observe Helen and Maddy through the glass, noticing, no doubt, how well acquainted they seemed. After a moment, she turned round to face me. 'I came here to tell Maddy something,' she said, 'something I just can't stop thinking about. But maybe . . .'

'Go on,' I prompted her.

She lifted her eyes to meet mine. 'Maybe she already knows.'

I waited.

Her eyes swam with tears. 'I couldn't stop thinking about what he did to you, Tate. You were fourteen. *Fourteen.*' She shuddered. 'I hadn't even kissed a boy when I was fourteen. My parents were strict. I was still . . . you know . . . so naïve, so protected. I'd barely stopped playing with dolls at fourteen. I just couldn't get it out of my head that he had sex with you, with both of you, when you were the same age I was then. And then I started to question everything . . . everything I'd heard him say, everything I'd seen him do. I started to think about him liking young girls and whether I'd seen anything . . . whether he might have hurt anyone that . . .' She shook her head, her voice dropping to a whisper. 'And then I remembered. I saw him with Emily.' She paused. 'You know, Maddy and Dan's daughter.'

I drew a breath. 'What did you see?'

'She came into the office a few months ago. Dan wasn't there and she knocked on the door of Jerry's office and . . . he asked her in, and I remember seeing them sitting there together. They seemed very . . . familiar with each other in a way that made me . . . uncomfortable, I guess. She had her feet up on the sofa and she was wearing her school uniform. Her skirt was short and her legs were bare and I remember noticing the way they were looking at each other and laughing. It was . . . too friendly, if you know what I mean.'

'I know what you mean.'

'I didn't think about it enough to . . . to realise,' she continued, a flush creeping up her neck. 'Not there and then. I knew that Jerry and Dan saw each other out of work and that their families had dinner together now and again, so Emily knew him, and so I suppose I didn't think too much of it. It was only after you told me what he did to you that it hit me and . . . and now I feel so guilty for just . . . ignoring it. For not saying anything.'

'You shouldn't feel guilty,' I said.

She squeezed her eyes shut. 'Believe me,' she continued, 'I've really, really struggled with this. But Dan's in Paris with Jerry and I felt it couldn't wait. I felt I had to talk to Maddy.'

'It's OK,' I told her. 'She already knows.'

Hayley slowly shook her head. 'So it's true, then?'

'We think so,' I said. 'But we can't prove it.'

'So Maddy hasn't spoken to Emily about it?'

'No.'

Tears welled in Hayley's eyes. 'I feel so bad.'

'Why do you feel bad?' I objected.

'For being a coward. For not going to the police. For not doing anything.'

'Hayley, you're not a coward,' I protested. 'He's a powerful man.'

'He's an evil, sick bastard,' she said angrily, tears running down her cheeks. 'That's what he is.'

'I know,' I agreed, putting an arm around her and giving her a hug. 'I know.'

Hayley looked through the window at Helen and Maddy, who were watching us. 'Is Emily here?'

I shook my head. 'No.'

Hayley wiped her eyes. 'Whatever it is you're doing, I want to help.'

'Hayley, it's fine,' I said. 'We're just talking it through at the moment.'

'Then let me talk it through with you.'

'Look, we're just—'

'Maddy doesn't think Emily will tell the truth,' Hayley interrupted me. 'Does she? And without Emily, there's no case. She doesn't think she can do anything about it.'

I nodded. 'That's pretty much where we've got to.'

'Then let me help.'

I fell silent, thinking. Our plan was in the early stages. We hadn't yet had a chance to work it all through. But what we were planning was huge and it was illegal and the risk was enormous; we needed to keep our circle of trust as tight as we possibly could.

On the other hand, Hayley already knew plenty. She knew about Emily, about Jerry. She knew that we all had a grudge against him. If we went ahead without her – if Maddy died and Jerry got the blame – it wouldn't take Hayley long to work out what had really happened. And then what? Would she tell anyone her suspicions? She might hate Jerry and she might be glad to see him locked up, but she might not agree with what we'd done.

There was only one way of knowing for sure and that was to tell her our plan. I'd have to run all of this by Maddy and Helen, of course. We'd only been writing our story since the previous evening. There were plot holes – multiple plot holes. There were many, many issues we still hadn't had a chance to address. If we told Hayley what we were doing, we could gauge her reaction. If she didn't like it, we would have to abandon it; it was as simple as that. But if Hayley could be convinced – if she *was* on board – she would have a unique perspective. She knew the CPF office, she knew the entire building. She had a wealth of knowledge that none of the rest of us had. In fact, she'd only just this week mentioned to me that Dan had been having issues with the security guys, which could prove really useful. Without a doubt, she knew things that none of the rest of us did.

'Whatever you're planning, I can help you.' Hayley's voice cut into my thoughts. She clenched her jaw and whispered, 'You're right. I'm not a coward.'

'What is it that you think we're planning?'

She narrowed her eyes. 'I don't know.'

'Maybe it's best that you *don't*.'

'Maybe it's best that I do,' she said. 'Just because I don't want to go to court, doesn't mean I'm a coward, Tate.'

This was the second time she'd said this and it made me wonder about that. So I asked her if she'd mind going down to the Tesco Express on Union Road and buying us all some sandwiches while I consulted Maddy and Helen. She agreed eagerly, refusing our money. 'You don't know me very well, Tate, but I'm quite creative. You may be surprised,' she said as she left.

I smiled and said that if there was no cheese and onion, then she was welcome to surprise me, and she gave me a look that said, 'Please don't tease me. Please take me seriously,' and then she walked down the front path, past the bushes I'd hidden in and out onto the street.

But we *were* surprised. Hayley was more than creative: she was brilliant. It was her idea to tell the police that she'd seen me lurking in Dan and Maddy's garden and about the missing diary and photograph. It was her idea to make up an additional story to tell the police: that she'd seen me slouched down in my car outside the restaurant in Soho on the day that Dan had left for Paris. It was her idea to tell them that she often caught me watching him. It was Hayley who invited me with the other secretaries to the bar in late November where we could watch and take notes on everything that Jerry did, smoked or drank. And it was Hayley who volunteered to take on the one remaining role that neither Helen nor I could have managed. In fact, the plan couldn't have worked without her. Hayley Allbright is definitely no coward. She's one of the bravest people I've ever known.

48

Saturday, 10 December

I woke early that morning, unable to fall back to sleep once I'd remembered what day it was. It was still dark outside, so I got back into bed with a mug of tea and my laptop and pulled up the website for St Katharine Docks. I clicked on the 'What's on' page to make sure that the dockside party was still going ahead that evening, the one that Helen was meant to be going to. The same announcement was there:

> *There will be a fabulous selection of festive treats and drinks on offer, including mince pies, mulled wine and hot chocolate. Guests can look forward to all the warmth and good cheer of a Christmas evening. Tickets cost £30 (plus booking fees) and are still available to buy by clicking the link below.*

The photos were enticing: happy, smiling people mingling, their faces lit up by the glow of the lights that were strung along the marina and across the water. The doors of the eighteenth-century dockside pubs were open and welcoming in the background, inviting you to step inside and enjoy the warmth of a cosy open fire. It looked like fun, the kind of party I'd like to go to if this were any ordinary Saturday in mid-December. The thought of a party going on in this normal, carefree parallel universe was suddenly hard to think about. I pushed my laptop aside and lay back against the pillows, closing my eyes and taking a few long, deep breaths. There was no going back now. From the outset, Maddy had been clear that this was what she wanted, and there was no way in the world I was going to let her down.

I finally dozed for what must have been a half hour or so. When I opened my eyes again it was light outside. I felt my stomach flutter as I got out of bed, dressed in jeans and a thick sweater and went out to check the car. It was a cold, bright winter morning and there was a thin layer of ice over the windows. I scraped it off, screwing up my eyes against the piercing white sky, then got in and started the engine, running it for a bit.

When I got back inside, Helen was in the kitchen with a bag of Danish pastries.

'Car's good. Running just fine,' I smiled, kicking off my trainers and standing in the doorway.

We looked at each other for a long, strange moment, then Helen heaved a sigh and we wrapped our arms around each other and held each other tight.

'This is it, Hel,' I whispered in her ear.

'I'm so nervous.'

'It's good to be nervous,' I told her. 'Not too nervous,

obviously, not stage-fright nervous. But the day I stop getting nervous is the day I stop acting.'

Helen picked up the pastries and followed me into the living room, putting them on a plate on the coffee table. I helped myself to one and ate it while I did some stretches and lunges. The cold air had woken me up and I suddenly had lots of pent-up energy. Helen sat down in the armchair and curled her legs up underneath her.

'You know what's making me nervous?' she said. 'You.'

'I'm just warming up, that's all,' I told her.

'I mean, what you said to Jerry. I can't believe you called him a prick.'

I grinned. 'You should have seen his face. "*Ristry*"!' I mimicked.

Helen stifled a smile and shook her head. 'You do like playing with fire, Tee.'

'He didn't remember me.' I stopped lunging and sank down onto the sofa.

'I know, but what if it hits him later?'

'Well . . . good,' I said. 'I want him to realise who's done this.'

'No, you don't!' she said.

I shrugged. 'What could he do? He'd have to admit what he'd done to us. He's hardly going to do that.'

She shot me a warning glance. 'Just be careful. Stick to the script. No more ad-libbing. OK?'

The day passed slowly. Helen and I spent it in the exact same spot in my living room, eating crisps and half watching an old Hitchcock thriller whilst exchanging messages with Hayley and Maddy on the old black Nokias that Hayley had picked up for us from a phone shop in Streatham. ('Prepaid. No contract. Paid for with cash. Can't be traced,' she'd told us simply.) All was going well, it seemed. There had been an incident between Emily and Dan just before he left for the office party that had resulted in Emily being grounded and her phone confiscated, following which it had then been 'lost'. Maddy now had it safely in her possession. She would start sending the messages soon.

At four o'clock, Helen went upstairs to get dressed up, then came back down again, looking lovely in her red coat and killer heels. We waited. By five, it was pitch-black outside the window. It felt like a million years since the crisp, bright morning I'd woken up to. At five thirty, I typed a message to Maddy. Hey. How's it going?

All good. I think I've caught him! came her reply, and my stomach flipped.

She said she'd get back to me in a minute. I sat as still as a statue, my knees drawn up against my chest and my head resting on my forearms, while Helen sat equally still in the chair opposite. A few moments later, the phone bleeped and I grabbed it from the coffee table.

It was Hayley. OK. We've got him. Time to go.

'It's time,' I breathed, looking across at Helen.

She immediately leaped into action. Picking up the car keys from the basket on the table, she gave me a hug and left the flat. I got up shakily and opened a tin of Sheba for George, then got my bag and my coat ready. It would take Helen fifteen minutes at most to drive to Kenrick Place at this time on a Saturday and then another five to park and call a taxi to bring her back.

Twenty-five minutes after she'd left, my phone rang, my real phone. I answered.

'Hello, Tate,' Helen said, speaking rapidly, her voice unsteady. 'I'm really sorry about this, but I need to get to the point. I've lost an earring. I've looked everywhere, but I can't find it. It must have fallen out of my ear last night.'

'Oh no,' I said. 'Were they expensive?'

'They're diamonds!' she exclaimed. 'They're precious. Unique. And irreplaceable. They were the last thing my gran gave me before she died. They're . . .' She paused, then I heard a sob. 'They're all I have left of her. I have to find it. I have to get it back!'

I smiled. Her acting was good; she sounded really upset. We said the rest of our lines and then I went downstairs and there was the cab, idling outside the building with Helen in the back. I got in next to her and she gave the driver the office address. As we headed through Mayfair, I told her all the stuff about how we should warn security that we were coming and she begged me not to and then she told me how she'd got fired from Cowan McCauley and that if we found the earring, she was going to buy me a very large drink. All the while, we made sure the taxi driver could hear us. I squeezed her hand. I was proud of her and I knew she was right; there should be no ad-libbing. This would all go to plan if everyone stuck to the script.

49

Up on the roof terrace, it was cold and dark, the single motion-sensor emergency light having cut out several minutes ago.

Where are you?!! His message was frantic.

On the roof.

Are you kidding me? What are you doing up there?!

The view is amazing! It's such a long way down.

Em, you need to come down from there!

Hayley looked up at Maddy. They were reading and typing the messages together, huddled up close on the cold, hard gravel behind the skylight, the screen of Emily's Samsung lit up in the darkness.

'Let's leave it there. He'll be worried now,' Hayley said. 'He'll come up to find you.'

Maddy nodded, breathed in deeply for a moment, then pulled Dan's coat tightly around her, zipped it up and drew her snood up around her throat and chin.

'It's not too late to change your mind,' Hayley said softly.

'We've got the messages now. We can confront him together, call the police.'

Maddy shook her head. 'The messages aren't enough.'

'I know,' Hayley said, her voice trembling with emotion. 'I just need to be one hundred per cent certain that this is what you want.'

'I'm certain,' Maddy whispered, then smiled up at Hayley. 'And extremely grateful.'

'Me too.' Hayley wiped a tear from her eye. 'I'm so glad to have known you, Maddy.'

'I'm so glad to have known you too.' Maddy smiled weakly, then powered the Samsung off and held it out to Hayley, who opened her rucksack pocket. Maddy dropped the phone inside and Hayley zipped it up.

Maddy pulled her hood around her face, then stood up shakily and stepped out from behind the skylight. A gust of wind blew hard and Hayley saw Maddy struggle a little to regain her footing. A second gust of wind blew her hood back and she had to grab hold of it and pull it forward. As she secured it tightly, she turned to face Hayley for a brief moment. She then walked round the corner, out of sight.

They waited in silence, Hayley shrinking down into the shadows on the far side of the skylight. Finally, Hayley heard the metal door to the fire escape opening and the security light blinked on.

'Em.' His voice. 'There you are. What are you playing at? Come away from the edge.'

A pause. Footsteps.

'Jesus, Em,' he said. 'You've had me worried. What's going on?'

Hayley was incensed. The casual, familiar way that bastard spoke Emily's name. And – as the scent caught the breeze and wafted across the rooftop towards her – was that aftershave? Was he wearing aftershave for a fifteen-year-old girl? The smell of it combined with the nervous tension that was already gnawing at her stomach made her want to retch.

She inhaled deeply and held her breath for a few seconds. And then she heard it: Maddy was launching herself at him. 'You bastard. You filthy, disgusting bastard!' she screamed.

His neck, Maddy, Hayley pleaded silently. *Remember? No marks on his face. Just his neck.*

There was the sound of wrestling, and Jerry's voice yelling out in shock and surprise, 'What the fuck are you doing? Get off me, you crazy bitch!'

Hayley heard a heavy thud as they landed against the skylight. She clenched her fists, dug her fingernails into her palms, raging, yearning to run out there and help her friend. As they moved, the security light blinked off, on, off, then on again.

'You bitch,' Jerry snarled. 'I'm bleeding!'

'My daughter!' Maddy sobbed. 'How dare you prey on my daughter? How dare you use me and Dan to get to her, you sick fuck!'

'You're a fucking psycho,' Jerry countered. 'I don't know what you think you know, but I was concerned about Em. I just wanted to make sure she was OK. If you were a better parent—'

'Liar!' Maddy yelled. 'You came here to have sex with my daughter!'

'Don't be ridiculous,' he spat.

'You've known her since she was a baby!' Maddy cried. 'We trusted you! You were like an uncle to her! Did you touch her then? When she was a baby . . . a toddler? I mean, where do you draw the line, Jerry? How young do you actually like them?'

'You're off your head, do you know that?'

'What,' Maddy said, between clenched teeth, 'have you been doing with my daughter?'

'I haven't done anything to your daughter,' he sneered. 'You're a fucking lunatic. I don't know how Dan puts up with you!' But there was a tremor in his voice that Hayley knew revealed more than anger. Behind his rage was a layer of fear.

'You fucking bastard!' Maddy cried, launching herself at him again.

There was one more thud against the skylight as he pushed her sharply backwards, then Hayley could hear him striding away.

'I'm out of here,' he called to her, shakily, as he crossed the roof terrace towards the inner fire escape. 'And you'd better get out of here too, before I call security.'

The metal door creaked open, then swung shut again.

Hayley let out a breath. Jerry wouldn't call security. He'd be running scared; he'd want to get out of the building without being seen. He'd be wondering exactly what Maddy knew, what she could prove, trying to remember if he'd said anything truly incriminating in any of those messages to Emily. He'd be wondering if Dan knew about the messages, if Emily knew that they knew and, if so, what she'd told them. He'd be wondering why Maddy, alone, had confronted him on the roof of his office, of all places, instead of knocking his front door down or calling the police.

He'd figure it out soon enough, of course.

But, whatever Jerry did or didn't do, they needed to act quickly. Hayley waited until Maddy stepped round to the side of the skylight where she was crouching in the darkness. When they were sure Jerry had gone, Maddy moved over to the wall, reached down and pulled the wine bottle from the gap between the wall and the skylight. She handed it to Hayley, who took it in her gloved hand.

Hayley hesitated.

Maddy nodded.

Still Hayley waited, wanting to be sure. She stifled a sob.

'Please,' Maddy said gently. 'You have to do this for me. For Emily.'

Hayley nodded and swallowed, pushed her courage into reserve, then in one swift movement raised her arm and broke the bottle against the skylight. She stepped forward, tears streaming down her face, and they moved together to the edge of the building and scrambled up the skylight and onto the wall.

The bottle struck Maddy's cranium on the left-hand side above her ear. She began to sink down, to slip. Hayley threw the bottleneck down amid the splintered shards, and quickly took hold of Maddy, lifting her, supporting her and finally levering her so that she was bent double over the railing.

Hayley took a deep breath, her heart breaking into a thousand pieces as she rocked Maddy gently forwards and watched her go.

50

I heard her hit the ground from the shop doorway I'd chosen as my lookout behind the building. Or maybe I heard nothing. Maybe my mind has embellished it since, in the same way that it has persisted in taking me to the edge of the roof terrace, as if I'd been there when it happened, looking down. Maybe my brain is still trying to join the dots, to make sense of the fact that, by the time I saw her next, the living, breathing woman I'd known as Maddy – the woman I'd spoken to just a short while ago when she'd called me from the rooftop – was now nothing more than a broken body slumped on the pavement with a misshapen leg and a missing shoe.

Her landing was an eerie, shocking thump, followed closely by a single scream, some frantic shouting and the slamming of car doors. Helen told me later that she'd heard it too, from the lobby inside the building where she was standing by the desk with Kevin from security, getting directions to St Katharine Docks. Even though she'd known it was about to happen, the shock had been more real than she could have imagined, she said, and her reaction was natural and unscripted. Once outside, she'd messaged and confirmed what I already knew to be true.

She's on the ground. A second message said: Kevin's outside. No sign of Elvis.

At the rear of the building, my fingers trembling, I typed, Nor here. Are you both OK?

A single word came back from the rooftop. Yes.

Yes, typed Helen. You?

Yes.

I waited, and watched the exit. Finally, I saw him. He'd pulled his coat up over his head and was striding up the slope of the underground car park, looking around him in all directions as he came out onto the street and walked quickly away.

Elvis has left the building, I typed into the Nokia. Greystone Way, heading for Turn Again Lane. I pressed send.

Still out front with Kevin. Lots of people now, Helen replied. Security from other buildings all out here.

OK. Coming down, said Hayley.

I stepped out of my hideout behind a stack of cardboard and followed Jerry at a distance, knowing it wouldn't be long before he realised that something had happened in the adjacent street. I could already see that there was a stream of traffic queuing up Turn Again Lane. At the junction, he turned left down the lane. I ran to catch him up. Meanwhile, he'd reached the junction with Eastcheap and had stopped. He stood still for a moment, staring in the direction of the office and scratching his head, then turned and walked quickly back up the lane again. I leaped into a shop doorway. When I looked out, he'd turned left and was heading away from me, towards Monument. I waited for several moments until I couldn't see him any more, then walked back down Greystone Way, going round onto Eastcheap in the opposite direction.

As I rounded the corner into the street, my heart hammered in my chest and my knees grew weak in anticipation of what awaited me. My eyes were immediately drawn to the scene on the pavement in front of the building, where a protective layer of security guards stood around Maddy's body to keep back the crowd that had gathered. People were milling around in the road and on the pavement, standing talking in small groups, expressions of shock and disbelief on their faces. One or two people had their phones out and, to my disgust, were holding them up in the air.

Shakily, I circuited the crowd, crossing the road and walking over to the opposite pavement. I looked towards the entrance of the office building, searching for Helen, but I couldn't see her. Seconds later, she appeared silently behind me and poked me in the back. I glanced briefly around to check it was her, then pulled my Nokia out of my pocket. I felt her fingers take it while I looked away.

'Good luck,' she said under her breath. 'I'll see you later.'

I nodded and watched her as she weaved her way through the traffic and the people and headed east, disappearing from sight. I crossed the road towards where Maddy was lying, to where the security guards were standing. I could hear the siren of the police and ambulance vehicles in the near distance, getting louder and louder. This was it, then. This was my moment.

I took a deep breath and began to push my way through.

51

Hayley quickly reached for Maddy's handbag and threw it over the railing after her. She then stepped carefully around the splintered glass to the other side of the skylight where she'd left her rucksack, desperately trying to shut out the memory of the thud she'd just heard and the ensuing commotion from down below. Her phone bleeped twice. It was Helen. She was out front with Kevin from security. Hayley shook with grief when Helen said that she'd seen Maddy on the ground, but resisted the urge to ask any questions.

Are you OK? came the next message.

Yes. A tear landed on Hayley's screen as she typed.

She moved into the orbit of the emergency sensor to gain some light, then, still wearing her leather gloves, quickly removed her blood-soiled, glass-splintered clothes and shoes. It was bitterly cold and Hayley shivered in her underwear as she pushed everything into a large grip seal plastic bag and then took off her gloves, dropping them into the bag too, before zipping it up. She then pulled her clean clothes and shoes out of the rucksack and put them on. As she did so, the Nokia bleeped twice.

Elvis has left the building. Greystone Way, heading for Turn Again Lane.

Then another text from Helen. Still out front with Kevin. Lots of people now. Security from other buildings all out here.

OK, she typed back. Coming down.

She pushed the grip seal bag into her rucksack, then slung it over her shoulder. She pulled up her hood and hurried through the emergency exit and down the fire escape, then followed the corridor round to the stairwell, where she descended rapidly, taking the steps two at a time. When she reached the ground floor, she propped open one of the double doors to the stairwell with her shoe, ran along the corridor, then dropped to her stomach and slid underneath the security turnstile. She crawled on her hands and knees, skirting the desk from the rear. The lights were dimmed and the lobby was in shadow. She sneaked into the security office and slid into the chair behind the desk, then checked the central panel that controlled the revolving doors. Kevin had already locked them remotely. No one except Kevin would be able to come back in, and if all had gone to plan, he should now be fully occupied outside.

Hayley tapped the keyboard in front of her, moved the mouse, slid the controller up and down until she found the part of the footage she wanted, then reached into the box that housed the hard drive to reset the time and start the footage recording again. She checked against the time on the Nokia as she did so, then looked up at each camera, one by one. On each, the hour was set at 18:40. The real time was now 19:40.

The footage had begun to overwrite. Everything that had happened in the hour since she and Maddy had arrived at the rear entrance would be wiped by the time the police came for the footage. She selected the cameras in the stairwell and lower-ground-floor corridor, then switched them off, along with the camera that pointed at the exit to the car park at the rear.

Crouching on the floor again, Hayley crawled out into the shadows of the darkened lobby. As she reached the desk, the sirens outside became deafening and the lobby was flooded with blue light. She bolted behind the desk and slid on her stomach, head down, underneath the turnstile, then pushed herself up to her feet and sprinted along the corridor of the inner quadrant and out into the stairwell, retrieving her shoe as she went. Once in the underground car park, she let herself out of the building with the Temp One security pass, pulled up her hood and ran.

52

The golden hour. That's what they call it. I saw it on one of those police shows on TV and it immediately got my attention. It's not really an hour. It's the critical period straight after a crime is committed – the quicker the police can preserve the evidence, the greater their chance of catching the perpetrator. But an hour was just about all we needed. Whilst I did my thing outside – pushing my way through the small crowd, forcing Kevin the security guard to grab hold of me and hang on to me as I implicated myself in the death of the woman on the pavement – there would be plenty of time for Hayley to destroy the CCTV evidence and turn off the ground-floor cameras. There would be more than enough time for Jerry and Hayley – and, of course, Emily's phone – to disappear.

I turn to Sarah, who's listening intently, her head tilted to one side. 'Do you remember how you told me that I changed the way the police dealt with the investigation?' I ask her. 'How they would treat it as suicide based on what I told them?'

She nods. 'With a suicide, all the police have to do is

produce a couple of statements for the coroner. It would be a different investigation entirely. They'd delay sealing off the building and making it a crime scene. They'd fail to look for suspects or to prevent them from leaving the scene.'

Of course, it wouldn't be too long before they found Dan's security pass in Maddy's pocket and her handbag hanging on a nearby railing with her purse and bank cards inside. These would give them a lead as to her true identity, which, of course, needed to happen. But, for a few hours yet, they still couldn't be certain who the handbag belonged to or how the security pass had ended up in the victim's pocket. Only when Dan identified the body later that evening would they know for sure that the victim was Maddy. And by then, I would be the prime suspect, Hayley would be about to become a key witness against me, and Jerry wouldn't even be on their radar. Why would he be, when they had me?

Not that they had enough to arrest me – not yet, not that night. But I knew the moment DC Gallagher entered the room with her notebook and pen, pulled out a chair and sat down in front of me, that she suspected me. From this point on, it was all down to me. This was a huge responsibility, of course – and scary. Acting innocent whilst trying to appear guilty is not as straightforward as it seems. (*Maddy?* Bewildered look. *It was Maddy who fell from the roof?* The girls had made me go over that scene a lot of times during rehearsals.) It's like acting drunk; the trick is *not* to try and look drunk. Instead, you have to try extremely hard – too hard – to look sober, and it's the same with acting guilty. You have to try to appear innocent and let what you say and do fulfil the task of arousing suspicion.

For instance, give conflicting accounts to witnesses. (*I was there inside the building with her* / *I didn't know she was inside the building.*) Struggle with the security guard. Try to leave the scene of the crime. (Kevin was telling the truth. I did struggle. I did try to leave.) Lie to the police. (Make it a credible lie, but one you'll be caught out on. *I swiped someone else into the building.*) Give them the name of an alternative suspect they'd find no trace of. (Helen Jones. A fake name if ever there was one!) And then, of course, I needed both opportunity and motive – and I had the perfect motive: love.

That one was an inspiration – all Hayley's idea, of course, based on the genuine suspicions she'd initially had about me. We knew it wouldn't take the police long to speak to her, and once they did, my motive for killing Maddy would become crystal clear. All those times I'd lurked outside Dan's office, inside Dan's office, outside his home, and – according to Hayley – outside the restaurant before he left for the airport. With the benefit of hindsight, it would make perfect sense to her that I had an unrequited obsession with our boss, and she was right – we could use this to our advantage. (It would be a full-blown affair, not an unrequited obsession, if you believed my account, but, again, I had to make sure no one did.)

As for Jerry, as soon as word reached him, as soon as he realised that I had been there that night, that I had the hots for Dan (but not for him – always a problem for someone with a big ego), that I was the police's number-one suspect . . . well, he'd delight in implicating me. Why wouldn't he? Admittedly, humiliating him on the lower roof terrace on the evening of the office party wasn't part of the script. (I went out on a limb there. My bad, I know.) But even without that, he'd need to account for his security pass being inside the building and this would be a golden opportunity to pin it on me. So what if it was a lie that it had been stolen? He didn't kill Maddy, did he? He might have had an argument with her, but she was alive when he left the roof terrace, and what was the office temp doing in the building on a Saturday evening, anyway? She must have done it. Besides which, after my antics on the smoking terrace, I was obviously a complete bitch. In his mind, the end would justify the means.

Both the end and the means would be his undoing, of course. Helen had researched it: even if we didn't get him for Maddy's murder, he'd have committed a whole string of other offences.

I look up at Sarah.

'Perverting the course of justice,' she agrees. 'With aggravating features: leaving the scene of a crime, misdirecting the investigation.'

'Pressuring his wife to give him an alibi,' I say. 'Although she may not have needed much persuading. "They've already got the person who did it, darling, but for the sake of the bank, the shareholders, you know . . . it's better that I don't get caught up in any of this. Better to say that I was at home."'

'He'd be looking at seven years for that alone,' Sarah says. 'And then there would be the messages, which would prove that he'd been attempting to have sex with a fourteen-year-old. He could serve ten years in prison.'

I consider this, biting my lip. We wanted him for murder. He'd get more for murder. A minimum term of fifteen, probably more like twenty, Helen had told us after she'd researched it fully, and he'd have to serve all twenty in prison.

But failing that, ten would do.

Sarah hesitates. 'But you've also perverted the course of justice,' she reminds me. 'And conspired to do so. You know that, right? You could also get a long stretch in prison – all of you.'

But only if we got caught.

I eye her carefully. I want to know what we have forgotten, what we have missed.

'You've taken a huge risk, Tate,' she continues, 'I'm sure you don't need me to tell you that. Framing yourself for Maddy's murder—'

'I never set foot inside the building,' I remind her. 'They'd never be able to prove I was on the roof that night.'

'You told them you were there,' she points out.

'Maybe I was confused. Maybe I'm one of those people who blame themselves, confess to things they haven't done.'

She looks at me for a long moment, then nods. 'So,' she says, 'that's why you put yourself inside the building – to account for the Temp One security pass?'

'Someone had to be there with Maddy at the end,' I say. 'Like you said, hitting herself with a broken bottle would be a tough thing to do. She could have passed out on the roof. We needed someone there to help her. We also needed Hayley to reset the CCTV and turn off the cameras. We had to get her in and out of the building without anyone knowing she was there. Putting me inside the building with Temp One would solve that problem. And it would also make me the prime suspect, which we needed in order to divert any attention away from Jerry. After all, his pass was used too.'

'And you expected him to say you'd stolen it?'

'We expected him to say he'd lost it and then I would say that Helen had had the opportunity to steal it and needed a pass to get in.'

'So that was Helen's purpose? To account for Jerry's pass?'

'Yes. And to build me a defence. We needed the focus of the investigation to stay firmly on me, so we made sure the police wouldn't believe me about Helen's existence. But at the same time, there was a third pass used inside the building, so it would confuse things as to who was using which pass until we were ready for Jerry to come under suspicion.'

'And if anything went wrong or things went too far,' Sarah guesses, 'Helen could come forward? Corroborate your account that you went there with her to look for the earring?'

'If I needed her to, yes,' I agree. 'Of course, the police would never find her if we didn't want them to. There is no Helen Jones – she doesn't exist.'

'And did she go to the party at St Katharine Docks?'

'No. It was enough that there was a party there that night she intended to go to. We didn't need to prove she went. She met Hayley two streets away at the place where Hayley and Maddy had parked my car.'

'I thought your car was in Kenrick Place?'

'It was. That's where Helen met Hayley and Maddy earlier in the evening and handed them the keys. They drove my car to the City and parked it nearby. After she left Eastcheap, Helen went back to the car and waited there for Hayley, ready to drive her straight home. Hayley was unlikely to need an alibi because her own security pass was never used inside the building, but she needed to get back home quickly, just in case. The minute she got home, she used her phone to make a call so that it would cell-site to her home address. She'd left her own phone at home, of course. And then her next job was to get rid of her clothes and dispose of all the Nokias. She had Helen drop them in the Regent's Canal on her way home. She'd already wiped all the laptops. Then it was just a case of waiting for the police to call Dan. And we knew it wouldn't be long before Jerry found out that the security guy had messed up and overwritten the CCTV—'

'Which would let Jerry know he was in the clear?'

'Exactly. That would be his cue to breathe a big sigh of relief and start working on his alibi. And all that was left after that was to find a good hiding place for Emily's phone.'

53

They discovered the phone at ten o'clock on a Sunday evening in mid-February, when Kevin from security was doing his rounds. Out of the blue, it started ringing from inside Jerry's office. Kevin glanced through the glass, but couldn't see a phone on the desk. He found this suspicious. Why would you leave your phone in the office all weekend without coming back for it? He also knew that Dan's wife had been using a phone the night she died that had never been found. Dan had asked Kevin to keep his eyes and ears open for it as he did his tours around the building, so when Kevin called Dan, Dan immediately said he would call the phone himself. Dan did so; Kevin confirmed that it was ringing. Dan called it a second time, then a third time. Each time, it rang again.

The police were called and Jerry's office was opened up and his sofa turned on its side and examined. Emily's missing phone was inside, tucked through a phone-sized rip in the fabric and hidden inside the frame. The police carried out an overnight forensic download and found the messages – six hundred and fifty-three in total. Kevin was now a hero. (We chose this for him, to make up for what we did to him over the CCTV. We felt bad about that, but we knew Kevin would now be super charged and keen to help the investigation in any way he could.)

By the time Jerry arrived at work the following morning, Gallagher and Heaton and three uniformed officers were there waiting. He got out of the lift and walked through the glass doors as if it was a normal Monday morning, only to have a police officer step out of his office to greet him and read him his rights. I listened, smiling insanely, as Helen phoned to tell me this. Later, when it was safe for me to speak to Hayley, I insisted that she tell me all over again. I wanted to hear every little detail first-hand, and so she told me how Jerry had frozen in the doorway to the office, how his face had fallen, how his eyes had moved quickly past the police officer towards his room, to the upturned sofa and the messy search that was still going on inside.

He'd tried to get past the police and into his room then, and two uniformed officers had moved to block him, had taken hold of his arms.

'Get the fuck off me!' he'd roared, lashing out at the one with the handcuffs.

Gallagher and Heaton had stepped forward.

'You're under arrest, Mr Seager,' Gallagher had told him. 'For the murder of Madeleine Blakely. You need to come—'

'You stupid fucking bitch!' Jerry had cut in, sneering. 'You're going to regret this. You've just made the biggest mistake of your career.'

He'd struggled hard, trying to stop the handcuffs from going on, and had to be taken to the ground in front of the interns, in front of the associates, in front of Hayley and Maria, his secretary of twenty-five years.

I could picture his expression as he was dragged to his feet and escorted out of the building. I could imagine his terror, his humiliation, as he was taken down in the lift to the foyer and out through the revolving doors. He'd have spent the past two months in some kind of purgatory, no doubt, hearing about my arrest and bail status from Dan and paying a keen interest, initially wondering if his life was about to unravel, but as the weeks went by growing steadily more secure, more confident, more hopeful that his secret would remain safe. And now, here it was – the reversal of fortune that would turn his life upside down.

54

We'd waited for two reasons. Firstly, I needed to have been on bail long enough for a court to recognise the true impact on me of Jerry's lies: the time I'd spent on bail, the restriction on my freedom, the fear of being arrested again at any moment, of being sent to prison. I'd kept a diary during that time detailing my ordeal, which would later become a victim impact statement. We needed it to be crystal clear that I'd been the victim of Jerry's lies; never could it cross anyone's mind that it might be the other way round.

Secondly, we needed Maddy released by the coroner. That was our cue. As soon as she was safely in the ground and it was too late for Jerry's defence team to ask for her to be cut open again, Hayley would take Emily's phone out of its former hiding place, charge it and slip it down the back of Jerry's sofa, through a hole she'd made in the fabric – something she could quite easily do when she was alone in the office after hours. She would call the phone at an opportune moment when she knew Kevin would be doing his rounds.

Not that Jerry's defence team would find anything helpful that the original post-mortem hadn't uncovered. But we didn't want Maddy cut open a second time, and we especially didn't want Jerry to have any say in that being allowed to happen. The first post-mortem would conclude that she'd been violently attacked with a wine bottle; now the bottle would prove to have Jerry's DNA all over it. Soon, they'd find Jerry's fibres on her clothing and his DNA on the scrapings taken from underneath her fingernails. Her defensive wounds and bruises would complete the picture. The death was suspicious. There was no way a second post-mortem could conclude differently.

So, we'd agreed that until Maddy was buried, I'd remain a suspect. The fear I felt during this time was real, the impact huge. Helen had come down the evening before my arrest to comfort me. She'd brought us a Chinese takeaway. We'd had wine and I tried to eat, but the whole time I was wondering if there would be a knock on the door.

'What if the police come for me this evening? They can't find you here,' I'd told her.

By then, Helen was the calmer of the two of us. 'Stop worrying,' she'd said. 'We'll see them out of the window. I can be out of the door and up the stairs before they get to the communal entrance.'

But in the end, I'd been too nervous to eat and Helen had gone back home.

I was frightened but glad when the police knocked on my door the following morning. The wait was finally over. The biggest acting job of my career had begun.

Later, released on bail, awaiting the results of the forensics,

I knew I was lucky to be able to spend Christmas with my family, but deep inside, I felt cut off from the world around me. I was living in limbo. I couldn't see or talk to Hayley. I had Helen to confide in, but we had to be careful in case the police came back, or in case anyone saw us together. We were restricted to talking on the phone. I couldn't tell Fern or anyone else the truth. I'd done this for Maddy, for Emily, for Hayley, for Helen and for myself, too, and I didn't regret it for one moment, but I hadn't anticipated the paranoia and the isolation I'd feel.

The weeks went by and on the day of the funeral, as we imagined the flowers, the coffin, the hymns inside the church, the procession to the graveside, Helen had reassured me that my ordeal was drawing to an end. But it wasn't until I got the phone call from Helen three days later to say the phone had been found and Jerry had been arrested that I began to breathe again.

Hayley had come through for me, for us all.

55

'So, that's it,' I say. 'The whole truth. I've told you everything.' Sarah doesn't speak for a moment and so I add softly, 'Do you hate me?'

Sarah's eyes meet mine and it's then that I realise: she's not angry. She's not pissed off with me. I'd known at the police station that she wasn't stupid – far from it – and I'd known when Fern offered to keep her working for me that there was a risk she might figure a few things out. But I'd expected her to be angry. I'd expected her to resent the hell out of me for all the lies I'd told her. And yet the expression on her face says other-wise. Her expression is one of empathy. It's certainly not one of judgement or blame.

'I don't hate you,' she says, after a beat. 'I understand your reasons.'

'And if he goes down for it?' I ask uncertainly. 'For murder?'

There's a pause. She moistens her lips. 'Then he'll be an old man when he comes out.'

Our eyes meet. 'How long?' My voice sounds thick and strange.

She picks up her phone from where it's sitting on the table-top in front of her. She taps and scrolls. I wait. Eventually, she stops scrolling and reads for a moment. 'Much will depend on how the prosecution presents the case.'

'But?'

'But if a jury is persuaded that Maddy confronted Jerry with what she knew about her daughter and that he killed her to shut her up and hid the evidence . . .'

I catch my breath. This is what we'd been banking on.

'. . . then that would fall under Schedule 21, paragraphs 3(1) and (2)(d) of the 2020 Sentencing Act.'

'Which says . . . ?' I ask, feeling myself starting to shake.

She lifts her eyes from her phone. 'That he'd get thirty years in prison.'

'Thirty years?' I gasp. 'Are you serious?'

Sarah nods. 'If it was apparent and provable that the murder was committed to obstruct the course of justice, then, yes, you would be in the category of a thirty-year tariff.'

We look at each other silently across the table and I can't help but notice the glimmer in her eyes. I feel rooted in the present moment; it's as though I'm in a vivid dream. I'm suddenly aware of the low hum of voices in the room with us, as if it had all been muted and now the sound's been turned back on. I look towards the bar, where a small crowd is gathering. The room is filling up. Guests are arriving for dinner. Two white-haired women in expensive coats with expensive shopping bags are being shown to a table not far from ours.

'Are you still my lawyer?' I ask. 'I mean, am I still going to need one?'

Sarah inclines her head. 'Honestly, Tate? I don't know.'

'You found out that Helen was living in Clare Henry's flat,' I say, leaning forward. 'So the police could too? Is that what you're thinking?'

She looks dismissive. 'I was trying to find Helen,' she says. 'They'd have to be looking for her to make that connection, and they don't seem to be doing that.'

'Clare's back next week,' I inform her. 'Helen's moving out. She's found a flat in Highbury, not far from where Dan lives.'

Sarah thinks about this. 'Well, I can't see why the police would start looking for her now – and once she's moved, how they'd find her. They'd be looking for a Helen Jones, not a Helen Milo—'

'Milocewska,' I agree. 'So,' I ask tentatively, 'what have we missed?'

Sarah thinks for a moment, then says, 'I'm afraid I can't answer that. I'd be crossing a line.'

I nod. I understand. 'So what happens now?'

'The police will contact you to sign the bail forms, but that's just a formality. You're already free to get on with your life.'

'And can I call you?' I ask. 'If anything happens? If I still need a lawyer?'

She nods. 'Yes. You can call me if you need me.' She pauses, then looks me in the eye. 'I hope you don't, though. I think you've been through enough.'

We leave it there. I don't need to tell her how it feels to

know that what happened to Emily, to Helen, to me and to Hayley was important enough for her to listen and to care and to understand.

She stands, pulls her handbag over her shoulder and picks up her laptop bag and we walk towards the door. Out in the lobby, Fern is walking from the lift. She notices us standing in the doorway to the bar and looks surprised. 'You're still here?' she asks. 'I thought you'd have left ages ago.'

Sarah lets me answer.

Fern waits, smiling, her eyes moving back and forth between us.

'We were waiting for you,' I say quickly.

'Really?' Fern looks sorry. 'All this time?'

'We wanted to say thank you.'

Fern scoffs, waving her hand at me. 'So, what else have you been talking about?'

I glance at Sarah. Beyond her, through the glass door that borders the street outside, there are flecks of white sleet floating gently down to the ground. 'It's snowing,' I say, as a diversion.

'Tate!' Fern presses me. 'What's going on?'

Sarah and Fern both gaze at me. I wonder what my sister would say if she knew the truth. Would *she* understand?

'After we left you, I got a call from Dan,' I say at last.

I sense Sarah stiffening beside me. Her face is expressionless, but she must be thinking how easily the lies trip off my tongue.

Fern doesn't notice any of this, but her face clouds over at the thought of me talking to Dan. She still thinks we were having an affair and doesn't approve of this connection between us, which would, indeed, be distasteful in all the circumstances if it were true. I don't want to have my sister think badly of me, of course, but my supposed affair with Dan has been integral to how things played out. And in a funny kind of a way, even though our relationship was an illusion, I have felt very close to Dan and it feels natural that he would be the one to bring me the news that we've all been waiting so long to hear.

'What did he want?' Fern asks, frowning.

'He wanted to tell me that they've got the person who killed Maddy.'

'You're kidding me? Who? Who is it?'

I tell her that it's Jerry and she smiles and smiles.

56

Sharon Seager has withdrawn her alibi. I know this because Dan called to tell me (really). Everyone at the office now believes that I was set up by Jerry, and Hayley has gently and carefully encouraged this. She had a whip-round and they bought me a present: a very beautiful, very expensive blue glass dish with stained-glass daisies, which now sits on the table in my living room. Hayley insisted that she be the one to bring the gift round to me in person. She wanted to apologise, she said.

'Hayley, please,' I told her, showing her into my hallway, keeping up the pretence until the door had fully closed behind her. 'I understand how it looked. Honestly. He fooled you like he fooled all of us. I don't hold it against you.'

'Well, you're very kind, Tate,' she said as the door slammed shut. 'And very magnanimous.'

She stumbled over the word and we both laughed out loud and then started crying, and we threw our arms around each other and held one another tight. We stood like that, clinging to each other, for what felt like a long time and then we finally broke apart and walked into the living room and sat down.

'Was it awful?' I asked her, wanting to know, but not wanting to know.

'It was quick, Tate,' she said, sparing me. 'And she was barely conscious. I don't think she would have felt too much, you know.'

I nodded, my throat tightening. 'I don't know how you did it,' I told her. 'I don't think I could have been that brave.'

'Tate,' she protested, her voice hoarse from crying. 'What you've done ... I couldn't have done that. You've been ... amazing.'

'We've all done our bit,' I said. 'Helen too. But what you did was truly courageous.'

Hayley looked pleased and said that she'd wanted to do it, not just for Maddy and for Emily, but also for Helen and me. When I'd told her what Jerry had done to us when we were fourteen, it had triggered her own guilt about things that had happened at school when she was a teenager. A girl in her class had got pregnant and all the other girls at school had been vile to her. Hayley had felt bad for the girl and had wanted to be supportive, but she hadn't stuck up for her because she'd been too afraid. In a way, she said, this felt as though she'd been able to right that wrong, and I said that it was strange how things sometimes went full circle because at school, as word got round about Helen and me, we had also been bullied by all the girls. Having Hayley tell me this, it felt as though that chapter of my life had been closed.

When I later told Helen, she agreed.

Now, Hayley said, it was time for her to move on. It was hard for her to go back to that office every day, and I could understand that. She'd found a job working in the IT department at Handelsbanken, based at their headquarters in Stockholm, and she was looking forward to making a fresh new start. She'd always wanted to learn a Nordic language, she said, and it would be an excellent career move for her. She was due to start in two weeks' time and was ready to leave, but would return for the trial.

We agreed to stay in touch and I showed her out an hour later, each of us parting, I imagine, with the same strength of feeling that arises from having connected deeply with another human from a place of extreme vulnerability. I knew that no matter where she went or how infrequently we met up again, we would have a lifelong connection. She, Helen and I now shared a secret that was written in Maddy's blood and which would go with us to our graves.

Dan offered me my job back so that this was on record, but he knew I'd refuse. I didn't want to return to the office either, not even to say goodbye. It would have been too upsetting for me and I want to put it behind me. Besides, I'm working for Fern now as her assistant manager. I'm really enjoying helping her run the hotel and I'm really good at it. She allows me time off whenever I need it for auditions, and if I get an acting job, that's fine too. This arrangement works perfectly for me and Fern is also happy with it. She'll often email me contracts to look over or invoices to pay and she trusts me to prioritise my workload and fit it in around my acting work. I feel as though my life has balance at last, that I'm getting to earn decent money doing something that makes me feel valued, whilst at the same time I'm able to follow my creative dreams and just see what happens, without pinning my hopes on whether I'll 'make it' as an actress – without being 'attached to the outcome', I think the expression is. Besides, I'm still waiting for the outcome of my most recent performance, which is the only one that matters to me now.

Dan gets regular updates from the police liaison officer, who's still a frequent visitor at the house and will be until the trial begins in June. Jerry has been remanded in custody, so the trial has to happen quickly. When Dan tells me this, my heart skips a beat. The police can't tell Dan everything, of course. We'll have to wait for the trial to know exactly how Jerry's going to try and wriggle out of it all. But Dan's been told that he protested his innocence at the police station and that he pleaded not guilty at the first court hearing, as we expected, so we will have to wait a little longer. But there is satisfaction in knowing that he's suffering and wondering who's done this to him as he sits in his cell or paces up and down in the prison yard.

He'll suspect me, I think. Maybe he'll suspect Maddy. Maybe he'll even suspect Hayley. But he'll never suspect all three of us, and unless he remembers me, he won't even think about Helen. Even if he does, even if he wakes up one day and works out exactly why this has happened to him, he'll never be able to prove it, and as I said to Helen, if he thinks about it hard enough to remember me as the fourteen-year-old girl called Tee who he had sex with in the back of a van all those years ago, he'll never want to tell a jury about that.

And besides, his DNA is all over Maddy's body. He was there. He left the crime scene and lied about it. An innocent person doesn't flee a crime scene. Who will believe him now?

57

I've had a visit from Gallagher and a superintendent called Gail Armitage who is Gallagher's superior. I was doing the washing-up when they arrived and I saw them out of the kitchen window. I let the plate I was holding slip down into the bowl of water and took off my rubber gloves, watching them as they slammed the car doors shut, crossed the street and walked down the steps. When they buzzed on the intercom, it floored me for a moment, transporting me back in time to the day I was arrested. I froze, then picked up George and hugged her to me, trembling as I picked up the receiver, fumbling and dropping it and having to retrieve it again.

'Can we come in, Tate?' a strange female voice said.

I buzzed them in, walked into the hallway and slid back the catch.

I don't know what I was expecting as I opened the door, but I could see immediately that they looked sorry. Armitage was smiling somewhat weakly and Gallagher looked genuinely remorseful. She was holding a large sack, which she handed to me. I could see my coat and my favourite blue jumper through the clear plastic.

I shook as I stood back in the hallway, put George down and took the sack from Gallagher, dragging it inside. I waved them into the front room.

They each took a seat, Armitage on the sofa and Gallagher in the chair. I sat on the pouffe near the window while they told me that Jerry Seager had been indicted on five counts, which, they said, meant that he'd appeared in the dock at the Old Bailey and the charges had been read out.

I raised my eyebrows. Five counts.

'Murder, of course,' said Armitage. 'Perverting the course of justice, assaulting a police officer with intent to resist arrest, meeting a child after sexual grooming, and sexual activity with a child.'

'Sexual activity?' Tears sprang to my eyes. 'You mean he . . . ? He managed to . . . ?'

'One of the texts suggested there had been kissing,' she said. 'Dan's daughter doesn't want to make a statement, so we only have the phone messages. But in the context of everything else, it's very serious. We're confident that he took Maddy Blakely's life in order to silence her. And making a statement which caused us to believe you were responsible is also very serious. I want to apologise that we got it so wrong.'

'It's OK,' I murmured – because, of course, it was.

58

The trial begins in Court Five of the Old Bailey on a hot June morning. The sky outside is cloudless, the courtroom airless and warm. I sit in the public gallery with Hayley, Dan and Emily and a number of others from the bank, all of us providing a little bubble of solidarity around Dan and Emily, but around me too, the wrongly accused. It's too risky for Helen to come, but it's natural that Hayley would fly back from Stockholm to support her former boss and his daughter, and her presence ensures that I am made to feel welcome by the associates and secretaries. Every time someone gets up to let me by, I'm given a pat on the back or a smile. I've gone from being a nobody to a celebrity and I must admit it feels good to be one of the crowd.

The prosecution's opening is like being told a story and it's pretty much the story we wrote, in fact, but it sounds so much better delivered by a bespectacled barrister dressed in a wig and gown. Maddy confronted Jerry with the messages to her daughter, we are told. Jerry tried to snatch the phone from her;

Maddy fought back. Jerry hit her with the wine bottle. Maddy fell to the ground and didn't get up again. Jerry panicked. Knowing there were no cameras on the roof, he picked her up and pushed her unconscious body over the edge of the building, thinking the gash to her head could be explained away by her fall and intending to make it look like a suicide.

As I listen, I can't help but imagine what Helen and I would have thought, had we known as schoolgirls that one of our creative works would end up being dramatised in Court Five of the Old Bailey; it all feels very grand. Not that I'm proud of what we've done – far from it. Emily's bowed head and swollen eyes keep me grounded. We have taken a huge risk. I will never be complacent, and when Hayley and I meet outside the courtroom, there are no words between us – there can't be – but I know that she, like me, is quaking inside.

The defence case is weak. Jerry is unable to explain the messages and he attempts to cover his lies with more lies. When the verdict comes in, there is no sign of Jerry and the courtroom is so quiet that I begin to wonder if something has gone wrong because it's taking ages for him to be brought up from the cells. For several moments we wait and I am filled with trepidation; I am so nervous that my limbs go numb. But then there is the sound of a door opening and an all-too-familiar jangling of keys and Jerry, head bowed, appears in the dock. He is convicted on all counts and he accepts the verdict with the same lack of dignity that he exhibited on his arrest.

Three weeks later, when he is sentenced, he is again led kicking and screaming out of the courtroom and into the cells.

I watch his face, his eyes bulging in fear and fury, and my heart sings. I daren't look directly at Hayley, but we're sitting just a few seats away from one another on both occasions and our eyes flicker to meet each other's for a very brief second before moving away.

When it's over and I have hugged Hayley and Dan and Emily and the others, I wander down the passage to the square outside to recover my equilibrium, to sit and be calm. I've come to like it here, behind the Old Bailey. I'm soothed by the collision of arches and slopes, by the sombre stillness that surrounds me. But I break that stillness as I put the phone to my ear and tell Helen softly, 'Thirty-three years. Minimum of thirty to be served before he has any chance of parole.'

The CPS lawyer later tells Dan that Jerry's counsel had advised him that there were no grounds for an appeal.

'What about Emily?' Sarah asks me when we speak again. 'How will she cope, knowing that the man she loved and trusted has gone to prison for killing her mother?'

I tell her that Emily now hates him, and this time she really won't ever see him again. She has woken up from whatever spell she had been under and is mortified that she could ever have been charmed by him. Of course, she is devastated by the loss of her mother and I feel bad about that at times. But, as I said to Sarah, it's a better ending, don't you think? She can remember her mother the way the world remembers Princess Diana – young and beautiful. Far better than watching her throw up, lose her mind, become incontinent and constantly reel in and out of pain. And far better than having to go to court and see that pig get maybe five years at most for stealing away her childhood and her self-esteem and messing up her life the way he messed up Helen's and mine.

I've been seeing a counsellor lately. I haven't told her the whole story, of course, but I felt it was time to talk about what Jerry did to me when I was fourteen. His conviction was closure of a very big kind, but sometimes something needs to be said out loud enough times for it to remain outside of you instead of locked up in your head. I don't call him by his name for fear that a connection will be made. I just refer to him as *he* or *him*. I talk about the intense shame I have lived with all my life, how it is repeatedly resurrected, triggered in the present day by everyday events, mistakes, conversations and encounters. She tells me repeatedly that it wasn't my fault. I know this, of course, but I need to *know* this. I need my body to know this, because I've met someone and I'd like to get closer. He's an actor who stayed at Scott Street recently. Our eyes met over the coffee jug at the morning breakfast buffet and we couldn't stop talking. Anyway, the counselling seems to be working, because we're now on our third date.

As for Maddy and my flashbacks, the counsellor tells me to imagine her being lifted away by angels instead of hitting the ground and I find this has helped. Now, as I close my eyes, I still see her falling, but I find that the more I practice, the more able I am to conjure up the angels who carry her up and away into the sky and out through space, where she is now at one with the universe.

Dan told me recently that Emily has done well in her GCSE exams in spite of everything, and that she and Rosie have joined a theatre group, which is where they now spend all of their time. It pleased me immensely to hear this and I'm going along next week to run a workshop. I hear that there's some boy Emily likes there. Dan has met him and finds him entirely suitable. I think he now feels nothing but relief that she's attracted to someone her own age and is actively encouraging her to go out.

Dan is heartbroken, pale and drawn, but unwavering in his desire to stay strong for his daughter, and although he is now a hard-working single parent, he is generous to me with his time. Since I stepped in to help Maddy conceal her illness that day and subsequently supported her through much of her treatment, there has been a bond of sorts between us that has been strengthened by my own suffering following the false accusation against me. I get the sense that, in his eyes, we are united as victims of his former boss, who abused his trust and mine. So, he calls me from time to time and we meet for a coffee, and on each occasion he seems just a little bit stronger than the last and I am so, so pleased to see that he is doing OK.

So, mostly, and for almost all of us, life goes on. Every now and then, as I walk down the street, I see a police car and my heart backs into my lungs and stays there until it has passed. But a moment later, the memory of how close I came to spending time in prison is no different from any other memory I'd like to forget. I hurl myself back into the present and focus on the task in hand: learning the lines for my next play, the ad I need to place for more kitchen staff at Scott Street, what to wear on my date on Friday, whether I should cook chicken or fish. I walk with Helen on the Heath or sit curled up on the sofa, drinking wine with her in her new living room, and I look at her and think about how he tried to divide us, but how fate brought us back together. When I eventually lie next to my new boyfriend, I will remember that time is a great healer and that no matter what I have done, I'll now be so much richer for the experience of having truly lived.

When I think of *him* and what *he* did, I now replace the memory with a better one. I remember how, at one point, his eyes had wandered across the courtroom from the dock towards us and landed on me, met mine. He looked at me blankly and I could read nothing there, but I wonder and wonder if there's a part of him that recognised me, is still wondering where he knows me from, who I am. I know we got what we wanted and this is all that really matters, what's happening in the here and now. But a part of me still wants to believe that it will hit him at some point, that one day it will come to him like a bolt from the blue as he paces around the prison yard, or that it might wake him suddenly, like a small, icy hand clutching at his heart, in the cold dark hours of the night.

Acknowledgements

Thanks a million to my small team of early readers: Ian Astbury, Simon Kingston and my dear sister-in-law, Karen Draisey. Your feedback has been invaluable and I am so grateful to you for giving up your time. Thanks also to Marie Brackett and to fellow author Abi Silver for your input on one or two scenes, and to Patricia Marquis, Catherine Scammell, Amy Eastham and Hazel Scott-Towers, and to my niece Shannon and my brother Mike for answering my medical, technical and other questions and for all your support and encouragement. To all the other friends and family who have cheered me on, thank you so much.

Enormous thanks to my dear agent, Judith Murray. Within half an hour of talking to you it felt as though I'd known you all my life! Your insights and enthusiasm have been amazing, and you couldn't have found a better home for me than with the brilliant Selina Walker. Thank you, Selina, for everything. I'm so enjoying working with you! Thank you also to Kate Rizzo and Imogen Morrell who read *The Woman on the Ledge* first and passed it to Judith, and to everyone else at Greene &

Heaton. Huge thanks to my eagle-eyed copy-editor Caroline Johnson, proofreader Sarah-Jane Forder and to Katya Browne, Charlotte Osment and everyone else at Century, and also to Gráinne Fox at United Talent Agency and to Sarah Stein and David Howe at Harper in the US. Thank you all so much for believing in me.

My gratitude to Nigel Cook for answering my numerous questions about CCTV. I often meet forensic and other experts through my work as a lawyer, but Nigel didn't hesitate when I told him that this wasn't for a client but for a story I was writing. The work you do is so interesting, Nigel, and your passion for it really shines through. Thanks as always to Paul Organ for his advice regarding police procedure, and to Dr Jonathan Rogers of the University of Cambridge Faculty of Law for sparing the time to talk to me and share his knowledge and research on the out-of-date law which forms the basis of the storyline in the second half of the book.

Huge thanks to my colleagues at Tuckers Solicitors, past and present, who gave me a second opinion on the legal aspects of the plot, and especially to James Turner and Alex Walsh Atkins in the Birmingham office and to Fiona Dunkley in London. A special thank you to Fiona Walsh, my lovely colleague and dear friend in our Manchester office, who told me: 'Go. Write. I've got this,' and who continues to hold the fort in our little file review team. Also to Barry Tucker and Ralph Williams, and to Adam Makepeace before him, all of whom made it possible for me to continue to pursue both the careers that I love.

To my husband, Mark, for also making that possible by looking after our boys and for putting up with a lot of weekends and school holidays at home. I promise you, you will now start to have all the fun and freedom you deserve!

And finally to my dear mother, Marsha, who taught me to read and who inspired in me the love of stories, and who later taught me how to overcome trauma and to see angels instead.

Bringing a book from manuscript to what you are reading is a team effort, and Penguin Random House would like to thank everyone at Century who helped to publish *The Woman on the Ledge.*

PUBLISHER
Selina Walker

EDITORIAL
Charlotte Osment
Katya Browne
Caroline Johnson

DESIGN
Glenn O'Neill

PRODUCTION
Helen Wynn-Smith
Faye Collins
Sinead Ussher

AUDIO
Meredith Benson
James Keyte

UK SALES
Alice Gomer
Olivia Allen
Kirsten Greenwood
Jade Unwin
Evie Kettlewell

INTERNATIONAL SALES
Richard Rowlands
Linda Viberg

PUBLICITY
Rachel Kennedy

MARKETING
Sarah Ridley
Hope Butler